Royal Mysteries of the Stuart and Georgian Periods

Royal Mysteries of the Stuart and Georgian Periods

Timothy Venning

PEN & SWORD
HISTORY

First published in Great Britain in 2023 by
Pen & Sword History
An imprint of
Pen & Sword Books Ltd
Yorkshire – Philadelphia

ISBN 978 1 39905 424 9

A CIP catalogue record for this book is available from the British Library.

Typeset by Mac Style
Printed in the UK by CPI Group (UK) Ltd, Croydon, CR0 4YY.

MIX
Paper | Supporting responsible forestry
FSC® C013604
FSC
www.fsc.org

Pen & Sword Books Limited incorporates the imprints of Atlas, Archaeology, Aviation, Discovery, Family History, Fiction, History, Maritime, Military, Military Classics, Politics, Select, Transport, True Crime, Air World, Frontline Publishing, Leo Cooper, Remember When, Seaforth Publishing, The Praetorian Press, Wharncliffe Local History, Wharncliffe Transport, Wharncliffe True Crime, White Owl and After the Battle.

For a complete list of Pen & Sword titles please contact

PEN & SWORD BOOKS LIMITED
47 Church Street, Barnsley, South Yorkshire, S70 2AS, England
E-mail: enquiries@pen-and-sword.co.uk
Website: www.pen-and-sword.co.uk

Or

PEN AND SWORD BOOKS
1950 Lawrence Rd, Havertown, PA 19083, USA
E-mail: Uspen-and-sword@casematepublishers.com
Website: www.penandswordbooks.com

Contents

Introduction

The 'Royal Mysteries' associated with the Stuart line of Scotland, who came to the throne of England (plus Wales and Ireland) on 24 March 1603 in the person of Queen Elizabeth I's cousin King James VI of Scots as James I of England, are generally regarded as being less 'high profile' than those of the later medieval and Tudor eras. This is partly due to the comparative lack of focus by the literary or visual media on them, which has kept them low in public consciousness – there have been only a few British TV series on the Stuart royal family and Court despite the complex and fascinating characters of leading 'players', and the usual murky mixture of sex and politics plus the occasional murder. The intimate 'bedroom politics' of the Courts of James I – a quirky, paranoid, and high-spending would-be 'New Solomon' (ie master of wisdom) with slovenly personal habits, a thick Scots accent, and a fondness for emotional displays of devotion to a succession of good-looking and greedy young courtiers – and the 'ins and outs' of his reign are as fascinating as those of Henry VIII and Elizabeth I but have attracted less attention.

Indeed, as an emotionally and possibly active homosexual King – the first to rule England since Edward II, or possibly Richard II – with a Court notorious for scandal, drunkenness, vicious feuding, and excess spending, he is arguably a more 'modern' figure than the Tudors. He headed an uneasily multi-national Court of mutually hostile English and Scots courtiers and lacked the then prevailing ideological hostility to international Catholicism, preferring peace-making and mediation to his MPs' demands for (expensive and risky but to them morally desirable) war on the 'evil empire' of Spain and the 'international religious threat' of the Papacy and its fanatical, murderous secret agents. The latter, especially the Jesuits, were played up by 'scare stories' in the printed media and added to an underlying culture of anti-Catholicism – which had a long-term impact on perceptions of the Royal Court as a 'safe haven' for real or alleged Catholics. A perceived threat by an expansionist and ruthless 'foreign' religion intent on world dominance, plus its allied English 'home-grown terrorists' (intent on murderous atrocities) incited by fanatical priests, was a part of early seventeenth-century life in terms reminiscent of the twenty-first century – but by Catholicism, not extreme versions of Islam.

The Stuarts' rule in England opened with the most famous of these attacks, still commemorated on Guy Fawkes' Night – the 'Gunpowder Plot' to blow up the entire English elite at the State Opening of Parliament in 1605. As with most of the major dramatic events of Tudor and Stuart history at this time of shifting and multi-faceted allegiances and double agents, there are still doubts over the truth of the plot and its 'surprise' discovery – how soon did the King's chief minister, Sir Robert Cecil, know about it? Did he unofficially 'keep an eye on' but not arrest (or even incited?) the naïve and fanatical conspirators for a while to maximise the politically useful horror of their exposure? Was it used – or even a 'set-up' – to ruin the chances of tolerating Catholicism in England? This was not really a 'Royal' scandal and I have chosen to sideline it and to highlight other instances of the murky relationship of seeming or real religious fanaticism and 'seditious conspiracy' against the Anglican-led ruling system of Stuart Britain involving the Stuarts – and the political use made of this sort of sensation, which has long obscured the truth. Did Charles II really intend to convert to Catholicism to win French support for his shaky throne, or was this a 'con' to win overseas (French) promises of help in case of a revolt? Did he deny, or his Catholic brother James VII and II 'cheat', his ultra-Protestant eldest son, the Duke of Monmouth (executed by James in 1685) of the throne? Did James really intend to bring Britain back to Catholicism – as argued by the sections of the political elite who deposed him with Dutch military assistance? The latter scandal even saw the bizarre episode of James' opponents alleging that his son James Francis Edward, 'miraculously' born to be his longed-for or feared Catholic successor in 1688, was a fake smuggled into the birthing-chamber in a warming-pan by the 'stop at nothing' international Catholic conspiracy to secure a long-term Catholic Stuart dynasty. The episode is an early example of widely-believed 'fake news', 'spun' by the King's enemies; the 'mystery' here is not whether the future 'Old Pretender' was really a fake but how and why it was so widely believed that this was so.

The ruthlessness of the royal 'establishment' – and its enemies – is one constant theme here, from the scandalous murder – and then the cover-up of it – of James VI and I's 'toy-boy' Robert Carr's wife's 'out of control' 'fixer' in the Tower of London in 1615 to the first of the Hanoverian dynasty's scandals, the disappearance of future King George I's erratic wife's lover and her own incarceration for life in Hanover in 1694. Indeed, the long history of the Stuart dynasty in Scotland before 1603 had been as violent (and more openly so) than that of the English sovereigns which I have covered in earlier books. King Robert III's elder son and heir David, Duke of Rothesay, had been imprisoned and (probably) starved to death by his crown-seeking uncle the Duke of Albany in 1402; his brother King James I had been stabbed to death in a drain under his Perth residence while fleeing his murderous cousin's 'hit-men' in 1437; his son James II had personally despatched the potential rebel Earl of Douglas in a scuffle at Edinburgh Castle in 1452; and his son James III had been defeated in battle by his rebel son's noble backers in 1488 and then stabbed to death as he was fleeing the battlefield. The career and misfortunes of Mary Stuart have already been dealt with in my Tudor book.

The seeming 'softness on the Catholic threat' of the Stuart kings, most of them with Catholic wives, one of them an open and unrepentant Catholic (James VII and II), and most with Catholic courtiers of uncertain allegiance, was a bonus to their enemies. It helped pro-Royal politicians and the majority of the monarchs in their hostility to attempted 'interference' in their choice of friends/servants and their religious policies as anti-monarchic subversion, a block to any political compromise. The religious and the political mixed with the personal in the complex world of seventeenth-century politics, and as we shall see underlying religio-political motives need to be examined for much of the 'evidence' both for and against the 'official' stories of assorted royally connected scandals – and indeed of the policies of the monarchs, which were often more 'short-term' and 'personal' in tone and in underlying reasoning rather than carefully thought-out or coherent. The easy-going but at times naïve and bumbling James VI and I, a man whose reign at times descended into farce and whose activities at times embarrassed normally strong defenders of the monarchy (not least his homosexually-tinged sentimental admiration for his male 'favourites'), the well-intentioned but devious, personally shy and 'stiff', and arrogant Charles I, the complex and subtle rake and shrewd tactician Charles II, and the narrow-minded, formal, and dictatorial James II, were all intriguing and still controversial characters. Their personal beliefs and friendships (with both sexes, especially in Charles II's case) determined how Court and national politics turned out. This was also still an era when national politics was centred on the Court and the King, who could try to rule as a semi-absolute ruler (and at times hankered after theoretical autocracy too), until the 'Glorious Revolution' of 1688 when the blundering James II was driven off his throne by a mixture of elite rebellion and invasion by his Anglo-Dutch nephew/son-in-law William III for supposedly trying to re-convert Britain to Catholicism and create a tyranny.

The visual media has tended to focus more on the better-known Tudors (or the feuds of the Yorkists and Lancastrians in the mid-later-fifteenth century), and though the licentious Court of Charles II has been occasionally portrayed in film or TV the period is short on portrayals 'on screen' – with the open violence and struggle for power ending in regicide in the Civil War preferred for films, e.g. the 1971 film *Cromwell* with Richard Harris in the title role and Alec Guinness as the enigmatic and untrustworthy Charles I. Back in the infancy of British TV 'historical drama' in 1969, a (now largely forgotten) series on the career of Winston Churchill's dynasty-founding ancestor John Churchill, first Duke of Marlborough (1650–1722), featured the Court intrigues of Charles II, James II, William III and Mary II, and the latter's sister Queen Anne. Written by the team that created the BBC's masterpiece *The Forsyte Saga, The First Churchills* also starred the latter's 'break-out' star Susan Hampshire as Marlborough's wife Sarah Churchill. More recently, Rufus Sewell has starred in a historical TV series on the story of Charles II's reign (*The Power and The Passion* (2003), also starring former 'James Bond' Timothy Dalton, which notably had far less public success than the various Tudor series that featured better-known figures, and the intrigue-ridden Court politics of Anne's reign – a time of another Stuart ruler accused of excessive and embarrassing partiality for a ' same-sex favourite', this time John Churchill's wife Duchess Sarah – were more successfully portrayed in the recent film *The Favourite,* starring Olivia Colman.

Anne, indeed, was to be accused of a lesbian relationship with her next 'favourite', Abigail Masham, a so-called 'dirty chamber-maid', by the allies of the side-lined and vengeful Sarah Churchill, and at this time the Stuart dynasty may have had to rule in line with the current political party majority of MPs and peers in Parliament (Whigs or Tories) but still had great powers of patronage and policy leadership. The less politically-important Court of their 'Hanoverian' successors, who came over from Germany as reliably Protestant to head the British state after Anne died childless, still had its scandals, as will be seen, even if their outcomes were (usually but not always) less politically crucial – featuring the usual run of secret marriages, royal bastards, and occasionally murders. The public, spurred on by a ravenous and sceptical media with papers and books to sell, and at times by their political agendas, still lapped up tales of sex and violence in high places. At times, such as the Regency era, the British royal family was to be notorious, with a bevy of high-spending and debauched princes, with their hangers-on. Not much changes in the world of Court intrigue, and 'fake news' – the bigger the lie and the higher-ranked the offender, the more likely it was to be believed – were as common in the seventeenth and eighteenth centuries as nowadays. In this book I shall be looking at a series of these scandals and political controversies from 1600 to the early nineteenth century, some comparatively well-known and others obscure but no less important, commencing with one of the most bizarre episodes associated with James VI and I and ending with the stories of bigamy aimed at the seemingly morally upright and strait-laced George III.

Chapter 1

James VI and I and the Gowrie House Conspiracy, 1600. Royal Kidnap Plot or Royal 'Honey-Trap'?

The toxic mixture of intrigue, double-crossing and sporadic violence that accompanied the career of Mary Stuart, was exacerbated by her claims to be the legitimate heir to the English throne when Mary Tudor died in November 1558 and were heightened as a result of the 'Protestant vs Catholic' ideological struggles that developed across the British Isles and Europe in the mid-late sixteenth century. Not only was the identity of the true sovereign of England as well as Scotland 'up for grabs' in an era of the principle '*cuius prinicipo eius religio*' (i.e. 'the ruler's religion should be followed by his / her subjects'), with Protestant subjects often uneasy at being ruled by a Catholic and vice versa, but both Mary Stuart (a determined Catholic) and her son and successor James VI (born to two Catholics, but brought up as a boy-King by his ministers as Protestant) had a legal claim on the English throne and were genealogically 'next in line' to Elizabeth Tudor. Mary's father King James V had been the eldest child of Henry VIII's elder sister Margaret, though he had excluded this branch of the family from the throne in his will of 1544/5, and that claim – which led to Mary's father-in-law King Henri II of France provocatively proclaiming her Queen of England when Mary Tudor died, as her half-sister Elizabeth's parents' marriage was not recognised by the Catholic Church. This claim passed to her son James VI, though Elizabeth was too insecure (or too wise) to name either of them as her heirs in case ambitious men flocked to cultivate their goodwill (or put them on her throne), and in addition Mary's second husband, James' father Lord Darnley, was her cousin and the elder son of Margaret Tudor's daughter by her second marriage, Lady Margaret Douglas. As a 'respectable' Protestant, and indeed brought up in the strict and theologically 'advanced' Calvinist ideology by his tutors, James was a 'safer' heir to England and its remaining Protestant than the Catholic Mary, though he showed some interest in conciliating Catholicism at home and abroad and bringing its practitioners into his court and government from time to time in both Scotland and (after he came to the English throne in March 1603) in England. He was far more politically skilful and canny than his rash and impulsive mother had been, and usually balanced the many mutually antipathetic factions at the Scots court far better – and he lasted as king of Scotland from his accession aged under a year to his death aged fifty-eight. But his reign in both Scotland and in England, as we shall see, was not without its political crises, violent struggles for power, and murder mysteries any more than his mother's was, though these were generally less 'high profile' and the awkward, obsessively learned, personally untidy and uncouth, and politically 'slippery' James was a far different person and has attracted far fewer admirers. A mixture of skill, good and bad luck, and often outright farce indeed marked his turbulent reign – which was quite the norm for Scotland, where adult as well as under-age rulers had been kidnapped, murdered, cheated, and slandered (and had fought back violently against their enemies) for centuries. James was indeed the first of his line to die at a reasonably advanced age of natural causes since the hapless and often marginalised King Robert III in 1406 – and every sovereign since then had died young, all but one of them by violence. The Scots court had long been even more violent and faction-prone than that of the English Plantagenet and Tudor sovereigns, though this is much less well-known.

Following the effective end of the Earl of Morton's regency in 1578, the then thirteen-year-old King James' growing self-assertion was reflected in his partiality for his cousin Esme Stuart d'Aubigny (born 1541), handsome cadet of the line of the Earls of Lennox (a junior branch of the royal house), who had been living in France and was a gentleman of the bedchamber to King Henri III. The death of the late Earl Malcolm (Stewart) of Lennox's younger son, King James' father Lord Darnley's sickly brother Charles Stuart, in 1576 (leaving an infant daughter, Arbella) left Esme's uncle Robert Stuart, elderly Bishop of Caithness, as heir to the Earldom of Lennox and James gave him the title in 1578. But the exile of the leading Hamiltons, the Catholic dynasts of royal blood who had backed Queen Mary in the 1568 revolt against the regency, brought Esme back from France in the late 1570s to challenge Robert for the Lennox estates. He was accused by indignant Protestant 'hard-liners' of being a Catholic and the agent of ex-Queen Mary's 'ultra' cousin, the ferocious Duke of Guise who led the French Catholics in their civil wars, but James showed him strong physical affection and he became the first of the King's so-called male 'favourites'. A homosexual element to this relationship was hinted at later and was made much of by the King's often ultra-Calvinist, rigidly conventional critics, and – as with the contemporary 'smears' against Queen Elizabeth I, her late mother Anne Boleyn, and prominent courtiers – it should be remembered that enjoying scandalous gossip about the 'great' (preferably involving sexual impropriety) is not just a modern phenomenon. The identity and motives of the critics also have to be considered, in a politically and religiously polarised age where a sovereign's choice of religion and personal friends often pointed to their international 'alignments' – Protestant or Catholic, and how fanatical about converting their country too in each case? The French upbringing and cultural as well as religious interests of Esme Stuart were seen as meaning that he 'must' be an agent of their current government, a regime continuing the same politico-religious alignment of current king Henri III's late brother Charles IX who had ordered the notorious St Bartholomew's Day Massacre of Protestants in 1572. Great nobles in Scotland who were accustomed to being major political 'players' (often as their hereditary 'right' on account of their ancestors' closeness to past kings) but were out of favour at the current Court were all too capable of sinking to 'smears' – or outright violence – to rid Scotland of the ministers and courtiers who they saw as blocking their way to power and the perks of office. As of the early 1580s it was the former '*junta*' of the Protestant regency for the infant King James (1567 to 1578) that were the 'outs' and were likely to target Esme Stuart and other newcomers to the King's favour, fairly or not. Also, the government of Queen Elizabeth had been a strong ally of the regency in the joint Protestant cause of keeping French and Spanish Catholic influence in Scotland to a minimum and were likely to encourage the overthrow of any 'pro-French' ministers – as they had helped the Protestant 'Lords of the Congregation' to overthrow the French-backed regency for Queen Mary in 1559–60. Nor was French influence, real or imagined, popular in Scotland as it had propped up the now derided 'Papist' Catholic old order in the Church until the rebellion of 1559–60 brought the Reformation – and the seizure of church property, led by the monasteries, by secular lords who would now fear that any new Catholic regime would seek to reverse this. The question of Catholic influence on King James needing to be stopped, by any means necessary including violence, lies at the heart of the assorted coups and plots (real or exaggerated) that afflicted Scotland in the 1580s and 1590s – and is the background to the first 'Royal Mystery' in this book.

It is more likely that James was merely showing enthusiastic affection for the dashing and sophisticated international courtier Esme Stuart than that he was involved in a sexual affair with him, or that there was any serious intent by Stuart to promote a Catholic restoration to power as a 'French agent'. Lennox was much older than the King's other apparent 'boyfriends' of the next forty years or so; though he shared their good looks and fondness for showy dress and courtly manners, he was more of a father-figure to him. Lennox showed him more regard than his ruthless guardians, the successive regents who had used him as a nominal 'front-boy' since he was one year-old, or his stern tutor, the ageing ultra-Protestant historian George Buchanan. In March 1580 James induced Earl/Bishop Robert to surrender the Lennox title and transferred it to Esme, and a Dukedom and Privy Councillorship followed. The new Duke of Lennox duly became the lynchpin of those councillors opposed to the still-powerful Morton, who had been a leading member of the regency from 1567 onwards and its leader from 1572, and was seen as a determined (and brutal but effective) mastermind of the Protestant nobles' political ascendancy. Morton was arrested on 31 December 1580 on a charge of involvement in the King's father Darnley's murder in February 1567, the most notable 'Royal Mystery' of Mary Stuart's reign,and was attainted as a traitor and executed (by the prototype for the guillotine, which he had introduced to Scotland) in June 1581. Ex-'Marian' leader Lord Maxwell's group (including Mary's ex-secretary Maitland's brother John Maitland of Thirlestane and lords Seton and Kerr of Ferniehurst) formed one faction at Court and were still favourable to sharing power with the exiled ex-Queen Mary, still in custody in England as of this date, as a stalwart enemy of the radical Protestants. The latter included Morton's nephew the Earl of Angus, the Earl of Glencairn, and William, Lord Ruthven (Earl of Gowrie from 1581), the equally ruthless son of the late Patrick, Lord Ruthven who had dominated the coup that murdered Mary's Catholic Italian secretary David Riccio in front of her in March 1566 and had famously led the murderers into Mary's supper-room at Holyrood to seize the victim, wearing armour over his nightshirt. This grouping were backed by the militant Presbyterian clergy, who saw them as a better guarantee of their religion's dominance of Scotland than the young king. Against the religious radicals stood the Catholic leadership of the Northern nobility, political and religious conservatives such as the Earls of Atholl (died 1579), Caithness (died 1582), and Crawford (head of the Lindsays) and the young Earl of Huntly (head of the Gordons of Buchan); the Catholic cause was backed by the Guises in France, Mary Stuart's mother's family, and their ally King Philip of Spain. To make matters more complicated the ultra-Catholic Guises, who had their own lands in Lorraine beyond the French borders and were junior members of the French royal house, were not natural allies of the current King Henri III, a mercurial and sophisticated bisexual who had started his adult career as the elected King of Poland (and had run away from Warsaw in secret when his brother Charles IX died in 1574 to take over France) and had been long-term foes of his powerful Italian mother, Catherine de' Medici. The Guises were close allies of France's overbearing neighbour, King Philip of Spain, and sponsored the fanatical 'para-military' armed Catholic faction of the 'Holy League' in the 'on-off' French civil wars, even to the extent of intimidating the monarchy. Indeed, Henri's reign was to end with him killing Mary Stuart's cousin, the Duke of Guise, in 1588, in an effort to rein in the 'League'.

The Spanish embassy in London proceeded in the 1570s and 1580s to use the current Jesuit mission to reconvert England to send Jesuit priests to Scotland too, to stir up the northern nobles against the Protestants in power and to rally support for a scheme of 'Association' of Mary recalled from her house-arrest in England to join James on the throne. Hopefully Mary, allied to the ultra-Catholics in France and Spain as a source of troops, could then persuade her son to convert to Catholicism – and it was alleged that this was the new Duke Esme of Lennox's role too as a 'Papist agent'. But the more ideological Protestant ministers at Elizabeth's court, such as her Secretary of State and spymaster Sir Francis Walsingham, failed to persuade their Queen that Lennox was a danger to England and must be driven out of Scotland. Although he managed to survive a plot by the Earl of Angus (who fled to England) his open profession of Protestantism failed to convince the Presbyterian clergy. While the King ignored the protests of the Church and of English ambassador Thomas Randolph about Lennox, a group of nobles led by William Ruthven, Lord Gowrie (born 1541), a leading landed figure in the 'ultra-Protestant' part of the new ruling circle, and the King's foster-brother Mar (son of the late regent who had brought James up at Stirling Castle) took direct action. This was to have implications for the Gowrie House incident too, as the King's chief kidnapper was the father of the alleged 'kidnap or murder plotters' in that case and people then and since have been able to link the brutally coercive behaviour of the father with the apparent intentions of the sons. The notedly timid and paranoid James could logically have feared violence from the latter (justly or not) and taken action to stop this given what their father had done.

On 22 August 1582 Gowrie and his allies intercepted the King's party *en route* to Perth on a northern tour, while Lennox was unsuspectingly holding judicial proceedings in Edinburgh. He seized the King's horse's bridle and forcefully 'invited' him to accompany him to Ruthven Castle for a banquet in his honour, and next day James was prevented from leaving and held prisoner (the 'Ruthven Raid'). He was taken to Perth and forced to issue a proclamation that he was not being held against his will which fooled nobody, and Lennox fled to Edinburgh, tried to protest his innocence of Catholic plots to the Assembly of the Church, and then moved to the safety of Dumbarton. The rebel lords moved the King to Stirling Castle and an English embassy arrived to show him written proof that Lennox was in league with the French, and despite James' delaying tactics the Council finally ordered Lennox out of the country in December.[1] The duke fled back to France, dying there in 1583; his son Ludovick Stuart soon returned to Scotland from France, in company with Mary's devious representative Patrick Gray (the famously unreliable intriguer 'Master of Gray'), and stayed out of politics as the King's trusted cousin and lieutenant (he died in 1624). James remained effectively prisoner of Gowrie's faction and their Presbyterian Church backers as their puppet-ruler, another naked assertion of Scots magnate *'realpolitik'* as had humiliated James II, III and V, but like the other kidnappers Gowrie, soon faced dissent from excluded nobles. Huntly, Atholl, the new Earl of Bothwell (successor of Mary Stuart's late third husband), the Earl of Montrose, and Lord Seton formed a conspiracy against him, and James' custodian Sir James Melville reluctantly agreed to his sovereign's insistence that he help an escape. In June 1583 James was allowed to accept a seemingly innocuous invitation from the Earl of March to come to St Andrews for some hunting, and *en route*, March and the town's Provost met him with some of his armed supporters in tow, firmly took him over from Gowrie's surprised royal attendants, and escorted him to safety. Gowrie and his allies set out in pursuit but were given a proclamation banning them from the Royal presence, presumably with some private assurances of goodwill as they obeyed, and they were soon pardoned; the Council was remodelled and Huntly, Argyll, Maitland, and Crawford now emerged as leading figures.[2] With them, to reassure radical Protestants, was the buccaneering figure of Captain James Stewart of Bothwell Muir, new (1581) Earl of Arran and ex-protégé of Morton, who had led the ex-regent's arrest and had temporarily been an ally of Lennox at that point – possibly as he had less hopes of influence from allying with the 'old nobility' Gowrie faction. Mar ended in exile after allying with Angus, Lords Claude and John Hamilton, the Master of Glamis, and other dissidents to seize Stirling Castle (March 1584). The King led a large army on the castle in person, the rebels fled to England which had not sent them any troops, and the captain of the castle was hanged for treason, and Arran proceeded to have Gowrie (not involved in this plot) rounded up and executed for treason. The execution of Gowrie on 3 May 1584 may have been a 'warning-shot' to the other, now temporarily exiled members of his faction that the King would be as vigorous in defending his rights as his purge-organising ancestors, a personal blow by him to the man who had humiliatingly held him captive, or mainly a personal vendetta by Arran. But it provided observers and interpreters of the murky events at Gowrie House in 1600 with a motive for the alleged plotters trying to kidnap or kill the man who had executed their father.

There may also have been a subterranean current to the ongoing clashes between the King and the Gowrie family, in that a story was later current that Gowrie's wife Janet, the daughter of the junior Stuart dynasty member Henry Stuart/Stewart, Lord Methven (d. 1555), was really not the daughter of Methven's second wife but of his first one – the King's grandmother, Margaret Tudor (widow of King James IV and older sister of Henry VIII of England). The middle-aged Margaret had married the much younger Methven after finally breaking up with her over-ambitious second husband Archibald Douglas, earl of Douglas (and the overbearing regent for her son James V), and although there is no evidence for her having a daughter by him this was rumoured – and she was said to be Gowrie's wife – after the 1600 incident. By the 1680s it had reached the ears of the Presbyterian cleric and political activist (and later historian) Bishop Gilbert Burnet, who included it in his history of the period. He alleged that when the Gowrie brothers had confronted and threatened the King at Gowrie House James had assumed on this account that they were after his throne as semi-royal Stuart/Tudor descendants and had warned them that if he was killed the public would lynch them.[3] The story is far-fetched and probably just lurid gossip, and although Janet was indeed born illegitimate and only legitimated later this was because her father Methven had not yet been divorced from Margaret Tudor when he made her mother pregnant; he married the latter. If James had been killed, he had a small son available to be nominal king, and Burnet was a foe of King James' equally autocratic grandson James VII and II; but the theory of the Gowrie House 'plot' as some kind of intended coup by typical Scots noble violence (involving killing the King or not) owed much to the precedent of the 'Ruthven Raid'.

Arran (John Knox's brother-in-law so with good religious credentials for the suspicious Presbyterian clerics) now became Chancellor and Maitland Treasurer, and the more radical Presbyterian preachers who had backed the 'Ruthven Raiders' were prosecuted – which has implications for their successors' hostility to the King's explanations over the 'Gowrie House incident' in 1600. The Edinburgh firebrand preacher Andrew Melville, who had been insolently hectoring the King for his fondness for ungodly Catholics and neglect of his duty to back up God's church, fled to England with around forty others. The authority of the King and his bishops over the church was now asserted in the 'Black Acts', restoring discipline and ending the threat of political defiance of the monarchy by autonomous local preachers and their congregations. But Arran was not able to exert the grip on power that Morton had done as the King was now semi-adult, and there were subterranean struggles for influence on the impulsive, secretive, and justifiably nervy young king – with Catholic nobles and their foreign backers angling for the restoration of Mary as co-ruler in the 'Association'. The exiled 'Ruthven Raiders' tried to stir up Elizabeth against Arran as a potential ally of her foreign foes – though it should indeed be remembered that in this era many claims of Scots faction-leaders having sinister foreign allies were no more than political 'smears' by their foes in the hope of attracting English aid. This applies to the case of the 'Gowrie House conspiracy' too, given that one theory had it that the Gowrie/Ruthven brothers were linked to English ministers in London who feared Spanish/Catholic influence on James. The ideologically anti-Catholic English minister Walsingham accepted their argument that by exiling Presbyterian clerics James and Arran were aligning themselves to the Catholics. The Queen chose to send a new embassy headed by her cousin Lord Hunsdon to negotiate with the Scots regime (August 1584), and this accepted James' desire for a new treaty. Elizabeth agreed to let the refugee 'Ruthven Raiders' go home and attempt to overthrow Arran by force, apparently persuaded by Patrick Gray that the King would abandon him to a determined assault, and on 2 November 1585 Mar, Angus, Glamis, Lords Claude and John Hamilton, and their allies appeared at Stirling Castle with a large armed escort to demand that James dismiss Arran. The King, lacking troops, had to agree to sack and demote Arran and restore them and their exiled clergy allies to their positions and estates. This ended the somersaults of political fortune in Scotland, and the English treaty was duly signed on 5 July 1586; it assured James that Elizabeth would not directly or indirectly prejudice his claim to the English throne provided that he remained friendly towards her. That claim, it would turn out, was James' principal ambition in his English policy – and Mary's claims to both crowns were abandoned again. The King made no move to save Mary and risk endangering the treaty when she was arrested for her part in the 'Babington Plot' to murder Elizabeth and put Mary on the English throne, and Mary's trial and her execution at Fotheringay Castle (8 February 1587) proceeded without James threatening to break off the treaty. James steered clear of involvement with either side in the Spanish Armada crisis of 1588, with Philip II intending to put his own daughter Isabella (a descendant of John 'of Gaunt') on the English throne and regarding Mary Stuart's son as an untrustworthy Protestant.

But despite James' own Protestant alignment there were still powerful ex-'Marian' Catholic nobles ruling unmolested over their tenants in the north and these had the manpower to intervene in national affairs if interested – with the Spanish and the Jesuits keeping in touch to plot a Catholic revival in Scotland. The most dangerous of these was young earl of Huntly, due to his Court connections – he had married the late Esme Stuart's daughter, from a family still in James' favour, and became Captain of the Guard. James balanced ministers and courtiers from the two religions, keeping his international links on both sides open. The King had been negotiating with both King Henri of Navarre, Protestant leader in the French civil war and heir to the French throne, and King Christian IV of Denmark (descendant of James IV's mother's brother) for the hands of their sisters – Catherine of Navarre, eight years older than James, and Anne of Denmark, eight years younger. The Danish match was chosen in autumn 1588, with a more certain dowry, but Princess Anne and her entourage, escorted by the Earl Marischal, failed to arrive from Copenhagen on time and with unusual daring James decided to emulate his grandfather James V and sail to his bride's homeland for the wedding. He and his party arrived in Oslo by sea and the marriage took place on 23 November; James was twenty-two (old for marriage by contemporary practice) and the bride fourteen. Anne was to give James a large family, commencing with Prince Henry in 1594, but never matched her husband's erudition or cultural interests; she became a secret Catholic and in 1596 had a major row with her husband over his insistence in handing Prince Henry over to the Earl of Mar to be brought up away from Court at Stirling Castle (as he had been). This spilled over into Court factionalism, and may have played a part in rumours over her sympathy for the 'Gowrie House plotters'.

The unstable and violent Earl of Bothwell, nephew of Queen Mary's final husband, was accused of consulting witches and wanting the King killed and was arrested but escaped to the Borders (June 1591). Claiming that it was a 'put-up job', the angry Earl raided Holyrood Palace on 27 December 1591 with a posse of armed retainers to scare the King, killed his stabler, and smashed up doors in the Royal apartments before being driven out by a posse of citizens.[4] He managed to maintain a degree of popular support as a victim of alleged Court conspiracy, with the possibility of meddling by Presbyterian extremists annoyed that the King had gone back on his promises to cancel all the so-called 'Black Acts' of 1584 which had given ecclesiastical authority and disciplinary mechanisms to the 'Popish' office of bishops. In April 1592 James had to accept a Parliamentary Act to allow the free development of the system of 'low-level' presbyters in the Church, allowing 'grass-roots' radical local evangelists to bypass Episcopal control and a national-level General Assembly. His critics now managed to use the murder of the popular new Earl of Moray, James Stewart of Doune (husband to the late regent Moray's daughter) by his Buchan rival Huntly in a quarrel over land, to allege that James was behind it. The 'Bonnie Earl' was supposed to have been killed off by the jealous King's order for paying court to Queen Anne[5] – which also has implications for the theories about the killing of the earl of Gowrie and his brother in 1600 as that too was rumoured to be a royal 'hit' to eliminate a potential threat. Nor did James bother to have Huntly hunted down for this blatant gangsterism, unlike he was unsuccessfully endeavouring to do to Bothwell, and the latter defied the King to his face again by attacking the Court at Falkland Palace and besieging his sovereign in a tower for several hours. Huntly, Erroll, and their new ally the tenth Earl of Angus (a recent convert to Catholicism) were now accused of a serious Catholic plot, as a conspirator heading for Spain was arrested and found to be carrying blank documents signed by them and others, the so-called 'Spanish Blanks', which invited Philip II to send 20,000 troops to assist their 15,000 volunteers in an invasion. Was the King's failure to arrest them a sign that he sympathised? With the church fulminating about the international 'Papist' threat and its local allies James finally put together a force to march on Buchan in February 1593, but the rebel leaders fled to Caithness and were not pursued. Bothwell now allied himself to the church as a stalwart foe of the Catholics, his ex-allies, and burst into the King's apartments at Holyrood – illegally armed – to stage a melodramatic confrontation with and deliberately terrify the King. Assuring his goodwill and offering the King his sword to stab him if he preferred, the Earl eventually agreed to withdraw from Court and turn up for a trial on the witchcraft charge if his acquittal was promised.[6] This dramatic scene and the way that an armed and clearly emotionally unstable noble came within inches of the poorly-protected King, implicitly threatening violence and no doubt terrifying him, has to be borne in mind when considering the 'Gowrie House plot', given the similarities between them. At the least it suggests that the apparent attempt to intimidate the King would 'tip off' a panicked and violent reaction from the latter, justified or not, and might make it more likely that if the Gowrie/Ruthven brothers threatened him he would let or encourage his attendants to kill them.

Edinburgh's loyalty could not be guaranteed either, with James being accused of suspicious weakness towards Catholic magnates, and this was to recur in 1600 as leading clerics expressed scepticism about James' explanation for the Gowrie House incident and made alternative, scurrilous suggestions about cover-ups and a royal 'hit' on two critics. In autumn 1593 James had to fulfil a promise to the citizens and clergy to march on the Catholic rebel Huntly, who the clerics had excommunicated – with an army largely made up of townsmen from the burghs rather than the usual entourages of nobles. By now Bothwell had left the Borders to join Huntly in Buchan despite their divergent religious views, and despite Huntly managing to outmatch the Royal advance-guard under the Earl of Argyll at a skirmish at Glenlivet (3 October) Huntly put up no resistance to the King when the latter arrived and submitted. Huntly was exiled but was allowed to return in 1596 and even became Presbyterian. Ultimately, the monarchist Huntly was less of a threat than the disrespectful Protestant Bothwell – who fled abroad and never returned. The international and domestic situations gradually became more stable in the late 1590s, the French civil war having ended in 1594 with Henri IV (Henri of Navarre) triumphant but turning Catholic to appease his Catholic subjects and the Anglo-Spanish war winding down after naval expeditions in 1596–8. Philip II died in 1598 and his son's near-bankrupt government had less interest in reclaiming England for the Faith, so a Catholic-run Scotland ceased to be a side-door into England for them. Elizabeth still refused to openly name James as her successor, but the likelihood of this eventuality was recognised by rival factions at her Court who kept a channel of communication open to James for their mutual benefit. The only realistic alternative to James as the next king was the English-born Arbella Stuart, son of Darnley's consumptive brother Charles (died April 1576) by the Countess of Shrewsbury's daughter Elizabeth (died 1582). The grand-daughter of James V's half-sister Margaret Douglas and of the formidable Countess of Shrewsbury, the farmer's daughter turned acquisitive matriarch 'Bess of Hardwick', she lived with the Countess and was a neglible factor in Scottish dynastic matters but in England was reckoned legal 'second-in-line' behind James by Cecil's advisers in a secret memorandum in 1601. Suffering from Queen Elizabeth's hostility towards potential heirs, short of cash and supporters, and at the mercy of scheming relatives and courtiers, Arbella could have been in with a chance of the English throne had the Queen backed her; and her existence as an adult alternative to James as the next King of England is another factor to be considered in investigating the murky background to the Gowrie House incident. She never gained the English throne – but as of 1600 she (or James' elder son Henry, born 1594, as an under-age king) was a potential successor to Elizabeth had she or any of her ministers wished to dabble in the apparent plot to remove James. This possibility of Arbella being a factor in the 'Gowrie plot' was also involved in later rumours about it, as one story had it that the earl of Gowrie had fallen in love with her on a visit to England (he made only one when she was adult, earlier in 1600) and wanted to make her queen by removing James and then marry her. This wild theory also has no evidence.

The second earl of Gowrie, John (born c. 1577), was allowed to recover his father's seized estates and title by act of parliament in December 1585 and was not victimised by the King, inheriting the late earl's role as a leading nobleman in Angus with a town-house in Perth (the site of the 1600 incident) and becoming a marginal figure in the murky world of court politics. But he seems to have willingly taken up his father's other role as a member of the more radical pro-Presbyterian affinity of nobles like his father and grandfather despite what had happened to the latter and the threat of their plots affecting the King's attitude towards his reliability – and making him more vulnerable to the insinuations of ill-wishers who might want him ruined. He did not have the sense as a teenager to keep himself well away from the turbulent and violent Bothwell, perhaps due to wanting revenge for his father's execution, and he had already come under royal displeasure over his support in April 1591 for the King's cousin Ludovick Stuart (earl of Lennox)'s illegal 'abduction' of and marriage to his sister Lilias. The King had banned the marriage, possibly out of fear that his cousin and potential heir Ludovick would be drawn into a Gowrie plan for reasserting their influence at court – or even replacing him? – but Gowrie and his mother, the Dowager Countess, abetted the (probably willing) 'abduction'. In the event, Lilias died in childbirth in 1592 so the Gowrie-Stuart alliance ended, but by this time Ludovick's godfather Sir William Keith (a privy councillor and trusted by the King to help organise his marriage in 1589) had also become involved with the Gowries by marrying the Dowager Countess later in 1591 despite a royal ban. Due to the King's hostility Keith then joined the Bothwell faction ahead of the shocking December 1591 raid by the earl on Holyrood House Palace. On that occasion it was noted that the raiders gained entry to the palace via Ludovick's private stables – had he let them use this to coerce his un-cooperative cousin? In October 1593 the King's distant Stuart kinsman the Earl of Atholl, a friend of young Gowrie's, staged a 'rebellion' (or more accurately an armed protest aimed at intimidating the seemingly heedless King) against the growing and unchecked influence of the Catholic and allegedly pro-Spanish faction, led by Huntly, who had not been indicted for the murder of Moray, and Gowrie joined him along with his sister's father-in-law the earl of Montrose. The nervous King refused to let them approach his court at Stirling, and when James brought an army to confront their assembly at Doune they ether surrendered or retreated into the countryside. Their army broke up and the King was able to arrest Montrose; Gowrie surrendered and was not prosecuted as he was only fifteen or so and was judged to have been influenced by his seniors.[7] But the following year Gowrie, now a student at Edinburgh University which had a strong Presbyterian tone, initially agreed to join his new ally Bothwell for an armed protest/rebellious assembly over the power and intentions of pro-Spanish nobles in the 'Spanish Blanks' affair (see above), only to back out of it and not turn up at the rendezvous at Leith. He and the earl of Atholl did sign a written declaration in support of Bothwell asking the Edinburgh clerics currently holding a meeting at Dunbar to assist the revolt which amounted to sedition,[8] but they took no direct action; Bothwell was left short of support and as seen above fled to England and later even joined Huntly. After this Gowrie stayed out of trouble and went off to France and later to northern Italy, studying at the university of Padua, but his past record and his family tradition would have earned him royal suspicion. His long stays in Italy and then France in 1594–9 led to the Edinburgh clergy, to whom he had acted as a friendly patron like his father had done, sending an envoy to see what he was up to and urge his return. Were they afraid that he might desert their faith for Catholicism as so many of those Scots and English studying on the Continent had done? His visit to England during his journey home in spring 1600 (the Queen received him in London) aroused a different type of suspicion, at least in retrospect after the autumn's forthcoming disaster for his family. It was rumoured that he had had contacts with English ministers and courtiers who were not necessarily in favour of King James 'current' stance on religion or hopes of the succession to England. This duly led to suggestions that he might have been approached by English political figures – secretary of state Robert Cecil, who he met, or the semi-disgraced royal favourite the earl of Essex? – about assisting a plot to kidnap or otherwise remove James. But this, though a logical guess, appears to be *'de post facto'* rationalisation though there is evidence that might support the theory of English collusion with Gowrie's apparent plans; and it would be normal for either Cecil or Essex to summon and question Gowrie while he was in London as he could provide information on the activities of 'loose cannon' Scots Presbyterian noble friends of his. 'Sounding out' Gowrie to see if he could continue to provide intelligence back in Scotland would be normal; anything further such as plotting to use him to remove James in favour of his young son Henry has never been proved.

The questions of violent aristocratic threats to royal power, a possible repeat of the 'Ruthven Raid' coup to forcibly neuter 'Catholic' influence on the king, and serious distrust of James' intentions (both by the plotters and of the king's subsequent explanations) marked the bizarre incident of the so-called 'Gowrie House Conspiracy' on 5 August 1600. The King was on a hunting trip at Falkland Palace, with a small entourage – nobles including his foster-brother Mar and his cousin Ludovick Stuart (ex-brother-in-law of Gowrie), and formal royal attendants or court hangers-on of lower rank who he trusted such as Thomas Erskine. The King's subsequent published explanation of the incident was as follows. As he prepared for the day's hunting Alexander, Master of Ruthven (younger brother and heir to the Earl of Gowrie), aged twenty, approached him and said his brother the earl had found a treasure in his nearby house at St Johnstone (the original name for Perth). This was about fourteen miles from Falkland. The house, the largest in the then small town, was at the end of the main thoroughfare, South Street, between it and the river Tay and had gardens leading down to the latter. From the river end of the street, the main gate (with a resident porter, who played an important role in the coming events) directly ahead led into the courtyard, with the main house to the right; the near end of the house, with the 'turret' room where the apparent attack on the king took place, faced the street adjacent to the gate. Apparently, the earl had been tipped off, as an honorary town official in Perth, that a mysterious foreigner had turned up with a large sum of money – something that in that feverish political era in turbulent Scotland might imply a link to a plot or subversion of leading men, most obviously by the Spanish given the 'Spanish Blanks' affair. Gowrie and Alexander had duly located and arrested the man in Perth and confiscated his 'treasure', and Alexander now invited the king to go over for dinner at the Gowries' house in the town, take a look at it, and interrogate the man. He urged the King to keep quiet about his reasons for going to Perth and bring as small an entourage as possible – which could seem sinister in retrospect (was it in order to make sure the brothers could kidnap or kill the King without immediate interference and rescue?) but was logical in order not to alert any court associates of the 'foreigner' to his capture. One of the later theories for the reason behind the strange events now to unfold, backed by the nineteenth-century Scots historian Andrew Lang (best known today as a collector of fairy-tales), was that Alexander's secrecy and desire that James be secret too was not malevolence or intended murder/kidnap, but because he wanted to get the King on his own and talk him into transferring the lease of Scone abbey, usually held from the King by the head of the Ruthven family, from his brother the earl to himself. The earl had refused to do the transfer, so Alexander was now intending to go behind his back – and as such his invitation to the king to come to dinner at Gowrie House was made without the earl's knowledge. James agreed to come, and dismissed his senior companions the earls of Lennox and Mar (which would suggest that he had no idea of danger). The interview between the king and Alexander occurred at around seven in the morning, as confirmed later at the official enquiry by a minor royalist laird in attendance, witness Drummond of Inchaffray.

Alexander now sent his servant Andrew Henderson – a dodgy character with unclear motives, whose subsequent statement to the authorities after his arrest may have been 'fixed' to exonerate the King as alleged by Gowrie partisans – to Perth to warn his brother that the king was coming there, which was again only interpreted as 'sinister' in retrospect. There was also some disagreement between witnesses in the Ruthvens' employ at Gowrie House over whether Henderson had in fact been as far as Falkland that morning to attend on Alexander or had lied about this. The question could be asked as to why if Alexander had sent him to tell the earl that James was coming the earl did not make earlier preparations for dinner and have it ready for the royal party on arrival. Did the earl not actually know James was coming until much later, and if Henderson did not ride straight back to Perth and inform him at once (which would have been around ten that morning) why not? The king's own narrative of events did not mention Henderson being in attendance on Alexander as the latter came to see him at Falkland – which was used to aid both the 'Henderson was framed' case (to say that Henderson's part in luring James to Perth and being the armoured man who helped Alexander at Gowrie House later was invented) and that 'Alexander was guilty of a plot but his brother Gowrie was not' case (to say that Alexander did not tell his brother via Henderson that James was coming). But there is a logical explanation, i.e., that Alexander only spoke to Henderson out of James' sight – or that his other attendant that morning, Andrew Ruthven, delivered the message. Andrew Ruthven was accepted as having been with Alexander at Falkland but was never arrested or blamed for being part of the plot – which would argue that James was not wildly looking for scapegoats and accusing all possible culprits but focussed on Henderson and did so on account of his role at Gowrie House later.

The brothers' supporters' later printed 'Ruthven Vindication' claiming that it had been James who took the initiative to tell Alexander he was coming to the Gowries' Perth house for dinner, and that there was a large entourage of fiercely pro-royalist Murray clansmen waiting in the town (ie summoned beforehand and ready to go into action) who joined the king's party as it arrived at Gowrie House or were lurking nearby. This allegedly amounted to around sixty men – i.e., enough to storm the house and dispose of the brothers. In fact, the king's party was agreed by other witnesses to be no more than twenty,[9] and though some Murrays did take part in the subsequent fight with Gowrie in the street after James called for help and then ran after the earl into the house these were only a few men. The party of Murrays who were in the town that day came there for a family wedding.[10] The king had sent messengers to Gowrie and his brother a few days earlier; but this was normal for the era with him keeping in touch on various matters with leading nobles and nothing unusual, let alone a sign that he was luring the brothers into a carefully planned 'hit'.[11] Nor did James hurry to Perth, as he apparently spent up to four hours hunting that morning before heading there in time for dinner – which does not suggest that he was unduly anxious and keen to get on with any 'plan' to surprise, trap or kill the brothers, rather that he was taken by surprise by events in Perth.

The earl of Lennox and Mar plus other members of the royal entourage who were not invited to join the king in Perth, were however uneasy about him going off with so few attendants – logical, given the era's royal kidnappings and the attacks on the king in recent years by the ultra-Protestants, Bothwell (an old ally of Gowrie as seen above) in particular. They followed the king's party and joined it later at dinner downstairs at Gowrie House. Notably, the dinner was delayed by around an hour after (around one p.m.?) the King's party arrived, suggesting that the earl of Gowrie may not have expected the King then or at all, and hence he had not lured him to Gowrie House even if Alexander had done so on his own. The earl had apparently dined earlier, possibly intending to go out that afternoon, with his nearby Dirleton castle being mentioned by his defenders as a possible destination, and if he had intended to go out he had not been told by Henderson at around ten o'clock that James was coming – though his traducers could then say he had intended to carry off the king to Dirleton as a hostage. His horse was not currently in the Gowrie House stables – was it awaiting him somewhere for his (cancelled) ride? He had apparently only received information that the King was arriving shortly while he was at a pre-arranged meeting with the Perth town officials later that morning and excused himself to them on that account, returning to his house for his own dinner around twelve – and presumably belatedly ordering dinner for a larger party. The pro-Gowrie 'Vindication' also mentioned that Alexander had been intending to go to Dirleton next day until the king 'lured' him into the Perth confrontation.

When the king arrived, Alexander lured him away from dinner to go upstairs to 'look at the confiscated treasure', and the others at dinner continued to eat. The King later said that he had intended that once Alexander had shown him the treasure his page John Ramsay would be summoned to join him; he had asked Alexander to fetch Ramsay and the latter had gone off for a few minutes but from the outcome had not done as he had been asked. The official version of events from the King's side in his 6 September statement and his later elaborations had it that the earl of Gowrie then told the arrived Mar and Lennox that James had left Gowrie House already, sending his servant Cranstoun (who later joined him in the fight with the King's men) out to the orchard to inform them as they were looking at his cherry-trees. But this was a lie as the earl well knew – and it could easily be confirmed by the nobles checking with the house's porter, which they did, and/or seeing if the King's horse had left the stables outside. (It was still there.) The surprised porter, Christie, replied that he did not think James had left or else he would have seen this from his position at the main gate, which logically Gowrie should have realised – so was his apparent, faulty explanation for James' absence a hasty improvisation? If he was making this sort of basic mistake, it suggests that he was not carrying out a careful plan to kidnap or kill the king; this is a point in his favour, or at least suggestive that any sinister plan was Alexander's and he only brought his brother into it at the last minute. There is also the question of Lennox's evidence at the November enquiry that Gowrie replied to the porter that the King must have left via the smaller back gate, to which the porter retorted that he could not have done so as he had the only key to it and had locked it earlier. The earl then apparently offered to check upstairs to see if the King had left, and after a short absence (too short to have searched every room) came down to say that he had gone – another lie. If he had not searched properly, however, this is not proof that he knew his brother was currently trying to kidnap James so he wanted the inconvenient nobles and attendants to leave – he may have been 'covering' for Alexander while he believed the latter was making some private request of the king (which in fact had turned into a row?). There is no evidence for the pro-Gowrie claim that Christie was a royal agent who had recently joined the household as part of James' plans. But the pro-Gowrie 'Ruthven Vindication' account was also full of improbabilities, as this had it that the villainous king, planning to get the brothers alone for a planned 'hit', had his men confiscate the keys of various rooms between the ground floor and the upstairs turret room where the confrontation and then the killing occurred. The various witnesses in the royal entourage, led by Lennox, all agreed at the November enquiry that they could not get into the turret-room to 'rescue' the King at first as at least one of the four (?) doors in between was locked when they rushed upstairs. The delay between James' witnessed yells for help at the window and the timing of the fight agree that a pause occurred between them – the royal 'posse' did not rush straight upstairs without hindrance, so someone had locked at least one door. Also, the first royalist attack on one of the brothers (Ramsay's on Alexander) did not feature the main rescue 'posse' at all, but a man who had been out in the yard further away as James yelled for help and had followed them indoors. This argues that

Ramsay was being truthful about having found Lennox and co. unable to open a door so he had to find another way upstairs.

According to the King, Alexander locked various (three or four?) doors behind them as he took his sovereign upstairs, which was logical for 'security' to prevent eavesdroppers for some secret investigation of a 'treasure' but also logical for a planned confrontation. In the final room that they entered, with a turret overlooking the yard via one window and the street via the other, the king said that Alexander drew his dagger and threatened to kill him in revenge for the execution of the brothers' father in 1584. This was apparently 'out of the blue' and so a sign of a planned assault, but alternative versions had it that the King and Alexander were looking at a portrait of the latter's father when James said that the late earl had been a traitor and had deserved to be executed. Alexander then became angry and threatened him – which James could have covered up so as not to put himself in the wrong, as a piece of calculated royal 'spin'. (As we shall see in the next chapter on the 'Overbury Murder' in 1613, James was to be expert at deflecting attention from his own mistakes by emphasizing his own innocence and his foes' malevolence.) James said he tried to calm Alexander down but was physically attacked, and the royal account of events in November has it that he asked the latter why he was doing this and Alexander said that 'Sir, it is but a promise' – presumably to his brother to assist a plot to kidnap or kill the King.[12] According to the arrested 'henchman' Henderson's later account, Alexander had told him he intended to kill the King to take revenge for his father.[13] Alexander attacked the King and apparently tried to call on his accomplice in the room, a man in armour, to help (the latter refused). The accomplice was identified in the royal accounts as a man in armour (with a visor on so his face could not be seen) who Alexander had stationed in the room to intimidate the King into not resisting, and as we shall see Henderson later 'admitted' to being that man while claiming he had been tricked into going there. But it is unclear if the account of Alexander explaining his reasons to the king was true, or if Alexander drew his dagger and told the King he would be killed if he opened the window but would not be harmed otherwise. Henderson later claimed he had disarmed Alexander of his dagger before he wrestled with the king, but this may just be an excuse to show his interrogators that he had helped the King so he should not be executed.

The man in armour was subsequently identified as Henderson after an initial idea that it might be one Robert Oliphant, and he admitted it after his arrest, providing the detail of Alexander's supposed statement of his intentions to the king as above. But his participation as the 'man in armour' and what he was supposed to have or have not done may have been a 'fix'. His admitting it and providing details may have been a royal ploy to get the 'confession of the villains' chief accomplice' neatly arranged from the main low-ranking suspect in custody. His capture and confession were announced to the public by an old acquaintance of his, former Perth cleric, Patrick Galloway, who was now the King's chaplain and so would be linked to the official explanation of events. The King also later claimed that Alexander had briefly left the room – to alert his brother that he had carried out the entrapment? – and while he was away James questioned the man in armour, who did not seem hostile but bemused and claimed that he had been told by Alexander, his employer, to report to this room dressed in armour but had not been told anything about the king being there. (Henderson later claimed that he had been told he would be needed to help arrest an anonymous Highland malefactor who had been spotted in Perth.) Alexander then returned and tried to tie up the king, but apparently paused to take off his garter (found on the floor later) so he had something to bind the King's hands. He had not prepared for the 'plan' by bringing cord – so was there a plan at all or was it improvised after his unexpected row with the king about the portrait? Struggling to the window overlooking the street, James shouted for help and was seen and heard by a group of his followers milling around in the street below, including Lennox and Mar who had gone outside to see if the King had left with his horse and if so to saddle up their own horses to follow. But as the room where the attack took place overlooked both the street and the yard, there was a good chance of help being at hand within earshot from part of the royal entourage (a larger part if the brothers had pretended the king had left Gowrie House as then the entourage would be saddling up outside). It was the wrong room to arrange a quiet royal kidnap in, and this again shows a lack of basic planning and a suggestion that the 'attack' – which seems to have occurred as all the witnesses agreed that the king, not a natural actor or with strong nerves, was visibly distressed and shouting about murder – was not arranged beforehand and planned.

The king's followers outside the house now ran inside and tried to get up the main stairs to the turret room but found at least one of the various doors in their way locked. This was probably the door out of the great gallery, the main room on the first floor, to the room adjacent to the turret. They seized a ladder and tried to break the door down, but it broke instead, and they wasted time trying to beat a panel of the door in. Quick-thinking royal attendant (page) John Ramsay, who had been out in the yard and seen but not heard the words of the King, had followed the Lennox/Mar group at a distance and heard that the last door before the king's room was locked. He now looked round for another staircase on the ground floor, found a narrow one (the 'Black Turnpike') leading up to the turret, and ran up it. He found the right room ahead of the others, a nearby servant (evidently not ordered to stand in the way of the royal party or else losing his nerve) opened the door for him, and he ran in to find James and Alexander struggling. James called on him to stab Alexander, and subsequently admitted to the brothers' sceptical Presbyterian clerical ally Robert Bruce that he had encouraged Ramsay to kill not just wound Alexander, but it was his life or his attacker's. Ramsay drew his dagger, wounded Alexander, and pushed him out of the room and down the staircase; those who followed him into the room were led by Thomas Erskine and the lame and slower Dr Hugh Herries, who now despatched the wounded Alexander on the spot. (Herries had apparently been to Gowrie House on unknown business a few days before so pro-Gowrie apologists were able to argue later that he was a secret 'royal hit-man' and had been ordered by James to kill the brothers.)

The Earl of Gowrie, via Cranstoun, had told Lennox and Mar that the King had left a few minutes before and had left them – presumably, so the King was able to imply later, to assist Alexander in kidnap or regicide. But the earl was not in the upstairs room as they were out in the yard seeing the King yelling for help and when Alexander was fighting the rescuer Ramsay; he and Cranstoun apparently witnessed the scene from the yard or the street. Precise movements are unclear, but it appears that Thomas Erskine and his brother tried to seize Gowrie – presumably arguing that as the house's owner he must be behind the attack on James – but he escaped with the aid of some servants who rushed to his aid. Given the frequency of brawls and stabbings in sixteenth-century Scotland, this need not be proof of villainy as it could have been just self-defence, as was Gowrie then drawing his two (as was fashionable in courtly fencing) swords. A group of Murrays further down the street tried to intervene and seize Gowrie, but his men hustled him back to safety in his house, as testified to later by Cranstoun. They then ran for the turret room's stairs, and when they saw Alexander's body, they ran up to attack the king and were pursued, trapped, and killed by the royal escort as the Erskines and then Lennox and Mar's group reinforced Ramsay. Later accounts also had it that as Ramsay had rescued the king by stabbing Alexander a few minutes earlier the latter's blood spurted over James so that when the Lennox/Mar group arrived they thought that the King had been badly wounded and killed off both Alexander and the earl of Gowrie in revenge, or that Ramsay gained a vital few seconds by pretending to Gowrie that the King was fatally wounded. (He had persuaded James to hide in the adjacent turret annex out of view.) This caused the attacking Gowrie to pause, and Ramsay lunged forward with his dagger and seriously injured him, enabling Ramsay to push his target out of the room and causing Gowrie's servants (how many?) to flee.[14] Cranstoun's later account confirmed that he had been in the earl's party rushing upstairs, they had seen Alexander lying at the foot of the stairs before they ran up, he had not seen the King in the turret-room but had fought Ramsay, and after the latter had injured him, he and other servants had fled downstairs. It is clear, if the King's men are to be believed, that the sword-brandishing earl had first attacked Ramsay with murderous intent, but if James was out of sight in the adjacent annex he may not have been targeting the King but the royal aide who had stabbed his brother – without bothering to stop and consider what was going on, where James was, and if Alexander had treasonously attacked him .

The melee ended with both Ruthven brothers dead, and the 'man in armour' (Henderson or not) fled downstairs in a panic to save himself during the fight and 'went to ground' in Perth where he was eventually tracked down by the king's men. His acquaintance Robert Oliphant, the first suspect to be identified as the 'man in armour' but quickly able to provide an alibi, was later to claim that Henderson had lost his nerve; possibly Ramsay's arrival and attack on Alexander gave him a few moments unobserved to bolt. Assorted Perth citizens who ran up to and into the house to investigate the fracas confirmed to the enquiry that they had seen Alexander's body at the foot of the turret stairs, and one said that he had seen Henderson jumping over it and running out of the house. The rescued king announced to an arriving assembly of confused and alarmed Perth citizens, who had heard wild rumours of what had happened and given the Gowries' patronage of their local town might easily have turned hostile and violent, that he had been the subject of a murderous attack by the brothers who his men had had to kill, and on the 7th, two days later, the bodies of the two 'plotters' were publicly hung and quartered at the Mercat Cross in Edinburgh as appropriate for condemned traitors. Their heads were put on spikes at the Tolbooth prison. Their younger brothers were sought out but managed to escape to France, all of the family were banned from coming within ten miles of court, and the family titles and property were confiscated.

The 'official version' of events referred to above was that which James put out within twenty-four hours in a message sent from himself at Falkland to the government ministers in Edinburgh and was elaborated in subsequent explanatory publications. The story was then passed on to the English ambassador Nicholson so an account of it could be sent to Queen Elizabeth in London. The story was already mostly contained in the first version, and no major details were changed – so if it was a fraud James had quickly decided how to cover up what had really happened. But to his annoyance many people – led by a group of Presbyterian clerics in Edinburgh who were linked to the 'Ruthven Raiders', Bothwell, and other past and current critics of his supposed sympathies for Catholics and political control of the Presbyterian Church – refused to believe it. James and the court arrived at the Mercat Cross on 11 August for an official religious service to give thanks for his escape from the 'wicked plot' and his chaplain Galloway gave the official version of events and denounced the attack which clearly God had caused to fail, and then James spoke too. But this was not greeted as warmly as expected. Those Presbyterian clerics who later wrote or spoke about it to attack the royal version included Robert Bruce, the Edinburgh church's envoy to the earl of Gowrie in France in 1599 and probably on good terms with him from this role – so not exactly unbiased? As seen above, the King had been curtailing the church's independence and seeking to censor sermons and ban unofficial, uncontrolled assemblies of clerics in recent years, so there was a political motive for asserting that James was a perjurer who had wickedly killed the church's 'godly' defenders, the Gowrie brothers. Fortunately, the potentially dangerous meddler Bothwell was a spent force, in exile in France. The details of the 'plot' story were now picked over and claimed to be inconsistent and unlikely, and Bruce was summoned to the King to be told to accept his version of events but refused to give way. He replied reasonably that he could give thanks for the King's escape as some violent danger to him had clearly happened, but not for the defeat of a 'plot' as this was yet 'unproven', and accounts were disputed. The offending preachers were threatened by the Council and banned from Edinburgh; those who repented and apologised publicly were allowed back but Bruce was exiled to France. They were presumably involved in the release of the written 'Ruthven Vindication' defending the brothers, which was widely enough circulated to get to the English authorities in Berwick later in September. Cranstoun was arrested and executed, which defenders claimed was a 'fit-up', and surprisingly Henderson was not tried but was let loose quietly and did not even lose his official job as chamberlain of Perth. Did he 'turn king's evidence' and keep quiet about what he knew, or did James accept that he had been tricked by the brothers into taking on the role of the 'man in armour'? A minor local connection of his, Robert Oliphant, was later arrested in early December for apparently talking boldly in a Perth house (while drunk?) about him being allowed to go free when the more innocent Cranstoun was unfairly hanged – and Oliphant also claimed that a few months before the incident the earl of Gowrie had offered him the role of the 'man in armour' assigned to help intimidate the King. He had supposedly refused. The man who he had been complaining to, tailor John Lyn, was also questioned. Although Oliphant prudently made himself scarce from Perth he was later picked up by a royal agent called Patrick Heron in London in 1608 after being spotted there as the king was alerted to his importance, locked up in the Gatehouse prison at Westminster, and sent to Edinburgh – where the Privy Council questioned but released him. What did he know and was he silenced in a 'deal'?

The forfeiting of the Gowrie estates which followed certainly made an example of a notoriously obstreperous dynasty which had been involved in Royal coercion in 1566 and the early 1580s, but it is unlikely that their partisans were correct that the King cleverly 'set them up' for summary execution using himself as 'bait' given his timidity – unless all the Royal retainers who witnessed the skirmish in the upstairs room at Gowrie House were lying. The story that the 'kidnap' had been a spur of the moment affair after the King had been insulting to the brothers' father's memory as he had seen a portrait of him upstairs at the house, Alexander had turned angry and abusive, and he had then feared royal revenge and decided to kidnap the king was heard by and/or spread by John Preston, the Scots ambassador in England. It was also heard and repeated by the north-eastern English magnate and Borders official Sir Walter Bowes, who had extensive contacts in Scotland, in a letter in September 1600 – i.e., soon after the events.[15] He apparently heard the story from the ambassador sent by James to London to explain events to Elizabeth, as the man passed through nearby Newcastle. In fact, there were portraits in an upstairs room at Gowrie House, though in which one is unclear (probably the gallery next to the room where the fracas occurred), and Ramsay had been looking at them earlier in the visit. An alternative story had it that Alexander had got the King alone to seek the grant of his brother's lay abbacy of nearby Scone Abbey or some other lucrative grant or post, possibly that of Gentleman of the Bedchamber (i.e. one of the King's closest and so influential attendants in his private apartments), and done so against the earl's wishes – possibly not telling him that the King was coming at dinner hours earlier as was claimed later by Henderson, so he could guard against the earl interfering with his planned private interview. The king had refused his request angrily and became heated, and Alexander had lost his temper and manhandled him[16] – again, a logical explanation that takes account of the botched nature of any 'kidnap plot'. But that leaves out the question of what the armed man was doing in the turret room and why the earl of Gowrie pretended that the King had left when his horse was still in the yard available for inspection – and why Gowrie and his servants ran upstairs, armed, to assist Alexander rather than restrain him, got into a fight with the rescuer John Ramsay, and the earl ended up dead. Did Ramsay mortally wound Alexander thinking he was an intended kidnapper or regicide and Gowrie, finding him dying, attack Ramsay and/or the king in retaliation?

On 15 August, ten days before the official account of the fracas was released, a well-connected English resident in Edinburgh, Roger Aston, gave his account of what he had heard in a letter to a friend who was seeking official Scots employment. His account backed up James, in that he heard that Alexander had called on James to report finding a mysterious stranger in a field near Perth with 'treasure' and also letters of credit addressed to various Scots nobles – an echo of the 'Spanish Blanks' affair. The letters, if real, were not referred to again – so if Aston had heard correctly was this incident 'hushed up' to save embarrassment to those involved, or did James take possession of the letters and hold them over the accused to ensure their future good conduct?[17] Aston was brother-in-law to Lord Ochiltree and son-in-law to Lady Gowrie's sister, so he had good access to sources, and he had been working on and off for the

Stuart dynasty and feeding them useful intelligence since the 1560s; James paid him the large sum of £5,000 for his services during the decade from 1590–1600. He also reported some wilder theories led by one suggesting that the good-looking earl had been involved with Queen Anne, who by this point was semi-estranged from her husband and often apart from him (though they continued to have children and at this point she was pregnant with the future King Charles I). Aston claimed that when he was dining at court after the incident his table-mate Sir George Home, a leading and trusted royal courtier and minister and later earl of Dunbar, had referred to Anne's secret part in the incident.[18] This might be taken as implying that the King was jealous of his wife showing attentions to Gowrie and was thus hostile to the latter and glad to have an excuse to get rid of him, though the evidence for the struggle in the turret-room makes it unlikely that this ultra-timid man used himself as 'bait' to trap the brothers. It is more likely that his suspicions would lead to him having the row with Alexander referred to as a possible cause for the latter's sudden violence. One rumour about the real version of events had it that Gowrie was suspected of being Prince Charles' real father, another that the homosexual king was having an affair with Gowrie or Alexander that went wrong – but these are both unlikely and probably the result of wild and later guesswork.[19] The rumour about a homosexual affair was known to the Gowrie family by the modern era and may be family tradition.

Another theory (perhaps inevitably) involved one of the favourite 'wild cards' of conspiracy theories, namely the Freemasons – then emerging as a secret society of genuine masons and ambitious court and Edinburgh figures with their first known 'lodges' and rituals. The royal 'Master of Works' Roger Scheves was a leading Mason. This version had it that Gowrie was connected to the Masons and had dug up or otherwise acquired a secret Masonic treasure, which the greedy King sought to confiscate by eliminating him. It may well be true that James did join the first Masonic 'lodge' in Perth on his next visit there, in April 1601, with the episode ironically occurring at the new building which had replaced the confiscated Gowrie House; but this seems just to be an elaboration of the story about a mysterious treasure. An alternative version, discovered by nineteenth-century historian Maurice Lee, had it that the 'treasure' was in fact secret intelligence documents relating to the Gowrie brothers' underhand dealings with important figures in London – possibly secretary of state Cecil – and that James went to Gowrie House on his own initiative to catch the brothers out and find evidence by a quiet search there. Alexander became suspicious, panicked, and tried to kidnap him. This is possible and would fit in with the evidence referred to below of the brothers having 'active' contacts in London, whether or not with the intention of kidnapping James (later?), but the King does not seem to have been very successful or secret in his search if this was what he was planning to do. Another version linked the King's alleged 'plot' to target the Ruthven brothers with the fact that he owed their family large debts from the time that the brothers' executed father had been his treasurer in the early 1580s; these debts were still unpaid but if James could execute the brothers and seize their property for treason he would not have to pay. James was undoubtably both greedy and devious – but this explanation does not cover the question of Alexander luring James upstairs to see a non-existent 'treasure' at Gowrie House or what the 'man in armour' was doing and it assumes that Lennox, Mar, Ramsay and co. were all blatantly lying about the course of events.

The apparent reference by Sir George Home to the Queen's involvement need not mean that the latter and Gowrie were suspected of having an affair, as now that James had one son (Henry, born 1594) the Scots political situation lay open for ambitious men to repeat the coups of past centuries when an adult King or Queen had been deposed in favour of their young heir to create a lucrative regency. This had happened to strong-willed and autocratic James III in 1488 and to the current king's mother Mary in 1567, so could he have been the intended victim of another such plot and his deposition been intended? In that case, the goodwill of the Queen would be important to the plotters and she would have been able to regain influence lost due to her husband's recent neglect, though it was unusual for a young monarch's mother to actually lead or take a major role in a regency and Queen-Mother Joan Beaufort had been side-lined in James I's regency in the late 1430s and early 1440s by great nobles while Archibald Douglas, earl of Angus, had struggled for power with Queen-Mother Margaret Tudor under James V after 1513. James had recently removed his son Henry from Anne's care and she was furious, so she might have been planning with ambitious nobles – possibly Gowrie's old associate the earl of Montrose, or even Home himself – to use Gowrie to depose James and install Henry as king under their own regency. Montrose was at Gowrie House in the royal entourage on the day of the attack and was later accused by the countess of Gowrie of betraying their family – by not aiding the plot and by assisting the King instead? The prince's new guardian as of summer 1600 was Lennox so the plot could have been aimed at him too, and there was initial talk after the incident of ferreting out the plotters' unnamed secret associates, but nothing happened.[20] Did the king's men find no hard evidence, or did James just 'warn off' potential allies of the plotters such as his wife? However, her apparent estrangement from her husband, the unusual nature of their problems arising from his partiality for good-looking young men which could well have left her feeling humiliated, and her separate court (and her reputed dabbling with Catholicism) were bound to lead to rumours, or even to abortive intrigues or attempts to 'smear' her by ill-wishers. This plus the inevitable speculation following a sensational court incident probably account for the rumours of the Queen having recently sent a letter to the earl of Gowrie urging him to come to court (which could well have been true but entirely innocent and just aimed at recruiting him as an ally) and the story which reached Cecil from Edinburgh of gossip about her being locked up once she had given birth to her next child. No credence can be placed on the unattributable romantic story circulating by the later eighteenth century of the King discovering a ribbon which he had given the Queen round Alexander Ruthven's neck when the latter fell asleep in the Falkland Palace Garden with his collar open. (It has echoes of the French court story, used by Alexandre Dumas in 'The Three Musketeers', of Louis XIII's wife Anne of Austria giving a diamond stud to the English duke of Buckingham and having to retrieve it.) As seen by the account of events at Gowrie House, there are major obstacles in the way of alleging a coherent and well-planned 'kidnap attempt'.

The question of who might have wanted James kidnapped and/or deposed also brings in the matter of ill-will to him in London, 'official' (i.e. by a worried Queen Elizabeth or Cecil on account of James' indulgence for pro-Spanish Catholic nobles?) or 'unofficial' (e.g. by a side-lined and royally snubbed Essex desperate to regain royal goodwill by removing the Queen's untrustworthy cousin?). The apparent reception of and talks with the earl of Gowrie by Cecil as the earl headed home from Paris in April 1600 – after the English ambassador in Paris, Neville, had recommended him – might seem to give this credibility. The earl had also met the anti-James earl of Home, an ally of his old connection Bothwell, in Paris – though Bothwell was currently plotting with Spain and this sort of Catholic alliance was in contrast to Gowrie's Presbyterian allegiance. This leads to the matter of the later allegations by one George Sprot, a thoroughly untrustworthy attorney of the Lothian port of Eyemouth who was a dabbler in secret intelligence and by all accounts was capable of inventing stories to earn money from interested parties by confirming their suspicions and/or to make himself seem important and well-connected. But he did have connections in high places, especially via his friend and business associate Logan of Restalrig (see below), so he was able to pose as being well-informed. According to his later stories there was a genuine plan to kidnap the King at Gowrie House and smuggle him out of Perth down the river Tay to a waiting ship that would take him to a secure stronghold in Lothian, probably Fast Castle on its isolated rocky 'stack' (owned by Logan) which was difficult to besiege. James would then supposedly be collected by an English ship and removed to imprisonment in England on behalf of his detractors there – and a suitable ship was currently in place at the English border town of Berwick-upon-Tweed, built with convenient haste recently by governor, Lord Willoughby d'Eresby.[21] Was this intended to be used to remove

James to London? Indeed, it was not unknown for a Scots monarch to end up a hostage in England while his successor 'regency' collaborated with London as this had happened to the declining King Robert III's boy-heir James (soon to be King James I) in 1406. Afraid of the boy being kidnapped or murdered after his older son David had already suffered this fate, Robert had tried to send James, aged twelve, off to safety in France to be brought up there, but an English ship had intercepted him and the boy-king had ended up as a hostage of English Kings Henry IV and Henry V, interned at the English court or in secure castles until 1424 while a pro-English regency under his uncle Duke Robert of Albany (d 1420) and cousin Duke Murdach (executed by James in 1425) had governed Scotland. Mary Stuart, deposed sovereign of Scotland and James VI's mother, had famously been interned in England for life after she fled there seeking help against her son's regents in 1568 and had ended up executed, and at one point while she was in prison the English government had considered ridding themselves of this political embarrassment by sending her home to govern as the puppet of a pro-English faction while James took her place in England – ready to be sent home in her stead if she showed signs of independence. Kidnapping James and putting Henry on the throne was thus in line with past English policy, and the disgraced earl of Essex was duly to accuse his foe Cecil of being behind the Gowrie House incident. But this might just be guesswork based on the fact that Cecil had met Gowrie while he was in London in March 1600, and/or a 'smear' to embarrass Cecil.[22]

As it happened, Lord Willoughby knew Gowrie too as he had met him in Padua in 1594 while the earl was studying there[23] – but this may be coincidence too and he had been absent from Berwick when Gowrie passed through on his way home from London in spring 1600 so he had not seen him recently. His hastily-acquired ship at Berwick was supposed to be for use against pirates from Dunkirk preying on English shipping in the North Sea. The most that can be said about Willoughby joining in a kidnap plot is that he had used Logan of Restalrig (a former Marian agent and a cousin of the arch-intriguer Patrick, Master, i.e. heir, of Gray) to acquire intelligence and do other 'dirty work' in Scotland, and back in 1599 he had arranged the kidnap of secret agent John Guevara, his own (half-Spanish) cousin and a 'go-between' between the Spanish and their English Catholic sympathisers, from Leith golf-links and had had him bundled into a carriage and removed to Berwick. Willoughby was an old friend of Essex rather than of Cecil, and Essex is even less likely to have wanted James removed than Cecil given that he had been having a productive secret correspondence with him for years and could look for rehabilitation when James inherited England .The 'Scots co-conspirators' in the alleged plot to smuggle the king out of Perth to Fast Castle were named by Sprot as Sir James Scrymgeour, provost of Dundee, and local landowner Sir Harry Lindsay whose Kinfauns Castle was on the Tay downstream from Perth so a useful place to hold the king or transfer him to a ship. There is however a question over Sprot's apparent source for the 'kidnap by ship plot', the multiple plotter and betrayer Logan of Restalrig, a minor Lothian laird who had dabbled in treason for years. He was part-owner of Lord Willoughby's new ship and was supposed to have planned to sell up his interests in Scotland in 1600 and go abroad in a hurry – to avoid repercussions if the plot failed?[24] By 1608 he was conveniently dead, so he could not confirm or deny what Sprot said about him; according to Sprot he had seen a letter from Gowrie to Logan dealing with the kidnap plan which Logan's (illiterate) servant passed on to him. The role of Logan in general and the naming of Lindsay of Kinfauns, Willoughby and co. relies on the far from trustable words of Sprot himself when he was arrested for forgery in 1608 and interrogated by the Scots government. He claimed that Logan had been in correspondence with the earl of Gowrie and Alexander and he, Sprot, had copies of the letter – but this was never published and there is no proof that it existed. Sprot was hanged as an accessory to the Gowrie plot, and contemporary observers such as future archbishop John Spottiswood did not believe him.

The death of Queen Elizabeth at Richmond Palace on 24 March 1603 finally brought James to the English throne. Her cousin Sir Robert Carey rode through the night northwards on a relay of horses to present James with her signet-ring as proof (and secure rich rewards for himself), and on 4 April James left Edinburgh for his new realm. The new king of England would return home only once, in 1617, and as he proceeded to utilise his new power and opportunities in his usual idiosyncratic way the mysterious affair at Gowrie House receded into the past. The extra weight of English resources gave James' so far turbulent reign greater stability and no more major plots against him in Scotland seem to have occurred, while his long-range 'government by pen' kept a firm grip on Scotland with Sir George Home among the main beneficiaries. The disgrace and final eclipse of the Ruthven brothers was largely forgotten until after the collapse of Stuart rule in England and Scotland during the post-1637 crises, when (as again after James VII and II's removal in 1688–9) criticism of the dynasty and its past alleged misbehaviour became safe again. As seen, the incident and its possible ramifications were so marked by uncertainty and conjecture that little of the 'evidence' is safe, though it is unlikely on the grounds of his character that James was staging a deliberate 'hit' against the Ruthvens by luring them into attacking him. It is more likely that something went badly wrong with someone's plans, be it a royal kidnap or James' investigation of his unreliable vassals, but more probable that if Alexander was indeed aiming at coercing his sovereign this was done on the spur of the moment in reaction to an unexpected quarrel with him. The mystery continues.

Chapter 2

James I's Bisexual Favourite, His Mistress, and the Poisoning in the Tower: The Overbury Scandal

Was James complicit or instrumental in a major 'cover-up' and miscarriage of justice?

From spring 1603 the new King James I was resident in England rather than his old realm of Scotland, with his Queen (Anne of Denmark, embarrassingly a secret Catholic convert), and children soon following him. The respect and obedience traditionally given to a monarch in England, plus the much larger revenue available and the greater Royal control of a bishop-dominated church, were much to the new King James I's liking after his turbulent reign in Scotland – as was the large collection of royal residences that he inherited from Elizabeth I which far outmatched those available at home. He had a collection of country estates useable for hunting – one of his great passions to the point of obsession – in the Home Counties was especially appreciated, as the King settled down to enjoy his new status as the fount of honour and patronage in a major European monarchy – and the head and 'supreme governor' of a deferential Anglican Church rather than a ruler who was barely tolerated as head of the decentralised Scots Calvinist Church and was frequently lectured by its grim and critical clerics. Unlike his loathed Catholic mother Mary he had been brought up as a Calvinist from his infancy by 'reliable' tutors and was no direct political threat to its power-hoarding clergy, but his fraternising with some of the surviving Catholic peers (mainly Highlands clan chiefs with useful large private armies of retainers) at his small court and the temporary ascendancy of his French-educated and Catholic cousin Esme Stuart, Duke of Lennox in the early 1580s had been viewed with deep suspicion. Fears that he could convert and ally to Spain – and perhaps pursue his claim to the English throne that way – were stoked up by ambitious and unscrupulous Calvinist lords seeking English aid to constrain him by yet another internal Scots coup.

As seen, this feverish atmosphere was prevalent and led to all sorts of wild rumours about plots and attempted coups around the time of the 'Gowrie House Incident' in 1600 – and Scotland had a long history of arrogant nobles kidnapping and forcing their wishes on kings, especially under-age ones during a regency. The intelligent and devious James, lacking a standing army, had managed to keep his rival factions from uniting against or constraining him again and had duly inherited England in March 1603, and after that huge increase in his power, resources, and international prominence he was determined both to make the most of his opportunities and – like his grandson Charles II after his return from impoverished exile in 1660 – to enjoy himself. With the resources of the English Crown, as aggrandised by the acquisitive Henry VIII, at his disposal he had enormous amounts of patronage to disperse and a much larger income than as ruler of Scotland, despite the debts run up by Elizabeth's government during the long Spanish war which he now brought to a swift conclusion. In return, much was expected of him by the ambitious nobles and gentry who flocked to greet him as he made his leisurely way down through England to London and then set up his court – both from existing Elizabethan courtiers and office-holders keen to keep their places (and cash) and from those excluded from power and influence under the late Queen. The victims of the unsuccessful and blunderingly botched attempted coup against Elizabeth in February 1601 by her disgraced ex-favourite, the charismatic Robert Devereux, Earl of Essex, also expected rehabilitation – and had old scores to settle against the current chief minister who had crushed the coup, secretary of state Sir Robert Cecil. Indeed, as the vain and psychologically unstable Essex (who had responded to his political marginalisation by Cecil by attempting to seize the person of the Queen and have his faction arrested) had been in regular contact with James for years as the Queen's unnamed but presumed heir, her next of kin once Mary Stuart was dead, James had reason to respond to the support the Essex faction had given his candidacy by freeing the survivors and restoring them to favour. This was duly done once James was King, though in an uneasy compromise the Cecil faction also retained power, led by Sir Robert as Secretary of State (in effect in charge of bureaucratic patronage and foreign policy) and from 1607 as Lord Treasurer. Cecil had been regularly corresponding with James for years too and promising to smooth his way to the English throne and help him govern once he achieved it, in a successful bid to rival Essex's offers and keep himself in power once James was King – though he had to do this secretly so as not to annoy the paranoid Elizabeth who did not like any mention of who was to succeed her.

Once James was safe on the English throne, those who had suffered in the purge of Essex's faction in 1601 were pardoned – though the ultra-devious Cecil remained alert to the danger of vengeful rivals from the Elizabethan court trying to have him sacked. He was probably behind the unexpected disgrace later in 1603 of his old rival, the swashbuckling and blunderingly incautious Devonian courtier/privateer/explorer Sir Walter Raleigh, who was accused of responding petulantly to his marginalisation on the new King's accession by plotting some sort of coup. Raleigh was supposed to have been planning with Lords Cobham and Grey to wipe out the Royal Family and install James' cousin Arbella Stuart – the daughter of his father Lord Darnley's younger brother, who had been a 'long shot' candidate to succeed Queen Elizabeth pre-1603 as a descendant of Henry VII and unlike James born and bred in England – on the throne. This was an unlikely gamble even for the notoriously hot-headed, arrogant and swashbuckling Raleigh, even granted that James had sacked him as Captain of the Guard and confiscated assorted money-making Court licences so he could expect his many debtors as well as his assorted Court enemies to close in on him. Nor were the King's principal informants about Raleigh's 'crimes', Cecil and the devious Catholic nobleman Henry Howard (earl of Northampton), exactly unbiased about Raleigh – but James had him convicted for treason, nearly executed, reprieved at the last minute, stripped of his estates, and thrown in the Tower of London anyway. Was his mixture of fear of a 'loose cannon' Elizabethan Court troublemaker and desire to set a harsh example to scare off other 'plotters' similar to his behaviour over the 'Gowrie Plot' (see previous chapter)? Among those who had confiscated lands and access to Court returned in 1603 was Essex's young son Robert Devereux (born 1593) – who was in due course to become a central figure in the murky 'Overbury Affair'.

The legally dubious annulment of the new Earl of Essex's marriage to leading courtier Earl of Suffolk's daughter Frances, as arranged for her benefit by the King and his advisers, enabled this young woman, one of the prominent Howard dynasty and a niece and probable protegee of Raleigh's enemy Henry Howard, to marry her lover (the King's admired Scots protégé Robert Carr) under the King's indulgent auspices. Frances and her new husband were at the centre of the Overbury scandal, when their former close friend Sir Thomas Overbury, a minor but well-connected courtier and writer, took against his former patrons and threatened to expose their secrets. He ended up (probably) murdered by poison in the Tower of London, after a bungled earlier attempt to silence him which did not lead to his alerted gaoler protecting him any better, and the King's own role in this was 'covered up' as were official attempts to 'shut down' the case. Though many details were unclear then and remain dubious, it is clear that at the very least the fetid and intrigue-laden atmosphere of James' extravagant court and its mixture of vicious rivalries and financial (and moral) chicanery enabled the Overbury affair to take place with the indulgent King showing very poor judgement. The unique British circumstances of his assumption of a second major throne and his move to England however produced special circumstances that raised the risk of a subterranean struggle between factions at court. James had to bring a suitably large and socially impressive escort of Scottish nobles to London to help staff his merged Anglo-Scots court there, quite apart from his personal need for people he already knew and trusted. The nature of the English court meant that there was a large 'Privy Chamber' of noble and gentleman attendants on a reigning male monarch, as used as a centre of intrigue and power-seeking under Henry VIII, with its occupants in close attendance on the King and so able to corner influence and jobs for themselves and their clients – always a major source of prestige and funds for ambitious men in an era of intense social and political competition. Elizabeth had not had a Privy Chamber, nor had her sister Mary Tudor, and their brother Edward VI had been a boy operating as king under a succession of actual or unofficial regents, so there had been no Privy Chamber since Henry VIII died in January 1547 and the new King's revival of this institution was eagerly expected to provide a major source of power and influence. In the natural course of events there would not be enough jobs for all applicants and those who lost out were bound to be resentful while successful new courtiers would be undermined by jealous enemies seeking their posts. So the risk of some scandal – real or invented – being used to undermine major figures at court was a permanent hazard after 1603, especially with such high expectations that the parsimony and relatively close grip on patronage by Elizabeth (and to a degree Cecil as her chief adviser after his late father Lord Burleigh died in 1598) would be relaxed.

A new king unused to the niceties of English politics and social behaviour presented a heightened risk, though arguably this was mainly Elizabeth's fault as – like Queen Anne with the Hanoverian heirs to her throne after the Act of Settlement in 1701 – she would neither let her presumed heir visit her country nor meet them in person and any courtier who went to call on them faced deep suspicion of currying favour in hopes of future preferment and so insultingly neglecting their current sovereign. James could only find out what was going on in England and who to rely on at its court ahead of his accession via ambassadorial visits to London and his correspondence with Cecil, Essex and others – all of whom would tell him what they wanted him to hear and undermine their rivals. Despite James' intelligence and shrewdness, his personal behaviour was such as to attract criticism, particularly of his appearance and slovenly habits – probably exacerbated by snobbish English disdain for the 'uncouth' Scots as a people. The potential problems had already become apparent during the relatively successful and more (but not that) stable years of his rule in Scotland from the late 1590s, as he and his younger wife Anne of Denmark grew apart and started to maintain separate courts though they continued to produce children. Anne became a spendthrift, with a love of theatrical masques to the Scots Presbyterians' horror, and by the late 1590s was largely living apart from her husband as well as there being rumours that she had privately converted to Catholicism which would be as problematic to English as to Scots Protestant zealots after the heightened anti-Catholic hysteria of the 1580s. The King was already being accused of undue partiality for handsome young men and homosexual tendencies, as alluded to in his public declaration explaining his decision to marry, and his relationship with Esme Stuart had come under candid scrutiny and hostile rumour in the early 1580s given the new favourite's good looks and charisma and James' enthusiastic hero-worship for him. The King's attitude to Stuart/Lennox was probably more to do with a desire for affection and uncritical support from a 'father-figure' after a harsh childhood as a closely-controlled puppet-king, but it was arguably unwise and angry ultra-Protestant nobles ended up kidnapping James in the 'Ruthven Raid', making him a puppet again, and forcing the favourite's exile. Critics of Esme and his Catholic Continental background, honestly fearing he would 'corrupt' the impressionable James into converting or determined to allege this for their own advancement by ruining him, were bound to paint the favourite's behaviour in the worst possible light – illegal homosexuality being a useful weapon as a 'smear' – and would use exaggeration to induce the alarmed Elizabeth and her rabidly Protestant chief ministers, Burleigh and Walsingham, to help them overthrow and exile Esme.

Despite his greater political skill as an adult and an apparent absence of any more influential good-looking male friends for a decade or so, James did not see fit to rein his feelings in permanently and his 'weakness' for dashing, handsome young courtiers was often remarked on. Once he was away from grim Scots Calvinist scrutiny in London and had plenty of money to lavish on his handsome young proteges the problem resumed and his conduct, as with his drinking, became worse with age. (He had also fallen victim to one of the age's leading superstitions, the fear of witchcraft, and sought to examine and understand the phenomenon in learned detail; he came to believe that the storms which had delayed him and his Queen on their journey to Scotland in winter 1588–9 had been due to witches and that a coven of Devil-worshippers at North Berwick had tried to sink his ships and in 1590–1 over a hundred alleged witches were investigated and many were burned.) His self-acclaimed role as the nation's supreme scholar and his undoubted extensive learning were not to the taste of many of his contemporaries, and his notorious fear of cold steel and assassination was something to be scorned. His wearing thick clothing to prevent stabbing and his slovenly habits attracted ridicule, especially after 1603 in England; a speech impairment from an over-large tongue added to this though the sources that specify the extent of his social imperfections may have been exaggerating due to malice. Even the flattery that he was a 'new Solomon' due to his learning was turned against him, with wits saying that this was appropriate as he was the 'son of David' (i.e. his mother's murdered Italian secretary David Riccio).

These imperfections plus his lack of detailed knowledge of England and its elite were bound to be utilised by critics, his paranoia about plots after his poor treatment by his Scots nobles opened him to insinuations from the crafty Cecil about who he should fear most (e.g. Raleigh), and as disenchantment set in with hopes from the new regime being disappointed it laid him open to both inevitable and avoidable criticism. His Bedchamber appointments of large numbers of Scots were one early source of criticism as it became clear that the ambitious English office-seekers would have to share the fruits of patronage with people who they had long looked down on as uncivilised northern savages; the Scots were supposed by their indignant excluded English rivals to be sucking up Royal patronage. The official Bedchamber which he set up in 1603 had four Gentlemen, six Grooms and six Pages, a mixture of English (pre-1547) and Scots practices, with James' loyal and 'non-political' cousin Ludovick Stuart, duke of Lennox and son of Esme, as the First Nobleman of the Bedchamber and honorary supremo – but real authority, organization and patronage with the captain of the Guard, Sir Thomas Erskine, as First Gentleman and Groom of the Stool. The latter famously had the exclusive personal access to the King and concurrent opportunities available from attending the King in the lavatory, along with sleeping at the foot of the royal bed and dressing the King with his more intimate garments. In fact his duties now could be shared if he and the King so desired with other Gentlemen and the Pages of the Bedchamber, though he still had the closest attendance on the King including in his coach while travelling, and this sharing of opportunities now extended to keeping the King's 'Privy Purse' (i.e his personal expenditure), which was now usually done at first by Sir George Home (earl of Dunbar) and having the ability to seek the King's signature for privately submitted warrants.[1] Under Elizabeth, with no Bedchamber, the secretary of state and his clerks had had this vital access for private approaches to and patronage from the monarch. All of the four Gentlemen of the Bedchamber formally appointed in 1603 were Scots, headed by Sir John Ramsay (who as seen above had played a major role in the Gowrie House incident and was totally trusted by the King) and by Lennox's brother; one of the two new members added that July was an Englishman from a major noble family, Philip Herbert (later Earl of Pembroke and Montgomery), who was the only Englishman thus honoured until 1615.[2] In addition, Dunbar had extra duties, perquisites and access as Master of the Wardrobe, as he was already in Scotland. All the Grooms of the Bedchamber were Scots until the appointment of the handsome young Northamptonshire gentleman Sir George Villiers (later his chief adviser, the Duke of Buckingham) in 1617, and when the future leading character in the Overbury affair, Robert Carr/Kerr, was transferred from his first post as Groom to be one of the Gentlemen in 1607 that made it seven Scotsmen to one Englishman as Gentlemen.[3]

These posts were seen at the time as crucial for access to and influence on the King, as a complaining petition to James' son Charles I by the side-lined Gentlemen Ushers (who had had close access to the sovereign under the Tudors) in 1603 dated the transfer of influence and close royal access to the Gentlemen of the Bedchamber to the appointments of May 1603.[4] Moreover, since the reforming Household 'Eltham Ordinances' of Henry VIII's reign only the personnel of the Bedchamber, not Privy Councillors or any other office-holders or courtiers, had the right of access to the King's inner apartments – the 'princes of the royal blood' technically did but James only had two, under-age sons pre-1610 and after that his teenage heir Prince Henry lived away from court at St James's Palace and Richmond. Away from his palaces, the King mostly spent his extensive leisure-hours hunting at his suburban residences or on royal summer 'progresses' – he was estimated at having spent about half his reign doing this and so being away from the court.[5] He liked to be attended by his lively young boon companions the Grooms of the Bedchamber (all active and good at riding) on the hunt too, not interrupted by importunate ministers with business, though the Gentlemen and some of the royal guards were also in attendance. This gave a new importance to the King's private hunting-lodges, such as his new buildings at Newmarket – where favoured companions like Carr were given rooms close to the King[6] – and Cecil made over his rural Hertfordshire family mansion of Theobalds, where the King often went to hunt, as a gift to him. (In return he received the Cecils' chief residence to this day, the royal palace of Hatfield House, and rebuilt it.) Business was duly severely delayed at times, and access to the King much less than that to Elizabeth with resulting frustration and resentment from excluded courtiers and importunate favour-seeking visitors. Even the Privy Council now did not have automatic access to the King, and with him frequently away from court there were fears over potential loss of influence and who might be inducing him to carry out what measures, grants and appointments – even Cecil was notably uneasy at this and bemoaning his lack of access to the King a few months into the reign.[7] His solution was to place his own men in the King's inner sanctum as Gentlemen of the Bedchamber and so have extra access to the King and an 'early warning system' of potential problems, i.e. firstly the young Scots courtier Sir James Hay (later earl of Carlisle) and soon Cecil's own nephew, Philip Herbert.[8] Another Gentleman, the Scots-domiciled English adventurer Sir Roger Aston who was James' Master Huntsman and had aided Cecil by letter in arranging his written access to James pre-1603 and the succession, was also a vital help to him.[9] He also arranged lucrative grants to the King's favoured (mostly noble) companions at his small size 'holiday retreat' courts, such as Lennox, Dunbar, and lords Fenton and Haddington, who duly helped him. Others lacked Cecil's ability to get access to the King and also joined in the new rush to shower gifts on those who might help with this and put in a good word with James, and favoured Scots were more than willing to exploit the situation and offer access and royal favours in return for bribes. Resentment at the influx and greed of these Scotsmen was notable in Jacobean satires about the corruption of the new court, as most notably written by the xenophobic Sir Ralph Weldon, and did the King's reputation great damage within the circle of its readers – and this problem would have been at least minimised with more royal care and subtlety. Similar sentiments were quoted by Guy Fawkes as a reason for his attempt to blow up the King and the entire Protestant elite in Parliament in November 1605; he had written an attack on the monopoly of access to the King by his countrymen as earl as summer 1603.[10]

This all raised the risks of scandal at a laxly-supervised court composed of nationals of two mutually mistrustful countries, the 'alien incomers' being resented for unfair monopoly of patronage (though that was to be expected given the new and deeply mistrustful King's reliance on people he was familiar with), the dangers of rumour and malice stoked up by xenophobia, and the risk of a notably careless and emotionally impulsive King giving his trust to those who were unworthy of it. James was not careful of his courtiers' reputation and willing to crack down on real or perceived misbehaviour, unlike Elizabeth who had famously guarded the chastity of her ladies-in-waiting like a hawk and sacked or otherwise punished those who became pregnant and/or married without her permission, plus their seducers. The ever-reckless Raleigh was famously in trouble with and disgraced by Elizabeth for his seduction of her young attendant 'Bess' Throckmorton, but in trouble with and imprisoned for a decade by James on political grounds, whether or not he was 'framed' by Cecil. Some of the most notorious incidents of rowdiness and mass drunkenness at James' court, which have been retold disapprovingly for centuries, would have been inconceivable at Elizabeth's court and after his death his son Charles I was to order an equally stringent crackdown. The most famous of these was probably the extravagant and party-laden visit of his wife's brother King Christian IV of Denmark, as heavy and enthusiastic a drinker as the King, in July-August 1606, when disapproving courtier Sir John Harington recorded the scenes of drunken debauchery at the shambolic masque that was meant to show the visit of the Queen of Sheba to the court of King Solomon (the latter being a tribute to the King given his nickname of the 'new Solomon'). The participants were too intoxicated to play their parts properly and staggered around the stage or started fighting drunkenly, the lady playing the 'Queen of Sheba' tripped up as she was climbing the steps to the royal seats to present gifts to King Christian and tipped them in his lap, the latter then tried to stand up and dance with her but collapsed drunk and had to be carried out, and the following 'parade and courtly dancing' of the participants was ruined by their drunken incapacity.

Many ended up collapsing or staggering out to vomit, and Harington was duly disgusted as he compared this with the far seemlier proceedings at Elizabeth's court.[11] This was perhaps an extreme case, Harington had a point to make to his correspondent at the time about the degradation of court life and his desire to escape from it, and King Christian was a notoriously hard drinker. But the overall tone of the court was much laxer – and thus open to discredit and people making the most of its potential – than the Tudor court, and it was also worrying that James was famously indulgent to the behaviour of those with whom he was friendly. Both the principals in the Overbury case, Carr and his lover/wife Frances Howard, were young and lively favourites of the sentimental King – and Frances' family, closely related to Queen Elizabeth but marginalised since she executed their head the Duke of Norfolk for supposed treason in 1572, were among what would now be called the 'fast set' at Court. Frances' father Thomas Howard, the duke of Suffolk and a younger son of the executed Norfolk, had been cold-shouldered by Elizabeth but was back in favour under James and as of 1614 was to become Lord Treasurer – and to prove himself hopeless at reining in the already burgeoning royal spending. Allegations of corruption were also rife against him, though his main 'sins' of accepting gifts in return for using his influence and spending the King's money on building his own large mansion (Audley End in Suffolk) were normal for a courtier of that era and under Elizabeth both secretary of state/ Lord Treasurer Burleigh, Cecil's father, and royal favourite/chancellor Sir Christopher Hatton had built mansions out of the perquisites of their salaries. The worst problems with Suffolk's time as lord chamberlain (i.e. in charge of Court spending and appointments) and later treasurer – which spill over into consideration of the Howard family's part in the Overbury murder – were the timing of his lavish spending (which came after Cecil had been trying to balance the books and stop the growing deficit of income to spending by a deal with Parliament in 1610) and his laxity in dealing with 'over-spend' and perquisites. His laxity also extended to governing his own family, given the number of his children involved in minor or major scandals. Notably, the austere and hard-working – and more religious – Prince Henry was to impose strict rules, rein in unsupervised expenditure, and ban drunkenness at his court once he was able to set one up in 1610, a reproach to his indulgent father. The scene was set for a potential major scandal, with a greater risk due to the King's recklessness and failure to enforce seemliness on enthusiastic hedonists at Court to the same degree as his earnest five Tudor predecessors.

One of the major Scots 'players' in James' English Court (and to a lesser degree in government) was a central actor in the forthcoming Overbury scandal, though his degree of culpability seems to have been more of foolishness and going along with stronger personalities than malice. This was Robert 'Carr' (actually Kerr), a handsome young Borders nobleman from the extensive Lothian dynasty of Kerr of Ferniehurst who had been one of the main 'second-ranking' Border families active in local events for the past century, ranking behind the peerage. A fourth son (his father Sir Thomas of Ferniehurst had died soon after he was born) so with no prospects of family money or land, the good-looking and ambitious Carr had followed the King south in 1603 along with many others of his type, aged probably around seventeen and as a minor Court page. He owed this role to the patronage of his previous employer, the eminent Borders magnate and government minister George Home, earl of Dunbar – the Homes had been patrons of the Kerrs for generations. At the time he did not apparently come to the notice of the King, who was lavishing patronage and friendship on the older and more experienced James Hay, lord Hay (1606) and later earl of Carlisle, who was more discreet and shrewder at keeping out of trouble. Indeed, James – whose partiality for handsome young men was already attracting unfavourable comment and moral disdain in England – was supposed not to be too deeply attached to Hay, and to prefer younger, more stunning-looking, and more androgynous young men – into which category Carr fitted better. James was also soon seen to be spending time with and giving gifts to his first English Gentleman of the Bedchamber, the more good-looking Philip Herbert, a skilled jouster and hunting-enthusiast, who as noted above was a careful 'plant' in his inner circle by Cecil – and who was soon married off to the latter's niece, Lady Susan Vere, with a lavish wedding-present from the King.[12] Carr was to follow this pattern exactly, and unlike the rather proud and bad-tempered 'entitled' aristocrat Herbert (nephew of the late poet Sir Philip Sidney) was supple or servile enough to subordinate his interests to the King's, dance attendance on him whenever the demanding James required, and be polite to courtiers who sought his help in approaching the King with requests. It is unlikely that Carr made some '*faux paus*' at Court and was sent home to mend his manners as rumour had it, but he may well have returned home for a while and only been recently back in London when he came to James' attention. Unlike 'reigning favourite' Hay, who had recently grown a beard and so may have become less attractive to the King who preferred epicene young men,[13] he was beardless and was becoming noted for his looks, and in the annual court tournament held at Whitehall Palace to celebrate the King's accession day (24 March 1607) he was a page and 'shield-bearer' to one of the participating aristocrats, possibly Hay himself. (The tilting-ground was on the site of the current Horse Guards Parade.) As Carr was riding into the tiltyard to dismount and present his patron's ornamental shield to the King his horse reared and threw him, breaking his leg; the King was apparently 'struck by' him and became enamoured enough to pay regular visits to him while he was laid up. This duly attracted bitchy comments at this worthless latest royal 'toy-boy' owing all his success to a freak accident not any personal qualities,[14] but the incident may have been a minor (but the first public) catalyst to an attraction that was already underway despite the legend. Carr duly started to amass gifts of land and possessions from the smitten King, as with Hay and Herbert before him, and on 23 December 1607 became a knight and a Gentleman of the Bedchamber.[15] He now eclipsed his predecessors as the King's regular and much-valued companion – and the object of fake admiration and respect from greedy courtiers wanting him to put in a good word with the King or secure a grant from him. Already in receipt of an annual pension of £800 per annum, in January 1609 Carr was given the prestigious estate of Sherborne Castle in Dorset with its new mansion there erected by its Elizabethan grantee, the disgraced Tower of London prisoner Sir Walter Raleigh. The latter had intended the estate as the secure new home of his (minor gentry) Devon family who were unceremoniously evicted, the King ignored their personal appeals, and it passed from one resented 'jumped-up' provincial social climber in royal favour to another – arousing criticism at the time but par for the period. The King did not even keep to his plan, as within two years he had made Carr hand Sherborne back in order to give it to Prince Henry and had fobbed him off with £20,000 instead.[16] Carr (probably hated worse as being a Scots 'interloper') was soon the object of profound loathing for the King's embarrassingly public relationship with him as the besotted James kissed and fondled him in public, and comments about how disgusting this was are scattered through contemporary sources along with criticism of his epicene looks and 'unmanly' frizzled hair[17] – which have been recycled ever since to his detriment and made him out to be some sort of unscrupulous catamite exploiting the susceptible King. But the initiative in the relationship and the public affection clearly came from the King's side, with even the relatively restrained contemporary commentator Bishop Goodman writing that he had never seen such public displays of adoration, and although Carr's duties involved him sharing the Royal Bedchamber and he may have shared the royal bed at times there is no definitive proof of a physical homosexual affair. Such relations were illegal at the time, punishable by hanging under a statute of Henry VIII (rarely enforced) so people would be wary of alleging in print that their King was guilty of blatant breaches of his own laws, but it is not clear that the affair went beyond an embarrassing emotional dependence by the increasingly incautious King – whose public affection for and gifts to his subsequent favourite George Villiers after 1618 would be even more blatant. On that occasion, the two appear to have shared a bed at least once, as revealed in the King's letters. At the most there may have been some embarrassing letters from a love-smitten and sentimental James to Carr that had proof of more than an emotional attachment. After Carr was arrested over the Overbury case in 1615 and his correspondence was officially seized by the Lord Chief Justice (Sir Edward Coke) and examined, something may have been discovered to the King's discredit as the (well-connected but later) author and MP Sir Simonds D'Ewes alleged that Coke found some highly damaging letter by the King to Carr that he 'hushed up' but kept hold of. Allegedly Coke was incautious or indignant enough to let it be known what he had found, and this was why the furious King later dismissed and 'cold-shouldered' this talented and principled constitutional lawyer[18] – though in reality Coke was too inclined to follow his conscience rather than royal orders to be trusted by James, who preferred servility. Carr even later became Secretary of State after Robert Cecil (by then also Lord Treasurer) died in May 1612, though this was more of a matter of the King entrusting the vital job of handling his official correspondence and foreign affairs to a man who he could trust totally and who did not have the skill or willpower to start taking his own 'line' on policy or to try to manipulate him. The 'downside' of this was his lack of knowledge or ability to assess useful from useless persons and proposals. A boon companion rather than a politician, Carr was probably not one for taking the initiative in anything beyond a degree of swollen-headed greed for the good things of life and a desire to show off his success. But the fact that such a politically inexperienced and naïve young courtier was the object of the King's eager patronage, and the attentions of courtly flatterers were to make matters a good deal worse than they could have been for the King in the Overbury affair. A more cautious and sensible man, or an experienced English aristocrat with a major family to back him like Herbert, would not have committed such mistakes.

All three royal favourites became earls, Hay (Carlisle) and Carr (Somerset) thanks to James and Herbert both thanks to James (Montgomery), and later by succeeding his brother (Pembroke, in 1630). Hay's nobly-born wife Lucy Percy was a mistress of intrigue and 'backstairs' influence who was to play a greater role in politics than her husband and may have changed history, as an unofficial 'secret agent' of ambiguous loyalties in the Civil War period who allegedly tipped off her lover John Pym MP that Charles I was about to arrest the 'Five Members' in 1642 and so enabled them to escape. But Carr was the only one to end up at the centre of a murder mystery, thanks to his entanglement with the stronger-willed and manipulative Lady Frances Howard, a classic amoral Jacobean court beauty who has an even worse reputation than him. She was convicted of the eponymous murder in 1615 at the height of the Overbury scandal, with her husband's ex-friend Sir Thomas Overbury having been thrown into the Tower largely due to her and her new husband Carr. He subsequently died in agony after eating a 'gift' of tarts which she was reliably supposed to have sent him and the 'smoking gun' of means, motive and commissioning the gift were all traced back to her – though she was not executed but reprieved and was later quietly let out of prison by the King. Frances has had a poor reputation for centuries and it is still far from clear if she was innocent or guilty whereas at the most the feckless Carr seems to have known about the crime after it occurred and covered it up to protect her – technically 'misprison'. Unlike other more famous Early Modern court ladies at the centre of sordid political/criminal goings-on at court, such as Anne Boleyn's sister-in-law Jane Lady Rochford who helped to condemn her relatives, she has not been given the posthumous benefit of a degree of exculpation in fiction. To add to her crimes, it is not certain that the convenient annulment of her previous marriage to the young Earl of Essex was a fraud, connived at or indeed arranged by King James, and that Frances was being honest when she successfully accused Essex of being impotent and requested an annulment. By this point Carr was her lover, so at the least she was an adulteress who sought to rid herself of her legal husband and she could be presented in more moral ages as a scheming, lust-driven whore who would stop at nothing to get what she wanted. But, as investigated in the analysis of her part in the scandal in Anne Somerset's book *Unnatural Murder* (Weidenfeld and Nicolson, 1997) it can be argued that she was caught in a loveless marriage to a young man who she had not wanted to marry, arranged by her parents and the King, and by modern standards had some right to attempt to have this unfortunate and painful situation remedied by any legal means – even if this meant bending the rules. Essex himself was to assure the legal enquiry into his marriage's validity that he had been in love with Frances when the King arranged the match ahead of the formal ceremony in January 1606, and Frances was spoken of by observers with no 'axe to grind' as a great beauty and seems to have had a degree of charisma too, quite apart from her useful connections as daughter of the earl of Suffolk and niece of the brilliant but universally mistrusted crypto-Catholic master intriguer Lord Henry Howard (earl of Northampton and from 1608 Lord Privy Seal). The worst that the more biased and gossip-prone Jacobean court observers, such as Anthony Weldon, had to say about her ahead of her marriage and 'shameful' annulment was that she was conceited, fond of praise, lacking in morals, and bred to all of this by the bad example of her mother the countess of Suffolk – who was libelled as a secret Catholic (like Henry Howard) and accused by both Weldon and the French ambassador Tillieres of being James' chief minister Robert Cecil's secret mistress.[19] The only practical evidence of the countess' misbehaviour came during her husband's legal prosecution for gross corruption and embezzlement as Lord Treasurer a decade later, when her letters were seized and read out in Court and she was shown to have demanded bribes for using her services for petitioners – not exactly an unusual practice for the era. It may also be worth noting that Frances' sister Elizabeth was also accused of sexual laxity, in this case using her lover Lord Vaux not her husband Robert Knollys to father her children; was their family's lifestyle somewhat lacking in moral guidance from their self-enriching courtier parents? Given the poor reputation of the dazzling and extravagant Jacobean court – itself a sharp contrast to the 'austerity' and tight control of the last years of the ageing Elizabeth – any of its prominent and 'pushy' gallants and beauties were bound to have a poor press from those bemoaning the 'good old days' before the Scots and their uncouth and Catholic-favouring, seemingly homosexual King arrived in London. Also, women who did not show proper modesty and submissiveness in line with the current ideals of seemly behaviour would be the targets of moralistic/idealistic 'Puritans' and outright misogynists, and in the next generation the sharp divide between the social and political tones of 'Court' and 'Country' would end in civil war so 'opposition' writers would play up the way that the 'rot had set in' at James' seemingly immoral court. Later literary critics of the decadence of the Jacobean Court were often pro-Parliamentarian or outright 'rebels' in the 1640s, e.g. the acute and acerbic female memorialist Lucy Hutchinson (wife of the regicide Army ex-governor of Nottingham Castle), and a prominent and 'showy' young Court beauty from a dubiously pro-Catholic family would be a prime target. This should be borne in mind when considering Frances Howard's culpability and motivation, as she has not exactly had a 'fair press'.

As Essex and his fiancée were only fourteen or fifteen at the time of marriage (Frances probably being a few months older) they did not live together until after he had spent some time on a foreign tour perfecting his knowledge and courtly manners. He returned home in 1609 and they set up house together, but soon proved temperamentally poles apart – with Essex's steward and literary defender Anthony Wilson alleging that the earl still loved her when he returned but she had been corrupted by the 'fast' social life at court into vanity, selfishness, and demands for the sort of intense social life that he could not stand.[20] Essex was not the sort of man to indulge in courtly flattery and romance, unlike his notoriously 'courtly', sociable, and womanizing father, the executed second earl Robert Devereux (who had neglected him and may have sparked off his noted moroseness), and he was both socially awkward and known to prefer the company of men to that of women. Wilson admitted that he lacked both grace and eloquence. As a result, it is no wonder that the demanding Frances, used to far different treatment and fond of courtly devotion and flattery, was soon both bored and repulsed. There was some difficulty over consummating the marriage too, though given the issues at stake and the desire of both parties to appear in a good light the embarrassingly frank details raked over in the 1613 annulment case cannot be taken as all true. Frances claimed that her husband was impotent so the marriage had not been consummated and should be declared void; Essex could not deny problems but claimed that he was rendered useless by his wife's frigidity and repulsion from him, and she had refused to assist his efforts – he would have been fine with another woman. The resulting lawsuit provided humiliation in public amidst gossip and sniggers for the allegedly impotent and maritally useless Essex, a proud and tragic figure whose father had been executed for treason and family stripped of their lands and titles when he was eight – which James had good-naturedly remedied. Arguably he is deserving of more sympathy than Frances, who was determined to get what she wanted no matter what the cost to others although she had been landed with a husband of a disastrously uncongenial temperament by her parents and the King (and possibly also the manipulative Cecil who had played a role in arranging other marriages among the court elite to bind together various rival families as his hopefully grateful clients).

It is ironic that Essex (already accused of being 'cold', stiff-necked, and uncaring by his wife) went on to show his stern principles and opposition to an allegedly 'corrupt and Papist' Stuart court by co-leading the Parliamentary opposition to James' son in the House of Lords in 1640–2 and then commanding the Parliamentary army in the field in 1642–4. Was this unconsciously a means of seeking revenge for the humiliation which the Stuarts had heaped on him in the law-courts? The marriage of Essex and Frances was a match of polar opposites who were temperamentally totally dissimilar, though in this era, aristocratic marriages were a matter of families linking up for social, political, or financial alliances, with children often being married off under-age by their parents (though not co-habiting until they were older) and love or compatibility were rarely considered. Men took mistresses if they were disaffected, wives were supposed to keep quiet and bear it (and bear plenty of children to keep the dynasty going) though a few no doubt consoled themselves with lovers too, and in Essex's and the Howards' world of aristocratic marital alliances the way their relationship was set up without the participants having any say in it and collapsed was nothing unusual. Cecil and the King had helped to arrange a similar marriage between Frances' brother Theophilus Howard (the dynasty's heir) and the heiress of James' leading Scots minister, the earl of Dunbar, and between Cecil's son and heir Lord Cranborne and Frances' sister Katherine, with both of these pairings marrying as young teens then living apart for several years, and indeed Essex was supposed to have been lined up originally as Katherine's bridegroom but had successfully expressed a preference for her better-looking sister Frances. The King apparently learnt from the mistakes of his naïve 'early teens' marital arrangements of the 1600s and later expressed his belief that people should wait until they were older, and compatibility was more obvious – but Suffolk and his wife never expressed any regrets and they seem to have ruthlessly played the useful 'game' of dynastic alliances to benefit their family's status without any concerns.

Annulment – as opposed to divorce, which meant that a marriage had been fully legal for the term of its length instead of legally flawed and so null and void – was unusual and was likely to be resisted unless both parties were resolved on it as any financial arrangements made for the marriage would have to be declared void and money returned. But it could be arranged with goodwill or appropriate evidence, if the church courts were willing to co-operate, and with the King backing an annulment, the lawyers and their clerical superiors would know what result was expected and if they valued their careers would rule accordingly. The disaster arising from the Essex/Howard annulment was not due to the actual case as such, unusual though that was, but to the way that the affairs of the unfortunate but rash and loud-mouthed minor courtier Sir Thomas Overbury became entangled in it. Indeed, the involvement of Overbury and his resulting suspicious death originally came about due to Carr's good nature and desire to improve his poor reputation rather than by any malicious action. Carr was alarmed at the abuse hurled at the King's Scots courtiers in general and himself in particular and sought to show off his Anglophilia and desire to live like an English gentleman and have English friends to improve his reputation.[21] Unfortunately, but as someone less naïve might have expected, it did not win him many English friends (not least as he still had a strong Scots accent) while many Scots courtiers were infuriated at him 'deserting' his own people and toadying to their English detractors. As a result, Carr had few friends at court able or willing to put in a good word for him to the King when the scandal broke, and the King started to distance himself from Carr.[22] In fact Carr had already met Sir Thomas Overbury, the Oxford-educated son of minor Gloucestershire squire Sir Nicholas Overbury of Bourton-on-the-Hill, before James' accession in 1603, when Overbury (four or five years his senior) had been on his travels after leaving the Inns of Court and had stayed for some time in Scotland. Carr had then been in the service of the Earl of Dunbar, and when the Scots royal court came south, he and Overbury renewed their acquaintance; it was clearly close though Overbury's referring to it as 'love' need not mean anything untoward as such terms were used more vaguely then and covered a close and emotional friendship.

Overbury ended up as Carr's closest English friend as the rising courtier sought to show his own goodwill to his hosts and his Anglicization, and as he was rather more intelligent and worldly and could navigate himself through the treacherous world of elite society Carr came to rely on him. He also travelled on the Continent around 1609 and made the most of his acquisition of knowledge and expertise, writing learned works on the countries he had visited and no doubt seeking to impress important people as to how useful he could be if they employed him – though it is uncertain how many if any foreign languages he learned. He had literary pretensions too and some (minor) success as a poet, though his ambitions and probably his conceit outmatched his actual talents. Indeed, his poetry had some bearing on the forthcoming scandal, as his only well-known work (posthumously) was a 'witty' collection of advice to young men on what to seek out in the ideal partner, *The Wife,* in which he condemned the idea of marrying a well-educated, intellectual and assertive female and proclaimed that to be a successful wife the woman must keep to her domestic duties – and have an unsullied reputation for dealings with the opposite sex. Like Caesar's wife, she must be seen to be above suspicion as well as being so in fact. This sort of demure and submissive paragon hardly fitted the character of Frances Howard, the strong-willed girl who had made up her mind to end her unwelcome marriage, and indeed it was later claimed by Sir Nicholas Overbury that the poem was written around 1612 and was meant as a literary statement of his son's private advice to Carr not to marry Frances, whose turbulent and failing marriage was already attracting attention.[23] Whether or not the determined and indiscreet Frances was saying openly that she intended to acquire a nullification, and this was being reported around court, may have been seen as 'trouble' and Overbury may have accordingly warned Carr, in vain, against marrying her once she was free. If this was the case and Frances found out about the poem it could have aroused her enmity and started the fatally downward path of their relationship – but there is no certainty that the poem was about her or that its 'message' about independent-minded women really referred to her.

Whether or not Overbury had upset Frances in this way, he was clearly tactless and inclined not to care about who he offended and such a person – particularly one with his high opinion of his abilities – was likely to arouse antagonism at court unless he operated carefully. But this was not his style, and when Carr acquired for him the post of 'sewer' or server to the King around 1607 his proximity to his royal master at the daily public royal meals brought him to greater notice among courtiers. Rather than making himself pleasant and behaving modestly he appears to have tactlessly enjoyed showing off his eminence and offering his advice to Carr, who the King now made Viscount Rochester and began to consult on appointments. Contemporary observers agreed that Overbury's worst faults were a mixture of arrogance and showing off his talents and influence, with 'impudence' and pride frequently cited, and the later seventeenth-century writer and mass-biographer John Aubrey reckoned it a near thing between Overbury and Sir Walter Raleigh as to which of them was seen as the more detestably arrogant – with Overbury probably ahead.[24] Both men were ambitious minor gentry who had pushed their way to the top at court and so would attract sneers and jealousy, and both ended up ruined by their enemies – but they clearly attracted hatred by their bumptiousness. Overbury's connection to the hated Carr as the latter's trusted lieutenant and self-declared 'fixer' did not help either, whether or not he took bribes to introduce petitioners to his friend (taking small 'gifts' to do this was normal for the era but this practice could go too far), and despite Overbury's new role close to the King, the latter did not warm to him and his knighthood. Some minor grants to his family were not followed by any major success, and possibly Overbury showed off his knowledge too much or was not sufficiently ingratiating to James. Also, the Queen soon grew to hate him as much as she hated Carr, and rumours spread – probably exaggerated – that Carr and Overbury's emotional dependence on and lavish praise of each other was proof of an illegal homosexual affair. Indeed, the fact that Overbury was so detested made it more tempting for his enemies – Frances or not – to kill him and so precipitate the scandal, as they could reckon that such an unpopular character would not be missed, and nobody would bother to enquire into his demise too deeply.

Around 1608–9 Carr also acquired the idea that he could make himself useful to the King on matters such as foreign policy – and who better to advise him on this than the widely-travelled master of international expertise Sir Thomas Overbury? To the King it might seem that the 'unpolitical' and down-to-earth Carr, whose interests centred on hunting and parties not politics, did not have an 'axe to grind' in matters of state, unlike ministers such as Cecil (now earl of Salisbury and treasurer from 1608–12) and was not trying to manipulate him into adopting particular policies. But the favourite's initiative duly aroused Salisbury's wrath as interference in his own field of expertise, although he tried to remain on good terms with Carr for as long as possible due to his influence with the King. When Parliament started to enquire into the King's 'excessive' grants of gifts to unworthy persons (without attacking the prickly sovereign directly) in 1610 the King and Carr felt threatened, and James was furious at the impertinence of MPs daring to query his right to make grants where he sought fit. Salisbury made attempts to negotiate a long-lasting financial settlement with the MPs, the 'Great Contract', that would grant James a regular, secure income – in return for surrendering his feudal rights – but this would entail some greater control and scrutiny over the munificent King's rash extravagance and Salisbury may have thought (or been seen by James and Carr as intending) that this would cut down on the favourite's acquisitions. The 'Contract' was stymied over agreeing details plus royal reluctance to make a bold and cost-cutting move to please his MP critics, and as rumours spread that the Commons would next require the extravagant King to cut his costs by sending all other Scots home, pressure was mounted by alarmed Scots courtiers, led by Carr, on James to dissolve Parliament and put an end to it.[25] The dissolution of Parliament later followed this crisis, and it was supposed to have permanently shaken James' trust in Salisbury – possibly as hoped for by

Carr (and behind him Overbury?) who had rash hopes of more lavish grants if the miserly treasurer was sacked. In the event Salisbury survived, in declining health and spirits, to die in office in May 1612, but Overbury's apparent attempt to steer the less able and naïve Carr into greater political influence set them both on a dangerous path as making Carr a 'political actor', not just an embarrassing 'toy-boy', would arouse formidable and much more expert rivals. Possibly this even set the pair of them on the path to ruin, though the death of Salisbury (aged only forty-eight) was to make matters worse by elevating one of Carr's most trenchant critics, Frances' father the Earl of Suffolk, to be Lord Treasurer.

Already Overbury had been temporarily banished from court for a few months in May 1611, after some unknown slight which they had made to the Queen, who apparently spotted him and Carr behaving disrespectfully to her in the palace garden when they saw her looking out of a window at them. She was supposed to have become hysterical and threatened to go back to Denmark unless both men were sent packing, but James would only banish the less important Overbury.[26] Whatever happened it suggests arrogant carelessness and probable mockery of her by one or both of them, not caring what she thought as the King's favour made them untouchable, and once Carr, the new earl of Rochester, was a Privy Councillor (April 1612) and being consulted on important matters of foreign affairs problems would multiply. In the initial stages of Carr's relationship with the now free Frances Howard probably in 1611–12, Overbury acted as a 'go-between' and lent support with his poems and Frances seems to have been on reasonable terms with him, but things were to change. The surreptitious affair between Frances and Carr also brought the former into the company of the disreputable character who was later to provide the tarts which were supposedly used to poison Overbury, and so set up one vital ingredient in this disastrous cocktail. This was Mrs Anne Turner (nee Norton), the shrewd and unscrupulous Catholic widow of a well-known physician (the treasurer of the Royal College of Surgeons) now living on her wits in London, who made extra cash by offering her services and her dubious connections to needy members of the elite and may have worked earlier in the Howards' household as she claimed to have been close to Frances for many years. The latter evidently trusted her for discretion, ingenuity, and lack of concern for the law, and they exchanged correspondence on affectionate terms ('gushing' by modern standards but normal for the emotional written exchanges of the time). Mrs Turner had been trying to induce her long-term (and usefully wealthy) lover Sir Arthur Mainwaring, carver to Prince Henry, into marriage after her cuckolded husband died, and as he was not interested, she apparently sought the services of dubious astrologer and reputed necromancer Dr Simon Foreman for predictions of the future and for love-potions to ensnare Mainwaring. (Using 'cunning men', astrologers, or wizards for various secret uses was a common problem of the era, and Frances was among those accused of doing so regularly; in 1616 Lord Chief Justice Coke duly conducted a legal purge of them.) Foreman had genuine medical skills if in somewhat unorthodox practices, clearly had knowledge and a degree of independent –minded 'vision' of his trade, and given the lack of competence of many contemporary doctors a proven medical 'success story' could be invaluable to alarmed seekers for remedies, but he was rather too keen to indulge in more dubious practices and secure large sums of money from his desperate clients and had been said to raise spirits and pose as a prophet. He apparently provided potions to Frances via Mrs Turner, either to stimulate her lover Carr's ardour or to make her husband impotent and help her subsequent legal case,[27] though it is unclear if he was also asked to use his occult powers to assist the lovers' sexuality or keep Essex impotent, but he died in September 1611. (Mrs Turner then did her best to search his house and reclaim assorted incriminating letters, presumably from Frances asking for help.)[28] After this, Mrs Turner apparently sought out other 'magicians' to help her mistress/ friend, though the evidence of this is less clear, and arranged secret assignations for her and Carr. Meanwhile Carr's new if unofficial prominence in organising state matters for the King and helping with his correspondence (on foreign policy in particular) plus his role as an intermediary with English and overseas political figures in 1611–12 seems to have gone to his head to a degree, though he was more restrained in his public showing off and his demands for 'presents' in return for his help than Villiers was to be later. As he was not that intelligent or well-informed he relied a good deal on Overbury and the latter made the most of it, even boasting that he would soon fill the vacant second secretaryship of state (not realistic as the King disliked him); once he realised this was impossible he tried to get the post for his friend Sir Henry Neville, although this was in fact quite logical and sensible as Neville had useful Parliament allies and some powerful peers like Pembroke agreed with this plan. It was said at this point that Carr governed the King and Overbury governed Carr.[29] This got to the ears of the King, who blamed Overbury for it, and Frances' father Suffolk was among those who made angry outbursts against the insolence used and power wielded by this pair.

Given the toxic state of hostility to Overbury as well as Carr and the fact that the former was a 'safer' target for foes than Carr as the King was not besotted with him, it seems that potential foes who might be willing to remove Overbury by underhand means were not lacking. Carr was now aided by the expert patronage and goodwill he received from the devious master of court machinations Henry Howard, earl of Northampton and Frances' uncle. With Cecil/Salisbury dead in May 1612 and so one major rival removed the earl was seeking to assert his unofficial power and influence at court and made up to Carr in order to obtain his help in undermining the earl of Pembroke (with whom both were currently on bad terms). However Overbury apparently resented Northampton – who was also accused by contemporaries of homosexuality and had no wife and various young male admirers – for 'muscling in' on his relationship with Carr and making the latter less dependent on him; Overbury claimed expertise in foreign affairs from his travels and had various overseas contacts but Northampton had been dealing with Spanish and French power-brokers and receiving and passing on intelligence for decades and was far better-placed to help Carr. (His loyalty to England, or at least to Elizabeth's Protestant regime, had been suspect in the 1590–1604 Spanish War and he probably kept his options open in case Spain won.) Overbury showed his hostility to Northampton, who reciprocated and was a dangerous enemy – and it seems that Northampton also now turned his nefarious talents to helping out Frances' relationship with Carr so the latter would be tied to the Howard clan, duly grateful for Northampton's arranging his marriage to Frances, and would keep away from Overbury. Northampton was thus a major 'behind the scenes player' in advising Frances in the manoeuvres at Court and seeking of royal backing that now led up to Frances' ceasing to cohabit with Essex (late 1612?) and her father Suffolk's formally seeking an annulment of the marriage a few months later. Northampton duly claimed to have been the prime mover in bringing Carr and Frances together,[30] and whether or not he used his persuasive charms on the King, or this was left to Suffolk the church courts case followed. The prospect of this succeeding and Carr's marriage to Frances following apparently alarmed Overbury so much that he had a major row with his friend about it in a late night encounter at the Privy Gallery in Whitehall Palace in March 1613, warning him against throwing away all that he had achieved (which rested on the flimsy basis of the King's personal infatuation) by marrying 'that base woman' and saying that if Carr did so Overbury wanted no more to do with him and would appreciate the swift payment of some £1,500 due for his past services. Overbury declared that he expected Carr's influence to collapse without him to help it, and a furious Carr shouted back that he would happily manage on his own.[31] In the event, though the men's friendship ended Carr was apparently wary of going too far and alienating Overbury, logically as the latter had some information that he could use to ruin him and/or block his marriage by halting the Essex annulment, and indeed evidence that Carr and Frances had committed adultery would have caused the church court (as influenced by the strictly moral and Calvinist archbishop George Abbot of Canterbury) to halt proceedings. The threat of Overbury doing this, or blackmailing Carr, caused the latter to seek help from Northampton, and the devious earl may have been behind the idea of offering some prestigious diplomatic posting to the vain 'foreign policy expert' Overbury that would pay him off and would get him out of the country for a year or two. (Frances had a less pleasant plan, to persuade one of Overbury's hot-headed court enemies to challenge him to a duel so he would break the law against duelling and the King would put him in gaol.) As a result, the King offered Overbury a diplomatic embassy, either to France, Spain, or Russia, but in a highly unusual move Overbury turned this down. Given that a diplomat would not have a very high salary and was expected to meet the expenses of his travel and overseas stay from his own pocket a minor gentry figure of no great wealth would have financial difficulty sustaining such a post without help, though in secret Overbury might have made enough money out of his recent 'influence-peddling' to manage this. The boost to his prestige and ranking at court would however have been expected to have led him to accept the offer, and Carr clearly thought that he would. Instead, Overbury defied the King's express wishes with his usual churlishness, delivering a blank refusal to James' representatives, and the King was furious as someone with more sense would have expected. As a result, on 21 April 1613 Overbury was arrested and sent to the Tower for insulting the King[32] – and Frances' solution of having her foe locked up rather than sent abroad had succeeded.

With the potentially indiscreet or vengeful Overbury locked up in the Tower, the annulment proceedings could go ahead – though there were still plenty of enemies of Carr and the Howards at large who might try to disrupt them by pointing out problems and inconsistencies (or even evidence of collusion by the two parties, which was enough to halt matters). The Queen loathed Carr and had quarrelled with Frances' uncle and current adviser Northampton (who had allegedly once told her sharply that she was as much a subject of the King's as he was), so she might seek to embarrass them and stop their plan for a new link to be forged between them through the Carr/Frances marriage. Nor was the moody and notoriously 'prickly' Essex keen to help matters by admitting that he was impotent with all women as opposed to being so with just Frances – and if he claimed the latter, this might be because she was withholding her favours and/or seeking to put him off her. Suspicious or pedantic church lawyers could then claim that she might have wrecked the marriage (rather than being the innocent victim of a medical problem in Essex as she claimed) and pretended it was all his fault to cover up her plans to remarry once she was free, which amounted to fraud and might imply adultery by her. Essex was reported as having boasted to male friends in private that he was perfectly capable of having sex with other women and shown them proof, and this and other embarrassing matters of their private life was pored over. He implied in his evidence that on some occasions Frances had rejected his sexual advances, rather than being their passive (non-)recipient. As he was also equivocal over whether he believed

Frances to be a virgin, the usual panel of expert matrons (including some of appropriate noble blood to match her status) and midwives were called in to examine her. This was apparently at the Howards' request, which seems odd given her record of adulterous meetings with Carr in the preceding year or so – but she requested to remain veiled throughout the proceedings to preserve her modesty so there is probably truth in the claim that a friend or relation took her place. Alternatively, the examination may have been brief and incomplete; at any rate she was proclaimed '*virgo intacta*' which was clearly inaccurate and indicates a mistake, collusion or fraud.[33]

Both Essex (who made a formal complaint that was carefully ruled inadmissible and destroyed) and the Bishop of London apparently believed that the verdict was wrong, perhaps because the gentlewomen on the panel had not been experts and had had to accept what the midwives said, and the latter had not looked closely enough.[34] Also, the scrupulous Archbishop Abbot was worried that if he granted this nullification, he would be besieged by other men trying to rid themselves of their wives for dubious reasons and it would cause chaos.[35] Essex had said that he could be capable of intercourse with another woman so he was not totally impotent and if it was Frances' cold behaviour that put her husband off she could remedy that and save the marriage. This was not what the King wanted to hear, but as he sought to 'encourage' (or in effect require) Abbot to listen to Frances' version of events more sympathetically the archbishop burst out that she was an immoral woman, and he did not trust her word.[36] Nor did Abbot change his mind when various other commissioners judging the case decided to treat Frances' version with more sympathy or consider that they might have based this on the weight of the evidence, as he furiously accused them of selling out in return for royal favour. In the end the King summoned the entire commission to Windsor to discuss the matter on14 July and made it clear what his view was of the evidence, which amounted to 'leaning on' them and was treated as such by the truculent (or honest and impartial) Abbot; the King took him aside to tell him that he had been behind Suffolk's submission of the case which shook Abbot but did not move him. He made it clear that he would follow his conscience, and as James would not let him resign from the commission as he asked – which would have increased the chances of a pro-Frances verdict but led to public comment on a 'fix' – James had to order them to adjourn if they could not reach a unanimous verdict. This duly happened.[37] During the delay while the King was away on his summer progress two more pro-Frances bishops (Bilson and Buckeridge) were added to the commission to put Abbot clearly in the minority and add to pressure on him to give way, while to add to the drama Essex had a violent quarrel with Frances' brother Harry Howard that looked like ending in a duel – with Northampton (did he encourage Harry?) probably hoping that Essex would be killed and the problem be solved that way. When the commission reconvened in mid-September Abbot was still fulminating about the fraud which he suspected, and when Essex was not allowed to give further evidence by order of the King Abbot rightly suspected that this was designed to help Frances and made a public outburst at the outrage of 'these people' (not naming exactly who) arrogantly expecting all to be sorted out to their convenience regardless of the truth. He had planned to use the commissioners' right to each deliver their reasons for their verdict in full legal detail to launch a devastating attack on the Howards' case and the 'cover-up', but instead the King would only allow them to state their verdict and Frances won by seven votes to five – with the two new members of the commission giving her the verdict which she and Carr wanted.[38] With the King bending the rules (perfectly legally) in their favour and most of the commissioners in fear of royal displeasure this was perhaps inevitable, but it was a poor day for justice and as biased as the notorious 'political' state trials of the monarchs' critics under the Tudors. Whether this first stage of the Overbury scandal had much impact outside the capital and the literate upper social classes is dubious, but within these it was no doubt seen as more proof of the moral decay at the heart of the elite and compared unfavourably to the situation under Elizabeth (though her court had had its sexual scandals, the Queen had always been on the side of propriety in public). The case gave rise to several satirical poems with lewd comments about Frances as a slut[39] and acerbic comments from commentators and diarists, eg John Chamberlain, and the King did not come out of it well – not least given his subsequent shunning of his more honourable Archbishop.

Overbury remained locked up in the Tower at the King's whim, and as with James's son Charles' treatment of the 'impertinent' and politically inconvenient House of Commons troublemaker Sir John Eliot, MP after 1629, the royal intention seems to have been to leave the prisoner to contemplate his folly in defying royal wishes and let him rot until he apologised. Overbury was the last person to give way, Frances and his ex-friend Carr were probably too nervous about what he knew of their adulterous relationship to let him go free and report what he knew to the archbishop in case the annulment suit was then reopened, and Overbury had made too many enemies at court for anyone else important to intervene in his favour. The latter might not have done any good as James was stubborn on matters of 'security' or a perceived personal slight and was keeping Sir Walter Raleigh in the Tower for over a decade on a dubious charge of pro-Spanish treason despite the appeals of his own son, Prince Henry ('Only my father would keep such a bird in such a cage'). It remains unclear whether Carr just wanted Overbury to be 'put out of circulation' (in the modern terminology) until he had either learnt his lesson and ceased to threaten his marriage or the danger of the annulment being reconsidered had passed; and it is also logical that Carr and others may have hoped that Overbury would see sense and apologise to the earl of Suffolk for his slights on Frances' honour then ask him to intercede with the King. It appears from the Lieutenant of the Tower, Sir William Wade/Waad, that both Frances and her uncle Northampton sent him frequent letters concerning Overbury's treatment, but it is not clear what they said.[40] These may have just dealt with making sure that Overbury's letters were read and any visitors who he was permitted strictly watched so that he could not pass on damaging information to Archbishop Abbot about the annulment case being fraudulent (or to any other enemies of the ever-controversial Howards), and indeed Overbury was (unusually for his minor and non-political crime) declared to be a 'close prisoner', which banned him from having visitors or sending letters. This was to the Howards' and Carr's benefit, not a legitimate matter of state security, and Carr claimed it was nothing to do with him; he had secured his ex-friend decent rooms in an airy tower to help not punish him. After Overbury died suddenly on 15 September the detail of the Howards' letters to Wade was cited eagerly as proof that the wicked pair – and Carr too – had been planning his murder all along. The 'prison will pressurise Overbury to apologise' theory was now twisted as being 'Stage One' of an elaborate murder-plot; first he would apologise and restore Frances' reputation and then the Howards would double-cross him and instead of having him released, murder him. This was seen as 'par for the course' for Northampton, who had operated in the shadows of murky Late Tudor politics for decades distrusted by Elizabeth.

Wade seems to have had doubts over the justice of Overbury's treatment, and even invited him to come and stay at his own lodgings – which was perfectly within his rights. Northampton promptly complained about this, and coincidentally or not on 6 May 1613 Wade was suddenly sacked and was replaced by someone more likely to do what he was told by the prisoner's enemies – minor Lincolnshire gentleman Sir Gervase Elwes, a witty but unimportant minor figure with no appropriate experience but an apparent link to the Howards, who had helped him when his gambling debts drove him to London to seek a lucrative court job and who had secured him a minor job as a Gentleman Pensioner. He was also considered by his acquaintance John Chamberlain, the diarist, as too mild and timid to cope with high office – so was he selected as a biddable Howard lackey, short of cash and needing to please his master, who would do what he was told and keep Overbury secure – or help to murder him? It is clear that Northampton promoted Elwes' unlikely candidacy for the job and sought assistance from both Carr and influential peers (e.g. Pembroke and Shrewsbury) to press his case; and once Elwes had been appointed he had to reimburse those who had helped him to the tune of a first instalment of £1,700, pushing him further into debt. (£1,400 went to

Northampton, as shown at the later murder trial when he was already dead so unable to interfere, but Carr wriggled out of trouble.) Once Elwes took over the Tower, assorted 'genuine' and potentially dangerous state prisoners were allowed more liberty to exercise, thus making their new gaoler popular, but Overbury was kept locked up in his rooms. Worse, an unsavoury associate of Frances' long-term assistant Mrs Turner, the venal Richard Weston who she had enlisted to help take letters between Frances and Carr during their affair, now turned up as a client of Northampton's co-plotter Sir Thomas Monson (who also helped Elwes get his new job in return for cash) and the latter 'asked' Elwes to place him in a job at the Tower as Overbury's personal warder. Thanks to his earlier role in the adulterous meetings Frances (presumably behind this move) and Mrs Turner knew that he would be discreet and would do anything for money; but was he chosen just to keep Overbury under strict surveillance, so he did not 'spill any beans' or because he was a willing murderer? According to his testimony at the later trial, Mrs Turner made it clear from the start that in return for his job he was to deliver and administer various unspecified foods or drinks that the Countess of Essex would give to her to be given to Overbury. Within days of his appointment, he was reporting to Whitehall to be told that he was to receive a first vial of 'a water', being told in person from Frances, with Mrs Turner in attendance; he was told it was harmless, but he should not drink any himself. He suspected it was poison, and it arrived a few days later by the hand of his son who worked at a London haberdasher's frequented by Frances.[41] Nervous at what he was probably about to do, he consulted his employer Elwes, who was appalled, and claimed later that he put the fear of God and divine damnation into the wretched warder who promised not to administer it. Elwes was too shaken to remember to confiscate the liquid, but next day he made sure that Weston poured it away in his presence.[42] This episode apparently frustrated a first murder attempt, if we are to believe the later testimony of two frightened men keen to avoid being hung and desperate to say what the government wanted in return for their lives. But Elwes, too frightened of the Howards' reach to report what had happened to his superiors and risk their revenge on him or at least being sacked and pursued for debt, kept quiet about what had happened and claimed to the later enquiry that he reckoned that Weston had been scared out of committing murder and removing him from his job would alert the Howards – who might easily suborn whoever replaced him. Another version of events had it that the wretched Elwes, caught in a political cleft stick, had told Weston that if he had to murder Overbury, he should do so without letting him (Elwes) know anything of it – to protect his own skin he was prepared to sacrifice his prisoner.[43] The equally scared, but craftier, Weston pretended to Mrs Turner that he had administered the liquid as asked and Overbury had been very ill but not died, then asked for his promised reward; Mrs Turner refused to pay him while the prisoner lived (or so he claimed). The accounts of the trial proceedings then have it that Mrs Turner hired a dubious Yorkshire 'low-life', possible conjurer and reputed poisoner who had helped her before with love-potions, 'Dr' James Franklin, and asked him to use his expertise to provide a slow-acting poison that could be given to a victim gradually so they would slowly waste away and appear to be suffering from a natural disease. (The cramped conditions and proximity of the Tower to the River Thames would make this sort of fate for Overbury seem quite natural and not arouse suspicion.) Franklin duly helped her, provided some noxious concoction (possibly a form of arsenic or nitric oxide) which she tried out on a cat to make sure it would work plus a variety of others, and liaised at a tavern near the Tower with Weston, according to whom Franklin heard from him that Overbury was taking a lot of medicine brought by apothecaries and decided then to use a 'new apothecary' to deliver the poison to his victim. Weston then supposedly warned Elwes about this and the latter promised to keep his prisoner safe.[44] The impression given is of both Elwes and Weston anxious to clear themselves from blame after Overbury did die and to please their captors by stressing the wickedness of Frances and Mrs Turner – but can anything they or Franklin said be believed?

The scandal of the annulment had been unprecedented – especially as acted out in court in public – for the English court elite, at least since the 1540 church court proceedings involving the annulment of Henry VIII's marriage to Anne of Cleves which touched on the similar matter of a repulsed husband unable to perform his marital functions. (That however had involved the paranoid and violent king, so wits and critics had to be careful what they said and wrote.) The crisis was also involving a controversial family at the heart of the court, the cousins of the Boleyns and of distant royal blood, and the son of England's famous and much-lamented late courtly hero the executed Earl of Essex. What Archbishop Abbot said in private to the King was not in general 'circulation' but the plain fact of a small majority verdict of the court members for annulment spoke for itself, and now the crisis (and its concomitant sub-text of a sleazy and faction-ridden royal court) escalated as Frances Howard's enemy Overbury conveniently died. As seen, the demise could have been avoided had the weak-willed, dithering and self-protecting Elwes had the sense to go to his superiors and warn them of the first murder plot, though the devious 'power-monger' Northampton had him in a cleft stick over his debts and ambition so he would have had to be careful to avoid immediate victimization. (The notion of crucial Tower of London posts with security implications being decided by court patronage may seem shocking today but was quite normal for the patronage-ridden sixteenth century and seventeenth century though it was usually the King or a serving senior minister like the secretary of state who did the selecting of their clients for posts.) Overbury's possibly obsessive regard for his health and reliance on medical assistance for it from outside personnel, many of whom in that era would have been 'quacks' peddling dangerous or useless remedies, made him an easy target – though if Elwes had done his job properly the Lieutenant could veto his contact with problematic figures. The whole question of how Frances' apparent hirelings were able to plan to infiltrate the Tower via Weston and poison Overbury – and who was ultimately behind this – is a major element of considering who was behind the murder, as the dubious characters of Mrs Turner, Weston and Franklin makes their (later) evidence unreliable. Also, by that point the government (in the sense of the King and his senior ministers, not least the embarrassed Suffolk) had a 'narrative' to present, or even a set of rival 'narratives' given that men like Suffolk hated Carr and would be quite happy to see him implicated or used as a scapegoat and even executed but the King was more concerned to keep his (by then discarded) 'favourite' away from the execution-block. Non-Howard ministers and courtiers might be willing or eager to see Frances get the blame, and there is also the question of Northampton's involvement – which as he had hired Elwes in the first place was crucial. By the time of the investigation in 1615 he was dead so he could logically have been used as a scapegoat too, but that would reflect badly on his nephew Suffolk and others of his large and royally favoured clan; and as a veteran of ruthless Tudor intrigue and double-dealing with Spain he probably destroyed crucial written evidence as a matter of course. Also, given the vagaries of infection in the prisoner-crammed Tower in 1613 – open to all sorts of diseases which gaoler Weston might have accidentally passed on to his prisoner – and the mixture of dodgy 'medical remedies' that Overbury was buying for himself it is possible that he could have died naturally, with his decline due to some infection or 'quack' remedy that damaged his inactivity-weakened system. The remedies of the era included many ingredients that have subsequently been identified as poisonous, at least if ingested over the long term. Alternatively, some such infection or 'accidental poison' remedy could have been responsible for weakening him and Weston's poison finished him off – with Weston assuming that the poison supplied by Mrs Turner was entirely responsible and thus stating this to his interrogators.

The 'pattern of events' supposedly established by the 1615 investigation thus has its problems and cannot be taken as entirely accurate, but at the least it can be said that the crucial low-level plotters around Mrs Turner were connected to and employed by Frances already by the time of the apparent poisoning and Elwes had been put in post to help the plot by Northampton; both these senior Howards were thus intending some harm to Overbury and murder is a logical conclusion, even if Mrs Turner's and Weston's stories cannot be relied upon. After the botched first murder plot, matters were complicated by someone, from Weston's evidence presumably Carr, sending gifts of tarts and jellies to Overbury in the Tower to supplement his meagre diet – though this looks suspicious in retrospect and Northampton was apparently warning Carr that Overbury remained hostile to Frances and had not learned his lesson, it was normal procedure for friends and family to send in food to wealthy prisoners. Letters were also hidden in some of the food, but that was standard procedure to get around bans on receiving letters and it was also a regular ploy in contemporary plays and books which might have appealed to Carr's theatrical tastes. He could have been communicating with Overbury on quite innocent matters or urging him to apologise to Suffolk and Frances so the King would relent, and toadying Elwes assured the 1615 enquiry that of course he carried out his legal requirements and intercepted and checked the letters and food. (Overbury was apparently also writing letters to Carr, foolishly abusing his wife and refusing to apologise; if he had done so, would he have been released by Carr going to the King and the coming tragedy averted?) The food was apparently harmless and known to Elwes to be harmless (who told him, Carr or Northampton?) as he let his family eat it when Overbury offered it to him, without any ill effects.[45] Subsequently more food, including jellies, arrived for Overbury – this time from Frances, apparently pretending that they came from Carr to lull his suspicions which is ominous; and Northampton's crony Monson's ex-employee Simon Merston brought them so Northampton may have been involved too. Weston claimed that Frances sent him a warning to let Overbury have them but not eat any himself.[46] According to Elwes's (self-protecting) version of events he intercepted these foods, put them in the Tower kitchen under observation and noted that they became foul-looking, and ordered Weston to tell the boy who brought them that Overbury did not want any more – and once Carr left London on the King's usual summer progress it was implausible to pretend that the food came from him so the gifts ceased. There was also the question of an incriminating-sounding letter that Frances allegedly sent Elwes at this time, later used at the 1615 trial, telling him to give the enclosed 'tarts' to Overbury, swapping them for the ones which he currently had, and not give any of them to his own family, and all would be well. Mention by Frances of someone asking her to write to Elwes in these terms was interpreted in the 1615 enquiry as meaning 'Carr' as he was then her husband and the only person in a position to order her about, but she claimed it referred to either Northampton or the gaoler Weston. There was a mention of smuggling 'letters' in the food to give to Overbury, which in 1615 was interpreted by the investigating Lord Chief Justice Coke as code for 'poison' when he read this, and a 'confession' signed by Frances then confirmed that the food contained poison and hence her guilt[47] – though she retracted this later. In a different version of her story which she offered to Elwes' trial for his part in the murder, she insisted that the tarts from her were intended to be substituted for those sent by Carr to Overbury, in order to have the secret letters that Carr was sending Overbury intercepted (and thus prevent Overbury from communicating with Carr to her detriment or pleading successfully for an appeal to the King?) but without alarming his suspicions that food was not arriving so it was being interfered with.[48] Was she hoping to make Overbury think he had been abandoned by Carr and so to make him depressed, willing to give in and stop threatening her? This is one solution to the question of why Frances was sending food to Overbury – and using her dubious but trusted associates of old to do so – if it was not to murder him. This solution and a resultant change of direction in the 1615 trial to exonerate Frances of the worst charges was not however taken up – as it was untrue, as it was disbelieved as far-fetched, or as it was politically inconvenient to let her off? To be fair to the judges, Elwes thought that there was a genuine poison attempt underway, though he may have been saying what he believed at the time due to the shock he had had earlier over Weston confessing about the first plot. Or was it Northampton sending the poison at this point, via Merston?

Poison or not, Overbury was seriously ill with fever and stomach-problems in mid-July though he recovered a little[49] – which might have been due to an infection in the Tower or poor food-preparation hygiene, and was common for the place and era. Also, his health had not been good for some time before his arrest, though this was carefully ignored at the 1615 enquiry which only seems to have used evidence that would fit the theory of wilful murder by Frances and Carr. The question of the competence of or damage done by those fashionable London doctors who Overbury was allowed to call in was ignored by the enquiry and was an issue that would not occur to most contemporaries, given that their understanding of medicine and the human body was seriously inadequate but was not recognised as such and their dodgy remedies were usually accepted with respect, not treated with scepticism. This applied to the then famous royal doctor who visited Overbury, Dr Theodore Mayerne, too, quite apart from his and others' obsessive reliance on letting blood from the patient which only weakened them; his prescribed treatment for Prince Henry's probable typhoid in November 1612 had been incompetent and bizarre and the heir to the throne had died. Overbury's brother-in-law Thomas Lidcote visited him while he was taking Mayerne's prescriptions in July and reported that he had said he felt dreadful, so was this making him worse or even a major cause of death? Overbury also relied on an unusual and possibly dangerous 'quack' medicine known as 'aurum potabile' or drinkable gold, invented by unqualified experimenter Francis Anthony[50] which was quite capable of poisoning him without any attentions from Frances Howard of Northampton – or making his condition much worse if their poisons were not effective and/or were usually intercepted by Elwes. There were also stories that Carr had been sending Overbury a supposedly beneficial emetic powder to deal with his health-problems but which was really disguised arsenic,[51] but this claim was made in the fevered atmosphere of 1615 when various high-placed court figures were keen to blacken his name and rid the court of him, so this is unreliable. At the time the majority opinion among the political elite was of deliberate murder by both Carr and Frances – and implicated socially inferior suspects were quite capable of telling the enquiry what they thought the latter wanted to hear. The man who first raised the matter was a servant of Overbury's called Lawrence Davies who referred to a small packet of white powder falling out of some letters that he was smuggling into the Tower,[52] and this might have been an innocent reference to a harmless (or well-intended but actually useless or harmful) emetic sent by Carr which eager investigators seized upon. Others suggest that Davies had old grudges to pay back and so stirred this up deliberately; or Carr might have wanted Overbury to fall ill so he could go to the King and say that he would die if he was not let out quickly. The 'genuine emetic sent by Carr' story was also backed up by Henry Peyton, Overbury's other servant, and by Carr's servant (and Overbury's cousin) Giles Rawlins in 1615. There may well be a perfectly innocent explanation for the allegedly suspicious visit that the warder Weston secretly made to Carr after Overbury died – not to confirm that he had administered the poisoned 'emetic' and collect his reward, as Carr's detractors assumed, but to ask for a pay-off for looking after and trying to protect Overbury.

Whether or not Overbury was being poisoned, he managed to survive the alleged attentions of Frances and/or her uncle Northampton (supposedly Carr too) for several months into September, though it must be asked what Northampton was doing reassuring Carr that the prisoner was in good health when he clearly was not.[53] Was he putting Carr off the scent to prevent him asking the King to release his sick ex-friend? Now in August Overbury – whether prompted by secret letters sent to him in tarts by Carr or by belated commonsense – finally wrote to the Earl of Suffolk at his treasury-funded new country mansion, Audley End, to offer his respectful apologies for being rude and impertinent about his noble family and ask for him to intervene with the King, and Suffolk sent back a friendly reply[54] – which was done in secret, but if it came to the ears of Overbury's enemies might have persuaded them to step up the poisoning and get rid of him quickly. Crucially, Overbury was still raging about Frances and her behaviour and angrily telling Elwes that he would never accept the Carr/Frances marriage, and he appears to have written the same to Carr himself – which may have doomed him if this made either Frances or Northampton realise that he was incorrigible and once he was released he would be interfering with their plans again.[55] Logically, Northampton or

Frances may have used this to warn Carr off trying to get Overbury released quickly by appealing to the King, or even speeded up a murder-plan.

Overbury had a fatal inability to know when to keep his mouth shut or to stop bragging, which may well have alienated enough courtiers with no 'axe to grind' against him to ensure that none of them came to his rescue and spoke up for him to the King despite his unusually close imprisonment and his declining health. Now, with his brother-in-law Lidcote warning him in late August that the Howards would never help him to be released whatever they assured him as he was a threat to the Carr/Frances marriage, Overbury apparently lost his temper again and sent Carr a threatening letter complaining that the latter had not really helped him at all and warning that he had written a long and revealing account of their relationship. This included details of how he had been the go-between in the Carr/Frances affair while she was still married to Essex, and hence it could be used as evidence of their adultery and cause the Essex annulment to be cancelled. Overbury had made copies of this explosive document and sent it to various friends, and would use it if needed to wreck Carr's reputation permanently – and Carr had better start helping him now 'or else'.[56] This provided the motive for either an alarmed Carr or Frances to seek to remove Overbury permanently before he could act, and was so interpreted by the enquiry in 1615 to accuse both of them of murder. It was after this that outside communication with Overbury became extremely difficult, whether or not this was due to a prompted person (Frances or Northampton?) telling Elwes to seize all letters, and Overbury became very ill again. But this time he had an ulcer or sore on his back which Dr Mayerne was called in to treat (from the post-death examination evidence), which suggests some different cause from the previous 'poison' and possibly an unrelated but convenient infection. Given that Dr Mayerne was not the most careful of doctors, hygiene was rudimentary, and the feverish Overbury was apparently shouting at and tussling with Mayerne as the latter changed his dressings, some infection setting in from a botched procedure or even gangrene might be a possible explanation[57] There was also the possibility of another enema from an apothecary finishing Overbury off, accidentally or not – Elwes claimed the man had been bribed to supply poison, citing a confession by Weston.[58] The (gossipy and unreliable) historian Anthony Weldon claimed in his 1650 memoirs of the King's court to have identified the apothecary's boy, Reeve, who brought the poisoned enema and then apparently fled to Brussels, and said that Weston then finished Overbury off by smothering him with the help of his dodgy associate Franklin – but this did not rely on proveable evidence.[59] Nor did Elwes, who was by his own account keeping a close eye on Overbury's visitors and who would be a likely scapegoat if the prisoner died, or Weston ever refer to the apothecary's boy in their own evidence in 1615, despite the advantage of this 'untraceable outside agent was guilty' theory to their own cases.

In any event, Overbury died on 15 September, hours after the alleged visit, and the Tower authorities who held the inquest conveniently claimed that it was due to natural causes. It amounted to a classic cover-up and was clearly arranged to protect a no doubt highly nervous Elwes, though there is no clear proof of them being directed by Northampton or any other highly-placed courtier endeavouring to protect the Howards let alone Carr or the King from embarrassment. In reality, contemporary chemical knowledge and tests were not advanced enough to detect the most common minerals used in poisons in a body so it is not safe to assume that the inquest jury were either bribed or intimidated into a fake verdict. In any case, as we have seen the evidence is so muddled that it cannot be assumed that Overbury had tasted any or all of the poisons sent to him (assuming that Elwes was not able to intercept all of these) or that he was not killed by incompetent medical treatment or some Tower infection. Given the gifts of 'poisoned tarts' and 'vials of poisoned liquid' alleged by Mrs Turner and Weston in 1615, it would be assumed – especially by those enquirers hostile to the Howards and Carr – that if any poisons were sent to Overbury they had worked and killed him, given how and when he died and the motives that the accused had to be rid of him. In the immediate aftermath of the event Overbury was so unpopular that his death was hardly noticed or much mourned, and the King went on to raise Carr to further honours on 4 November 1613 as Earl of Somerset – a step up the English peerage from his viscountcy which would have added to the rage of his English noble detractors and made them keener to get rid of him once his possible implication in the Overbury case was revealed. The new earl and his bride Frances Howard married in the Chapel Royal at Whitehall Palace on 26 December with the festivities hosted by the King – and with Frances shamelessly parading with her hair unbound in the traditional mode for a virgin bride. The King lavished them with gifts and hosted a magnificent reception,[60] which seems to show his connivance in the hypocrisy and lies of the Essex marriage annulment and at least displayed his ambiguous and sloppy standards of social conduct for his intimates. To consolidate the new Earl of Somerset's political 'rise' he was able and confident to continue working as a 'power-broker' without Overbury's help, and he succeeded in having his importunate ally Sir Ralph Winwood made secretary of state in March 1614. Rumour had it that Winwood had either paid cash for his help (£7,000?) or been financially aided by the Dutch mercantile elite who wanted pro-Dutch Winwood to have the King's ear and keep the latter away from their Spanish foes' influence[61] – but that was not especially unusual for the era, if more blatant than usual. Hence Carr could continue to be the King's most prominent if not expert adviser on foreign affairs and make sure that petitioners for the King's goodwill acted through him – until the wheel of fortune moved and the more clever and expert Winwood managed to usurp his (and Northampton's secret) role by proving more competent and adept at court politics.

The – probably reluctant – reconciliation with and help for Carr from his new father-in-law Suffolk, making the best of a bad job, also helped but tied him to the unpopular and financially lavish 'operating procedures' of the Howards' power-broking. But there were anti-corruption and more than the usual virulent anti-Scots speeches in the abortive and soon dismissed Parliament of 1614, which failed to reach any agreement with the King on financial reform and a stable long-term subsidy for him and was soon dissolved – though even Cecil had also failed to bridge the gap between cost-cutting MPs and the spendthrift King (1610) so Carr and the Howards were not to blame. On 15 June 1614 Northampton died (formally as a Catholic after decades of suspected unofficial loyalty to the Faith), aged seventy-four, which removed one adept if unpopular ally of the Howard-Carr group and countered the formal confirmation of Suffolk as lord treasurer in July – and Carr's now becoming lord chamberlain in Suffolk's place. The latter only formalised Carr's grip on court appointments and access to royal cash, but made this more obvious and 'official' and so heightened antagonism from those who did not achieve rewards or did not want to seek them through him – and as seen above he lacked either tact or prudence. Disappointed 'losers out' in the summer 1614 'reshuffle' of offices such as foreign policy expert Sir Thomas Lake, the young Earl of Arundel (head of the senior branch of the Howards), and the Earl of Pembroke (brother of the King's favoured courtier Philip Herbert, now earl of Montgomery), who had wanted to be the new lord chamberlain, came to blame Carr while the latter's old foe Archbishop Abbot, still fuming at the 'fit-up' and amorality of the Essex divorce proceedings, developed a hatred of him as a source of moral corruption which was exacerbated when he displayed pro-Catholic (or just religiously tolerant?) views and succeeded in having some arrested Catholic priests not executed but put under loose 'house-arrest' at Wisbech Castle in Norfolk. Carr was building up a dangerous list of powerful foes and was an easier target than Suffolk, not least as a hated Scotsman and a man without his own important English kindred or uncontroversial court allies, and this background helps to explain how the subsequent public unravelling of the 'hushed up' treatment and suspicious death of Overbury occurred. Rather than an idealistic quest for justice for a wronged man (as we have seen, Overbury was himself an arrogant and hated if minor court 'power-broker'), it was a move in the 'chess game' of court politics, and was a useful weapon to embarrass and try to bring down the now even more powerful Carr (and through his new wife, her father Suffolk). The possibilities to do this were obvious early on, as in August 1614 the King's progress in the Midlands saw him staying at the Northamptonshire manor of Apethorpe and becoming smitten by one of the guests at a reception there, the exquisitely handsome, well-turned-out, and charming young local gentleman George Villiers. A minor member of an undistinguished local gentry family but with distant noble connections, Villiers (aged twenty-two) was said to be the handsomest man in England and had been trained in courtly manners in a period at the French court, the most cultured and elegant in Europe; and unlike Carr he was intelligent, a quick learner, had useful – English noble – connections, and was able to adapt to his sudden good fortune without relying on such antagonising 'middle-men' as Overbury.

The King's interest in Villiers was quickly spotted by shrewd courtiers, and the chances of him being able to wean James' affections away from Carr were ruthlessly exploited as after the royal progress Pembroke and his brother Montgomery hosted a private gathering of anti-Carr nobles at Baynard's Castle in the City of London to agree on financing the impecunious Villiers' transformation into a dazzlingly well-turned-out young courtier.[62] Hopefully James would not be able to resist him, Carr would lose favour and perhaps be sent packing, and Villiers could then channel rewards in cash, grants, and office from the smitten King to his backers – which seems rather shameless to modern eyes but was no worse than the way in which assorted nobles (led by the then Duke of Norfolk) had dangled young women in front of Henry VIII in the 1520s-40s. The plan worked, and in November 1614 Villiers was made a Gentleman of the Bedchamber by the King. There was a new potential royal 'favourite' ready to be used to undermine Carr, and Carr fell into the trap by rapidly showing his jealousy and staging petulant outbursts of temper, accusing the King of neglecting and humiliating him by spending time with his new young friend. By playing 'hard to get' and turning jealous, spiteful and at times hysterical Carr would only alienate James sooner, though the latter was hurt and puzzled at first rather than angry and after a few months of this sent him a remarkably unguarded letter (unprecedented from a male British monarch to a male subject) assuring that he still loved and respected Carr and that he had nothing to fear but his behaviour was deeply troubling to the emotionally hurt James. Showing that he had some dignity left and knew what was his due from his subject, the King reminded Carr that he hoped that the latter would calm down and show him some trust and goodwill but if he did not behave better his attitude would cause the King to regard him as ungrateful and cast him off.[63] Carr failed to respond as wished. The reigning 'favourite' had thus fallen into the trap that Villiers' backers had laid for him, and the road lay open for a move to ruin him by his enemies in which they could be reasonably certain that the exasperated James would not intervene to save him – from dismissal at any rate.

Shrewd courtiers were now hastening to show their goodwill to Villiers and seek his support, a sign that the cracks in Carr's influence were becoming apparent and the usual sycophants were starting to treat him as a liability.[64] At this point, in July 1615, according to Elwes' later account whispers started to spread that Overbury's death would be investigated, though it is not known if this was coincidence or someone 'fishing' for dirt to use against Carr. The latter heard of them and hastened to make contact with Overbury's until now ignored ex-servant Lawrence Davies, presumably in case he knew embarrassing (or innocuous but distortable) details that could be used against Carr. Meanwhile the crucial witness if not actual murderer, Weston, had been unsuccessfully seeking a 'pay-off' from Mrs Turner, who claimed that Frances had no money to pay him – whether out of embarrassment at him reappearing, over-confidence that he could not 'finger' her or Frances with legally damning proof, or a wish that he would go away and keep Frances from having to become involved with the matter again. She was in attendance on Frances that summer while the latter was in 'retirement' in the countryside near Henley-on-Thames, pregnant, and probably as a result of their discussions about what to do with Weston Mrs Turner later met him again (at her initiative this time) and suggested what he should say if he was questioned – e.g. about why he had been chosen as Overbury's gaoler. As a result Mrs Turner sent Weston on a 'fishing expedition' to Elwes to find out what the latter knew or suspected and if he had talked, and though he found out nothing Elwes (by his own account) was uneasy enough in these weeks to seek out Northampton's sidekick Monson, who as seen above had been the devious earl's co-funder in appointing him to the Tower post. Elwes told Monson that he feared that Overbury's death had been suspicious, but Monson pooh-poohed it. Given the febrile atmosphere and possible multiple lies told to each other in 1613 by Mrs Turner, Weston, and Elwes, it is impossible to conclude that all this nervous checking up was due to guilt rather than wariness at who might (unfairly?) accuse whom of what – though Weston is the likeliest to have had serious crime to hide and if any reliance can be placed on any of his later evidence Mrs Turner (and behind her Frances) had at least made one botched attempt to poison Overbury in spring 1613. Nor can too much be made of Carr asking James at this time to grant him a royal pardon that would protect him from conviction for any past misdemeanours, though this was later interpreted as him trying to escape prosecution for murder and hence as evidence of guilt.[65] Unfair and 'rigged' charges were as likely as genuine ones when a Tudor or Stuart royal favourite or minister was brought down by his enemies, state trials notoriously bent or ignored inconvenient evidence, and exoneration in court was rare; other favourites and courtiers too had sought such protection. Lord Chancellor Ellesmere refused to approve the pardon, and it was dropped.

The investigation that now began was apparently launched by the new secretary of state Winwood, either (as per the contemporary memorialist William Sanderson) as a result of his hearing news from Holland of the 'confession' while ill of the fugitive apothecary's boy (that is, the person who had brought the fatal 'enema' to Overbury in September 1613) or (Anthony Weldon's version) as a result of a 'tip-off' by the disgraced Catholic Countess of Shrewsbury, mother-in-law of Carr's detractor the earl of Arundel ,who was a prisoner in the Tower and had heard disturbing gossip there which Elwes confirmed to her was correct.[66] The Weldon story that William Trumbull, the charge-d'affaires in Brussels (ie the Spanish Netherlands), brought the details of the apothecary's boy's confession to London and this started the enquiry is inaccurate; Winwood was making his first enquiries from Elwes before Trumbull returned home in late September. According to Elwes, Winwood used the earl of Shrewsbury (i.e. his informant's husband) to approach and 'pump' Elwes indirectly without making it clear what the 'casual' questions in the course of talk about other matters were about, and the nervous and self-protecting Elwes gabbled out more – though in terms to justify his own potentially criminal inaction in protecting Overbury – than Winwood had expected to hear (account of 1640s MP and diarist Sir Simonds d'Ewes). Shrewsbury then revealed that Winwood would be interested to hear what Elwes knew, the latter assured that he would co-operate fully and be happy to do so, and a meeting was set up. This was around 21 August, when the King was still away (at Beaulieu in the New Forest) – but he was kept informed and duly asked that Elwes be told to draw up a full written account. This document contained Elwes' version of events in 1613 including the alleged commission by Mrs Turner (on behalf of Frances) to poison Overbury and how Weston confessed that to Elwes and was warned off, as covered earlier.[67] The full enquiry now proceeded – with the King already 'cooling off' towards and irritated with Carr, but with no sign yet that the latter would be implicated.

Given that it was Winwood who set the wheels in motion, possibly Carr's quarrelling with and trying to assert authority over him was the final blow that led to the first 'leaks' about the killing coming out and being taken seriously. As secretary of state and so the recipient of foreign reports, the apothecary's boy's story would end up in his 'in-tray' – if that rather than what Lady Shrewsbury heard was the crucial detail. As seen, however, there were plenty of other foes ready to take a chance on any story that might bring Carr down, especially as the King was wearying of him and had Villiers available as a replacement. Nor did the initial evidence point to Carr rather than to Frances, though the latter might imply that her lover as of 1613 was involved too; and the matter of the 'fatal enema' of September 1613 might not have any connection to the apparent botched poison plot by Frances of late spring 1613. Indeed, as seen the evidence for the 'enema' or its fatal effect is dubious; Overbury might have been fatally weakened already, whether or not he was helped on his way by Frances, Mrs Turner, or Weston. The events that now snowballed had a political as much as legal traction, and the need for those under suspicion to try to minimise their own guilt and direct the government to blame others instead makes all 'sworn statements' as to what had actually happened in 1613 of dubious value. Nor was it a case of the King either 'covering up the truth ' to protect Carr and Frances or, alternatively, using the stories to provide a cast-iron excuse to rid himself of his now unwanted and petulant favourite (as was suspected at the time). The then attorney-general, Sir Francis Bacon, later wrote that James' initial reaction was that it was a 'smear' by low-born enemies of Somerset to ruin him and alienate the King, and that although James insisted on a full enquiry he was hoping that it would clear the Somersets and reveal who was falsely accusing them.[68] The actual 'royal cover-up' amounted more to James hastening to assert that he had been tricked (ie by scheming courtiers) into falsely imprisoning Overbury and putting him in danger, and Lord Chief Justice Coke hastened to stress this 'official line' in court. Weston was arrested and interrogated by the Privy Council in late September, though this hardened malefactor at first claimed that Overbury had just caught a chill sitting in the Tower gardens in poor weather and had declined in health thereafter, and once he was in custody Frances had the dodgy 'physician'/astrologer Franklin summoned to meet her and Mrs Turner in secret (possibly with Carr listening and being consulted in the room next door) and according to him told him that he must deny it all even if he was then hanged as she was not going to face that fate. Mrs Turner gloomily and accurately predicted that she would also be hanged to save her mistress.[69] Mrs Turner and Franklin were soon arrested too, and the King put Lord Chief Justice Coke in charge of the enquiry to emphasize its seriousness and his determination to get to the bottom of what had happened. The latter was both energetic and rigorous to the point of brutality, especially with the socially lower malefactors as opposed to the Somersets, but need not be written off as a royal toady who knew what was expected of him and what lines the King wanted to pursue and what not to pursue. He was notorious for his independence of mind and his own views of what constituted proper and traditional English justice, and was to clash with the King later over his equally rigorous (and learned) views of the legal restrictions on the royal prerogative. Coke's harshness towards the accused was probably at least partly due to the known or suspected Catholic leanings of most of them, given his anti-Catholic views and keenness to smoke out 'Papist agents', and he also made it clear that he was not going to give the King a full and regular picture of what he was discovering and he must be left to draw up his own conclusions and take the enquiry where he wished – citing what he had done and not done for Elizabeth, who had not interfered with him.[70] The accused never complained at his intimidating or trying to trick them – rather, his 'forte' lay in aggressive and emotional, generalised accusations in court which were designed to whip up the jury and public to follow his desired course of action which in this case centred on exposing a sinister Catholic conspiracy of diabolical wickedness. (This was not unusual for the era; it was only a decade since the 'Gunpowder Plot').

Coke's investigations and questionings led to the examination of Overbury's ex-servant Lawrence Davies in early October, and his revelations about the packet of white powder which Carr had sent to the victim soon before he died pointed the finger of accusation at Carr as an apparent poisoner. As explored earlier, the packet may have been innocuous or Carr may have had a plan to make Overbury seem seriously ill so getting him released would be easier – but for Carr's numerous circling foes this was a 'smoking gun' once it was known, which happened due to the alarmed Coke now requesting the King to add extra commissioners to his investigation as it was becoming so serious. These men included Carr's enemy Ellesmere – and the Duke of Lennox to keep a 'watching brief' for his cousin the King. Carr turned up at the King's hunting-lodge at Royston near Cambridge a few hours later than Coke in a failed attempt to appeal to James not to extend the panel – and as James refused and sent him packing the two of them would never see each other again.[71] In effect Carr was being thrown to the wolves, and he made matters worse by using his authority as a Councillor to send an official to search the house where the ex-gaoler Weston's son was lodging and recover a trunk of papers relating to Mrs Turner, which then seem to have disappeared. This was duly reported to the commissioners and treated in the worst possible light. Carr also burnt assorted letters which he had sent to the late earl of Northampton, which he had recovered from the latter's house, and he was duly placed under arrest. Weston was now tried for murdering Overbury, with Coke – already the magistrate who had been investigating the case – presiding and also intervening in proceedings from time to time, as far as the patchy accounts of the trial can be interpreted to accuse and abuse the prisoner. By modern standards this seems shocking, but it was normal procedure for the seventeenth century and would be seen later in other cases of 'political' trials, most famously by Judge Jeffreys in the 1680s. More unusual was the explicit linkage of both Carr and Frances, and moral abuse of the latter as a rare wicked member of a noble family who needed to be 'cut off' to preserve their stock's purity, by the prosecuting (ie State) counsel, Lawrence Hyde, who would presumably have been advised on what line to take.[72] The official line, whether or not due to disgusted and anti-Catholic moralist magistrate Coke as opposed to courtiers lurking in the background, was that Frances and her current husband were fully to blame, though if Weston, Mrs Turner, and Franklin were to be believed

Frances at any rate had made one attempt to murder Overbury in spring 1613. Weston, panicking or gambling to save his life, tried to stymie proceedings by refusing to enter a plea so the trial had to be adjourned, but he eventually gave in to pressure and entered a 'not guilty' plea; his eventual defence seems to have been rambling and incoherent, whether due to his overwhelming guilt or not. He was speedily found guilty and on 25 October was hanged at Tyburn, probably justly given the weight of evidence and his long history of lies and double-dealing though it is possible that he actually murdered Overbury by smothering not poisoning him despite all the emphasis placed on the latter in the trial and investigation. Nor is it clear that it was Frances rather than Northampton who put him up to it, if he did commit the crime. Elwes was now arrested too, though his crimes were more of omission and seeking to wriggle out of a difficult situation by lies and sacrificing Overbury than of actual criminal activity, and Carr was stripped of his offices in disgrace and on 2 November was put in the Tower. His wife, under investigation but pregnant, was confined to his Whitehall apartments.

The procedure of judicial investigation, trial and sentence now proceeded for the accused, with a grisly inevitability and seeming determination to read the worst possible interpretations into often obscure, dubious, contradictory and illogical evidence. A modern defence counsel would have torn some of the cases to pieces, but in this era the advantage – particularly with state-sponsored trials where a guilty verdict was probably required for political reasons – lay with the prosecution and 'detective work' as such by official investigators was sporadic and often absent. Anne Turner was prosecuted before the King's Bench court (as appropriate for her low social status) on 7 November, for assisting Weston in killing Overbury and not apparently even knowing that he had been convicted and hanged let alone what was in his statements. Apparently confident of acquittal and doing her best to look like a respectable widow, she was soon discomfited and past details of her association with dubious characters like Dr Forman (which were not relevant to the case but seemed to show the jury and public what a crooked and immoral woman she was) were dredged up. Magical paraphernalia used by Forman in allegedly endeavouring to create attraction (or lust) between his customers and their targets were produced to imply that she dabbled in witchcraft too, with prosecutor Lawrence Hyde whipping up public indignation about it all, and according to Sir Simonds D'Ewes Weston, Elwes and even Franklin had a more favourable public reaction as Frances' 'dupes' than did her seeming accomplice in crime Mrs Turner.[73] This was probably the prosecution's intention, whether or not it was manipulated to stir up hatred of her employer Frances too and increase the chances of the latter being convicted. The accused was duly found guilty and condemned to death, and afterwards (possibly at the King's request) she was questioned further by clerics to secure extra details, supposedly for the good it would do her soul to confess but more likely to try to find out information concerning exactly what had happened and what Frances' or Carr's role was. Her limited 'confession' included a few more details about the mysterious foods which she had transmitted to Weston for use in the Tower (though not who had made them) and talk in Frances' household that Overbury was doomed when he entered the Tower – and also Weston's reference to smothering the victim which could have 'proved' that he was not actually fatally poisoned after all. This was inconvenient so it was quietly ignored, and this inaction was not out of scruple that post-conviction evidence was inadmissible as what Mrs Turner had said on this occasion about the poisoned tarts was later referred to in court (generally) by Hyde. On 14 November the wretched Mrs Turner was hanged at Tyburn, with enthusiastic crowds including coaches full of society ladies in attendance. With her and Weston out of the way, Elwes was tried for assisting the prisoner too, on the grounds that when he had discovered Weston to have a vial of presumed poison he had not confiscated it, he had not stopped suspicious foodstuffs getting to his prisoner despite fearing that the latter was to be killed, and he had not sacked Weston which was within his power; he had also had confidential correspondence with Frances on the matter. Despite what both Coke and Hyde had said in their opening speeches about dramatic new evidence showing that the 'conspiracy' was wider and more serious than originally thought, this was not fully explained – was there any admissable evidence for it? – although Hyde did accuse Northampton of involvement on account of his correspondence which Carr had sought to secure and hide from the authorities. Incriminating extracts from letters by the late earl were read out and duly sounded as if he was a scoundrel up to his neck in the plot, but not full letters[74] – which would suggest that they were tampered with for dramatic effect, in the same way that the famous 'Casket Letters' had been tampered with by the English and Scots political elites in 1567–8 to incriminate the King's mother Mary Stuart.

But if Elwes was being set up as another scapegoat he did not play ball, and he kept his nerve and launched a bold and logical defence, assuring that he had saved Overbury's life rather than killed him – by ordering Weston to abandon the first 'poisoned food' plot when he discovered it in May 1613 – and he had only kept him on as gaoler out of charity. He had been remiss in trusting Weston but that was not worthy of death; he had confiscated all the apparently poisoned tarts and stored them in his kitchen to see how they developed – and as they had turned black and noxious they had clearly been poisoned. (If this was true, it argues for Frances' guilt on that occasion, as Mrs Turner would hardly have risked all on a poison plot without her mistress' orders, and if Northampton had commissioned the idea then Mrs Turner could safely accuse him once he was dead.) Elwes asserted – again, with logic and quite likely truthfully – that Carr had wanted Overbury locked up, but only to scare him into accepting his marriage to Frances and stopping his threats to disrupt it; Monson and even Suffolk had written to him confirming that intention and he still had their letters.[75] The public reaction in court seems to have been to believe Elwes and excuse him from guilt if not some naivity, but Coke now produced a convenient confession just acquired from Franklin stating that he had seen letters from Elwes to Frances discussing and not making any objection to the murder plan, plus extra details about the frequency of the attempted poisonings. Again, the supposed letters may have been selectively quoted or invented and they were not shown to the jury, but Elwes was visibly dumbfounded by the apparent quotes from his words that were read out. The jury reacted badly (as Coke or whoever had prompted him had intended?) and he was found guilty, and in due course he was executed too – admitting concealing the murder plot from the authorities, and so bringing Overbury to his death, and blaming Northampton and Monson for cozening him into it.[76] The undenied allegation that Elwes had once told Weston that he could kill Overbury if he had to but he should leave Elwes out of it, thus saving his skin and hopefully his job, was probably his worst crime apart from not sacking Weston – who could have been replaced by another killer gaoler anyway. Elwes was shifty rather than wicked, but the final accused to be convicted apart from the Somersets, the villainous Franklin, tried to bargain for his life by promising to reveal all sorts of unguessed-at wickedness in his post-conviction 'confession' and ended up accusing Carr of poisoning Prince Henry too, in 1612, and the earl of Suffolk of abetting the Overbury murder. If this was intended to please the authorities who were clearly out to convict Carr too, the plan misfired though it has provided extra ammunition for conspiracy theorists ever since. Franklin was executed, and the case against Monson (co-hirer of Elwes as the new Lieutenant of the Tower and close crony of Northampton) appears to have collapsed – and more important, been allowed to collapse – as when his trial opened at the Guildhall he threatened to call Suffolk in his defence and was probably going to assert that the Howards as a family had intended to pressurise Overbury in gaol into abandoning his enmity towards Frances and her intended marriage. This was 'near the knuckle' though it did not amount to any involvement with Mrs Turner or Weston, and Coke obligingly adjourned the trial after trying to intimidate Monson by accusing him of falsely slandering the noble earl of Suffolk of being a Catholic[77] (i.e. presumably a proven traitor).

This left the cases against Carr and Frances to be pursued or not, and though the extent of court dislike of Carr, the King's desire to show that he was not interfering in justice to save his nuisancesome ex-favourite, and anti-Howard intrigues all made it desirable to proceed with their trials the actual burden of evidence (such as it is) points more to Frances than her husband. His trying to corral and destroy evidence did not exactly help, but the reasonable case – made in court by Elwes – that he had been seeking to have Overbury locked up to protect his forthcoming marriage was deliberately ignored in favour of the interpretation that he had placed his ex-friend in the Tower so Frances could murder him. The evidence for his collusion in the poison plot was even more dubious, though much could be made of the various foods which he had sent Overbury and the attempt (if such it was) to make him appear ill so the King would release him earlier. As usual for a state trial, evidence that contradicted the 'official narrative' was ignored or side-lined.

The wheels of justice now ground into action against Carr and Frances – and as shown above, although it was a major achievement in impartial administration of the Law to indict people so close to the King this was in itself a piece of political 'spin'. It showed that the King was keen to see justice done against all offenders and did nobody any especial favours, thus offsetting criticism that he had showered favour on Carr and the ultra-corrupt Howards in the first place – and the 'public theatre' of the trial (presumably deliberately) ignored arguments that might have suggested that Carr had non-lethal reasons to send food (tainted or not) to Overbury or that Frances' assumed attempt to poison Overbury had not been the fatal one. There was also even a degree of political rivalry involved in the conduct of the prosecution, as the attorney-general (i.e. the man who would organise the prosecution case behind the scenes and then present it in court), the brilliant and shrewd but devious polymath Sir Francis Bacon, was at odds with and probably seeking to undermine the trial judge, Coke. Ironically, Bacon was himself a homosexual who had an entourage of good-looking young men in his household, like the King, and was to end up accused of accepting bribes and other corrupt practices as his tenure as Lord Chancellor (1618–21) ended in disgrace and indictment – so he was as guilty of illegal practices in the same ways as the King, Carr and Suffolk. The obsessive but perhaps genuinely revolted Coke intended to make much of the association of Carr and Frances via Mrs Turner with the 'witchcraft' of Dr Foreman, Franklin, and other shady characters to show what wicked people they were and so influence the jury and public opinion – and distract the latter away from blaming the King for favouring them and throwing Overbury in gaol? There were also stories arising from the Turner/Foreman investigation that these two or Franklin had possessed waxen images of the late Prince Henry, which could imply practising magic against him – which would be distressing to his grieving father and stir up rumours of him being murdered too. But Bacon argued that all this was not relevant to the case and counter-productive, and it might alarm Carr and cause him to go what we would now call 'off-script' in his defence to release embarrassing information. Bacon duly advised the King that it was indeed justifiable and useful to stir up public hatred of Carr as a wicked character who had committed many other unsavoury actions, as Coke intended, but much safer to just hint that these were – unspecified – political machinations.[78]

This evidence, hidden from public view, confirms that the tone and direction of the trial was as 'political' as other state trials of the era, not a fair judicial process, and also that Bacon was using it to show the King that Coke was unreliable and hence needed to be replaced – by himself? The trial in May 1616 duly saw Carr accused of being an accomplice before the fact in the murder, the eloquent Bacon hinting at the many other underhand crimes of Carr in secret political matters that were too serious to be explained in public, and the way in which Carr had abused the King's confidence by disclosing to and seeking advice on official matters from Overbury while he was acting as secretary of state. The two men had conspired to arrange Carr's marriage to Frances in order to satisfy the latter's lust and were as bad as each other, and Overbury was deserving of little sympathy despite his horrible end as he was as corrupt and amoral as Carr[79]– a new slant on the case that was probably crafted in order to deprive the victim of much public sympathy and give the King a good excuse to reprieve Carr after his sentence. The Attorney-General went on to craft a seamless 'narrative' whereby the imprisonment of Overbury, the choices of Elwes and Weston to guard him, the dabblings in poison of Mrs Turner and her villainous accomplice Franklin, and the gifts of food and drink that Carr had sent Overbury were all part of a coherent 'master-plan' to murder him, and Bacon also named the safely deceased Northampton as part of the plot too – but with Carr as equal in guilt to and working with him (which is very unlikely). The witnesses called included a friend of Weston's who had assisted Lord Chief Justice Coke in recovering some of the 'black magic' waxen images and who now obligingly asserted that Carr had in reality known Weston far better than he had pretended and had lied about not being the prime mover in Overbury's arrest – though this witness was unreliable and quite possibly 'bought' or pressurised, which was glossed over. Bacon appears to have lied himself in claiming that Northampton's ally Monson had testified that Carr and his late patron had been the cause of Overbury's arrest, as the actual record of Monson's interrogations do not contain this detail, and worse behaviour – though normal for the era – came from Bacon's supporting counsel, Sir Henry Montague, who whipped up feelings with his loud declarations of horror at the abominable nature of the crime and laid out the worst possible interpretations of the 'white powder' (i.e. arsenic?) and 'poisoned tarts' sent by Carr to his victim.

Carr did his best to defend himself but could not deny that he had sought to have Overbury locked up after the latter threatened his marriage, that he had tampered with evidence by trying to seize or destroy documents, and that Weston (who he had supposedly never met until Overbury was dead) had acted as a message-carrier between him and Frances, and after a stumbling performance and some confusion about his explanations was found guilty and sentenced to death.[80] However, there was no hurry to execute him – whether or not the threat was always a charade and he had been convicted as a 'political message' that the King was carrying out justice impartially. He was allowed to exercise and have other privileges in the Tower, though his possessions and titles were confiscated (the latter and some of the former only temporarily), and he had enough confidence of the Kings' goodwill or conceit to refuse a Council offer of a 'deal' that would entail his giving up only some of his lands permanently (and exchanging others for new if less valuable estates elsewhere) in return for a quick pardon – thus turning down a large potential income of £7,000 per annum.[80] He and his wife remained in the Tower, living in conditions of relative affluence and allowed visitors and various perquisites but politically neutered and ignored by the King which no doubt pleased their triumphant enemies, and ironically Frances' corrupt and negligent father Suffolk ended up disgraced and sacked as Lord Treasurer in 1618 after annoying the new favourite George Villiers (as of January 1618 marquis of Buckingham and as rich and fawned upon as Carr had once been). Suffolk even spent a short period in the Tower after his ruin before his pardon, leading to wits joking that there were now enough ruined Councillors in the Tower to hold a Privy Council meeting there, and in January 1622 the Somersets were released from the Tower. The most glaring omission of the case had been the failure to indict Frances given the amount of evidence against her, albeit coming from possible serial liars – but quite apart from the chivalric instincts of the King not to subject a noblewoman to the intense atmosphere and hysterical language of a seventeenth-century lawcourt, he and his advisers may have feared that pardoning her would be even riskier to their reputations than pardoning Carr. A charitable view would be that they had realised that Mrs Turner, Weston and Franklin were too slippery to be reliable witnesses and/or that Northampton had pushed Frances into acting or done so himself – a sceptical view would be that it was a 'cover-up' designed to deflect popular opinion against Carr.

A pardon followed for Carr (Frances had never been tried and so was free from judicial penalties) on 7 October 1624, though he never regained most of his lost estates let alone any influence at Court and the King notedly treated him as an embarrassment and cut him out of his life, never seeing him again. The disgraced earl had to promise to keep away from the House of Lords and seems to have settled in semi-isolation at his new house in Chiswick, amidst the perhaps inevitable rumours of infidelity by a bored and less than loyal Frances. Carr was also rumoured to have blamed Frances for talking him into their disastrous liaison and being the cause of his ruin, which if true was no more than she deserved; at the least she had shown a shocking lack of judgement, had no qualms about dealing with characters like Mrs Turner, Weston and Franklin (even allowing for their tainted evidence not being accurate), and been governed by what would nowadays be called a 'sense of entitlement'. The pair of them were clearly 'shunted aside' from Court and from any possibility of recall to prominence as an embarrassment to the King, quite apart from punishing them – which seems (as is so often the case in scandals in high places) to have been less important for the State's leadership than was 'keeping the lid on' the amount of information let out into the public domain and then protecting the King's reputation. Once the case came to trial Carr and Frances had to be 'sacrificed' to the proper legal procedure to appease elite and wider public opinion about their behaviour, but their lives were spared despite their misbehaviour – which royal 'grace' was not extended to political offenders who the King did not like, such as convicted and 'treasonous' Sir Walter Raleigh in 1618 after his blundering expedition to South America annoyed Spain. The mixture of double standards in the legal process, vengeful behaviour to personal enemies by an 'entitled' Court favourite, and a state desire to hide the truth is all too modern. It is far from clear – as far as anything is clear in this case of sleaze, intrigue, multiple betrayals, and murder at the heart of the Jacobean court – that Frances Howard had not made at least one serious if botched attempt to kill Overbury so if she did not kill him, it was not for want of trying. Though her husband was a victim too he was far from an innocent one and his conduct verged on arrogant stupidity at times and was as guilty of 'covering up' major crimes as the unfortunate and executed Tower official Elwes. But the tone of a court and what happens there depends to a great degree on the leadership (or not) provided by its presiding monarch, and in that respect James had much to answer for. The mixture of greed, betrayal, poison, and hangers-on at a viciously competitive Court who allegedly dabbled in black magic was a new 'low' for the English royal court, though an even more extensive poison-scandal was to hit Louis XIV's France in the 1670s, and it reflects very badly on James' priorities.

Chapter 3

Charles II and the Secret Treaty of Dover: Did he Really Intend to Convert to Catholicism?

In 1642 the Parliamentarians had gone to war with Charles I claiming that he was an ally of repressive and ungodly international Catholicism, helped by the semi-Catholic cultural tone of his court, his proselytizing Catholic French wife Henrietta Maria, and the number of both established and 'new convert' Catholics at his court. His attempt to shut down opposition to his divisive policies in the Commons by arresting the famous 'Five Members' in person on 5 January 1642 and subsequent flight from London and refusal to accept Parliamentary terms neutering his political independence seemed to confirm this charge to many of his citizens, and his reliance on Catholic northern English, Welsh, and later Irish, troops in the war added to it. After his defeat at Naseby in 1645 his correspondence was captured in the Royalist camp, and confirmed that he had been negotiating with European Catholic powers to hire troops, and his slipperiness and refusal to agree to the varying terms for a political and religious settlement put out by rival English Parliamentary, New Model Army, and Scots factions after 1646 duly led to his trial and execution. The claims of 'royal Popery' were in fact exaggerated and Charles' chief concern was to preserve the Anglican Church in England from a 'Puritan' / Presbyterian purge, and he was wary of granting the terms demanded by his rebellious but potentially useful Irish Catholic subjects for aid – but his mutually contradictory offers to different factions aided his enemies' blackening of his name. The executed King was able to be posed as an Anglican 'martyr' and a cult was built up of him as a victim of unjust 'fanatic' victimization once the Restoration unexpectedly occurred in May 1660 – yet despite Charles II's promises of defending the new Anglican-dominated Protestant order in 1670 his representatives seemingly signed a treaty with the current international Catholic 'bugbear' France promising to convert both himself and his kingdom, the negation of all he had assured he would do in 1660. How did this come about, and was he sincere in his apparent offer to his fanatically anti-Protestant cousin Louis XIV? If he did resort to this, was it just an 'insurance policy' in case his plot-threatened regime needed Louis' troops, and was it due to his own failings in not securing national reconciliation?

It is unfair to put all the blame for the political 'drift', religious repression, financial problems, and diminished international position of post-1660 Britain on an inadequately 'focussed' monarch and his squabbling ministers, although the role of the 'Head of State' was bound to be crucial as the fount of policy and patronage. Charles II, always a hedonist and after 1660 lacking in concentration and 'thrust' compared to his formidable political predecessor Cromwell, was a 'hands-off' ruler, who put more energy into his already notorious private life and his rising number of (often emotionally and financially demanding) mistresses. The young king who had been ruthlessly prepared to 'sign up' to be an obedient puppet-king of the anti-Cromwellian Covenanter religio-political clique ruling Scotland in 1650 in order to enlist their political and military resources for reconquering England, defying his Catholic mother and most of his advisers, had not been lacking in 'thrust' or determination then. Nor had he stinted in his military leadership and risk-taking as he asserted his influence and rallied the Royalists (Covenanter Royalists devoted to a Presbyterian Church as well as 'old' 1640s Anglicans and Catholics) in Scotland after the hard-line Covenanters' defeat by Cromwell at Dunbar in September 1650, preparing and leading a desperate invasion of England. While Cromwell's vastly superior military 'machine', the New Model Army, was overrunning the heartland of Scotland in late summer 1651 Charles risked all on an invasion of England via Carlisle to try to rally the defeated Royalists and disgruntled Presbyterians (hostile to his late father but not in favour of regicide and the new English republic), and ended up defeated by Cromwell when the latter caught up with him at Worcester on 3 September, the anniversary of Dunbar. Famously, the King then survived many exciting but hair-raising adventures and 'near misses' as the Cromwellians hunted him down across England, protected by a network of often Catholic loyalists as he made his way in disguise from Worcester to Brighthelmstone (the nucleus of later Brighton) to take ship for France – a story that he often repeated to listeners in later years and which served as the centre of a new heroic royal myth. Despite all the odds he struggled on abroad as an exile and sought overseas aid to overthrow Cromwell, even when his young French cousin Louis XIV's minister Cardinal Mazarin chose to expel him and sign an alliance with Cromwell instead – and when Cromwell died and the military-led Protectorate imploded into civil conflict and coups Charles successfully presented himself as the agent of stability and reconciliation to coax the divided Anglo-Scottish elites into accepting his return in 1660. So far he had seemingly not put a foot wrong and showed an impressive mixture of courage, flair, and shrewd good sense as he emerged as the man who had ended civil war and political chaos – rather like his equally licentious but brilliant French grandfather Henry IV, the Protestant who had turned Catholic to win over his doubters and who had 'thought Paris worth a Mass'. There were great hopes – and sheer political exhaustion and fear of more chaos – in Britain in 1660 which aided Charles' position, yet within a decade he was apparently in such concern over domestic instability that he was prepared to seek French military and financial aid from the 'hard-line' Catholic proselytizer Louis in return for a promise to declare himself Catholic in the secret treaty of Dover. How on earth did this seeming 'volte-face' and betrayal of the anti-Catholic majority of his (English and possibly Scots but not Irish) subjects come about? Was he just involved in another of his notorious political 'cons' of people whose goodwill he needed for the time being – as he had done to the Scots Covenanters in accepting their equally 'hard-line' demands in 1650?

The government's political and financial position in the early 1660s was bound to produce major problems given the priorities and constraints of the Restoration settlements. Some of the wide diversity of hopes for the new regime's policies were bound to be disappointed and grumbling to start – financially ruined or exiled and long-sidelined 1640s Royalists (mostly Anglican but also Catholic) and their heirs were out for revenge for losing the 1642–6 and 1648 Civil Wars, and the crushing of republicans and ultra-Protestant religious 'fanatics' were major priorities. They expected 'no compromise' once the King was back on the throne and had sufferings and huge outputs of blood and resources for their late 'martyr' King Charles I to avenge, not implementing the politically wiser promises that Charles II had had to make in the 'Declaration of Breda' in spring 1660 to secure his recall. (He had not won his throne back by warfare, after all, but by catastrophic and vicious internal feuds among the divided elite of the 1649–60 'Commonwealth' and the now internally feuding Army once Cromwell was dead.) For them, the 'Act of Indemnity and Oblivion' limiting legal reprisals – though breached by Parliament in 1660–1 by its extended list of those proscribed – was 'indemnity for the King's enemies and oblivion for his friends'. For moderate Cromwellians who had in some cases backed a potential Cromwellian monarchy (including the future Carolean naval supremo, admiral Edward Montague) and anti-Army civilian republicans (including 1650s Council of State member Anthony Ashley Cooper, Charles' future bugbear) the untried King represented their best hope of stability and keeping the Army generals and the wilder republican and religious radicals at bay; for the defecting Army commander in Scotland who masterminded the Restoration, General George Monck. Charles could secure both political stability and toleration for Monck's moderate Presbyterian allies and help him 'de-fang' the unstable Army – which was now purged and mostly paid off. Many of the one-time Parliamentarian political elite of the 1640s who had defeated Charles I but not wanted him dethroned or killed had been 'betrayed' (as they saw it) by the Army coup of late 1648, regicide, and republic or else had gone along with this reluctantly to end up with Cromwell evicting the last remaining part of the old legal Parliament (the 'Rump') in April 1653 and imposing his own dictatorial rule. They thus swung round to Restoration to avoid more military rule in 1660, and hoped for the best from the King's moderation and his 'Act of Indemnity and Oblivion' – only to see a brutal purge of many non-Royalists from political influence and Presbyterians from any sort of religious toleration, and to have to watch as leading regicides earlier promised their lives were hunted down and executed in a blatant betrayal of faith (led by Royalist MPs rather than the King but accepted by him). All sides could feel that they had been let down by the messy imperfections of the Restoration, and given the reduction in size of the Army, the abolition of Cromwell's system of regional military control of England and blatant occupation of Scotland, and the limitations of the 'reach' of the unwieldy and limited Stuart government 'machine' (and secret service) new uprisings and plots by angry ex-military and religious radicals were a major fear. Indeed, despite their amateurish incompetence and limited support there had already been some revolts after the Restoration – commencing with the botched religious radical 'Fifth Monarchist' attempt to seize London in late 1661. In an age of rumour and vivid memories of recent chaos, was it so unlikely or unrealistic that the embattled (and under-resourced) King would seek a source of long-term stability wherever he could find it?

One area of criticism for the new regime and of a potential source of instability – and hence a Royal search for a drastic solution like aid from Catholic France – was the heightened political quarrels over domestic and foreign policy and personal feuds at Court. But this was not anything new for the Stuarts or a sign of a particularly 'weak' King, as intrigue and factionalism were endemic at any Court. The difficult situation of the 1660s partly arose from the legacies of over two decades of conflict; formerly exiled or suppressed Royalist and former 1640s 'victor' Parliamentarians surviving from the Civil Wars were bound to distrust one another, with a legacy of bitterness from the sufferings of the defeated party and the disappointment of Royalist hopes of compensation in 1660–1. As with resentful Royalists who had regained office in the localities pursuing vendettas against their 1650s supplanters once they had the power to do so – and taking out their feelings on 'fanatics' in general – courtiers who had been in exile or financially ruined in the 1650s would dislike men who had served Cromwell, such as Anthony Ashley Cooper (whose case was made worse by his being a former Royalist who had changed sides in 1644). Monck had initially been Royalist as well, though he was not a civilian minister involved in formulating domestic politics as Cooper was. Even some aristocratic ministers like the Earl of Southampton, the new treasurer, had been – moderate – Parliamentarians, and in the early 1660s ex-Parliamentarian commander the Earl of Manchester, Admiral Montague's older cousin, and his fellow Presbyterian leader Denzel Holles (the latter one of the radical 'Five Members' who Charles I tried to arrest in January 1642) were still politically powerful and were sporadically consulted over policy. In the event, the only one of the 1640s Parliamentarians and 1650s Cromwellians at Court who was reckoned to be trusted by the King was Monck, the general who had enforced the Restoration and purged republicans from the Army beforehand ; the Earl of Annesley (a Presbyterian and Cromwellian but not as divisive for his 1640s role as Cooper) and Cooper, prominent in government, were not personally close to the King who may have found them not amenable enough to his suggestions. In Ireland, it is notable that late in 1661 the 1640s Royalist commander-in-chief in Ireland, the Marquis of Ormonde, was restored as Lord Lieutenant. This was a parallel to the simultaneous eclipse of 'moderate Cromwellians' from the 1650s by 'old Royalists' from the 1640s and their kin in England.

Charles seems to have resented being lectured by advisers, a drawback for the prosy and 'managing' Lord Chancellor Clarendon who as his 'Secretary of State' Sir Edward Hyde had been a leading moderate figure in the exiled Royalist court in the 1650s and had opposed the more risky military adventures (and seeking of extremist Calvinist and Catholic aid) that Charles and his swashbuckling officers had indulged in. In political terms, relying on the highly capable and experienced Clarendon to guide him would have been safer than listening to or indulging less capable, vain, and mutually hostile intriguing aristocratic courtiers, not least his own childhood friend and wartime companion George Villiers, second duke of Buckingham. Clarendon was a long-term political moderate who had started out as a Parliamentarian critic of Charles I's autocratic policies and suppression of dissent in 1640 only to turn Royalist in 1641–2 as he opposed outright coercion of the King and the danger of civil war. He had schemed for reconciliation with civilian moderate Parliamentarian critics of Cromwell within England and with the Presbyterians in the 1650s and seemingly backed a tolerant 'big tent' approach (as it would now be called) to the Royalists' old foes in 1660, but the suppression of religious dissent in favour of legal Anglican Church dominance after 1660 had been blamed on him – as the 'Clarendon Code' – rather than on the belligerent Royalist MPs and his 'capital' of support was running out as his health and political skills deteriorated. It is notable that in Charles' personal relationships too he would rarely put up with bullying or pressure, to which the much older and more experienced Clarendon was supposed to resort. The only person who could get away with an overbearing approach was the King's favourite mistress Barbara Villiers, a charismatic but overbearing young woman of impeccable Royalist background and insatiable greed who had the advantage of her sexual allure and even so lost her lustre during the 1660s due to her frequent tantrums. When the new Queen Catherine of Braganza attempted by sulking to get Charles to abandon his proposal that he make Barbara her lady-in-waiting he ignored her and took his mistress' side instead. Managing the King was of great importance for ministers and courtiers in promoting their causes, personal or political, and this is one reason apart from personal distaste for their religion why the (usually older) senior Presbyterian peers lacked success with him.

The most prestigious and 'noticed' wits and flatterers were almost exclusively ardent Anglicans (or Catholics) and 'ultra' monarchists, and often of a younger generation than the Civil War veterans. Those of the King's closest non-royal advisers as of 1660–4 who had been active in the 1640s were all dependable Royalists who had served his father loyally, led by Hyde/Clarendon and Ormonde; as was the non-governmental senior Court figure Bristol who as George Digby had been Hyde's militaristic 'ultra' critic as well as personal foe then. In Scotland, a mixture of political misjudgement as Commissioner and diverging from the King's interests cost the senior minister of 1660–3, ex-1650s Royalist commander the Earl of Middleton, his post and Royal trust in 1663. Middleton, a hard-drinking and ageing military officer not a politician, had made the classic mistake of using Charles' sporadic laziness and willingness to devolve major and minor business to trusted ministers to 'presume' on his goodwill on a matter of personal 'one-upmanship' in politics in September 1662 over the Scottish Act of Indemnity, namely who was to be on the list banned from future office. Middleton proposed a seemingly moderate solution of banning only twelve men – but then he arranged for his old foe the Earl of Lauderdale (John Maitland), a Covenanter leader and Commissioner to the Parliamentary regime in England in the mid-1640s, to be included. Middleton gave the 'Royal assent' to it in his role as Commissioner, and the list was then taken quietly to London for Royal approval by Middleton's agent Sir George Mackenzie of Tarbert. However, it appears that someone, probably Archbishop James Sharp's brother William, sent an urgent report of what had happened to Lauderdale in London, and the latter duly alerted the King and had himself taken off the list. Mackenzie was disgraced, and Charles sent Lauderdale to keep an eye on Middleton.[1] Nor was Charles pleased that Middleton had arranged for the Scots Parliament to ban the sons of attainted 'rebel' peers from petitioning the King to have their lands restored, as this trespassed on his prerogative of mercy. Foolishly, Middleton then added to his sins by trying to oppose Charles' orders to halt the collection of fines from those condemned to pay up for their political 'crimes' under the Covenanter regime and told the Scots Privy Council to resume collecting the money – which Lauderdale was only too keen to inform the King about. Middleton clung onto office in name for a few months but was replaced later that spring – according to Bishop Burnet after the King called an (English) Council meeting for this purpose.[2] His political partner and fellow-ex-general, Chancellor the Earl of Glencairn (John Cunningham), died in 1664.

Clashes were inevitable at any Court though the loose moral tone and open feuding at Charles' gave a poor impression, and the interest in specific policies (e.g. religion and foreign affairs) of senior non-governmental courtiers like Bristol (or the Duke of Buckingham later) would lead to this spilling over into matters of government. In that sense, the political result of the problems over Anglican MPs' block on religious toleration bills and penny-pinching MPs' refusal to grant Charles all the money he needed in May-June 1663 – Bristol 'going rogue' and trying to impeach Clarendon – was a return to normal Elizabethan or Jacobean politics, not a sign of chaos in government or Royal weakness. Charles was angry with Clarendon over his preferred religious measures for reconciling moderate Presbyterians and other sects within the Church being thwarted by a rash of MPs' bills to exclude them, and the Commons was seen to be 'out of control'. An ambitious backbench MP from a Royalist family who was short of cash and in need of Court office to earn some, Sir Richard Temple, offered to help Bristol 'manage' the Commons in return for office. Bristol apparently agreed, keen to show the King that he could succeed where Clarendon could not, but he and Temple soon quarrelled, and Temple joined the faction of MPs blocking the King's financial supplies. The angry King informed the Commons that Temple had previously been offering to control them in order to damage his credit with the 'opposition', and when pressed by MPs to name Temple's 'middleman' in the plan did so, 'fingering' Bristol. Temple insisted that it had all been a misunderstanding, and the vengeful Bristol sought to cover his position by launching an impeachment in the Lords against Clarendon – the charges including the supposedly corrupt sale of Dunkirk to Louis XIV plus arranging for Charles to marry a barren Queen so his daughter's children by the Duke of York would sit on the throne. This was all unproveable, and the impeachment was thrown out; Bristol was barred from Court as the King ingeniously reversed his usual policy of toleration and had the Earl arraigned as a Catholic recusant.[3]

The fiasco said nothing for unity at Court and played up inter-courtier feuding, but that was not new for Stuart politics – indeed, back in 1621 the present Duke of Buckingham's father had inspired the impeachment of his Court rival Sir Francis Bacon and in 1624 he and the late King had done the same to Lord Treasurer Cranfield. Nor was the Earl of Bristol accusing Clarendon of being a French puppet, using popular rumours, unique. Powerful courtiers and/or family groupings had also been associated with particular 'lines' in foreign policy before, such as the aggressively pro-Protestant and anti-Spanish Dudley/Sidney connection at Elizabeth I's court, who lobbied for war with Spain in the pre-1585 period, and the pro-Spanish Howards (either Catholic or crypto-Catholic) under James I who sought to keep him from a European Protestant alliance. The French birth and proselytizing Catholic sympathies of new Queen Henrietta Maria after 1625 had led to her Court allies favouring her homeland and the international interests of her religion under Charles I. In contrast, Lord Treasurer Weston and later Secretary of State Windebank, plus some Catholic courtiers such as Endymion Porter, had been associated (fairly or not) with the interests of France's enemy Spain. As yet, unlike with the nubile young Breton adventurer and alleged French spy Louise de Kerouaille at Court in the 1680s, none of Charles' mistresses was considered to have an impact on major policy matters; though Barbara Villiers/ Palmer, distantly related to Buckingham, promoted her large clan and secured a title for herself as Countess of Castlemaine. She also secured a large new house for herself next to St James' Palace – and the decaying Tudor fantasy palace of 'Nonsuch' in Surrey which she was accused of pulling down to sell for its building-materials. She was as much of a political actor as male courtiers and was valued by potential allies accordingly; Bristol formed an alliance with her against Clarendon. Her rival from 1663, the more honourable Frances Stuart, was less active in Court intrigue and was indeed reluctant to take on the role of a Royal mistress – though she was used by the Villiers' enemies to undermine Barbara. The way that Barbara's enemies hopefully dangled attractive young women under the King's nose to undermine the relationship was reminiscent of the use made of attractive young men like George Brett (and initially George Villiers) by ambitious courtiers under James I.

For the first time in the Stuart dynasty's rule in England, there were adult Royal male relatives with a major input in policy, at least in naval affairs and associated diplomacy – the King's brother James, Duke of York and Lord Admiral, whose capacity as a 'hands-on' head of the navy is evidenced by Pepys, and their cousin Rupert, former Royalist general and 1649–52 Royalist naval supremo. Given James' attraction towards Catholicism well ahead of his conversion in the early 1670s, this had led ever since to allegations of his 'sinister' influence on the King in that cause – and in 1679–81 a large political faction was worried enough about him to seek to bar him from the succession. The relationship between James and Clarendon was complicated by the fact that the duke had secretly married Clarendon's pregnant daughter Anne Hyde late in 1660, and their daughters Mary (born April 1662) and Anne (born February 1665) remained the King's next heirs after James; several brothers died as infants. Clarendon's enemies alleged that he had pimped his daughter to James in order to put his grandchildren on the throne and had landed the King with a barren bride too to improve their chances. In fact, the secret James/ Anne Hyde relationship seems to have embarrassed Clarendon, who had no idea of what was going on until after the marriage; indeed, some courtiers encouraged James to break off the relationship and offered to pretend that they were the baby's father instead. The 'official' story, by the editor of James' (augmented) 'Memoirs' decades later, was that the King sought to dissuade them from marriage, but James loyally persisted. In fact, it appears that a shabby proposal was made to marry Anne off to courtier Charles Berkeley, who falsely claimed that Anne had slept with him too and he was the father, and it was the King who insisted on the marriage to James taking place. Hyde then secured an earldom to raise himself to a more appropriate rank for a Royal connection.[4]

James had had his own circle of political allies at the exiled Stuart court in the 1650s and was used to operating independently of his older brother; swashbuckling naval commander Rupert had been the leader of the Royalist 'hard-liners' then and had favoured foreign Catholic help more than the circle of civilian advisers (e.g. Hyde) close to the King. Rupert now concentrated on his role as Governor of Windsor Castle and his scientific and colonial interests rather than politics. James and Rupert were major shareholders in the Royal African Company and promoters of its aggressive colonial ventures (and slavery), which brought about much of the escalating tension with the Dutch leading to war. As head of the Navy, James had the personnel and funds to arrange such ventures. The seizure of Dutch ships and outposts in Africa in 1663–4 by their Company's expedition was led by Rupert's former 1650s naval subordinate and continuing ally Sir Robert Holmes,[5] and it acted independently and in contrast to 'official' peace with the Dutch government. Quite apart from commercial opportunism, the lure of riches and a desire to stand up to the Dutch who were keeping the English out of the East Indies by force, some of the Company's leaders such as Sir George Cocke (as remembered by the Company's secretary Sir William Coventry) were explicitly prepared for the expedition to lead to war to curtail Dutch power, and the sooner the better. Similar English colonial clashes with a supposed ally had occurred in the 1630s against Spain in the West Indies, organised by powerful nobles at arm's length from the government (the Warwick/Saye faction's Providence Islands Company). It had also occurred in the 1650s against the Dutch in the East Indies – and a similar strong line had been taken to the authorities in The Hague then, by the same person as English ambassador (the anti-Dutch 'hard man' George Downing). The 'private war' carried out by the Royal African Company was evidently designed to put pressure on the Dutch and risked the threat of European war, and a substantial group of Royal advisors – including ex-Cromwellians Monck and Montague, the latter involved in similar Cromwellian naval intimidation of Spain and Portugal then – backed this official 'hard line'. So did some ministers, notably secretary of state Sir Henry Bennet, in defiance of Clarendon's cautious approach, and by 1664 the Commons was being stirred up with petitions by merchants affected by Dutch harassment.[6] The committee on trading problems that heard this was stuffed with clients of James and of Bennet, so they were sure of a favourable hearing.

Warning signs? Tilting foreign policy towards the autocratic Louis XIV of France: why?

Drift – or a deliberate move – away from the initial compromises of 1660–1 to a 'hard line' position was visible in mid-1660s foreign policy. The Protestant Dutch Republic, a long-term commercial foe with which Cromwell's republic had fought an indecisive war in 1652–4, and its shipping were treated with increasingly bold hostility by both private English shipping and the Navy, with the high command of the Navy led by the King's competent but autocratic younger brother James, Duke of York (not yet Catholic). The determination of overall policy and the general tone of orders sent to naval commanders was in the hands of the Privy Council and the ministers who implemented its orders. But a lot depended on the actions of individual naval officers 'on the spot' in determining whether English shipping would take a high hand with its rivals and spark an incident that could lead to war – and James was actively promoting former Royalists like ex-privateer Captain Robert Holmes. But the escalation of the potential for conflict in sending a fleet to the Mediterranean in 1664 to attack Dutch shipping and hopefully seize their wealthy Smyrna fleet as it brought goods back from the Ottoman Sultanate – in time of peace – was not that unusual either. It was a repeat of Cromwell's orders to his admirals (including Montague) to seize Spanish shipping and treasure-fleets in European waters in time of peace (1655) and do likewise to Portugal over a diplomatic dispute (1656).

The major war of Clarendon's 'ministry', against a Protestant commercial power and to the advantage of France, Holland's rival was started against his wishes at the instigation of his rivals at Court, and with the King standing back from backing either side in the argument but tacitly encouraging a 'hard-line' approach. It was not a 'trial run' for Charles' French alliance against the Dutch in 1670 – France was technically a Dutch ally in 1664–7. The hard line taken towards the Dutch by English ambassador Sir George Downing (an ex-Cromwellian who had notoriously handed his own ex-commander over to the King for execution) was not so much due to an eagerness to risk war as a hope that England's old rivals could be successfully persuaded to back down over points at issue for fear of war. The Amsterdam merchants had too much to lose from war and would therefore pressurise the De Witt government to give way. Those of the seven Dutch 'United Provinces' which had a strong party in favour of 'Grand Pensionary' De Witt's eclipsed rivals, the pro-Stuart aristocratic Orange dynasty, would not want war either. Downing was correct in his analysis as the Dutch did back down at first; although his hopes for an unwanted Anglo-Dutch crisis enabling the Orangists to overthrow De Witt in favour of Charles' under-age nephew William III were premature a major foreign crisis (with France) was to see De Witt lynched in 1672. There was also a major problem in the web of inter-state European rivalry that now hampered England independently of any 'amateurish' or 'unwisely anti-Dutch' behaviour by the Restoration government and its leading minister Clarendon – the latter being the favourite cause of blame for England's slide into war in 1665 without allies by many mid-late twentieth-century diplomatic historians such as Keith Fielding (UK) and Pieter Geyl (Netherlands). Charles' marriage-alliance with Portugal in 1662 obliged him to send troops to take part in the latter's ongoing war with Spain (against which it had revolted in 1640), and a force under Irish magnate Lord Inchiquin duly joined the war in 1663. This infuriated Charles' host in exile from 1656–60, Philip IV of Spain, who withdrew his ambassador from London and broke off contact, even apparently considering sponsoring a rebellion. With Spain and now the Dutch hostile, England was thrown onto the goodwill of Louis XIV, who coveted the Spanish Netherlands to add to his expanding country, was considering an invasion to secure parts of it, and needed Dutch rather than English goodwill for this. Accordingly when Louis invited England to join his new commercial agreement with the Dutch it would have had to accept the latter's demands on access to English waters for fishing, which Louis had backed, so this was turned down – and instead new secretary of State Bennet had to get Charles to try to mend his fences with Spain and send them an envoy.

Louis' hard line towards England in the early 1660s – he even insisted that Charles stop using his ancestors' claimed title of 'King of France' dating back to 1338 – meant that the Dutch regime was in no imminent danger of an Anglo-French alliance threatening them and so could afford to respond aggressively to English naval attacks. This played a part in the resulting Dutch resilience and failure to hurry to negotiate a commercial settlement of outstanding issues as the English government and navy piled on the pressure on the Dutch in 1664–5, though in any case the Amsterdam merchants would not have stood for any obvious diplomatic 'climb-down' that affected their commercial profits. They had been equally obdurate towards Cromwell despite needing his goodwill against the Spanish and Swedes. The corresponding 'hard-line' mood in London was partly driven by the same City interests linked to councillors in Whitehall as under Cromwell (but now with an added stake in the game due to the development of the Royal Africa Company that was challenging the Dutch commercial interest in West Africa), and partly the new factors of hostile figures among the English leadership and navy commanders alike. Both the Duke of York and Prince Rupert had major commercial interests in the Royal Africa Company and other commercial ventures that tangled with the Dutch e.g. the 1664 Corporations of the Royal Fishery (which sought to dominate the North Sea fisheries) – and so did the ex-Cromwellian commanders who were to join them in command of the Navy in 1665–7, Monck (now Duke of Albemarle) and Montague (now Earl of Sandwich). York was indeed identified by the French ambassador as the principal architect of the Dutch war.[7]

Instead of reining the navy in, Charles chose in summer 1664 to send a second expedition to the Dutch 'sphere of influence' under the equally incautious prince Rupert, a veteran and aggressive privateer commander. At the same time a separate expedition retaliated against Dutch piracy and smuggling based at New Amsterdam in North America by invading and overunning it – since which the defunct Dutch colony has been known as 'New York' after James' ducal title. To add to the danger of war following, Charles' (and before him Cromwell's) 'hard-line' ambassador to the Dutch, Downing, encouraged those London merchants who had grievances against the Dutch to present their claims to the Commons in 1664, with the intention of stoking up anger in the latter so a diplomatic compromise was implausible. In any case, the special post-1660 factor of a host of bored and belligerent young gentry and nobles at Court clamouring for a war so they could earn glory was pressurising Charles towards launching one, and Clarendon and other cautious veterans of the miseries and costs of war in the 1640s were left isolated. All of this duly made a Dutch war more likely, and in November 1664 the Commons duly voted for the sums of money in taxation which Charles told them were needed and the government subsequently ordered the seizure of all Dutch shipping on 18 December 1664. But the Privy Council later lost their nerve when the Dutch proved readier for a clash than expected and sent an expedition to retake the new English positions in West Africa; the councillors panicked, asked the King and York to arrange new talks, had Captain Holmes thrown in the Tower as a goodwill gesture, and tried to ask for French mediation.[8] (The primacy of aggressive English commercial interests in Commons thinking was a major factor in other contemporary matters too – the mid-1660s saw this 'lobby' blocking efforts for an Anglo-Scottish customs union except on extortionate terms and banning the import of Irish cattle to protect the English agricultural sector.)

Backed by the belligerent Commons and public, war was declared in March 1665 – though as seen this was hardly a result of a calculated 'pro-French' or 'pro-Catholic' policy by Charles II, rather a mixture of poor and 'short-termist' diplomatic strategy and careless bluster. Indeed, at the time France was a Dutch not English ally, for devious purposes of the French rivalry with Spain. War was not handled any better than peace; in practical terms it is surprising that experienced officers like Albemarle and Montague as well as the King and his brother expected the well-armed and resilient Dutch navy and its experienced admirals to be easier to crack than they had been in 1652–4. In retrospect, the drawn naval battles of 1665–6 could have been expected from two such well-matched fleets. English over-confidence was duly to lead to the lack of planning and security measures that enabled the Dutch to conduct their humiliating raid on the English naval bases in the Medway in 1667, when several major ships were sunk at their moorings and Charles' flagship was towed away to Holland.[9] This 'Pearl Harbor'-style disaster was luckily not a sign of an imminent Dutch naval descent to land troops on a woefully poorly-prepared English coast, as the Dutch navy and finances were as exhausted as the English by this point, and it was more of a 'warning shot' to demoralise the English ahead of immanent peace – talks at Breda. Charles and his brother had been aware of the threat to the Medway with its large dockyards and poor defences and had recently been to Sheerness to check the situation 'on the ground' and urged greater security-measures – though orders to improve matters were as usual slow, too late, and lost in a welter of bureaucracy. The first of the most shocking facts was that English intelligence in Holland had sent warnings beforehand that the Dutch navy was preparing to put to sea in force but was ignored, even when the Dutch were known to be at sea; the second was that Pepys' colleague at the Admiralty, Coventry (who pooh-poohed the rumours of an imminent Medway attack days before it occurred), was obsessively cutting costs and laying up rather than preparing fireships to use against attackers.[10] Pepy's own diary for the relevant days shows that he was not feeling any urgency about a possible attack but was busy with social concerns and minor business in London; at the usual Trinity House Monday dinner his fellow-diarist John Evelyn was more anxious. When the attack occurred and Pepys was sent to take charge, he was unable to carry out the imposing-sounding orders from Coventry to raise sailors to man the 'laid-up' English fireships and fight the invaders as due to manpower cuts to save money most of the sailors had been laid off and, unpaid and disillusioned, had left the area.[11] Nor was the veteran but somnolent and corrupt commissioner at the Chatham dockyard, Phineas Pett, any use – he had failed to move the 'Royal Charles' upriver to safety as ordered and when the attack occurred his main action was to call on dockyard workers to carry his own possessions to safety.[12] Meanwhile the nation's supreme military commander and most royally trusted ex-Cromwellian general, Monck/Albemarle, arrived post-haste at Chatham during the attack to find he had too few sailors available to fight back as the Dutch casually burnt and hijacked ships in front of him; he was left watching helplessly from the riverbank and had to be talked out of a brave but suicidal plan to take a few boatloads of sailors out to try to save some ships. The catastrophe showed up the slackness and poor management of the navy, and was a major blow for national confidence that could easily have turned into popular wrath given its contrast with national naval success under Cromwell (e.g. in taking the Spanish treasure-fleet in 1656). It was lucky that it came at the end of the war, not earlier or that the Dutch regime had no intention of using it to try to enforce 'regime change' as exiled republicans had sheltered in Holland; Louis XIV was a far greater menace to De Witt than was Charles.

This was another blow to morale soon after the Great Fire of London and could easily be turned into a spark to ignite opposition by the Restoration's foes unless action was taken; it could not be 'spun' as anything but humiliation and (luckily only a few) satires attacking the regime duly followed. It has been blamed on the amateurishness, 'short-termism' and intrigues of the 'high command' that was now led by inexperienced courtiers unlike in the 1650s. This was a favourite complaint of Pepys'; but the King and his brother (if not senior courtiers) were in fact more alert than the supposedly 'careerist' and less 'amateur' lower ranked officials like Pett, whose like had been in place for decades, and both Pepys (often seen as the master of new and efficient practice in the navy) and Coventry were complacent. The worst that can be said of the King's current actions is that he was too confident of his cousin Louis deserting his Dutch ally and putting cousinly goodwill ahead of cold-blooded French strategic interests.

The disaster in the Medway luckily had no serious military consequences as the Dutch were already preparing for peace and indeed De Witt's mercantile-republican regime was becoming anxious for an English alliance to counter rumoured French plans against it. The English leadership were already committed to peace before the humiliation, though as usual there was a court squabble over how best to achieve it. Clarendon preferred to concentrate on prising Louis away from his Dutch allies first to isolate the latter, aided by the King's French mother's chief adviser Sir Henry Jermyn who was with her in Paris, but Bennet preferred to tackle the Dutch first and offer to guarantee the security of the Spanish Netherlands so Louis could not attack Holland that way without English reprisals. Bennet, acting with the anti-French Holy Roman Emperor Leopold's ambassador in London, got his way but the Dutch snubbed him; and with Dutch and French privateer raiding cutting Charles' custom-receipts for 1666–7 to a third of those in 1663–4 and the seamen due £930,000 in wages (only £140,000 could be found) the King had to hasten to accept what terms the Dutch were prepared to offer.[12] Fortunately, Louis had just invaded the Spanish Netherlands on the first of his 'land-grabs' so De Witt needed a quicker peace. This meant abandoning Charles' claims to Pula Run in the East Indies, returning New Amsterdam (which was retaken by England in 1672), and giving up on all his boasted demands for commercial compensation for his merchants for various losses. Other major disasters that had a serious psychological impact were more a matter of bad luck than clumsy governmental leadership, such as the serious outbreak of the plague in London in 1665 and the Great Fire of September 1666 – but they left many of the capital's population dead or in flight and two-thirds of the capital in ruins and led to a general mood that the hopes of 1660 had gone horribly wrong and God was punishing the sinful English. This could easily turn against the government as the scared public sought scapegoats, and the physical effects on the capital (where the gunfire from successive naval battles could be heard during the war) made the danger to the regime more dangerous. The only good side-effect of the succession of crises was that the provincial hunt by Anglican JPs and their allies for 'fanatic' Nonconformist violators of the new penal laws was petering out by 1665–6, and prosecutions for violating the Conventicle Act dropped off. The new 'bogeymen' were the Catholics (again), who were blamed for the Great Fire of London which was supposed to have been started by 'Papist agents'.

The King's 'relaxed' attitudes and lack of control of his feuding intimates (and the absence of one dominant faction) meant that the Court was an unrestrained hotbed of seething jealousies and back-stabbing as well as the usual competition for office and perquisites. This all mattered in terms of the perceived 'drift' of policy in the early-mid 1660s, though even at the orderly and hierarchical Court of the unapproachable Charles I there had been rival factions and a noticeable lack of decisiveness over choosing a foreign policy between the rivals' suggestions in the mid-1630s. Crucially, it undermined the potential for dominance by the most powerful minister, Clarendon, whose impressive capacity for work and devotion to duty helped to cement the new government together and made up for Charles' only sporadic interest in matters of governance. The King was more prepared to attend to State business and more conscientious in his duties than has sometimes been suggested, and it is too simplistic to suggest that he had to be called to attend to Council business reluctantly by a schoolmasterly Clarendon who he came to resent. The effect of a bored King chafing at having to attend Council meetings and Clarendon – a figure from another generation who did not approve of his licentious lifestyle – chiding him for his inattentiveness can be exaggerated. It represented a clash of values, but a monarch bored with business and leaving the minutiae of official paperwork to a workaholic chief minister had been seen before – Henry VIII with Wolsey and James I with Robert Cecil, Earl of Salisbury. Neither was less able or willing to take initiatives in policy when they were interested, and the same can be said of Charles II. Conscientious administrator Charles I was the exception rather than the norm for recent adult male monarchs.

Clarendon, hampered by sporadic ill-health, was alienated from and disliked by many at Court even without the King encouraging this; did this add to problems? Logically, this alienation from the active (and often louche) young aristocrats around his sovereign dated back to Clarendon's experiences as a harassed and not always royally valued civilian minister during the Civil Wars, when he had first clashed with Bristol. His role as head of the future Charles II's administrative Council in the south-west had been under fire from impatient and more bellicose young nobles as early in 1645–6, when he had feuded with aristocratic generals. His lower social rank – he was from minor Wiltshire gentry – and lack of close aristocratic relatives to promote his reputation at Court or in the King's bed did not help either. Charles had ignored his advice over major policy matters before, notably in taking the gamble of signing up to the Covenant in order to be invited to Scotland in 1650. There had been tension between him and other senior advisors at the exiled Court through the 1650s, with Hyde (as he then was) as the King's chief civilian advisor at odds with some of the more daring or hopeless schemes for plots thought up by his companions in exile. He had also been at odds with the Queen Mother and her circle of Catholic or pro-Catholic advisers, such as the ever-intriguing Henry Jermyn, who had leaned towards the European Catholic monarchies as invaluable allies for the exiled King. The ultimate aim of this faction's reliance on either France or Spain as the best means of restoring the Stuarts had been to persuade them to invade England and put Charles on his throne by force, even if Charles had to convert to Catholicism to achieve this – and Hyde had seen the political folly of this and tried to 'downplay' Charles' reliance on Spain as its pensioner at Brussels in 1656–60. Such matters had not been forgotten by those courtiers who he had frustrated, though he had been vindicated by unexpectedly managing to have Charles restored by negotiations in 1660 and as of that summer had been the King's unchallenged chief minister. Maximum mischief was however created by his detractors as early as autumn 1660 – with noticeable impact and success – over the much-publicised allegation that he had sought to pander his daughter Anne Hyde to the Duke of York so that he could secure his grandchild as the next monarch-but-one rather than being unaware of and embarrassed by her becoming pregnant. The relationship between James and Anne dated back to her time as Princess Mary's lady-in-waiting at The Hague in 1659, when they appear to have gone through some private form of marriage ceremony (as Charles and his mistress Lucy Walter were also said to have done). After the Restoration it led to Anne becoming pregnant, and she and James married secretly at her father's London house on 3 September 1660 (six weeks before her child's birth).

Clarendon's efforts to counter Royal leniency towards the Quakers were not successful until the 'scare' caused by the Northern rising in autumn 1663, and his control of government policies was limited even at the height of his influence. There was no coherent 'Clarendon government' of England in 1660–7, and once his equally competent rival Sir Henry Bennet was Secretary of State (and spymaster) in 1663 his influence was further reduced though expectations of his dismissal proved premature. Bennet – allied to the Earl of

Bristol, who was seeking to alleviate the legal position of his fellow-Catholics, and probably to Cooper and Annesley over relief for Presbyterians – was able to plan measures to extend the Royal ability to 'dispense' with the laws against non-Anglicans in Parliament in 1663, in defiance of Clarendon's stance though without effect. As seen above he stirred up a harsher line against the Dutch in the Commons too, in defiance of Clarendon's distaste for conflict. In foreign policy in general the King relied on a group of advisers, including James, Monck, Lord Treasurer Southampton (against conflict with the Dutch on account of the cost), and Cooper (chancellor of the exchequer), not just Clarendon and the Secretaries of State, from 1663 Bennet and Morice. Clarendon's lack of languages (e.g. Dutch) compared to the linguist Bennet was a problem, though he had a translator ready to tackle foreign documents in Richard Belling. The lack of enthusiasm that Clarendon had for the Dutch war did not prevent him being the obvious political scapegoat for it when England failed to win any glorious naval victories, with the possible partial exception of the 'St James' Day' fight in 1666, and the costs began to mount – and his personal isolation at court and perceived haughty arrogance made him an easy target for ambitious courtiers with the King's ear like Buckingham. His apparent attempts to monopolise giving advice to the King and 'cut out' his rivals, though hardly unusual for early modern English courts, was said to be annoying the King, and on a less provable level of 'tittle-tattle' he was said to have infuriated Charles by encouraging the King's mistress Frances Stuart to run off with and marry the King's cousin, the Duke of Richmond, to put a stop to Charles pestering her. This may be just gossip and its main literary reporter was the 1680s pro-'Whig', anti-Catholic Scots politician Bishop Burnet, but Bennet reported that there was a major confrontation between the suspicious King and Clarendon's son Lord Cornbury after he caught the latter bringing a secret message from the minister to Frances.[13] Meanwhile the old rumours that Clarendon had been bribed by Louis to sell Dunkirk to him and had used the money to build his luxury new house in Piccadilly were revived, and angry crowds smashed the windows and pulled up the trees outside. Having been away from court ill with gout for several months in the winter so he could not defend himself, Clarendon was now left exposed by the death of his friend and colleague, Lord Treasurer Southampton, who was not replaced by any of his allies. Coventry, none the worse politically for his complacency over the Medway raid threat and with Pett the sole senior scapegoat to be sacked, boasted that he had persuaded the King to turn against Clarendon – though this may be exaggerated. Clarendon's enemies co-ordinated their efforts with Buckingham having useful allies in the Lords ready to ask embarrassing questions about his past supposed financial indiscretions, and his indictment by Parliament and flight abroad were to follow later in 1667.[14]

The lack of leadership that Charles took in matters of policy like the 'escalation' of the Dutch dispute in 1663–4 and his naivity towards Louis' priorities in both 1663–4 and 1667 was notable compared to Cromwell's approach, when whatever the disputes over the desired course of policy the government had held to one 'line' once this was decided. Charles, probably for reasons of personal insecurity, hung back from giving his full confidence to any one person or faction – and went against Clarendon's and Archbishop Sheldon's initiatives on the desirability of confronting the Quakers as 'subversives', at least until rebellion by other radical sects in 1663 hardened his approach to all non-Anglican Protestants. Determining what approach would appeal to the King was sometimes difficult for the ambitious and/or the sycophantic minister or courtier, though Bennet had success in his approach to formulating a pleasing foreign policy in the early-mid 1660s. Clarendon, by contrast, lost out by proceeding from principle rather than from a desire to please the King. Indeed, the impression received is that Charles – in genteel revenge for his minister's priggish tone? – took to enjoying going behind his back. Charles was more attracted to the wild and the risk-taking at Court than to the sedate and prosy, little though this affected policy; personal friendship for a politically ambitious 'rake' only seems to have had some importance in explaining the rise in importance of his long-excluded crony Buckingham in the mid-late 1660s. The latter played a major role in undermining Clarendon during the Second Dutch War and was reckoned to be one of the dominant group of advisers around the King in 1667–72, the supposed 'Cabal' – though he never achieved a major post, and his influence has probably been exaggerated. Charles was supposed to have reckoned this mercurial intriguer safer within the Royal circle, causing trouble for those outside it, than outside causing mischief for his ministers. But by proxy Buckingham did provide Charles with an invaluable asset for the 1670s, his Yorkshire client Sir Thomas Osborne (Lord Danby) who was the King's Lord Treasurer and agent in controlling the Commons after 1673. The '*secret du roi*', a notion of a private Royal foreign policy conducted via the backstairs, not the Council meeting, was to be as important for (the half-Bourbon) Charles as it was for his French relatives in the later seventeenth century and eighteenth century. As ambitious Spanish diplomats had sought the backing of the current Royal 'toy-boy' Robert Carr to influence James I, so Louis XIV was to seek to place a French 'agent' in Charles' heterosexual bed in the form of Louise de Keroualle, the Breton beauty despatched to Whitehall in 1670. An additional close connection with the French court arose through the early 1660s diplomatic meddling of Henrietta Maria, as ever politically disastrous to the reputation of her husband's family in England. Having failed to convert Charles II or one of his brothers to Catholicism in exile during the 1650s, she secured the marriage of her only surviving, youngest daughter

Henriette-Anne ('Minette') to Louis' homosexual younger brother, 'Monsieur', the Duc d'Orleans, in 1661. This had long-term consequences, given that Charles had already lost one brother (the Duke of Gloucester) and one sister (Princess Mary, still only twenty-nine so able to have children) in autumn 1660. Had 'Minette' been given a Protestant husband her children would have been the logical heirs to James' daughter Anne in the 'Act of Settlement' in 1701, not the more distant descendants of Charles' aunt Elizabeth of Bohemia. The House of Hanover would have been unlikely to inherit the throne had 'Minette' left Protestant descendants; instead, her daughters by 'Monsieur' had Catholic husbands arranged by their French uncle, Louis XIV.

The frequent correspondence between Charles and 'Minette' duly provided the culturally Francophile King with his own access to the French Court, with his sister acting as his unofficial ambassador to Louis and receiving Bourbon advances in return. She was not just a 'French agent', as sometimes crudely supposed, and clearly had brains; her suggestions for helping Louis to dismember the United Provinces in 1669 were presented as beneficial to England too, and as not excluding a later breach with Louis. The interests of a sovereign, with personal connections in the European dynastic network, and their ministers in foreign policy were still divergent in the period 1714–60 over the Hanoverians' involvement with their German Electorate's interests. Ultimately, this divergence between the King's 'personal' foreign policy and that of the government was to lead to the secret diplomatic initiatives for an Anglo-French alliance of 1668–70, which went against the diplomatic tenor of the 'official' endeavours to contain the growing threat of French expansionism in Europe. The 'Triple Alliance' of Britain, the Dutch, and Sweden in 1668, arranged by Secretary of State Bennet (Lord Arlington) after the humiliating end of the expensive Dutch War, was designed to offset Louis' aggressive Catholic militarism as well as to break up his alliance with the Dutch. In 1667 his massive army had wrenched substantial parts of the Spanish Netherlands from Spain, but the prospect of all his neighbours combining – Montague had just negotiated peace between Spain and Portugal – forced him to a quick peace. The English intervention to back De Witt and Montague persuading Philip IV to back down in his dispute with Portugal were crucial, though again Charles showed his naivety in trying to make up for the Medway disaster by blackmailing Louis into handing over his strategically valuable (but expensive) conquests of Ostend and Nieupoort on the Netherlands coast to England, which had been promised them under Cromwell.[15] Bennet now drew Sweden into the Anglo-Dutch alliance too, and Louis was forced into a quick peace with Spain to save his Netherlands conquests.[16] The 'Triple Alliance' was a seeming guarantee of England's commitment to its Protestant allies, the Dutch and Sweden, and thus a conciliatory gesture to the Protestant and not too Francophile MPs who held the national 'purse-strings' in Parliament; it would help to get finances back on track after the revenue-slump and large rise in expenditure during the war. Arguably Louis had shown his unreliability and Charles would have been wise to give up on him as an ally, except in a case of extreme need. But the new diplomatic order was shaky even without Charles yet considering abandoning it, and the impoverished regency for Philip IV of Spain's infant successor Carlos II (supposed to be helping to fund it) failed to come up with the promised financial aid to Sweden. When Louis first offered Charles a new alliance late in 1667, he refused unless his cousin abandoned his enlargement of the French navy and supportive tariffs for French manufactures, which were causing concern in London.[17] But this stand by him was not kept long-term, while shifts in power and office-holding at court were to the detriment of those hostile to France – though due to circumstance not any grand 'plot' or manoeuvres, least of all by the King's supposed 'secret adviser' Buckingham. Lord Treasurer Southampton, a sexagenarian Royalist courtier, had died in May 1667 and was replaced by a commission; Monck/ Albemarle, the mastermind of the Restoration, died in 1670 and his post of military chief (Captain-General) was left vacant while his other main post as Chamberlain went to Henrietta Maria's pro-French adviser Jermyn. Bennet's fellow-secretary of state, the Presbyterian William Morice (a client of Monck's), resigned in 1668 and was replaced with Bennet's protégé John Trevor; the veteran Presbyterian Earl of Manchester died; and senior court Presbyterian Anglesey was suspended as navy treasurer after complaints of his financial malpractices and incompetence (mainly in earlier duties in Ireland) then sacked from the Privy Council by the furious King for challenging his decision. These were the usual 'give and take' of ministerial and court life and did not affect the dominance of Bennet, so far, a critic of Louis.

But then Charles gave his secret backing to 'Minette's' suggestion – her own or prompted by Louis? – that a concurrent French alliance with Louis need not contradict the 'Triple Alliance' but complement it. This was first discussed in letters between Charles and Minette in late 1668, and then put by the King to a gathering of ministers on 25 January 1669 – though unfortunately our sole account of this meeting comes from the unreliable and propagandist post-deposition memoirs of Charles' brother, James, Duke of York. The latter an exile living in France and dependent on his co-religionist Louis' help to try to get his throne back, had every reason to allege that his own controversial 'pro-French' policies and attempt to revive Catholicism to a dominant (or at least major) role in Britain had been his revered brother's policies too. Accordingly, he wrote that on the 25th Charles had summoned him and two Catholic ministers/ advisers, royal secretary and future treasurer Lord Clifford and Lord Arundell of Wardour, to meet him and Bennet/Arlington and had told them of his earnest desire to convert to Catholicism and plan to set up this alliance with Louis as a first step. Due to James' biased views and the lack of other witnesses some historians have doubted if the meeting ever took place, and Charles was rarely if ever that open (let alone sincere) about his real opinions on religion – though he might have 'opened up' to this small gathering which was Catholic apart from Bennet (and the latter had just been shaken in his confidence in the Dutch by a private approach which the devious De Witt had made to Louis).[18] Charles might have been 'testing the waters' for a shift in policy away from the unreliable De Witt, though Louis was no less untrustworthy. It had the advantage of preventing Louis from accepting Dutch offers and wrecking the 'Triple Alliance' – it thus supported rather than undermined Bennet's policy. A private mission to France followed, led by Arundell who was both a discreet and loyal courtier (later to be used as a minister by James) and as a Catholic of ancient family congenial to Louis. The terms which Charles offered Louis have been lost, but from the French replies and contemporary correspondence were apparently for an offensive and defensive alliance based on Charles receiving men, money and ships in case of a war – which would tie Louis to backing him not the Dutch next time round, provide French ships to save English mercantile shipping from Dutch privateers, and reduce the threat of the cost of troops and plunging customs revenues causing bankruptcy. Louis would also halt new naval construction.

The French alliance which this planned in spring 1669 would not breach the Triple Alliance – which De Witt was already threatening by his devious underhand approaches to France – provided the Dutch played fair and kept it; the riskiest pledge was an apparent private offer by Charles to proclaim himself Catholic if Louis would pay him £200,000.[19] In practical terms, despite the political risk the cash would help England to balance its books after the Dutch war, and without such a cash boost the government was at risk of not being able to pay the interest on its current debts. It was a gamble, but it may reflect financial needs as much as a shift to 'pro-Catholic' policies by Charles – and by tying Louis to England it would stop De Witt rebuilding the 1665–7 Dutch-French alliance. It did not threaten the Triple Alliance; it was a balancing act rather than a 'treacherous' shift towards France against England's new Dutch allies, and presumably this was how the not noticeably pro-French Bennet regarded it. But the French King would now try to lure Charles into a rather more dangerous course of action, i.e. turning on the Dutch.

Stage Two of the Anglo-French plans. A new gamble by the unwisely 'Francophile' Charles, or reluctantly responding to a determined French initiative?

The conventional modern historical interpretation of the moves to the Anglo-French plans in the 1670 Dover 'secret treaty' runs as follows. Thanks to a mixture of English Court rivalries, Charles' dislike of the De Witt regime, and the efforts of his younger sister 'Minette', the Duchess of Orleans, Charles' willingness to confront his sister's bisexual husband Orleans' more formidable elder brother Louis XIV in 1667–8 was short-lived – despite the way Louis had refused to help him against the Dutch earlier. This duly frustrated the Whitehall proponents of a 'sensible' alliance with England's fellow-Protestant powers, the Dutch and Sweden, most notably the level-headed and highly capable diplomat Sir William Temple. Nor were the pro-Dutch and anti-French, anti-Catholic ministers in the so-called 'Cabal' ministry that succeeded Clarendon's in 1667–72, led by the veteran ex-Cromwellian earl of Shaftesbury (Sir Anthony Ashley Cooper), secure in Charles' backing against their rivals in an ever-shifting and disunited nexus of power. But this is arguably an interpretation which downplays the real threat of De Witt wrecking the Triple Alliance himself in 1669 and returning to the Dutch-French alliance of 1665–7 which had deprived England of French naval aid or money during the then war and so helped to undermine the English 'war effort'. Also, when Louis responded favourably (in general terms) to the Arundell mission and offered to send the £200,000 if Charles converted, plus guaranteeing the Triple Alliance and halting naval construction for a year, he insisted that any longer-term alliance centre on a joint attack on the Dutch. This duly stalled talks that summer – i.e., Charles would not rush into it and he was not as enthusiastic a Francophile and pro-Catholic as James' later account would make him. His government duly pushed a compromise settlement of the matter of the endangered Spanish subsidy to Sweden, and so kept Sweden in the alliance.[20] However, restricting English policy to an open promotion of the 'Triple Alliance' and loyalty to this and ignoring French offers would have run the risk of Louis and the Dutch combining against Charles, as they had done in 1665–7 (though Louis had not been actively at war with England despite the terms of his then Dutch alliance). Also, Anglo-Dutch tensions remained over such matters as the English evacuation of its South American colony of Surinam, which the Dutch had successfully demanded in the 1667 peace treaty. But if anyone 'sunk' the prospects for the Triple Alliance remaining in force it was De Witt given his approaches to France – and later in 1669 he offered to Louis that the two powers could divide up the Spanish Netherlands between them and 'cut out' England.[21] As ever, Louis' main interest was land and expanding France across the Low Countries towards the Rhine, and he did have a legitimate claim on some of the Spanish lands if the unhealthy boy-king Carlos II died (the latter in fact lived to the age of thirty-nine) given that his wife Maria Theresa was the boy's elder half-sister and presumed heiress. If Louis responded favourably it could threaten England again, so Charles had a pressing strategic reason to make a better counter-offer to the French even without 'prodding' to do this by 'Minette'. The latter duly sent Charles another letter in September urging him to make another tempting offer to Louis – with her words centring on the desirability of destroying the treacherous Dutch rather than on her alleged Catholic enthusiasm to convert her brother.[22] Was this just a shrewd assessment of what would appeal to Charles – or was it evidence that 'Minette' was thinking as a political strategist not the naïve religious zealot that her critics have called her?

Charles was won back to offering new proposals for a French alliance in December 1669, aimed at crushing the Dutch republic's commerce and replacing De Witt's republican regime with the Orange dynasty. As seen earlier, Charles' brother James (not yet Catholic but already sympathetic to them and long hostile to the Dutch), claimed in his later memoirs that the original initiative for the French alliance was Charles' early in 1669 and that the King enthusiastically envisaged converting to Catholicism in return – but James had his own reasons by then for asserting that. In drawing up the papers to be put to the French and then negotiating Charles used Bennet (who did not convert to Catholicism until his death-bed though he was by now exasperated with the Dutch and doubtful of Spain's ability to keep funding the Triple Alliance) rather than the more 'committed' and less clear-headed Clifford, though the latter did some of the 'donkey work' of writing. The King and Bennet went further than just securing a 'safer' offensive and defensive alliance with France that would tie Louis to backing England not the Dutch and keep him out of a unilateral alliance with the latter – but it should be remembered that only a 'good' and convincing offer would satisfy the hard-headed and arrogant French King. Charles raised his prices to demand £1 million as a 'down-payment' for alliance and then a subsidy of £600,000 per annum, which would balance England's books and offset military costs and the danger of Dutch privateering – and £1 million matched the English Navy Board's assessment of what they needed to equip their fleet and pay their debts for a year so it was a realistic plan not greed. Charles also wanted three ports in the province of Zeeland, on the Dutch coast around the mouth of the Rhine, to secure the Rhine trade for England, plus land or money to boost Charles' young nephew William III of Orange – but not definitively the overthrow of the Dutch Republic by restoring William III to his late father's powers as 'Stadtholder', as stripped from their family since 1650. Louis would guarantee the continuation of his peace-treaty with Spain of 1667 i.e., not annex any more Spanish lands, but if Carlos II died and his family secured Spain England would receive a large part of the latter's empire.[23] This set the scene for the manoevurings leading up to the controversial 'Secret Treaty' that followed – but with no clear and dateable commitment by Charles of when he would proclaim himself Catholic or any accompanying major promotions of Catholics to office to make the conversion backed up by a supportive 'bloc' of political allies. Was it all bluff to lure Louis into alliance and cut out De Witt, or was cynical Charles prepared to commit himself if the circumstances were right?

The mysterious and highly risky 'Secret Treaty of Dover' followed, but it was not a case of an eager Louis quickly luring a naïve or easily tricked Charles into signing away his religion so he could convert England too as a permanent junior ally. Instead, a five-month bout of haggling saw Louis offering to let England enter an attack on the Dutch with a temptingly – or dismissively? – small commitment of thirty ships for the initial naval campaign that would however entail the French, not the English navy, dominating the Dutch coastal waters. Spain would be lured into signing over its Netherlands to Louis in return for territory elsewhere, so Louis would have the best of both bargains. Charles insisted on committing sixty ships not thirty to the campaign, so making naval forces more even, and offered 4,000 troops for the campaign on land, which Louis accepted – and both offers were within the English government's current budgets, provided that Parliament paid a normal-size subsidy and Charles converted to secure the promised French grant too.[24] Crucially the war was only to follow Charles' declaration of conversion so he could find the right timing – and holding the war up gave him the time to come to a firm agreement with Spain in spring 1670, whereby the latter accepted the English occupation of Jamaica in 1655, so he had a 'fall-back' – if financially insecure – ally to rely on. Nor did Charles give in as Louis sent his foreign minister Colbert de Croissy over to England to try to ameliorate his insistence on making a larger naval contribution to the war and so cutting back French wartime naval dominance of the Dutch seas; he retreated up to Newmarket for the races, forcing the visitor to trail up there to see him, and refused to budge. Colbert de Croissy had to advise Louis to give in which he did, and agreement was reached on 2 May. The Anglo-French treaty was then signed – behind many of Charles' more disapproving ministers' backs – with Colbert de Croissy at Dover on 22 May 1670, during the King's sister 'Minette's' final visit to England. The King arrived from London with his brother James, eldest illegitimate son the Duke of Monmouth, and cousin Rupert plus the Queen and most of the court for the royal 'summit' at Dover Castle but most of the court had no idea of the political 'sub-text' of the meeting; 'Minette' arrived by sea with an entourage of over two hundred. The English signatories consisted of Bennet and three governmental Catholics – Clifford, Arundell, and long-term Irish Catholic intriguer Richard Belling (now an aide to Bennet) who had once worked for the 1640s 'rebel' Irish Catholic regime at Kilkenny and had been trying to persuade Charles to convert and rely on European Catholic goodwill since the 1650s. The personnel involved were just those involved in the talks (Bennet and Arundell), writing the documents (Clifford), and translating them (Belling). The King secured promises of French money and if needed troops as part of the alliance in case of an English rebellion, but there were political risks – the treaty was only known to pro-Catholic ministers, which could cause a political 'explosion' once it leaked out to anti-Catholic opponents like Cooper (now earl of Shaftesbury).

Charles' reliance on the maverick and arrogant Louis long-term was problematic, not least as Louis had deserted his cousin to sign up to a Dutch alliance before and was clearly not to be trusted – unless Charles assumed that his own offers to Louis would now prove irresistible in the long term, the Dutch were threatening to desert him for France, and he should abandon his previous 'balancing act' between the major European powers. The key to this, if it was Charles' reasoning, was religion given Louis' aggressive Catholicism and disdain for the French Protestants; the *'devot'* Catholic clerics at the French Court constantly worked on Louis to deal with the latter by forcible reconversion and they were to have their way in 1685. Thus Charles' seeming eagerness to turn Catholic could bring this influential body of advisers to back allying with him, and thwart the 'mercantilist' efforts of those of Louis' advisers (e.g. Colbert, the foreign minister's powerful brother) who preferred Louis to choose allies on more pragmatic and commercial/strategic grounds. With 'Minette' to give him the 'inside news' on how policy was decided in Louis' personal circle and who the French King listened to most, Charles had pragmatic as well as allegedly religious reasons to play up his keenness on Catholicism after the danger of a Franco-Dutch alliance. How much Charles' promises to declare himself Catholic and then reconvert England to that religion in return for French troops and money were sincere remains open to heated speculation. But it was a triumph of subterranean Court intrigue or the King's own personal 'gamble' over official ministerial policy-making by his official advisers, and was a sign of what had changed since the monarchy returned – though foreign policy was ultimately the prerogative of the sovereign anyway and the more effective of the two secretaries of state, Bennet, was fully 'on board'. The change was a return to the inner workings of the Court (especially the Royal Bedchamber personnel) as a centre of policy-making in the time of James VI and I, when the duke of Buckingham (senior) and the Howards had possessed great influence by means of personal access to the King rather than through office. Its international context was new, in that for a century it had been Spain that had been associated in the mind of English Protestants with the causes of imperialistic Catholic oppression and a 'Papist master-plan' for world domination.

The signing of the 'Secret Treaty' was not however the end of the diplomatic contortions of Charles' trying to lure Louis into an alliance on his terms ahead of the 1672 Third Dutch War. The potential political critics Buckingham and Cooper/Shaftesbury were currently alarmed at Dutch obstinacy over new commercial talks and were prepared to accept a closer link by treaty with France (which was publicly stated as being agreed at the Dover talks), but they had no idea of the clause about Charles converting. They were thus prepared to become involved in further talks which Charles soon planned. Logically and given the outcome, now Louis had 'signed up' Charles was deviously – or for his political safety? – trying to 'row back' from his promise to convert, or at least to push this back beyond the outbreak of a Dutch war. Matters were complicated within weeks, as tragically 'Minette' died suddenly at the French royal country palace of St Cloud on 30 June, aged only twenty-six, less than four weeks after her return to France from England.[25] She had been in poor health since the birth of her second daughter Anne Marie in autumn 1669 and the cause of her sudden stomach pain and subsequent decline was probably peritonitis and/or a burst ulcer and the doctors claimed it was cholera, but given the intense intrigue and treachery of the era and the feverish rumours poison was inevitably rumoured. Charles himself apparently suspected his sister's unstable and currently jealous husband, at least in his first shocked reaction.[26] Once the King had been reassured by Louis sending him the official autopsy report and things had quietened down, he sought to change the terms of the treaty to his benefit – and he used the naïve enthusiasm of Buckingham to join in the officially proclaimed 'French alliance' agreed at Dover (terms not all revealed) to send him as envoy to Paris for the next diplomatic meeting. Buckingham and his ally Shaftesbury thought the talks were to confirm and expand on an agreed 'Treaty of Dover' with a Dutch war but no mention of the King converting; so while the Duke was publicly dealing with the French on this basis, behind his back Charles was using private letters to Louis to hedge on when he would actually convert and to back out of any idea of a war in 1671. Having blocked Louis from the threatened Franco-Dutch alliance and secured the prospect of ports in Zeeland and loot from Dutch ships, Charles was able to postpone the war and induce his cousin to offer him two more Dutch islands in the revised terms that were now agreed. This new version of the plan, the 'Secret Treaty of London', was duly signed in December 1670 – but kept the King's conversion and the money he would receive in return out of the official, publicly-released clauses in a secret one.[27]

It was not clear in this treaty if Charles would convert before or after the attack on the Dutch, and Louis failed to 'nail him down' on this crucial question. Given Charles' ruthless subtlety, the King might even be able to deny that the 'conversion' clause even existed if he so wished, once the Dutch war began as he desired – and if Louis published it he could say it was a forgery. This was hardly either religious zeal by Charles to convert to Catholicism or a naïve 'pro-French' line; rather it was a mixture of cynicism about what was in his best interests plus a dangerous gamble on coming out on top without any angry English rebellion if details of the secret clause became public. The whole episode can be seen in one light as a shockingly cynical diplomatic comparison to the far more 'high-minded' Cromwellian approach to the harshly intolerant Catholiciser Louis XIV, with Cromwell prepared to annoy his much-needed French ally in the mid-1650s rather than let French state and church harassment of that nation's Protestant community (the Huguenots) go without English protests – and Charles prepared to turn a blind eye to Louis' religious policies and to exploit his desire to crush the Dutch republic in return for a share of the proceeds. Charles offering to convert to Catholicism in return for French aid would seem in this case to be the ultimate betrayal of the fiercely Protestant majority of both his subjects and his elite, albeit in the cause of securing stability in a still fractious nation that was only a decade away from twenty years of civil war and bloody factional disputes. The threat of 'Popery' taking over the State by 'insider treachery' by the unreliable King, the excuse for the 1688 'Glorious Revolution' against Charles' brother and successor, would seem to be correct as early as 1670 in this scenario – and Charles' (later) critics such as the earl of Shaftesbury to be correct. But the real motives of this most devious and 'opaque' of seventeenth-century royal statesmen are far from clear, and as far as can be reckoned Charles was playing a far deeper 'game' in this gamble. It is more likely that, unlike the more honest and naïve James, he would never have implemented such a scheme in reality unless driven to it by a serious rebellion in England that he could not suppress – and that he was 'playing' Louis for his own benefit by a vague promise to 'sign up' to the fanatically Catholic 'Grand Monarque's' religious plans. The arch-gambler Charles II, however, ran the risk that the documents would become public later to his reputation's detriment – though his risk paid off for the moment. Was this a classic case of 'short-termism' by a master-strategist who was rather too accustomed to rash gambling?

Chapter 4

Did Charles II Marry Twice – and Was the Duke of Monmouth his Rightful Heir?

One of the most pressing issues for the restored monarchy in 1660 was the issue of the King's marriage. Charles II was unmarried at the age of thirty, the oldest King or heir to be in this position until Prince Charles in 1981, and had been no 'catch' in the harshly realistic world of international European diplomacy during his years of exile. The exiled Stuart court (based in France until the Anglo-French treaty of 1655 when Cromwell required the latter to expel Charles so he moved to the Rhineland and later to Spanish-run Bruges) had actively considered various matches. But no European power had been willing to align themselves with a nominal monarch whose chances of returning to his throne seemed slim after the defeat of his Scottish venture and invasion of England in 1651. The Commonwealth, and from December 1653 the Protectorate of Oliver Cromwell, seemed firmly established in power despite numerous plots and had impressively large and successful armed forces. Republican England had defeated the Dutch at sea in 1652–4 and held the balance of power between a civil-war-afflicted France and the declining Spanish empire through the 1650s; it would make a dangerous enemy. Charles' cousin the 'Grand Mademoiselle' of France – Anne Marie Louise, Duchesse de Montpensier, daughter of the under-age King Louis XIV's uncle Gaston of Orleans – was put forward as a candidate by his mother, Gaston's sister Henrietta Maria, and Charles kept her company for dances in Paris in winter 1651–2 where he had the advantage of a heroic reputation from his invasion of England in 1651 and his dashing escape from the 'Roundheads' after the battle of Worcester. But the princess did not prove willing and turned him down, and her subsequent 'Amazonian reputation' after she personally fired cannons at the rebel-held Bastille fortress at Royal troops during a revolt in Paris in April 1652, did not help her chances.[1] The latter incident also blackened her reputation with the French court, as she was thereafter regarded with the same suspicion as her intrigue-prone father Gaston who had notoriously tried to overthrow his elder brother Louis XIII several times in the 1620s and 1630s. In any case, the French chief minister Cardinal Mazarin, an unpopular if brilliant Italian cleric – the target of the Duchesse's rebel aristocratic allies who were attempting to overthrow his regime – preferred to keep in with Cromwell than to assist

Charles and so countered the pro-Stuart sympathies of his mistress (reputedly sexual as well as political), Queen-Mother and regent Anne of Austria. The Anglo-French treaty in November 1655, vital to war- and rebellion-hit France to keep England's powerful New Model Army from assisting its foe Spain in the 1635–59 Franco-Spanish war, required Charles and his next brother Duke James of York to leave France. The only Spanish princess available in the years of Charles' resulting anti-Cromwellian alliance with that power in 1656–9, King Philip IV's daughter Maria Theresa (born 1638 so eight years Charles' junior), was to marry Louis XIV after the Franco-Spanish peace of 1659 and was probably already earmarked for him. The alternatives for Charles were limited anyway – Portugal (his eventual marital choice) was a weak state, at war with his Spanish allies and menaced by Cromwell's fleet, and Sweden had no princess of the right age. The former Queen of Sweden, the formidably intellectual Christina who abdicated in 1654 and was roaming around Europe after converting to Catholicism, was four years older than Charles, brought no political advantages, and seems to have been shunned by him.

Charles, son of the young Louis XIV's aunt Henrietta Maria and thus half a Bourbon, had initially been allowed to base his exiled Court at St Germain near Paris had had the nominal backing of the regency government of France, led by Queen-Mother Anne of Austria and her chief minister Cardinal Mazarin. But the commercial hostility between France and the Commonwealth, exacerbated by English republican meddling with French rebels and vocal Protestant support for the threatened and potentially rebellious Huguenots, had never escalated into open war. Mazarin then reluctantly agreed a peace-treaty with England in November 1655, leading to Charles' expulsion from France. Retreating to Spa in Germany, he was able to take advantage of the angry Spanish reaction to Cromwell's attack on its Caribbean colonies in 1655 as this led to an Anglo-Spanish war, and from 1656 to 1659 was based at Brussels in the Spanish Netherlands at Spanish invitation. Various schemes were launched to enable him to invade England, but nothing came of them due to the poor state of both English Royalism (heavily infiltrated by Secretary John Thurloe's intelligence-network) and Spanish finances and military strength. The King was never seen as more than a useful diversion to Spain's war with England, which in itself was less important to Philip IV's government than its long-term struggle with the French for dominance in Europe. The Anglo-French invasion of the Netherlands in 1657 put Spain on the defensive, and after their defeat at the battle of the Dunes in June 1658 (in which Charles fought in the Spanish army) the principal potential invasion port of Dunkirk fell to the allies and was handed over to Cromwell. Cromwell's death in September 1658 did not improve matters for the King, as the fatal spilt between civilian and military backers of the new government of Richard Cromwell which ended the

Protectorate in April 1659 did not lead to a swift revival in the Royalist party. The Royalist revolt that summer was a poorly-supported fiasco despite the growing instability in England, and the Franco-Spanish peace-treaty ended serious hopes of either government being willing to lend military assistance to a Royalist invasion. It was the collapse of the Commonwealth into factional feuding over power and the nature of the future constitution during the second half of 1659 that made the King's return seem feasible to important power-brokers as a source of stability, backed by popular demand for an end to military rule, and the decision of General Monck to use the Cromwellian army in Scotland to overthrow the military '*junto*' now ruling in Whitehall was the crucial move which opened the floodgates. To the surprise of most observers, Charles – carefully moving from the Catholic Netherlands to Protestant Dutch territory to minimise his unpopular European Catholic links – was duly invited to return to the throne and a peaceful settlement was negotiated. On 25 May 1660 he set foot in an England he had left nearly nine years earlier as a hunted fugitive after the battle of Worcester.

Neither of Charles' Catholic allies in the 1650s, France and Spain, had had an available Princess to marry off to him in a diplomatic alliance against Cromwell. His cousin and potentially closest ally Louis XIV (eight years his junior) only had one younger brother, and Philip IV of Spain had no available daughters. Nor had various potential Protestant allied sovereigns, most notably the unmarried Queen Christina of Sweden and her successor Charles X. The Dutch royal House of Orange was in political abeyance at the hands of the ruling mercantile oligarchy of Amsterdam following the death of Charles' sister's husband Stadtholder William II in 1650, and the new government under Jan De Witt was soon an ally of Cromwell. This dearth of available princesses continued after 1660, reducing the choices available to the restored King; if he was unmarried his heir was his next brother James, Duke of York, who was already rumoured to be sympathetic to Catholicism. James was unmarried too, though he had been abortively linked to the – Catholic – daughter of the exiled Duke of Lorraine (under whom he served as a military officer in the French civil war in the early 1650s). The surprise marriage of James to an English commoner, Anne Hyde – the pregnant daughter of the new Lord Chancellor, Sir Edward Hyde – late in 1660 was deeply unpopular among the latter's political enemies and led to inaccurate accusations that he had arranged the marriage and was keeping Charles from marriage to put his grandchildren on the throne.[2] The marriage took place privately in September 1660, apparently at Anne's father's house in Westminster, and given the date of birth of the couple's first child Anne was at least seven-months pregnant. Efforts were made to pretend that the marriage had not taken place because it was a private occasion with few witnesses – as with Edward IV's marriage to

Elizabeth Woodville. Similar allegations were made about Charles' 'marriage' to Lucy Walter when that became a political issue. It appears that Clarendon was opposed to the marriage lest it damage his reputation and make him seem to have pandered his daughter to James and had her get pregnant to persuade the honourable Duke to marry her and force an entry to the Royal Family for himself. James was probably more reluctant to marry than the bland 'official' story in the posthumous biography based on his memoirs had it, and his mother Henrietta Maria considered the match 'beneath' him and came over to England from her home in France to persuade him to abandon Anne. His sister Mary, the widowed Princess of Orange living in her late husband 'Stadtholder' William II's Dutch 'United Provinces', also pressurised him, and initially he agreed to renounce Anne – who the embarrassed Hyde had reportedly locked in her room and threatened to throw out of his house as a whore.[3] An obliging Court rake, Lord Berkeley, even offered to swear that he, not James, had made Anne Hyde pregnant and take her on as their wife.[4] It was Charles who insisted on the marriage, not Hyde, giving the latter £20,000 and a peerage (the Earldom of Clarendon) to sweeten the humiliation of the inevitable comments when Anne's pre-marital pregnancy was revealed. The marriage was accepted, the Royal Family was distracted by the sudden death of Princess Mary from smallpox (which in the long term prevented her from remarrying and having more Protestant children who could have succeeded Queen Anne instead of the Hanoverians in 1714), and early in 1661 Henrietta Maria retreated to France. Eventually a marital alliance was negotiated for Charles with Cromwell's ally Portugal, whose Catholic dynasty of Braganza had led a successful revolt against Spanish rule in 1640.The refusal of Spain to accept Portuguese independence meant that the latter were constantly in need of strong allies to assist their fight, and although the dynasty were pious Catholics everything possible was done to minimise the hostile political effects of England having another Catholic Queen. Firm measures were taken to ensure that the new Queen, Afonso VI's sister Catherine, would have a minimally Catholic household and the children of the marriage would be brought up Protestant. In May 1662 Catherine arrived in England and was married to Charles at Portsmouth Cathedral on the 21st ; her dowry included the Portuguese African port of Tangier.[5]

Catherine proved to be a far less influential or controversial character than the strong-minded Henrietta Maria, being firmly Catholic in her religion but quiet, modest, and uninterested in Court politics. The King's sexual habits already indicated that he would be more like his promiscuous grandfather Henri IV of France, the 'Evergreen Gallant', than his monogamous father Charles I, and his already-dominant principal mistress Barbara Villiers held and retained far more power at Court. (Ironically, she was to convert to Catholicism.) One of the few occasions when the new Queen displayed any spirit was when she discovered that she was expected to put up with Barbara as a principal lady-in-waiting to facilitate the latter's presence close to the King. She crossed Barbara's name off the King' s list of ladies-in-waiting for her that had been submitted to her, and the King put it back on at Barbara's angry insistence and typically chose to side with his mistress rather than his wife although his surviving sister 'Minette', now married to Louis XIV's brother Philip, regarded Catherine's anger as justified.[6] Clearly the King expected docility from his wife as was appropriate for a docile and convent-reared Princess imported as a Royal 'brood-mare', and regarded her tantrum over accepting his mistress as a childish irritant to be punished ; worldly and sophisticated sovereigns had and gave Court posts to their mistresses and that was normal courtly procedure (though not in the morally strict Portuguese court where devout priests held sway over Catherine's younger brother's regency). The feisty Barbara Villiers was a more independent and ruthless character, keen on collecting honours and goods for herself and in due course her children by Charles. Charles' court was already becoming notorious for its loose morals, as minutely chronicled by observer Samuel Pepys whose diary shows a sexual admiration for Barbara and fondness for seeing her underwear hung out on the Palace washing-lines. But the initial suspicion of the foreign Catholic Queen faded as it became clear that she was no religious zealot and had minimal influence on the King, and she became accepted by most of the nation. Hostility to influential Catholic womenfolk at Court revived, but centred on the King's Catholic mistresses – firstly the acquisitive Barbara Villiers and later the Frenchwoman Louise de Keroualle, who was popularly supposed to be a spy for Louis XIV. The Queen's importance in politics in the 1660s and 1670s arose from her failure to provide an heir, something which was clearly due to her infertility rather than her husband's as the number of his bastards paraded at Court multiplied. (He eventually acknowledged fourteen, and possibly had three others.) The Duke of York's rumoured conversion to Catholicism, a political nightmare given current English anti-Catholicism and his role as heir to the throne, was exposed by his failure to continue attending Anglican services, now a requirement for office-holders under the Test Act of 1673 – which itself was due to Parliamentary paranoia about the growth of Catholic influence following Charles' unwise abandonment of a Protestant overseas alliance with the Dutch and Sweden to attack the Dutch in alliance with France in 1672. James was a first-class administrator and more hard-working than his hedonistic brother, but he had to resign as Lord Admiral;[7] he had two Protestant daughters by Anne Hyde (who had secretly converted to Catholicism before she died in 1671) but he married a Catholic Italian princess, Mary Beatrice of Modena, as his second wife. He had been refused permission by his brother to marry a young widow who was socially his inferior, Susan,

Lady Belasyse, as this would be as unseemly as his first marriage[8] – though it might have diminished the furore over his religious policies as King if he had not had a Catholic son born in 1688 to succeed him. Independently of his marriages he had at least five 'serious' mistresses, including the rising courtier John Churchill (later Duke of Marlborough)'s sister Arbella, and the plain looks of some of his lovers led to a reported joke by Charles that James had his mistresses imposed on him by his priests as a penance.

Amidst rising fear of Catholic influence at Court and of the King's close relations with the new national enemy, the aggressively Catholic Louis XIV, Charles was urged to divorce his wife and marry a Protesant to provide a Protestant heir but to his credit refused to abandon Catherine.[9] England had not had a Catholic sovereign since the notorious Mary Tudor, the villainess of the still-popular *Book of Acts and Monuments* by John Foxe, and in an era when a nation traditionally took the religion of its ruler the accession of James was feared as inevitably meaning a renewal of persecution. The popular mood of the nation was rabidly anti-Catholic and the latter were seen as the instruments of a sinister 'Papist' conspiracy to undermine Englishmen's religion and liberties, whether directed by the traditional Elizabethan enemy Spain or now by the rising European Catholic power of France under Louis. The English were brought up on memories of episodes such as the Spanish Armada and the Gunpowder Plot, and anti-Catholic feeling sporadically burst into the open with outbreaks of hysteria whenever there seemed to be evidence of a 'Catholic plot' such as the Irish rebellion and massacres in 1641. The feeling that English foreign policy was being tied to French interests – to the detriment of the nation's natural Protestant alignment, aggressively promoted under the far more successful Cromwell – rose during the late 1660s and early 1670s, with Charles' aid to Louis' invasion of the Protestant Dutch 'United Provinces' in 1672 being more controversial than the previous Anglo-Dutch wars in 1652–4 and 1665–7. Unlike then, France was now seen as a major threat to European stability following Louis' aggressive 'land-grabs' on his northern and eastern frontiers, even though these were as much at the expense of his fellow-Catholics (the Holy Roman Empire and Spain) as of Protestants. Until the overthrow of the republican oligarchy that ran the Dutch state (led by 'Grand Pensionary' Jan de Witt) in the aftermath of defeat by England and France in the early stages of the 1672–4 war the Dutch regime was also excluding his nephew William of Orange from power; but their overthrow in a revolution brought William to military and political command as 'Stadtholder'.

The situation was complicated by the political marginalisation of some important government figures and courtiers, particularly the Earl of Shaftesbury, by 'pro-Catholic' ministers in the early 1670s. Shaftesbury, a 'self-made' man from the northern Dorset squirearchy born as Sir Anthony Ashley

Cooper, had commenced his career as a Royalist in the Civil War but deserted to the winning side in 1644 so 'ultra' Royalists were suspicious of him as an unscrupulous timeserver anyway, and after a period as a Commonwealth MP and a short stint on Cromwell's Council he had resigned office in 1654 (apparently disquieted at Cromwell's dictatorial powers and neglect of Parliamentary rights) and had re-emerged in 1659–60 as a moderate Presbyterian opposed to the '*junto*' of radical generals who seized power from Cromwell's son Richard. He was then a leading actor in the moves by moderate MPs and their allies to help General Monck overthrow the '*junto*', restore Parliament, and link up with the Royalists and invite Charles back as King in spring 1660. Like Monck (as army commander and mastermind of the Restoration) and Pepys' cousin Edward Montague (as commander of the navy) he reaped his reward at the Restoration with office and power, but was never at ease with Charles' more pro-Catholic, pro-autocracy, Francophile advisers and in 1672–3 broke with them. A constant thread of backing for a 'constitutional' and limited monarchy, be it Cromwell's Protectorate or a Stuart dynasty, and for religious toleration for Protestants can be seen throughout his career – but as his relations with Charles II deteriorated and he lost influence at Court he turned more to the 'politics of the street' for influence and duly played up his anti-Catholic credentials. Lucy Walter's son Monmouth was duly to become a major weapon in his struggle for power with James, Duke of York, and other Catholic court figures, as a means of keeping James from the throne. The Restoration dramatist John Dryden duly presented Monmouth and Shaftesbury in an unflattering light in his epic poem '*Absalom and Achitophel*', disguising them as the Biblical King David's spoilt, rebellious eldest son Absalom and the power-crazed mischief-maker who encouraged him to rebel, the King's treacherous minister Achitophel. In the Old Testament story Absalom launched a futile revolt and ended up being caught by his long hair in a tree as he rode underneath and accidentally strangled, and contemporary readers would have recognised the allusions – with many who feared a new outbreak of civil war and yet more deaths and misery blaming the pair for undermining national unity.

The so-called 'Cabal', an uneasy and informal alliance of competing interests in power after Clarendon's dismissal in 1667, gave way during 1673 to a pro-French ministry presided over by Lord Treasurer Sir Thomas Osborne (Lord Danby), who was believed to be taking bribes from the French to maintain a pro-French policy. The alienated Shaftesbury joined up with 'Country' critics of the Court's extravagance and French alignment in Parliament. There were rumours that Charles had signed a secret treaty with Louis' emissaries at Dover in 1670 under cover of a visit by his younger sister Henrietta Anne ('Minette'), Duchesse d'Orleans, which involved him re-converting England to Catholicism in return for French money and troops. (See previous chapter.) These were in fact true, though Charles was almost certainly playing a risky political gamble to obtain French funding rather than being sincere. Luckily for the King, Shaftesbury and his allies could not prove anything. Anti-Catholicism had played a major role in the crisis of 1640–2 that led to the Civil War, and the potent issue of a Catholic heir for England implying autocracy and persecution would explode into a new outbreak of hysteria over the 'Popish Plot' in autumn 1678. Then apparently ludicrous allegations were made by the unsavoury informer Titus Oates of a sinister Catholic cabal at Court, centred on the Duke of York's Catholic household, to murder the King and convert the nation to Catholicism. The King and Privy Council had to promise to investigate them for political reasons but seemed ready to politely dismiss them, and Oates was shown up as unreliable by the King during questioning – he could not describe men he had 'met' accurately. Luckily for Oates, the magistrate delegated to investigate the alleged plot – Sir Edmund Berry Godfrey – was discovered dead in a ditch on Primrose Hill outside London, confusingly both strangled and run through with a sword. It was claimed that he had been silenced by the plotters and he was treated as a martyr, although he was depressive so suicide was possible (as was murder by a personal enemy, such as the violent and paranoid Philip Herbert, Earl of Pembroke).[10]

An outbreak of public panic about an immanent Catholic coup and mass-killings followed, with Oates regarded as the hero of the hour rather than the shady opportunist which he clearly was. The favoured suspect at the time by the anti-Catholics among the elite was a Catholic peer, Lord Belasyse, but the King pointed out that he was too incapacitated by gout to go around strangling and stabbing an active magistrate and dumping his body in a ditch in what was then a remote rural location; one Miles Prance was arrested and tortured into confessing but later retracted his statement. The 'Country Party' of MPs and peers opposed to Catholic influence at Court, led by Shaftesbury, exploited the crisis to force the resignation and arrest of the Lord Treasurer Danby and then to try him for accepting French bribes as alleged by a disgruntled ex-ambassador to France, Ralph Montague. The dissolution of Parliament for new elections followed in the hope of the King securing enough loyal MPs to block further investigations and arrests, but the 'Country Party's' electoral organisation and nationwide propaganda campaign secured them a majority. Meanwhile the 'opposition' staged a seventeenth-century equivalent of a 'Nuremburg Rally' on the emotive anniversary of the 'Gunpowder Plot' of 1605 to stir up popular feeling, with a torchlit procession featuring a tableau of Godfrey being murdered by the current Catholic 'bogey-men', the Jesuits. A wave of arrests and executions (on dubious evidence) of assorted Catholics named as plotters by Oates and his associate Israel Tonge followed, with some men such as the aged Lord Stafford clearly innocent and the worst interpretations being made of admittedly indiscreet and dangerous boasts by James' proselytizing Catholic secretary Father Coleman. Charles was unable to protect the innocent men accused of being Jesuit agents for fear of the wrath of the 'Country' party, now under a new nickname as the embryonic 'Whigs' (called after Scots Covenanter extremists) lost control of Parliament. The King had to admit some of his leading opponents to the Privy Council in 1679. It was these men, led by Shaftesbury, who now raised the issue of securing a safely Protestant heir for the King by what was called an 'Exclusion Bill' (ie excluding James from the succession).

One solution was to set James aside in favour of his elder daughter Mary (born 1662), married in autumn 1677 to her older cousin William of Orange – the new Stadtholder since 1672 and the Dutch Protestant hero who had defeated Louis XIV's invasion that year. But the alternative candidate was the King's eldest illegitimate son, James Scott (originally Crofts), born on 9 April 1649 to his first known mistress Lucy Walter, daughter of a minor and impoverished Pembrokeshire Royalist squire.[11] Lucy Walter, as unconventional and daring as Barbara Villiers though in a different manner (and notably less shrewd or acquisitive), was one of a number of bold and adaptable young women 'thrown up' into unusual roles by the exigencies of the Civil War when the 'world turned upside down' and the financial ruin of once prosperous families – especially those caught on the losing, Royalist side – as well as ambition to serve their chosen side in the conflict led to them taking on unusual and daring ventures. This family financial catastrophe met the Walters' case, as Lucy's mother (Elizabeth Protheroe's) uncle, the Royalist general Lord Carbery, had garrisoned their Roche Castle for the King in 1644 and it had been stormed and sacked. However, the family was also one of those divided by choosing different sides in the war, and in this case Lucy's father Walter was a Parliamentarian and her mother a Royalist; they were quarrelling with and suing each other for custody of the children through these years and Walter accused his wife of being unfaithful. With her home burnt down and Pembrokeshire a major 'war zone', Lucy and her siblings appear to have been brought up in safer (but Parliamentarian) London in straightened circumstances – Walter won custody of them from her mother in 1647, helped by his Parliamentarian record, but Elizabeth did not hand them over. Lucy duly gravitated to the Royalist 'underground' after the war ended in 1646. Lucy, like the Royalist agent Jane Whorwood who sought to rescue Charles I from prison on the Isle of Wight in 1648, became a Royalist agent, in her case travelling abroad to the exiled Royalist court at The Hague in Holland in 1648 (aged eighteen) as 'Mistress Barlow' with her Essex cousin John Barlow, Royalist 'Master of the Ordnance' in 1648. She was assumed by the triumphant Parliamentarian regime in London to have gone as a Royalist spy, and after failing to intercept her they arrested her aunt for assisting the 'plot'.[12]

Prince Charles, having been at the head of his own Council in Royalist south-west England until the Parliamentarian victory in spring 1646 and then fled to loyal Jersey, arrived at St. Germain near Paris to join his mother's exiled court that summer of 1648. He was there for two years, while his zealous mother tried to convert him to Catholicism and to interest the regency government in supporting his cause; both failed. Negotiations were also begun with the Scots Covenanter regime for the Prince to go to Scotland as the captive King's representative for a war on Parliamentarian England, which would necessitate Royalist acceptance of the Presbyterian government and church (which had commenced Charles I's troubles with a successful revolt in 1637–9) and taking the Covenant. Charles I had sought this aid from the Covenanter army and their civilian allies in 1646 by handing himself over to them as the first Civil War ended, but had stymied talks by refusing to become a Presbyterian; many of the leading Covenanter peers were faithful to the idea of a Stuart monarchy providing that its King was religiously reliable. Would Charles' son be more amenable than him? Despite distrust of Charles I, his cousin the Duke of Hamilton and the 'Engager' party signed a secret treaty with him at Carisbrooke Castle late in 1647 to send an army into England on his behalf and persuaded most of the Scots Parliament (though not 'hard-line' clerics) to go along with it as they quarrelled with the English Parliament the following spring. The chances of this Scots expedition were dramatically improved when the Royalist risings in England in May coincided with the revolt of most of the English navy, which was currently stationed in the Downs off Kent. Parliament had attempted to replace the politically suspect commander, Sir William Batten, who fomented a mutiny in retaliation, providing Prince Charles with a naval force to challenge the government in London. He duly set off from St Germain to The Hague in Holland at the end of June 1648, to stay as the guest of his sister Mary and her husband Stadtholder William II while his acceptance on board the mutinous ships – now sailing to the Dutch coast at Helvetsloeys – as their new commander was negotiated. He arrived in The Hague by 12 July. The titular Royalist 'Lord Admiral' was Charles' younger brother James, now fourteen, who had just been smuggled out of Parliamentarian custody in St James' Palace in London (disguised as a girl) by the Royalist agent Colonel Bampfield and arrived at The Hague; he was the rebel sailors' first choice as their new commander but they were persuaded to let Charles take over. He sailed with the fleet for Kent around 22 July, though the attempt to link up with local rebels or overcome the remainder of the fleet loyal to Parliament was a failure and he had to return to Holland at the beginning of September. He then remained at The Hague over the winter, being there when the news of his father's execution arrived at the beginning of February 1649. It was this period of his exile when his involvement with Lucy began.

Once in The Hague Lucy settled there, and appears to have become the exiled Prince of Wales' mistress ; she may have met him already according to the contemporary memoirs of the Countess of Dunois and Baronne d'Aulnoy, in Wales in 1646.[13] The relationship of Charles (recognised as King by the Royalists when his father was executed on 30 January 1649) and Lucy was accepted by his sister and local hostess Mary, whose husband 'Stadtholder' William of the United Provinces was at this point alive and in power there, and at one point in summer 1649 the two of them and the boy born as a result of their affair on 9 April 1649 were living with her.[14] They also paid a visit to Charles' mother Henrietta Maria at the Palace of St Germain near Paris, a stickler for social propriety who would not have been so accepting had she suspected they were married.[15] A rumour of the marriage had however reached Charles' political confidante and Secretary, Sir Edward Hyde (later Earl of Clarendon) in 1649.[16] The question of a secret but legal marriage was to be connected in later stories to the existence of legal papers as 'proof', kept in a mysterious 'Black Box'. Charles' and Lucy's son was later removed from her custody by his father's agents after the end of the couple's relationship (see further below), and Lucy appears to have been a feckless mother who did not even bother to see that her son was taught to read and count properly. It is a moot point whether the fickle Charles (already known for his interest in women) became bored with her and 'side-lined' her or whether she drifted off on her own accord, but the main 'break' appears to have been when Charles returned to The Hague in Holland after a few months in Paris and Lucy was left at Henrietta Maria's court at The Louvre. Her main 'protector' – and according to Charles' brother James, who was hostile to her, her lover – at the court was Theobald, Lord Taaffe, an exiled Irish Royalist nobleman. He may have been the father of her daughter Mary, born in 1651 around a year after Charles' departure; at any rate Charles did not recognise the girl as his daughter. In the early 1650s Lucy was having an affair with the King's exiled Royalist courtier-ally Sir Henry De Vic, a versatile linguist then living in Brussels and later his 'ambassador' in Madrid – and so in charge of the crucial job of trying to persuade King Philip IV of Spain to lend him an invasion-fleet. Possibly Lucy thought of the shrewd and energetic Royalist 'fixer' De Vic as her 'insurance policy' should Charles refuse her a pension, but she was also constantly nagging Charles for money and seems to have found it difficult to manage her finances. Her maid Ann Hill was later to tell Cromwellian interrogators when their party was arrested in London in 1656 that Lucy was living well beyond her means. (This had a bearing on her claims about her 'marriage', as she might have been 'upping the ante' to demand a higher sum of money from the King.) Whether or not she was treated badly by Charles and his moralist 'Secretary of State' Sir Edward Hyde (later Earl of Clarendon and a major historian) who undoubtably disapproved of the more reckless and promiscuous exiles on principle and had been the constant critic of reckless Royalist nobles in the Civil War, she did not marry De Vic. Instead she ended up with a junior officer in Charles' sister Mary's service in Holland, Thomas Howard, younger brother of the earl of Suffolk. Their affair scandalised the moralist leading Dutch 'burghers', many of whom were republicans who did not like Mary's late husband 'Stadtholder' William II's (d. 1650) Orangist dynasty as 'tyrants' and used it to 'smear' Mary's court for immorality. There was one unsavoury incident when a maid tried to make money out of stories about Lucy's and Howard's immoral lifestyle, including her alleged abortions, and Lucy was supposed to have asked her lover to get rid of the mischief-maker by murdering her (by driving a needle into her brain as she slept?).[17]

As with the case of James Duke of York 'smearing' Monmouth as illegitimate in the 'Exclusion Crisis' in 1679–81, ulterior motives and 'spin' have to be remembered when considering how truthful any of the stories about Lucy were – the exiled Royalist court was a hotbed of intrigue and feuds and stories of Charles' mistress' behaviour were useful to both the Cromwellian regime in England and the current oligarchic, anti-Orangist Dutch mercantile regime led by 'Grand Pensionary' Jan de Witt. The question of what papers of Charles' Lucy owned and why he was so keen to get hold of them in the mid-1650s will be considered later. But it was significant that when Charles moved to the Spanish Netherlands in 1656–9 as a Spanish pensioner he would only give Lucy a pension (£415 p.a.) if she stayed in Antwerp well away from his court, although she was brave enough (or desperate enough for cash?) in 1656 to return to England on a mission connected with Royalist intrigue as well as claiming an inheritance. According to her maid at their June 1656 interrogation by Cromwell's 'secret police' in London, Charles saw Lucy before she left, so she was probably trusted enough by him to be given secret information to take to Royalist agents. After this visit, which ended when the Cromwellian secret service captured and deported her, she had a struggle with Charles and his courtiers over who was to control her son's upbringing, which Charles won by having the boy abducted (see later). She died in poverty in France in autumn 1658 – her foe James Duke of York alleged of syphilis, the common disease of her 'profession' i.e. prostitution – and did not live to see the Restoration. Her son James Crofts (called after the foster-father, Lord Crofts, with whom Charles placed him after kidnapping him) was brought over to London from Paris – where he had been placed by his father in 1657 to have a more secure and less raffish upbringing than with his mother. He was made Duke of Monmouth by his father on 10 November 1662, and was a prominent and popular young courtier with political links to Shaftesbury and his faction by the late 1670s. He had been trained in the French army but was unswervingly Protestant and as charismatic as his father although less politically astute. Ironically, in 1672 he had trained as an officer under Louis during his invasion of the Dutch state – along with his fellow-cadet John Churchill, later Duke of Marlborough, who like him was to make his name as a foe of the French Catholic state. Legitimizing Monmouth was one possibility, but instead rumours were spread that his mother had been secretly married to Charles and that the proof existed in a mysterious 'Black Box' which Lucy had had in her possession (As she had died in 1658 legitimising her marriage to Charles would not affect his current marriage.) This box of Lucy's, or another containing the written proofs of the ceremony by the priest who had conducted it, was supposed to have been passed to the daughter of Dr John Cosin, the late Bishop of Durham and as of 1648 Henrietta Maria's Protestant chaplain in exile – who was probably the man who was supposed to have married Charles and Lucy. Was there any truth in this story or was it another piece of 'spin'?

Charles and Lucy Walter: married or not? Was there a 'cover-up', or was the claim just wishful thinking?

The King never sought to deny that Monmouth was his son, only that he had been married to the boy's mother Lucy Walter when he was living with her on the Continent in 1649. The diarist John Evelyn, who saw her parading in Paris in early summer 1649 during her affair with the King, called her 'brown, bold, and beautiful' but somewhat insipid; the sauciness evident in her portraits was a trait which was to attract Charles to Nell Gwyn. Her activities in the 1650s show that she was an independent-minded young woman not overawed by her lover's status, but that she was somewhat rash and poor at planning (traits inherited by her son). If the birth-date later given for Monmouth was accurate, he was conceived early in July 1648. The later accounts of the relationship between his parents were mostly written at the time of the controversy over his legitimacy in the late 1670s and early 1680s, and there is no clear contemporary record. The 'Whig' accounts of the affair had an interest in showing that the marriage had taken place, to boost Monmouth's claim to the throne and make it easier to have his legitimacy recognised. The main pro-Monmouth account written on his behalf in 1683 needs to be treated with caution, particularly given its author – the veteran Scottish intriguer Robert Ferguson 'the Plotter', a master of propaganda involved in numerous plans against the Stuart regime. Originally from Aberdeenshire, Ferguson was a radical Protestant preacher, secretary to Shaftesbury, and foe of Catholic influence who was described by his more moderate 'Whig' colleague Gilbert Burnet (later post-1689 Bishop of Salisbury) in his history as a wild and desperate character, prone to think up or adopt fantastic schemes that were unlikely to succeed. After 'Exclusion' was blocked by the King and Shaftesbury had to go into hiding in fear of arrest, Ferguson resorted to vague and over-hopeful plots to assassinate the King and then seize power in a popular rising during the resultant chaos, either by ambushing Charles in the street or by stationing men underneath his box at the theatre to shoot him.

The fact that Monmouth would not countenance his father being murdered was irrelevant to this 'hard man' – the cause of saving Protestant Britain from a Catholic king demanded sacrifices. The story of a 'Black Box' emerged among Shaftesbury's group of pro-Exclusion radicals in a private social club that the earl and his intimates set up in the late 1670s after Shaftesbury's political disgrace and banning from Court, called the 'Green Ribbon' club after their trademark ribbons – in the colour of the ribbons that the famous 1640s Civil War democratic radicals (both in Cromwell's New Model Army and among their civilian allies in London), the 'Levellers', had worn in their hats. The Levellers, led by the veteran controversialist pamphleteer 'Freeborn John' Lilburne who had annoyed and been arrested by both Charles I's government pre-1642 and the triumphant but socially conservative Parliament after 1646 for subversion, had argued for a far more democratic resolution to the constitutional struggles of the 1640s than the leadership of either 'side' would tolerate. This had included 'one man one vote', annual Parliaments answerable to the electorate, and an end to administrative favouritism and corruption, and when their written proposals were brushed aside by both the army leadership and Parliament in the post-war constitutional negotiations some of them had tried to arrange mutinies in the army to force the shaky new regime's hands. That had ended up with Cromwell and the other generals suppressing one military mutiny at Corkbush Field in late 1647 and a larger one among the regiments stationed in Wiltshire in spring 1649 by force, on the second occasion chasing the rebels across country and cornering them at Burford, and rebel leaders had been shot as a warning and others cashiered from the army.

Some of the surviving Levellers, such as Major John Wildman, had now re-emerged to assist Shaftesbury and their commitment to any form of monarchy was suspect, given their past republicanism, but they and moderates from the aristocracy such as the Earl of Essex (a former Lord Lieutenant of Ireland and competent minister side-lined by the King and Danby) and the idealist aristocrat Lord William Russell could agree that Monmouth, a committed Protestant and now a foe of French 'Papist' and absolutist interests, was a safer King than James would be. The 'Green Ribbon Club' toasted Monmouth as 'Prince of Wales', ie the King's legitimate heir born in wedlock, but it is not clear if this was more than wishful thinking or making the most of vague rumours about Charles marrying Lucy 'Barlow' (Lucy's alias as a Royalist agent in 1648). The latter possibility was now to appear to be made more substantial.

By the late 1670s the circle around Shaftesbury were irrevocably hostile to the King's 'official' heir James, Duke of York, who now showed what could be expected from him as King when he ran a 'hard-line' and autocratic anti-Presbyterian government in Edinburgh as the King's representative there in 1680–1 after having to leave London during the 'Exclusion Crisis'. With James effectively exiled from London and the 'Exclusionist'-run Parliament putting Danby in the Tower on suspicion of treason by his corrupt and underhand dealing with France, the King had to accept a Council of State that included Shaftesbury (as its president) and Essex (as Lord Treasurer) in order to get his business through Parliament and provide his government with funds. For the moment the 'Whigs' (as the Shaftesbury faction were nicknamed, using a Scots slang term for the most radical anti-Catholic Presbyterian faction in the Lowlands, the militant 'Whiggamores') were in the ascendant, and rising young 'Royalist', anti-'Whig' ministers such as James' brother-in-law Lord Rochester and the financial 'fixer' Sidney Godolphin were prepared to work with them on the Council with Charles angry at being coerced but having to bide his time. Monmouth, who had in his role as a rising and dashing military commander suppressed a violent 'Whiggamore' attack on Glasgow at the battle of Bothwell Bridge but then generously pardoned many of the arrested radicals, was the darling of the anti-Catholic crowds and toured England showing himself to his admirers.

It was in this atmosphere that the story of the 'Black Box' containing Charles' and Lucy's marriage-certificate emerged in 1680 – with it now supposed to be in the custody of Bishop Cosin's son-in-law Sir Gilbert Gerard, a 'Whig' MP. It was not seen in public or presented to the Commons to back up the 'Exclusionist' cause, however, and it is possible that the exiled but still powerful James and his conservative and Catholic allies in London (including the French embassy) were content to have it talked about in the knowledge that it was entirely a myth so Shaftesbury and Monmouth would never be able to produce it and would thus by 'shown up' as liars. The months went by, and the box never appeared – and when Sir Gilbert Gerard was called before the Council and questioned about it in April 1680 he denied that it existed or that he had even heard of it or been given any papers concerning this matter.[18] Other 'witnesses' who were called to give evidence after referring to the box also denied having seen or knowing anything about it,[19] and the King firmly put out an official statement that he had never been married to anyone but Queen Catherine.[20] That would seem to have quashed the matter as far as 'evidence' was concerned, but Charles was notoriously untrustworthy and in the heated political atmosphere of 1680 both sides had too much at stake to give way. If

Charles admitted that he had been married to Lucy it would not only show up his seeming lack of decorum or judgement in 1648, in marrying his mistress who was a woman of too low rank for a sovereign (though hardly inferior to James' first wife Anne Hyde in social status), but infringe his prerogative to name his heir and replace his brother with a young man who was closely linked to the disgraced Shaftesbury and his allies – men intent on coercing the King to follow their policies (e.g. in breaking with France) and including republicans like Wildman.

Charles was always harsh to 'fanatic' subversives, the men who had hijacked the Parliamentary cause in 1648–9 to execute his father, had resisted Restoration in 1660, and who might yet spark off a new civil war (whose dangers were repeatedly played up in government propaganda about radical Protestant 'plotters' from the time of the January 1661 'Fifth Monarchist' fanatics' rising in London onwards). Notably, even in the post-Restoration period when a general 'amnesty and oblivion' for all past political crimes were promised, (this excepted the men who had signed Charles I's death-warrant, most of whom were ruthlessly hunted down and killed though the King pardoned Cromwell's regicide cousin Colonel Ingoldsby who had militarily assisted the Restoration. Charles II had unforgivingly targeted those republican leaders who had resisted his return – General Lambert, who had tried to stop it by leading a military mutiny, was imprisoned for life on the remote Channel Islands (and later on an islet in Plymouth Harbour), idealistic republican hardliner Henry Marten was locked up in Chepstow Castle for life, and leading anti-Royalist MP and ideologue Sir Henry Vane was executed after a rigged trial with Charles declaring that he was too dangerous to be left alive.

The initially lazy and (mostly) generous King was even harsher towards political threats as he aged, and Shaftesbury now fell into that category by his leadership of the 'Whigs' and exploitation of the 'Popish Plot' crisis in 1678–9 – quite apart from his having used pressure from the anti-Catholic London crowds to force Charles to try and execute innocent men accused of Catholic conspiracy by the unsavoury Oates. Monmouth was now keeping company with these would-be rebels and subversives who sought to constrain Royal power, as no doubt James continued to point out, and so it was impossible for Charles to concede to their demands whether or not any 'Black Box' in fact existed (or could be located if Gerard genuinely had no idea who if anyone possessed it). Nor did Shaftesbury's group shut up about the 'Box' after the Council seemingly disproved its existence; within weeks Robert Ferguson had produced a pamphlet, *'A Letter to a Person of Honour Concerning the Black Box and a Letter to a Person of Honour concerning the King's Disavowing His Having been Married to the Duke of Monmouth's Mother*, apparently drawn up by Ferguson in an alehouse in Chancery Lane in London. This threw down the gauntlet, accusing the King of lying and stating (with some truth) that a proper enquiry held by Parliament would have found it easier to get at the truth and would have questioned more reputable witnesses. The latter presumably included the senior 'Whig' plotter and friend of Ferguson, veteran Royalist captain Thomas Armstrong who had been in exile at Liege at the time of the alleged marriage and who stated that he had heard rumours of it at the time.[21] Ferguson even alleged that Lord Chancellor Clarendon (now deceased) had excused himself from the allegation of marrying off his pregnant daughter Anne to James in 1660 to put his grandchildren on the throne by insisting that Charles already had a legitimate son, i.e., Monmouth, and that James was using his knowledge of the marriage to blackmail Charles into denying it and so keeping himself as heir by threatening that if the story was proved Charles would be so humiliated that he could be deposed.

Even if the details of the marriage are suspect, Ferguson's account of the relationship between Charles and Lucy fits in with the few references made to her in independent contemporary letters. Lucy was supposed to have travelled to The Hague as a Royalist agent in summer 1648 with her mother's cousin, an Essex Royalist JP called John Barlow, and the State Papers show that Lucy's aunt Mrs Gosfritt was arrested and imprisoned at this time by Parliament for her niece Mistress Barlow's (ie Lucy Walter) illicit journey overseas. Lucy's relationship with the Prince followed – if Monmouth's birth-date was accurate it must have commenced before Charles sailed with the Royalist fleet around 22 July. It presumably resumed on his return in September, and Lucy was with the Prince some time that winter when he was his sister Mary's guest. A different account from Ferguson's was given by Monmouth's uncle and enemy, James, Duke of York, who said that Lucy had arrived in The Hague thanks to an earlier affair with the radical Parliamentarian MP Algernon Sidney (an arch-critic of the monarchy executed by Charles II in 1683). Sidney was currently governor of Dover Castle, but also politically active in London. James wrote that Sidney had told him that he had paid Lucy fifty gold pieces but been unable to recoup his investment as he had had to join his regiment; in fact the only time Sidney was serving in the Army was in 1644 when Lucy was only thirteen. Nor was James ever on good terms with the republican Sidney, a political enemy in whose arrest and execution in 1683 he was involved, though he might have met him on neutral terms while he was living as a Parliamentary hostage in St James' Palace in 1647–8 or around 1650 on a visit to Holland. The information is more likely to have come to James from Sidney's brother Robert, who was in James' sister Princess Mary's service in The Hague in 1648 when James arrived there – but it should be treated with caution as James had every reason to portray his rival Monmouth's mother as a slut and the mistress of a notorious republican. Seemingly having been Algernon Sidney's mistress in

London, she had transferred her affections to his brother Robert, Chamberlain to Princess Mary at her court in The Hague, and come to Holland to join him. Thus it was her presence at Charles' sister's Court which led to their meeting, and Robert Sidney probably introduced her to Charles.[22]

The third account of Lucy's sojourn at The Hague in 1648, by the equally antagonistic Royalist minister Sir Edward Hyde (later Lord Clarendon and in 1660–7 Lord Chancellor), merely said that she travelled to The Hague intending to seduce Charles for her own benefit and a Groom of the Bedchamber made the introduction. Clarendon, as father-in-law to the Duke of York and with his granddaughters in line for the throne, had every reason to denounce the idea of Lucy having married Charles. Why Lucy should think she stood a chance of success with an inexperienced prince of eighteen, not yet known as a womaniser, is unclear; some writers have speculated that she might have already met Charles while he was in nominal command of the west country in 1645–6 though he was only fifteen at the time. In the 1670s the Baronne d'Aulnoy wrote that Lucy had met Charles earlier in the Civil War when he was in Wales, presumably visiting her family home at Roche Castle.[23] Renewing an earlier acquaintanceship would seem less of a gamble for Lucy to carry out than attempting to seduce a complete stranger. She is unlikely to have been the unknown woman with whom Charles was supposed to have had an affair while on Jersey in 1646; it is not even certain that this incident occurred. The alleged product of the relationship on Jersey, the mysterious 'James De Le Cloche' who surfaced in France in the 1660s, may have been an impostor.

The Dutch authorities offered no military assistance to invade England and negotiations for Charles' acceptance in Scotland continued to stall, and in June 1649 he left for France to seek aid from his aunt the Regent, Anne of Austria. Lucy seems to have accompanied him, along with their son. After an unsuccessful sojourn with Anne and her son Louis XIV at Compiegne, Charles joined his mother at St Germain in July; she resumed her previous attempts to interest him in marrying his cousin the 'Grand Mademoiselle', daughter of Gaston, Duc d'Orleans. Although he turned this down he had not been interested in 1647 either, and nothing was said about a legal impediment; Charles only said that he would drop whatever attachment he might have formed as a bachelor once he was married. When he left France for Jersey in September his son presumably remained behind with Lucy, but when Charles' plans to be invited to Scotland finally bore fruit in 1650 the boy was placed with his grandmother Henrietta Maria at St Germain (according to the 1683 'Whig' account). He presumably remained there during Charles' Scottish adventure and the Worcester campaign, but later returned to his mother's custody; he (and a second child, Anne, born in 1651) was with her when she travelled to London on secret Royalist business in 1656.

Huntingtower Castle, previously known as Ruthven Castle. Home of the earls of Gowrie, where James VI and I was kidnapped and held hostage by the first earl in 1582. Seen as a template for what was believed was planned to happen at Gowrie House in Perth in 1600? (© *Arthur Bruce/Creative Commons*)

Falkland Palace. Where James was staying on a hunting trip when he was lured – or went of his own accord to set a trap? – to Perth to meet the second earl of Gowrie and his brother. (© *Mike Pennington/Creative Commons*)

Mercat Cross, Canongate, Edinburgh. Where the earl of Gowrie and his brother's bodies were hung as traitors after they were killed in the mysterious scuffle upstairs at Gowrie House. (© *Mary and Angus Hoare/Creative Commons*)

Site of Gowrie House, Perth, looking East down South Street to where its entrance gate stood. The King's retainers rushed down this street to help him when he appeared at an upper window shouting for help – but were they forewarned that they might be needed? (© *Dave Fergusson/Creative Commons*)

Fast Castle, Lothian. One theory had it that this isolated clifftop castle was where James was to be taken by sea after his planned kidnap – by the enigmatic owner, veteran spy Logan of Restalrig, or English agents? (© *James T M Towill/Creative Commons*)

King James VI and I. Genial master of conciliating rival factions, or master of cover-ups who over-indulged his proteges?

Robert Carr, Earl of Somerset,. James' rapacious young Scots favourite: spoilt and greedy, but how much did he know about his wife's apparent homicidal activities?

Audley End House, Essex. Childhood home of Frances Howard; built by her father, Lord Treasurer the Earl of Suffolk, allegedly with the perquisites of his office and Court corruption. (© *Richard Croft/ Creative Commons*)

Blackheath, London, where Charles II reviewed the New Model Army before paying it off on the Restoration, May 1660. But after dismantling Cromwell's military machine did he have enough troops to fend off plotters without needing to call on his cousin Louis XIV of France and so pretend to be a Catholic sympathiser? (© *Chris Downer/Creative Commons*)

Highgate Hill woods – site of the climax of Thomas Venner's republican Fifth Monarchist revolt , January 1661. This rebellion was put down easily – but did it lead to exaggerated Royal fears of more instability and so to repression? (© *Malc McDonald/Creative Commons*)

Dover Castle , where Charles II signed the mysterious Secret Treaty of Dover with Louis' envoys in 1670. Was he serious about converting to Catholicism or was this just an insurance policy and an attempt by this master-gambler to secure troops in the unlikely event that they were needed? (© *Chris Hilton/Creative Commons*)

Monmouth Beach, Lyme Regis. Where Charles' supposedly illegitimate eldest son, the Duke of Monmouth, landed in 1685 to proclaim that he was legitimate and the rightful King, and that his uncle James II had murdered his father. Was the supposed marriage-certificate real? (© *Neil Owen/Creative Commons*)

Site of the battle of Sedgemoor, near Westonzoyland, Somerset. Where the Monmouth rebellion ended in a bloodbath six weeks later, before the Duke was rounded up hiding in a ditch and taken to London for execution. (© *Ken Grainger/Creative Commons*)

Portrait of George I's disgraced and divorced wife Sophia Dorothea of Celle, his first cousin. Was her secret lover Count Konigsmarck murdered at the Hanoverian royals' palace in a 'hit' by George's family to stop them running away together?

Cliveden House, near Maidenhead. The luxurious summer residence of George II's eldest son Prince Frederick Louis, who died before he could come to the throne. His parents hated him – and there were rumours that he was a bastard. (© *Des Blenkinsopp/Creative Commons*)

SE corner of St. James' Palace London, the site of the former royal apartments where the Duke of Cumberland was attacked and nearly killed in 1809. His valet was found dead afterwards and blamed for it – but rumour had it that there were dark secrets being covered up, with the Duke accused of homosexuality and incest. (© *N Chadwick/Creative Commons*)

The birth of a daughter to Lucy (probably in 1651) has been taken as evidence that their relationship continued, though Monmouth's foe James, Duke of York, later claimed that an exiled Irish Royalist courtier, Lord Taaffe, was the father. By that time Charles was in Scotland in his failed attempt to present himself to the 'hard-line' Calvinist faction ruling that kingdom as a suitable 'godly' King and so induce them to ally to the ousted Scots Royalists and help an invasion of England. The suspicious Covenanters never gave in to his pleas, though their military defeat by Cromwell's army at Dunbar in September 1650 enabled Charles to muster enough Scots 'moderate' Royalist aid to invade England in 1651 – where he was defeated heavily at Worcester and memorably escaped back to France in disguise. (One modern suggestion has it that Lucy's daughter was born in 1654 not 1651, but his being the father is still doubtful.) He did not see much of Lucy in the mid-1650s and her main contact with him seems to have been to write demanding money, but she continued to be on good enough terms with his sister Mary to spend part of her time at the latter's court. This may have been more to do with her affair with Mary's Household official, 'Master of the Horse' Thomas Howard. Lucy is referred to as 'your wife' in two letters which Mary sent to Charles in June 1655, though this may well have been a private joke not meant literally.[24] She is also accounted this status in a reference in a letter that March by Charles' Groom of the Bedchamber, Daniel O'Neill, though the latter was a veteran Royalist plotter from his time at Henrietta Maria's court in London in the early 1640s and was apparently mixed up in Charles' plans to recover compromising papers from Lucy so his use of the word cannot be taken as unbiased (or as more than a private joke). Lucy seems to have been living at The Hague at Mary's court with Thomas Howard, rather than following Charles about as the exigencies of international politics took him from France to the Rhineland in 1655 and thence to Brussels as a Spanish pensioner in their conflict with Cromwell. By February 1656 O'Neill's letters indicate trouble between Charles and Lucy, apparently involving the King giving her instructions which he feared she would not obey and threatening to take their son from her.[25] It appears from comments made at the time that the Stuarts took over Monmouth's education that Lucy had not bothered to have him taught properly, so the King may have been anxious about that. O'Neill hinted that Lucy's conduct was potentially detrimental to Charles, though there is no indication if this meant she had been mentioning their secret marriage which would embarrass his efforts to find a Royal bride from an allied nation in Europe. Possibly the increasing concern to get the boy away from Lucy was merely to do with her being an inadequate and unreliable mother, but logically it could also be connected to fear of her using him as a pawn in any dispute with Charles – which might mean that she had documentary 'weapons' at her disposal, or was feared to do so. However the way that Lucy was manipulating her status also raises the question of whether she was so desperate for cash (or cunning?) that she was falsely claiming to have married Charles in order to secure a large 'pay-off', and the papers that O'Neill referred to might merely have been secret Royalist intelligence documents that she (as Charles' mistress) or her swashbuckling and intrigue-prone lover Thomas Howard had acquired in their time assisting Charles' agents.

Lucy's visit to London in 1656 was officially an innocuous private visit with her brother Justus, connected to her late mother's estate – and to her search for money. But it was also to meet plotters and arrange funds for the Royalist war-effort now that Charles was arranging an alliance with Spain and an invasion of England from the Spanish Netherlands was possible. Charles met her at Antwerp and gave her a valuable necklace to take to London according to what her maid Ann Hill told Cromwellian interrogators later, and she was escorted there by Charles' sister Mary's 'Master of the Horse' – her lover Thomas Howard. The latter was acting as an agent for Charles, Cromwell's intelligence-chief Thurloe, and the Dutch government at the time, and it is not certain if he was the person who tipped Thurloe off to her presence. She stayed secretly at a 'safe house', a barber's shop opposite Somerset House where her maid had arrived earlier, and met various agents; a propagandist pro-Monmouth account later claimed that she had been given a coach and treated with honour as the King's wife by local Royalists, being served on bended knee. But late in June she and her children were arrested and taken to the Tower; most of the story of her visit comes from the official dcoumentation in Secretary of State Thurloe's papers of her entourage's interrogation. The authorities deported her back to Holland, but made the most of her role in gleeful public references to her in their official newsletter as 'Charles Stuart's whore'.[26] Back on the Continent, the relationship between her and Charles finally broke down and the latter's followers appear to have planned to forcibly remove their son from her custody, presumably to prevent her using him as a bargaining-counter. A Colonel Slingsby offered to arrange for Lucy to be arrested for debt, and in retaliation she threatened to publish certain embarrassing letters – apparently including the mysterious marriage-certificate which is now mentioned for the first time.[27]

The subsequent drama suggests that Lucy certainly had some papers that Charles regarded as compromising and which he wished to retrieve, though it must be stressed that these may have been to do with intelligence, not her 'marriage'. According to the Royalist State Papers preserved by Clarendon, Charles' 'Groom of the Bedchamber' Daniel O'Neill suggested that Charles ask the Spanish Viceroy of the Netherlands to have Lucy's rooms searched for certain suspicious papers in Slingsby's presence. This followed an unsuccessful first call on Lucy by Slingsby, when she refused to hand over her son as demanded and fled with him into the street to yell out to passers-by that the boy was being kidnapped. The locals duly stopped Slingsby, who did not help his cause by blustering that he was acting for the King of England. The search was duly done by a group of Royalists and local Spanish officials, despite a promise by Lucy to hand over her son provided that neither Slingsby nor O'Neill had charge of him, and apparently the boy was 'snatched' and removed by Charles' men during the search while Lucy was looking for a paper. (This was the version of the 'Whig' agent Major Disney, later to assist Monmouth's revolt in 1685, in 1680.)[28] The boy was never returned, and the King gave him a new tutor called Thomas Ross who complained about the past neglect of his education. Lucy did not locate him for some time; he was duly placed in a Catholic Oratorian convent at Colombes near Paris under the guardianship of his grandmother Henrietta Maria, the nearest member of the Royal Family. (Charles and his brothers were banned from France under Cromwell's 1655 treaty with the government of Anne and Mazarin.) Lucy remained in exile among the Royalist community in France, and died in poverty in Paris in 1659.

The Duke of Monmouth as a political factor at Charles II's court

The boy was now called 'James Crofts' after William Crofts, in whose house at Colombes he was living while being educated at the nearby convent, but in July 1662 he was brought to Charles' restored Court in London in the entourage of the returning Henrietta Maria. Not politically vital to the dynasty at first as the King was expected to have children by his new wife Catherine of Braganza, he was nevertheless an object of interest as the King's eldest son and Charles made sure that he was quickly converted to the Church of England from his initial Catholicism. He was regularly seen about Court, and in October 1662 Pepys wrote that:

> 'What great faction there is at Court, and above all what is whispered, that young Crofts is lawful son to the King, the King being married to his mother. How true that is, God knows; but I believe the Duke of York will not be fooled in this of the three crowns'[29].

A wealthy and prestigious bride was duly arranged for James by the King's Scottish adviser, the Earl of Lauderdale, in the person of the Buccleuch heiress Anne Scott; factions opposed to the Duke of York (not yet a Catholic, but probably already known to be sympathetic to them) may well have hoped for Charles to legitimise James and proclaim him Prince of Wales. Lucy's death meant that there was no legal obstacle, though it would be embarrassing for Charles to admit that he had really been married and to a member of a minor gentry family – at a time when he had been seeking a Continental bride in the 1650s. There had been enough criticism of the Duke of York's sudden and secret marriage to Clarendon's daughter Anne Hyde later in 1660, the first Royal marital alliance to a commoner since Henry VIII's marriages, and this admission would further damage the dynasty's reputation. The Queen Mother appears to have been the principal opponent of any admission of a marriage to Lucy, threatening never to speak to Charles again if he affirmed that he had married Lucy.[30] Which did she regard as worse – the social disgrace of him marrying a non-royal or the threat of Monmouth succeeding to the throne? The boy was raised to the Dukedom of Monmouth in November 1662, given precedence at Court over all except York and the King's cousin Prince Rupert, and married to Anne Scott, heiress to the Border Scots dynasty of Scott of Buccleuch, in April 1663.[31] Pepys continued to report worries that if Charles did not have any heirs by Catherine of Braganza this would lead to Monmouth becoming his heir instead of James of York, which would require legitimation – though technically that need only mean a special grant of legitimate status to him, not a posthumous recognition that Lucy had been legally married to Charles, as in 1396 Richard II had legitimated his uncle John, Duke of Lancaster's (Beaufort) bastards by his mistress Katherine Swynford, born while John's previous wife Catharine of Castile had been alive. In any event, Pepys reckoned (no doubt based on solid stories as he was working for James himself at the Admiralty) that making Monmouth the heir would infuriate James[32] – so this was already expected long before the rising 'Catholic vs Protestant' and 'pro - and anti-French) factionalism of the 1670s made matters more serious and Monmouth's alliance with the 'Whigs' estranged Charles. The issue of the King's marriage to Lucy was never admitted, even when Henrietta Maria died in 1669, although the Queen remained childless and Charles refused to set her aside to provide a new heir by a second wife. The idea of Monmouth succeeding to the throne did not revive until the rising anti-Catholic tension of the 1670s coincided with the revelation of the Duke of York's Catholicism. But the question was still unresolved, and some time in the 1670s a prisoner in Newgate Prison, the Revd. Peter Bell, testified to the Duke of York's chaplain (Dr. Lake) that he had heard a story about a Mr Forder of Houghton-le-Spring, Durham, who had been steward to the Bishop of Durham, John Cosin, when the latter was Protestant chaplain to Henrietta Maria in exile in 1648. Forder had several times declared in public company that:

> 'to his knowledge the Duke of Monmouth was the lawful heir of the Crown of England; for he was present at the marriage of His Grace's Mother to the King, a Competent time before the birth of the Duke of Monmouth, of which he was, to the discharge of a good conscience, ready to make affidavit before legal authority'.[33]

The Duke of York seems to have been keen to discover the truth for himself, and in that case was not trusting any assurances that Charles had given him about not marrying Lucy. Clearly he had not been privy to any marriage ceremony in 1649 or told about it subsequently by Charles or Princess Mary. The latter had died of smallpox late in 1660, along with their other brother the Duke of Gloucester. Nor was York ever prepared to countenance Monmouth's succession, even before the linkage of Monmouth to the rabidly anti-Catholic faction around Shaftesbury from 1679 made it certain that Monmouth's succession would imperil James' Catholic co-religionists. The 'Popish Plot' furore did not commence the Duke's fear of his nephew's succession. James' much-lauded conscience and sense of honour did not extend to accepting that Charles had married Lucy Walter, even with adequate reason to accept that it might have occurred. The testimony of any Monmouth partisans to the marriage after 1679 could be discounted as politically motivated, but Cosin and Lake had no obvious reason to have made up the story.

The 'Exclusion Crisis' and the 'Black Box'.

The question became a major political issue with the 'Popish Plot' and the attempt to use the 'Country' party's new control of the Commons in the 1679–81 Parliaments to introduce an 'Exclusion Bill' which would legitimise Monmouth and make him heir to the throne, forcing the recognition on the King. Shaftesbury and his fellow 'Whigs' sought to coerce the King, and the vain and impatient Monmouth lent himself to the cause of proving his legitimacy despite his father's denials and started to tour the country to rally support for his cause as the impeccably 'Protestant Duke'. New witnesses were produced to testify to the legality of the marriage, though as this was part of a concerted political campaign their testimony could be questioned and the Duke of York was quick to do so. From now on the questions of the marriage and of Monmouth's claim became inextricably linked to an assault on Charles II's right to choose his own successor and avoid political coercion by the 'Country Party'. Thus Charles was even less likely to admit that he had married Lucy and that York was not his legal heir. At the most he may have considered an alternative form of 'Exclusion' that would achieve the opposition's political aim (neutralising York as fount of authority) without interfering with his right to choose his successor, namely allowing York to succeed but under a 'regency'. This would be exercised by York's heiress, his elder daughter Mary, and her impeccably Protestant husband William of Orange. But even this plan, 'floated' in 1681 and backed by a senior minister (George Savile, Marquis of Halifax), was abandoned and it may have been no more than an attempt to lure the 'moderate' part of Monmouth's political following away from him and Shaftesbury in vital votes in Lords and Commons.

The main issue was now the rumoured 'Black Box' containing the marriage certificate, which according to the Finch Papers (vol. II, p. 76) was supposed to have belonged to Dr. John Cosin – Henrietta Maria's chaplain at St Germain in 1648 – as the clergyman who had solemnised the marriage.[34] Later becoming Bishop of Durham but now dead, he had bequeathed the box to his son-in-law Sir Gilbert Gerard, a ' Country Party' MP.[35] The Earl of Dartmouth, a supporter of York and thus antagonistic to the legitimacy of the marriage, wrote at the time of talk of 'another successor in a black box' which was likely to be a 'Pandora's Box' of troubles.[36] But as mentioned above, when Gerard was questioned before the Privy Council in April 1680 he denied knowing anything about a black box 36 and so did various other alleged possessors of vital information. Charles duly put out another statement denying that he had ever married Lucy. Given Charles' habit of dissimulation, the word of the King was not reliable (as rhymed about by the Court poet Lord Rochester, who called him 'a pretty witty King/whose word no man relies on'). He had every reason to avoid the Whigs forcing a choice of heir on him – a curtailment of his prerogative. But it was unfortunate that Gerard could be written off by sceptics as a politically biased agent of Shaftesbury capable of inventing his story, not an impartial 'outsider'.

The King's action naturally did not halt the 'Whig' campaign to prove that the marriage had taken place. Quite apart from the King's known untrustworthiness and his desire not to be forced to change his chosen successor – his brother – by political pressure, it could be assumed that the Privy Council investigation was a 'cover-up' on behalf of York (now temporarily in exile in Edinburgh at the height of the 'Popish Plot' storm). Behind York would be the expansionist Louis XIV of France, who would much prefer a dependent co-religionist, York, as the next King to the Protestant and Whig-allied Monmouth. Possibly France was already offering money behind the scenes to Charles II if he stood firm against Monmouth, and in March 1681 Charles was to be confident enough of (eventual) French financial aid to risk shutting down Parliament – as it turned out permanently – at Oxford sooner than accept 'Exclusion'. In any case, giving in to the Whigs would amount to curtailing Charles' freedom of political manoeuvre, with uncomfortable overtones of how his father had been coerced in 1640–2 and 1646–8. In reply to the official investigation which 'rubbished' the 'Black Box' story, the 'Whig' propagandist (and Shaftesbury's chaplain) Robert Ferguson penned assorted pamphlets including *'A Letter to a Person of Honour Concerning the Black Box* and *'A Letter to a person of Honour Concerning the King's Disavowing his having been Married to the Duke of Monmouth's Mother'*. He said that a proper enquiry should have taken place in a more independent atmosphere, before Parliament, and witnesses been called.

Apart from Ferguson's colleague, Sir Thomas Armstrong, other backers of the legality of the marriage were said to include Lucy's aunt Margaret Sambourne, who was in possession of letters from Charles to Lucy but unwilling to testify publicly for fear of official retribution, and people who had heard Lucy's brother Mr Walter boast about the marriage while he had been serving at Court at the Restoration. Clarendon (also now dead) was said by Ferguson to have referred to Monmouth being legitimate in the House of Lords at the time of his impeachment in 1667; Ferguson 'the Plotter' believed Clarendon to have known more than most about the truth. In fact at the time (1649) Clarendon had written that he had been apprehensive of the Prince secretly marrying at the time that he and Charles had arrived in France in June 1649; the marriage was then being rumoured in London and he and other Councillors had warned the Prince earlier not to do it. This dating refers to the period before Charles left Holland in June 1649, i.e. the months around Monmouth's birth.

But were the rumours concerning Dr Cosin as the celebrant wrong, and so his son-in-law Gerard was being honest in denying having possession of any relevant material? Was the link to Dr. Cosin due to the story that he had been the exiled Royalist cleric in Paris in 1658 who gave the ailing Lucy spiritual consolation for her 'sins', though that might also mean that Lucy had given him secret papers then? It was rumoured in 1680 that it was Dr. Fuller, subsequently Bishop of Lincoln, who had carried out the wedding. Ferguson even alleged that York was blackmailing the King into keeping him as heir by threatening to reveal the truth and undermine the whole dynasty if he was disinherited.[37] In the second of his 'Letters to a Person of Honour…', Ferguson claimed that Henrietta Maria had reluctantly consented to the marriage in order to calm her son's immoderate desire and resulting (?suicidal) despair at not being able to marry his lover. It might be assumed that the strict Catholic Queen-Mother would only have agreed to be Monmouth's guardian if she thought him legitimate. But the 'Whigs' were still hopeful of forcing the legitimisation through Parliament in despite of the King's denials of the marriage, and the issue of the evidence was less important than their political campaign. It only became relevant again when Charles had succeeded in outmanoeuvring and dismissing his final Parliament in March 1681 without conceding 'Exclusion' and that avenue was blocked. The 'Whigs' now resorted to plots for an armed uprising and/or killing the King and York, with a fatal division between those who were prepared to go to any lengths to save the country from a Catholic King (including regicide) and the more moderate figures unwilling to shed so much blood. Monmouth was alleged to have insisted that the King be spared and tried to stop his allies from plotting to kill his uncle York too, with one plan involving armed 'Whigs' causing a riot in the City of London and then marching on Whitehall to seize the King and kill the Duke of York.[38] Ferguson and a number of former New Model Army officers were the most ruthless and were determined to be rid of the King as well as York by assassination which they knew Monmouth would not tolerate so he would have to be 'kept out of the loop' on that matter, but they did not prevail with the more restrained upper-class members of the group (such as Essex and Russell) and even the most bloodthirsty could not escape the suspicion that if they did kill the King (or York) Monmouth would sacrifice them later to assuage the public outrage that regicide would cause. But the plot never progressed beyond wild talk and was soon revealed to the government – who may have exaggerated its bloodthirstiness and the list of who exactly approved regicide in order to blacken the names of the leaders, Shaftesbury, Essex, and Russell given their elite status and political allies among the courtiers. All the leadership were either arrested or driven into exile and Monmouth was forced into hiding from whence he negotiated his surrender and pardon. Charles duly received him in secret, but his political influence was at an end and his main allies were executed (Algernon Sidney and Lord Russell), committed suicide while under sentence (the Earl of Essex), or died abroad as a fugitive (Shaftesbury). There is even a possibility that the most respected of the accused, Essex (son of an executed Royalist hero of the 1648 uprising, Arthur Capel, so with a potential appeal to the King who was usually loyal to his father's supporters who had sacrificed so much), did not kill himself but was 'silenced' by an agent of the pro-York 'hard liners' so the King would not pardon him and reinstate him in office later. But this, like the 'Black Box' story, may just reflect the extreme state of 'Whig' suspicion of the York faction in these years – and as their allies came to power when William of Orange invaded in November 1688 they were able to promote their theories and denigrate York at will thereafter.

Later induced to flee the country sooner than accept that he must give evidence against his friends, Monmouth was still abroad when Charles died suddenly on 6 February 1685 and James succeeded to the throne. He sought to regain his supposed rightful inheritance by invasion, landing at Lyme Regis in June, but was defeated and captured and ended up executed on Tower Hill. Tragically, Monmouth's accusations that the new King was seeking to promote Catholics to positions of power, overturn the Anglican monopoly of power, and institute a French-backed autocracy – which won little significant backing in south-western England and virtually none from the elite in June 1685 – turned out to be correct as James set about his reforms in 1686–8 and forced his co-religionists into senior positions in the State and Church – and in the Army. In the end, the unwelcome birth of a Catholic heir to James in June 1688 led to an invitation from alarmed members of the elite (including Charles II's ex-minister Danby) to William of Orange to invade and save Protestantism, and James' regime fell. Had Monmouth waited for two or three years, he could have had much more backing and possibly succeeded in his aims – unless his rival William, as husband of James' Protestant elder daughter Mary (the King's heir until June 1688), had removed him somehow. His failure was as much one of timing as of aims, and presumably reflected his impatience and lack of political skill – though at the time he was spurred on by the fact that his Scots ally, the exiled Earl of Argyll, was determined to invade Scotland in summer 1685 and Monmouth wanted to co-ordinate their attacks. He claimed to be the legitimate King in his proclamations during the invasion and said that the Duke of York had poisoned Charles II in February 1685,[39] but with no proof to display to the public. The charge of secret regicide by the Duke of York and/or men keen to assist his cause, intended to prevent the wavering Charles from recalling Monmouth to England in 1685 and giving him another chance of the throne, was also made by York's foe Bishop Burnet in his subsequent history of the period and by 1730 anti-Catholic historian John Oldmixon, presumably using contemporary rumour, so Monmouth did not just invent it in 1685 to add to popular paranoia about accepting a Catholic King.[40] But given that Burnet had had to flee Scotland under York's rule to Holland and 'sit it out' there until his new patron William of Orange's invasion in 1688, he had every reason to pump up the rhetoric in accusing York and his allies of hideous crimes.

Subsequent evidence in Monmouth's favour?

One final incident revived the possibility that the 'Black Box' had not been a mere rumour and the problem over its being proved 'real' in 1680–1 may have owed most to inaccurate belief that it was Gerard who was in possession of it (unless Gerard lost his nerve and hid it to save himself from arrest by the King's men). The editor of an edition of the contemporary memoirs of the Baronne d'Aulnoy, G. D. Gilbert, wrote that he had received a letter in 1905 from Sir Frederick Barnewall on what his friend Sir Bernard Burke had been told many years earlier by the Duke of Abercorn. The latter had been told by one of the Dukes of Buccleuch, a descendant of Monmouth and Anne Scott, that he had found a copy of the marriage certificate of Charles II and Lucy Walter in the muniment room at his residence, Dalkeith House: 'after considering the matter for some time he decided to destroy it and thereon threw it into the fire and it was burned'.[41]

Sir George Scott, son of the sixth Duke of Buccleuch, wrote in his biography of Lucy Walter in 1947 that a few years previously Sir Hew Dalrymple had come across a document in the Buccleuch papers which he had copied. This stated that:

> 'The certificate of marriage was found by Henry, Duke of Buccleuch [the 3rd Duke, who died in 1746]) and President Hope (Charles Hope, Lord President of the Court of Session) amongst some old papers at Dalkeith; and the Duke thought it best to burn it. It does not seem clear whether it was the original or a copy of one at Liege where they were married by the then Archbishop of Canterbury. I believe it is supposed that the other copy or original, whichever it was, might be found at Liege if looked for. And it is said Charles II would have acknowledged the Duke of Monmouth as his heir, if it had not been prevented by James II'.[42]

The final statement here agrees with the information Ferguson had about York blackmailing or at least influencing the King's decision, though it is possible that the copyist in the Buccleuch archives had merely read Ferguson's material and assessed it as accurate. The clergyman who carried out the ceremony would here appear to be not Cosin but William Juxon, Archbishop of Canterbury from 1660–3, or his successor Gilbert Sheldon; but neither is known to have been in the Low Countries at the time and if Ferguson's words about Henrietta Maria's involvement are accurate she is more likely to have sent her chaplain to carry it out. Charles and Lucy could easily have travelled to Liege from The Hague some time in winter 1648–9; this would fit in with Clarendon having heard rumours of the marriage and warned Charles not to carry it out some time before June 1649. It was Princess Mary, Charles' hostess at the time, who referred to Lucy as his wife in subsequent correspondence; she if anyone would have been his confidante about the incident. The question however arises of whether the document was drawn up for a ceremony that never took place, and if Charles had second thoughts but Lucy secretly retained a copy (or was given one later by an ally?) and planned to use it for blackmail in the mid-1650s.

If the document was genuine its existence and location raises other problems. As it was in the Buccleuch papers, it probably belonged to Monmouth himself – or else was acquired some time after his death by his widow Anne, who lived until 1732, or their grandson Francis Scott, second Duke of Buccleuch, her heir. If it was owned by Monmouth, why did he not publish it at the time of the invasion in June 1685 to show that his uncle York (now James II and VII) was a usurper? His reticence in his father's lifetime is more explainable, out of respect to the King and unwillingness to force his hand; but Monmouth would surely have mentioned the date and place of marriage to his confidants had he known them. Ferguson would then have mentioned the precise details in his pamphlets in 1680, instead of making vague hints. The 'original' of the marriage certificate (used for a ceremony that took place or just drawn up ready for one) would seem likely to have been the document in Lucy's possession which Charles was so keen to retrieve in 1657–8 when she was making threats about publishing certain details. Did the search by the King's agents when Monmouth was 'snatched' retrieve it, and if so how did it survive – surely Charles or his brother would have burnt it? Or were there two or three copies, only one of which had been possessed by Lucy? If Lucy managed to save the document then, how did it come into Monmouth's hands after her death given that he was not yet an adult in possession of a household or trustable servants which he could use to hide it? Did the certificate pass into the hands of her own family, who gave it to Monmouth when he was adult? The fact that the precise details of the marriage, which would have been on the certificate, were not being bruited about in 1680 or 1685 would suggest that the document at Dalkeith was more likely not to have come into Monmouth's hands, but been acquired by his family later. The placing of the ceremony at Liege – an independent Bishopric within the Holy Roman Empire, outside Dutch jurisdiction but within easy reach of The Hague – was known or suspected by Sir Thomas Armstrong by 1680/3 according to Ferguson. But why did the 'Whigs' not attempt to acquire a copy of the certificate there and publish it (abroad, as it would have been confiscated in England by the King's or York's orders) to back up Monmouth's claims?

Similarly, it would have been a vital weapon in Monmouth's cause when he landed at Lyme Regis in June 1685 to take the Crown. He set out his cause in a manifesto claiming that he was the real 'King James' and his uncle a usurper, adding that the latter had murdered Charles II (to prevent a rapprochement with Monmouth?). The most recent research indicates that Charles may have died of mercury poisoning rather than of a straightforward stroke, but this was more likely to have built up accidentally over years of dangerous chemical experiments than to have been deliberately administered by Catholic plotters.[43] The occasion of Monmouth's landing was surely the time to publish printed copies of the marriage certificate to prove his case, had the original been in his possession at the time. The rebellion was launched sooner than anticipated, due to a need to co-ordinate the rising with the exiled Marquis of Argyll's invasion of Scotland. But there was still time – and adequate local printing-presses – to print copies of the document in The Hague before Monmouth sailed. Failing that, its details could easily have been announced to all and sundry during the rebel advance, as Monmouth advanced across Somerset on Bristol. The rebels' failure to use this important piece of propaganda on the occasion when it would have been of most use argues against Monmouth possessing it at the time.

If it was genuine, it casts a different light on the murky politics of the 'Exclusion Crisis' and makes Monmouth's treatment by James II seem a particularly ruthless piece of '*realpolitik*'. Charles' unwillingness to admit to the ceremony for fear of the political consequences is more understandable, though even so he should have been determined to do his son justice by legitimizing him by Act of Parliament once it became apparent that York was Catholic (1673) and would prove a contentious successor. The fact that the witnesses to the mysterious document in the Buccleuch archives had no axes to grind in making the allegation of its existence argues for their sincerity. They had no reason to fabricate the story, and at the time the certificate was allegedly found (pre-1746) the Jacobite threat to the insecure Hanoverian throne meant that making up a story about George II not being the lawful King would have been treated as treasonable. The fact that the third Duke of Buccleuch was a – Protestant – Scots magnate made it particularly dangerous; the Jacobite invasion of 1715 would have shown the support that even a Catholic Stuart could rely upon in the country. So was Monmouth the honest victim of ruthless and self-serving 'spin' by an embarrassed Charles II (who refused to admit his youthful 'folly' in marrying Lucy) plus determination not to sacrifice the chances of a Catholic king who could 'do God's work' by James II? Or were Charles and James correct and Monmouth was inventing a claim – possibly in 'good faith' as he had been shown the certificate drawn up for an abortive planned marriage that Charles backed out of? In the case of the document being genuine and the marriage taking place, the correct legal heir to England after Monmouth's execution was his elder son by Anne Scott, ie James, Earl of Dalkeith (1674–1705). From him the line of descent continued via the latter's son Francis, Duke of Buccleuch (d. 1751) to the current family of Montague-Douglas-Scott, with the Dukes of Buccleuch followed in their right to the throne by their relatives by side-descent including Sarah, Duchess of York.

Chapter 5

James II – Progressive Promoter of Religious Toleration or Determined to Turn Britain Catholic?

The accession of James VII and II on 6 February 1685 was, as seen above, temporarily a smooth and seamless occasion which reflected the grip that the Stuart brothers had achieved on the British Isles since the 'Popish Plot' and the 'Exclusion Crisis' had threatened to get out of hand. Charles was able to pass on the throne to his presumed legal heir, and any claims that the disgraced and exiled Duke of Monmouth had to be his legitimate eldest son had been brushed aside by the political elite. Whether or not this was a 'stitch-up' arranged by the ambitious James and his backers to deprive the three kingdoms of a ruler linked to the 'ultra' radical Protestants and semi-republicans of the 'Whig' 'party' is unclear, but as seen in the previous chapter any evidence for Charles II having married Monmouth's mother Lucy Walter was dubious, largely circumstantial, and never produced in public. Nor was it a clear case of a sinister cabal of Catholics and pro-Catholics, 'French agents' included, wanting to use James to arrange the reconversion of England and Scotland to Catholicism (Ireland was still largely Catholic anyway, at least at lower social levels) and hoodwinking the passive, pro-royalist English elite into accepting this by pretending that James would defend the Anglican Church and political stability as his brother had done.

There had been serious alarm among provincial royalists and supporters of a stable political order over the turbulent and potentially coercive nature of 'Exclusion', with riots, inflammatory propaganda and obstinate Parliamentary defiance of the King's wishes in 1679–81 seeming to point to an alarming return to 'Forty and One' (i.e., 1641, the run-up to the Civil War). This had been played up by royalist propaganda to justify the King's closure of the 1681 parliament at Oxford and subsequent political 'crackdown', which even led to a number of high-profile executions of top Whigs and a purge of the provincial urban corporations. But in the minds of most of the national as well as provincial elites in 1685 the overwhelming need would have been to avoid a return to the disorders and bloodshed of the 1640s, even if this played into the hands of people hoping to use it to impose a stricter and more autocratic/centralised regime in England (and across Britain) and into the hands of Catholic evangelisers too.

Legality came first and James was the legal heir to the throne, and in addition the Anglican Church had been playing up the importance of obedience and 'non-resistance' by loyal subjects as a way of weaning people away from defying the authorities ever since 1660 and preaching that rebellion was a 'sin'. All of this was in James' favour, and the stability and military strength of the well-ordered and centralised monarchy of France across the Channel under the autocratic (and fiercely Catholic) Louis XIV was also a temptation to proponents of stability to look to similar measures of empowering the King and his ministers as a way of securing long-term peace in Britain after the 'Exclusion' crisis of 1679–81. The question at issue is thus partly whether James' (and his secular ministers') priorities were stability rather than 'Catholicization' – and if one was mistaken or misrepresented as the other, mainly by his opponents. After James – the beneficiary of all this desire for stability – had been overthrown in 1688 the new, aggressively Protestant and anti-French, regime of William III and Mary II and their Whig allies duly played up the 'threat to liberty' and 'threat to Protestantism' that James had posed – justifying his deposition. But how much was this 'spin' or a deliberate exaggeration?

As with the question of Charles II's alleged secret marriage (where the supposed 'cheated' legal heir, Monmouth, was now safely dead and William and Mary had taken over the claim to be rightful sovereigns), there was a political agenda in presenting a firm 'narrative' of events in 1685–8 that backed up the new regime and brushed embarrassing questions out of the way. Indeed, despite the naming of the crisis of 1688 as the 'Glorious Revolution' – the replacement of the autocratic 'Divine Right' Catholicising monarchy of James by the liberal, democratically accountable new monarchy of William and Mary, based on Parliament's invitation to them to assume the throne – the 'revolution' was often seen as a 'restoration' of the 'proper' traditional British order, not an 'innovation'. (The term 'revolution' originally meant 'turning full circle' ie a return to an original position, as with a rotating wheel, not a new order – though after the French Revolution it came always to mean a 'new' order.) By this definition, which was formalised in attitudes to the 1688 events at the time of the 1789 French Revolution by the conservative MP and political writer Edmund Burke, it had been James who was the innovator and the 'Revolution' had saved the old order from his autocratic and Catholicising innovations – a reassurance to traditionally-minded Englishmen that they could celebrate their 'Revolution' without implying that they were like the monarch-executing French and their bloodbaths of 1789–94.

Monmouth's alleged claim to the crown, truthful or not, ended up with him invading England in June 1685 in a failed bid to overthrow his 'Papist' uncle James – who by this point had not shown any signs of wanting to overturn the firmly Anglican religious establishment or fill secular and religious offices with Catholics – and he had not been able to rally enough support to challenge James on the battlefield or cause mass-defections. Unlike the cautious and brutally realistic William (already an experienced ruler and general by the mid-1680s) Monmouth had been shunned by the elite and ended up defeated by the king's army at Sedgemoor, fleeing for his life, hiding in a ditch near Ringwood, dragged out, and taken to London to be executed for treason. He was seen thereafter as a failure in the role of Protestant champion against James, whether or not his disastrous campaign had been due to his striking too soon rather than any notable incompetence, and although he left children to carry on his claim to the throne these were never considered as alternatives to James as the latter's policies started to cause major concern among his elite. It was James' legal heir until his second wife gave birth to a son in June 1688, i.e. his daughter Mary, and her husband William III of Orange, Stadtholder of the Dutch 'United Provinces' and in control of a usefully large and experienced army and navy, who was the focus of hopes as elements in the English (not Scots or Irish) elite planned to depose James. Indeed, as will be seen below, the new complication of the birth of a son and – presumably Catholic – heir to James and his Italian Catholic second wife Mary of Modena was ruthlessly side-stepped by the plotters, and by William and the anti-Jacobite political leadership as they declared the refugee James deposed and William and Mary to be the new sovereigns in February 1689. The baby was proclaimed to be a fraud, a changeling smuggled into the birth-chamber at St James' Palace in a warming-pan to replace a baby who had died at birth or indeed never existed at all in a fake pregnancy, and Mary as next – and safely Protestant – heir to the throne and her husband (on his insistence as many 'Tories' wanted Mary as sole ruler) were the new and fully legal sovereigns.

Thus the new regime's 'spin-doctors' could allege that there had never been a coup to depose James but rather the legal replacement of a tyrant who had cheated and deserted his people by the next heir, and this shameless distortion of events duly left out any legal claims by Monmouth's heirs – though to be fair the so-called 'Black Box' and its presumed contents of Charles II's and Lucy Walter's marriage certificate had never been produced. Their existence is doubtful if not impossible, as seen in the previous chapter, but William and Mary and their supporters had no more reason than James' elite to accept their reality and in any case the Dutch invasion had had far more political support in November 1688 than Monmouth's half-baked landing had done in June 1685 so many more people had invested in the new regime and its 'narratives'. The new 'narrative' of events left Monmouth and his claims as both rightful king and Protestant champion out in the cold – with some observers then and later even suggesting that William had let Monmouth go to his death in 1685 without any Dutch support to rid himself of a rival. But the main thrust of what became the established – and in modern terms the 'establishment' – explanation of the 'Glorious Revolution' of 1688 also distorted history in another useful myth, which later triumphalist defenders of the new and successful 'constitution' and expanding British power after 1689 were to promote for centuries in what became known as the school of 'Whig History'. James had been a treacherous and dictatorial ruler who violated his coronation oath to protect the Anglican Church and was planning to turn England Catholic, reversing the Reformation, so his deposition had been necessary and legal. This has been challenged by modern historians, who point out that in fact James was promoting non-Anglican Protestant 'Dissenters', the sects driven out of or not allowed to link up with the Church by the intolerant religious settlement at the Restoration in 1660–2. The so-called 'Clarendon Code' had established a hard-line Anglican list of religious beliefs to which all members of the Church of England had to subscribe, driven out all objectors from Church and secular state and provincial offices, and banned all other religious assemblies, with the enthusiastic 'High Anglican' royalist elite in Parliament (who had arguably forced this settlement on an unwilling Charles II) piling up stringent legislation in the 1660s and early 1670s (e.g. the Test Acts) and defeating subsequent royal attempts to get round this by personal royal grants of exemptions or 'Declarations of Indulgence'.

This harsh and divisive religious legislation had been challenged after 1685 by James, who had sought to bring alienated Protestant 'Dissenters' as well as Catholics into his national and provincial governments and had thus been a champion of toleration, and he had had good relations with leading 'Dissenters' such as William Penn, founder of the American colony of Pennsylvania. By this reckoning, the King was the victim of an unrelenting Whig-led political faction that sought to stir up exaggerated fears of his Catholicising tendencies, and succeeded – and once his nephew Monmouth had failed to overthrow him in summer 1685 they turned their attention to enlisting his son-in-law William of Orange. These plotters, aided by the Dutch ruler's fear of an alliance between James and Louis XIV to destroy him, intervened to overthrow James in November 1688 – and this time succeeded. Their success was due to their willingness to resort to violence and use foreign help, not primarily to James' own failures. So, was James really an enlightened and principled champion of toleration who had been unfairly targeted and overthrown by alarmed factions who disapproved of this and so exaggerated his commitment to Catholicism and enrolment of Catholics in his government and armies?

This has duly provided another 'Royal Mystery' crucial to understanding of what really happened in Britain in the 1680s – with 'knock-on' effects for centuries in Ireland (and to a lesser extent Scotland). What was the truth about James' intentions, and has his name been blackened unjustly – or, conversely, do enthusiasts for his 'toleration' take his reassuring public statements too much at face value?

James' accession on 6 February 1685 provided a useful myth for his foes of England having its first openly Catholic sovereign since 'Bloody' Mary I, the villain of the highly popular *Acts and Monuments* of John Foxe, and Scotland with its first Catholic sovereign since the Reformation. James, moreover, was not only Catholic but proceeded to advance the interests of his co-religionists, not merely by suspending the penal laws against Catholics but by reversing the additional discriminatory legislation that had been passed in his brother's reign (especially the 'Test Act' of 1673). He had a Catholic second wife, Mary Beatrice of Modena (born 1658), who was still young enough to bear children although they had lost several babies in twelve years of marriage. Fortunately for Anglican fears his two daughters by his first marriage (to Anne Hyde, Clarendon's daughter) were determinedly Protestant so James' policies should end with his death. Attempts could still be made by his zealous Catholic priests to convert them, but the elder and heir, Mary (born April 1662), was living abroad in the United Provinces with her firmly Protestant husband William – arch-foe of Louis XIV, the persecutor of the Huguenots as of 1685. The younger and supposedly more malleable Anne (born February 1665), resisted the arguments of her father's Catholic priests to convert her in 1685–6; she and her Protestant husband, the famously dim Prince George of Denmark, still lived at James' court. The latter, of whom Charles II famously remarked after first meeting him 'I have tried him drunk and tried him sober and there is nothing in him', was politically negligible but a major emotional support to his stressed and unhealthy wife as Queen, and his death in 1708 was a major factor in shifts of power at Court – Anne's closest friend/'favourite' Sarah Churchill shrugged off his death and so infuriated the Queen who was shortly to find a new confidante.

The King was in a very strong position as of Monmouth's defeat in late summer 1685, and despite his contentiousness as a Catholic heir had suffered no significant defections as a Protestant challenger had appeared. He had been as enthusiastically treated by his subjects as his brother at his accession despite his religion, with a plethora of loyal addresses sent to him by local communities.[1] Boroughs and county governance were both now usually in 'Tory' hands after the 1681–4 purges so these were probably organised, but there is no indication of a 'fix' against the wishes of most of the county and town elites – and no indication of mass approval for the King's challenger Monmouth even in the (mostly pro-Parliamentary in the 1640s) west country except to a point in the 'special case' of former 'rebel' stronghold Taunton. Ordinary and politically non-partisan commentators (Anglicans and Dissenters of all views included) almost all expressed hope of a 'positive' and settled reign at James' accession despite his religion,[2] and his gracious and (for once) astute promises to the Privy Council were taken at face value as proving his desire to continue his brother's policies.[3] Indeed the amount of public and private optimism would suggest that any theory of an overarching 'rabid anti-Catholic prejudice that refused to accept a Catholic king' in 1685 England is exaggerated, even if it did not take much to reawaken this. The most obvious alarm at what he might do was expressed by Quakers[4] who had suffered serious persecution from the Anglicans as subversives since 1662 and could expect similar behaviour from an autocratic Catholic king, though his public attendance at Mass in London raised some hackles and caused adverse comment.[5] James' public declaration of his determination to preserve the extant constitution duly led to extra enthusiasm in the 'loyal addresses' to him, albeit 'conditional' in that this was couched in terms of relief that His Majesty would preserve the existing politico-religious system.[6] The evidence of the county elections for the 1685 Parliament – where the late King had been unable to 'fix' the results by altering the voting lists or transferring organization to his loyal supporters as in borough elections – shows an unforced shift to the King's so far unconditional supporters, the 'Tories', with around seventy MPs returned in their interest and only around seven for the suspicious 'Whigs'.[7] (There had been around sixty-five county 'Whig' MPs in 1681.) Nor did the King's repression in Scotland as its effective viceroy in 1679–85, the notorious 'Killing Times' when his troops were quartered on and terrorised the Galloway Covenanters, cause major desertions in 1685 to the rebel earl of Argyll, hereditary clan-chief of the Campbells. His situation after Monmouth's defeat was strong – so did he throw it all away by over-confidence, and/or due to his missionary view of his religion?

He was now confident enough to launch active proselytising on behalf of his fellow-Catholics, and his partisanship now went beyond the expected appearance of Catholic priests and noblemen at his court, diplomatic relations with the Papacy, and suspension of the penal laws – reasonable enough actions for a Catholic King and Queen to take. He showed no concern at the poor image that would be given by removing unenthusiastic ministers such as the marquis of Halifax, the famous 'Trimmer' whose attempts to create a coalition of moderate ministers to stave off the worst excesses of 'Exclusion' in 1679–81 had annoyed James by being prepared to have his powers as King restricted and his daughter Mary made regent to reassure Protestants. He increasingly used the king's prerogative power of 'dispensing' with the laws in specific named cases to make exceptions for individual Catholics, who secured local and central governmental posts and seemed to threaten the loyal but anti-Catholic Anglican Tories.[8] Whether or not the latter were intolerant, greedy of monopolising office, and thus ready to take offence, it was unwise to alarm them and so reduce his field of support. Unlike Charles, James blatantly appointed many Catholic officers (seventy-four) to his army as early as 1685 in defiance of the Test Act and then had this absolved by Parliament in one act of Royal 'dispensation', just before it dissolved so there was no 'comeback'.[9] These actions, plus the (logically necessary for security reasons but unpopular) suspension of the '*Habeas Corpus*' right to a quick trial to help round-ups of rebel suspects, aroused early if limited resistance even in the House of Lords, and 'moderate' leader Halifax's sacking prior to this was a bad sign.

Typically, the insensitive and triumphalist James relied on the vicious-tongued and bullying new Lord Chancellor Jeffreys, fresh from his mass-executions in the west country, to intimidate the Lords – though as we have seen in accounts of the 1615 'Overbury Case' trials (connected to the poisoning in the Tower of London of an ex-confidante of King James VI and I's favourite Robert Carr) and the early 1680s Whig trials Jeffreys was far from the only judge to bend the law and bully defendants, witnesses, and jurors. Royal critics then proposed that the judiciary should rule on the legality of the King's dispensing power – and as James and Jeffreys had not yet had time to 'pack' the Bench of judges the King had to prorogue Parliament and remodel the judiciary before proceeding on this matter. The remodelled judiciary then obediently ruled that this disputed power was fully legal in the 'test case' of Godden vs. Hales (1686), four of the twelve Common Law judges having been sacked beforehand for refusing to accept that the dispensing power was legal. Lord Chief Justice Herbert declared that Kentish Catholic JP Sir Edward Hales was quite entitled to accept a commission in the army, as the laws were the King's to amend as he wished at his discretion.[10] A large standing army was built up despite the popular unease of 'arbitrary rule' which that had caused ever since the 1640s, and was openly encamped on Hounslow Heath near London every summer to intimidate the restive City. Nor was any attempt made to halt indiscipline by the soldiery, which in the West Country after Monmouth's rebellion was certainly used as an instrument of terror (notably by Tangier veteran Colonel Percy Kirke's ironically-named 'Lambs' who were used to intimidating Moroccan Muslims during their service at Tangier and now ran a virtual 'lynch-law' over rebel suspects). In practical terms, quartering the soldiery in private houses and inns in restive towns kept an eye on the behaviour of the inhabitants; and it was cheap. With the equivalent Catholic-led military forces in Ireland in view, it could be seen that James was installing ultra-loyal Catholic officers in English commands too. Notably, French ambassador Barillon reckoned that opposition to the latter was not based on a paranoid fear of their potential for a Catholic takeover – they were few in number – but on indignation that the King was blatantly breaking the laws by appointing them.[11] But their proportion in the army – around eleven per cent of the total – was far larger than their proportion in the nation, showing a clear desire to promote them at the expense of

Protestants, and James blatantly placed them in the major strategic commands in important garrisons and around London which increased suspicion.[12] The resentment of the newly large, extra-costly, and explicitly Catholic-orientated army led to public riots in places where the soldiers were quartered (a return to a provincial anti-military mood of the 1620s and 1640s), complaints at the undesirability of a standing army by those peers who were to invite William and Mary to intervene in 1688, and particular alarm in and around the volatile capital at the annual camps on Hounslow Heath.[13] James was thus deliberately stirring up 'sleeping dogs' that his brother had more carefully let lie.

Catholic priests had been told to be careful and unobtrusive at the start of the reign,[14] but from mid-1686 were allowed to proselytise openly with Royal support, with ambitious courtiers and ministers showing their loyalty to their master by becoming Catholic – the most notorious case being that of the King's political 'fixer', the devious earl of Sunderland (Robert Spencer). James especially hoped that using his powers of patronage to promote Catholics would encourage conversion, telling ambassador Barillon that it was more useful than any priestly arguments, nor was anti-Catholic pamphleteering permitted, though arguably this supposedly helped avoid stirring up prejudice as well as sedition. This had started as early as 1682, with the prosecution of cleric Samuel Johnston for his inflammatory *'Julian the Apostate'* (attacking James). The rabidly anti-Catholic 'Popish Plot' scaremonger Titus Oates was sentenced to an annual public whipping for his libels in 1678 (which may have sent innocent if indiscreet people to execution); the veteran Presbyterian divine Richard Baxter was fined for a 'seditious' work on the New Testament and Jeffreys shouted at him that he should have been flogged into obedience forty years ago; and 'Popish Plot' libeller Thomas Dangerfield was whipped and was stabbed to death during it by a Royalist fanatic. The Bishop of London, Henry Compton, was sacked as Dean of the Chapel Royal late in 1685 for speaking in the Lords against readmitting Catholic peers, and was suspended as Bishop in June 1686 for refusing to act against the rector of St Martin-in-the-Fields.[15] Either criticism of or lukewarm support for the King was thus equated with disloyalty, and the presses were rigidly controlled with hunts for seditious writings assisted by the soldiery. As far as early 1680s Whig supporters were concerned it was a reign of terror, comparable to (and inspired by?) the activities of Louis XIV's thuggish Catholic military 'dragonnades'. It was in fact no more repressive than James' father's rule in the 1630s – except that the latter had been patriotically careful to disassociate his repression from Catholicism. Charles' minister Strafford had been as fond of issuing violent threats as Jeffreys (though he had not been a judge).

James also showed internationally risky incaution in his public utterances, allowing his rising dislike of William (still his heir's expected co-ruler) to be known abroad. Arguably, the physical alterations to Whitehall Palace in 1686–7 also caused alarm, with an ominous sign in the first Catholic Chapel being constructed within the Palace precincts for the use of the Queen.[16] (Henrietta Maria's new chapels had been at St James' and Somerset House.) James also openly backed the notoriously unpopular Jesuit Order in their 'ultramontane' Catholic propaganda despite the public relations gift that this gave to his critics, approving the release of literature explaining that they were no longer the villainous regicidal fanatics of old and instead backed up monarchic authority. Indeed, 'modern' Jesuit and Jesuit-allied propaganda was now published explaining the duty of all subjects to obey their King and all his laws unhesitatingly, thus using them to back up the already extant 'complete obedience' writings of pro-Stuart 'High Anglicans' like Sir Robert Filmer.[17] Steve Pincus points out that this 'absolutist' Catholic approach to authority was a leading theme in French 'Gallican' Catholicism as promoted by and on behalf of James' cousin Louis XIV, not one present in all Catholic countries. Indeed 'Gallican' and pro-French Catholics dominated the ranks of James' Catholic advisers.[18] His closest spiritual advisers were Jesuits, famous and feared by Protestants for over a century as ruthless arch-converters lacking principles, with experts then and since agreed on his enthusiasm for their views.[19] The Jesuits were indeed treated with deep suspicion by the Pope, Innocent XI, who was a foe of Louis XIV and his autocratic claims to dominate the French Church.[20] The Pope was also a critic of Louis' decision to convert the French Protestant 'Huguenots' by force in 1685, which the Jesuits backed – which shows that James was not on the 'side of moderation' in this crucial matter. Indeed, Innocent disapproved of James as pro-French.[21] There was not a monolithic bloc of Catholic European states keen to back up any converting English monarch, as the insular English usually supposed; rather, the ultra-Catholic Habsburgs in Spain and the Holy Roman Empire had been hereditary foes of the French monarchy since before the Reformation and in the war of 1689–97 were to back the Protestant William III against Louis.

The absolutist Catholic views backed by James went beyond the normal 'High Anglican' doctrine of obedience to the King, and so unnecessarily added previously loyal Anglicans – lay and clerical alike – to the ranks of those alarmed by James' policies.[22] This would seem to imply that James was deliberately taking the 1680s Royal policy of 'State control' over political life to a new level. Close but Anglican advisers of long standing such as his brother-in-law Lord Rochester (Anne Hyde's brother) were encouraged to convert and sidelined if they did not.[23] James moved the anti-Dutch, pro-French ambassador to the Dutch, Bevil Skelton, to be ambassador to Paris and replaced him with the pro-French Marquis d'Albeville, who was in the pay of Louis' ambassador to England (Barillon), which arguably distorted his crucial group of 'foreign policy advisers' in a pro-French direction and ended his brother's even-handedness. Moreover, the creation of a new and specifically Catholic 'Cabinet Council' of the King's closest co-religionist allies, such as Richard Talbot, in his first weeks in power led not only to this body being called the real location of decision-making (probably inevitable in terms of Protestant fears of secret Catholic cabals) by his gleeful supporters such as Sir Edward Hales as well as by his foes.[24]

Recently Steve Pincus has analysed the King's policies in the administrative, political, religious, and even economic spheres in 1685–8 and seen them as a co-ordinated campaign of creating a centralised, autocratic state on the model of contemporary France.[25] Royal interference in long-established local autonomy extended to North America, where the disparate mainland colonies were to be brought under one central governorate controlled from London.[26] James, a patron of the Royal African Company in its (centrally-directed) colonial ventures since the early 1660s, also backed and strengthened the monopolistic position of the East India Company, now under its new 'High Tory' director Sir Josiah Childs, against any liberalising of trade to include new (and potentially Whig) merchants.[27] He was also lucky in the growth of customs revenues due to a boom in overseas trade in the early-mid 1680s, and was more actively responsible for a growth in revenues from the Hearth Tax by more efficient collection.[28] Overall Royal revenue rose by around a third in 1685–8, to around £500,000 p.a. – thus enabling expenditure on more tax-collecting bureaucrats and on a larger army.

James' allies also showed his lack of politic caution, and argued for his zeal for conversion, not just toleration. The Catholics who he relied on were enthusiastic zealots with little political realism, priests (e.g. Father Petre) or new converts (e.g. the Earl of Dartmouth) rather than the more cautious senior aristocrats of ancient Catholic families who were used to making themselves inconspicuous out of self-preservation and were thus against undue haste or provocation. Father Petre, James' closest priestly adviser, was regarded by all as keenly Francophile;[29] James naively tried to get the Pope to make him a Cardinal.[30] James was seen by international observers as being on Louis' side in his ongoing disputes with the Papacy, and under Jesuit influence. It was a return to the mistakes and bad luck of Mary Tudor, linked to the most aggressive Continental Catholics and to a power distrusted by the Pope. Both sovereigns had deep insecurities and were arguably thus less tolerant and clung to their faith, having lost a parent to political 'persecution' and been humiliated. James rid himself of loyal but cautious Anglican ministers whose presence would have reassured the majority community, such as Halifax in 1685 and his brother-in-law Rochester in 1687, and became trapped in a circle of committed Catholics who had a stake in his policies succeeding and told him what he wanted to hear.

Indeed, he declared that implementing policy in his brother's reign had been hindered by divided opinions in his Council and this should now be ended. Firstly Bishop Compton of London (December 1685) and then Archbishop Sancroft of Canterbury (autumn 1686) were thrown off the Privy Council in England, as was the Duke of Queensberry in Scotland;[31] French Ambassador Barillon commented that the King intended to remove all who would not obey unquestioningly from senior office.[32] Rather than seeking compromise and avoiding confrontation or inflammatory action on the contentious issue of religion, James even told his close ally the Earl of Dartmouth that he hoped to be martyred for his faith and that he would never dissemble.[33] This was of course in stark contrast to his brother, and pre-dates his gloomy statements about his role as a 'martyr' for his faith once he was in exile; he showed that he did not care if he failed as long as he had done his duty and tried to aid his co-religionists. He used the political skills of Sunderland and others to personally 'lobby' peers and MPs in favour of repealing the Test Acts, and – no doubt sincerely – argued that he was only seeking to grant equal status to all law-abiding, peaceful Christian denominations in his kingdom and thus was also in favour of more legal rights for the Dissenters. Crucially, those Lords Lieutenant or JPs who did not return sympathetic answers to his appeals for support for his religious measures were liable to be dismissed, which secured him the support of enough local office-holders who controlled the levers of power but ignored the fact that the new Royal nominees (often Dissenters and increasingly Catholics) had no strong support in their local communities.[34] It was no use having control of the machinery of local government if the men involved were not in possession of the support of their communities, as he found in autumn 1688.

James' alliance with those Dissenters who seemed prepared to abandon their position of the 1670s – political opposition to a strong monarchy and attempts to coerce the sovereign into toleration in association with the 'republicans' in the Whig agitation – was led by his chief 'contact' William Penn, the Quaker leader. It has been a major part of the arguments of his defenders ever since, showing his willingness to 'reach out' to men of differing faiths who his brother had abandoned to Anglican persecution. But Penn was far from having the support of most of his religious persuasion in working for a 'High Tory' Catholic King allied to the persecutors of the early 1680s, and was soon dubious as to whether James was moving too fast too soon in wanting laws formally repealed and so stoking up opposition; he and Father Petre became opponents over this.[35] By 1688 some thoughtful Dissenter leaders were coming to think that having toleration from James was no use if he was both suppressing civil rights and arousing majority Anglican hatred – the latter could rebound on them too. Some prominent Whigs and Dissenters who were approached to serve on the King's remodelled corporations or assist the election of pro-toleration MPs refused, preferring continued marginalisation to letting authoritarian Catholics share the new toleration.[36]

Some prominent Whigs refused to aid James' electoral campaign in winter 1687–8 as the King was the ally of reactionary Counter-Reformationary France and was thus a threat to Protestant Europe.[37] Most Whig pamphleteers – including Milton's nephew John Philips and the rising journalist Daniel Defoe – refused to have anything to do with James,[38] and in London the marginalised 'Exclusion Crisis' Whig leadership refused to work with him even if this meant guaranteed toleration for the Dissenters.[39] The exiled Whig ally thinker John Locke refused a pardon in order to return home, though at this point James' overthrow was far from certain; future moderate 'Whig' 1690s minister the Earl of Pembroke refused to help in return for toleration of his Dissenter protégés; and ex-Cromwellian advisers Colonel Richard Norton and Sir Charles Wolseley, now backers of toleration for Dissent, refused offers to join the Privy Council.[40] They clearly did not trust James and his priorities.

The Whigs mostly seem to have agreed with the view expressed by Lord Delamere, a future Williamite minister, that James would grant them religious but not civil liberty and so they could not trust him.[41] Civil liberty was the crucial issue for them, not least as many had defied their government over the issue of the succession in 1679–81; and James' use of the army and the law for outright intimidation outweighed his religious policy. By spring 1688 James and his advisers were aware of the hostile attitude of a majority of Dissenters, and were removing some from recently-granted offices.[42] This shows that his previous support was conditional, not based on immutable 'pro-toleration' principle. Indeed, even some English and Scots Catholics were to link up with anti-James plotting by Dutch envoy Dijkvelt in 1687, due to fear of James' link to the national enemy France. The leading Catholic in southern England's premier Catholic dynasty, Cardinal Philip Howard, loathed the Jesuits and opposed Petre's influence over the King, rather than being a 'cheerleader' for James' policies as might have been expected. Similarly, senior Catholics Lord Baltimore and the Duke of Gordon disliked and held aloof from the King and in autumn 1688 Welsh Catholic leader Lord Powis had his chapel spared by the Protestant London mobs as he hated the King's Jesuits. James' incaution thus kept him at odds with vital English Catholic figures who were his natural allies; he did not win support from even all his own co-religionists.

The King discounted the level of Anglican resistance to be expected too, assuming that their religious doctrine of obedience to the divinely-sanctioned Royal authority meant unquestioning acceptance of whatever he decreed. He seems to have misunderstood the nature of the doctrine, which when analysed shows belief in the inviolability of the Royal office but not necessarily of the man holding it. Some Anglican thinkers at least accepted that an imperfect King could be removed from power, as used to excuse abandoning James in 1688. By contrast, the inviolability of the King and demand for complete obedience in all circumstances was a mainstay of French Catholic absolutist thought, as preached by Louis' adviser Bishop Bossuet and supported by the Jesuits. James trusted in his ability to intimidate any opposition using the Royal coercive authority built up since 1681, which his enlarged Army and remodelled judiciary assisted. The 're-modelling' of local government and interference in the boroughs and counties that resulted was not new, having been carried out before to exclude Whigs in 1681–4, but now went further – and affected the Tory gentry and townsmen who had been the monarchy's allies on the first occasion. The Church was also threatened, with the attempt to ban 'inflammatory' Sunday afternoon clerical lectures – which James clearly saw as inspiring rather than reflecting intolerance of Catholics and Dissenters – leading to attacks on individuals such as John Sharp (later Archbishop of York).[43] At the time Sharp was rector of St Giles-in-the-Fields parish in London, a poor area of Soho affected by Irish Catholic immigration, and he cast doubt on the King's faction's promotion of Charles II's allegedly pro-Catholic writings as fakes; James ordered his superior Bishop Compton to suspend him from preaching and when he refused to do so without due legal process the King turned on Compton too and refused to accept Sharp's (limited) apology. He then set up a new 'Court of Ecclesiastical Commission' to use the Royal ecclesiastical powers without having to go through the (to his mind unreliable) bishops – thus returning to the issue of a 'prerogative' court, closed down by Parliament in 1641. Compton was suspended from his (ecclesiastical) powers and possessions to shut him up, with the King refusing to accept an apology. To the Anglican public mind, Compton was a 'martyr' not a defender of bigoted anti-Catholic preachers (as James' defenders then and later claimed).

General legal measures for easing the restrictions on the minority religious sects followed, using the legally dubious prerogative powers which had already backfired on Charles II as Parliament responded to the 1672 Declaration of Indulgence with the Test Acts. The first Declaration of Indulgence of April 1687 used 'Whig' political as much as religious arguments in explaining the need for and advantages of toleration, as a clever piece of 'spin' to maximise support.[44] But James' base of support was already narrowing by his own choice given his sacking of unenthusiastic ministers such as Rochester, he had finally closed the prorogued Parliament, and his heiress Mary and her husband William of Orange had given the 'thumbs down' to his proposal to abolish the Test Acts despite his sending 'Dissenter' leader Penn to ask for their support. Penn's pro-James stance was now (early 1687) being abandoned by most of the other Quakers. But James pressed on. Those Anglican clerics who resisted the support given to their Catholic rivals or the use of Royal legal powers for the minority religious communities were subject to harassment and intimidation that only made them appear to be martyrs. But the notion that James only wanted a 'level playing-field' to assist the peaceable enjoyment of their religion by all minorities – not only Catholics – from Anglican intolerance is dubious. At least the contemporary French observers close to his Court, such as Ambassador Barillon, reported that he repeatedly said his ultimate hope was the conversion of England to Catholicism though this would necessarily be long-term and due to the numbers of current Protestants might not be achieved by himself;[45] his most militant advisers were more 'short-termist'. When his heir was his elder daughter Mary, a Protestant (i.e., pre-June 1688), hopes concentrated on pressurising his next heir after her, her sister Anne, to convert.[46] Assisting the Dissenters and silencing anti-tolerationist Anglican zealots was a means to achieving this, not the desired goal.

Louis XIV used the Revocation of the (Huguenot-tolerating) 1598 Edict of Nantes and repression by his soldiery to convert his kingdom's Protestants, and James saw this as virtuous, if not the publicly embarrassing furore over the bloodshed.[47] In Ireland, he desired a monopoly of office for the Catholics rather than equality between them and Protestants – demographically just, possibly, but politically suicidal given the impact on English opinion. The Anglican Protestant landowner elite, loyal to the monarchy so not a threat to the Stuarts, had been left in charge by Charles II and the (numerically small) Presbyterian 'settler' elite of Ulster, who had mostly been anti-Stuart in the 1640s, and the Catholic landowners across Ireland who the CromwellIans had evicted from their lands had only partly been restored by Charles II after 1660. Neither were a viable threat to the Stuart monarchy as of 1685 – and even if James' abrupt 'swing' to including far more Catholics in the governing 'class' (the army's higher ranks in particular) was morally 'good' in ethical terms, it stirred up panic among Anglicans as well as Presbyterians. Was alienating the main base of Stuart support, which the canny Charles II had refused to do even after defeating the 'Exclusionists' in England and having a 'free rein', really wise? In Scotland James had already backed crushing the Covenanters and sacking lukewarm Royalist ministers before 1685, driving Argyll into exile under a death-sentence, and relied on the Catholic convert brothers, Perth (Chancellor) and Melfort (Secretary of State), both converted by Bishop Bossuet. His arguments had logic given the alarm caused to the government by the Galloway 'extremist' Covenanter rebellion in 1679, which showed their desire to coerce the government, and in his youth his elder brother Charles had been humiliated by the then governing Covenanter politico-religious faction (led by Argyll's father, who Charles had executed once he had the chance) as a 'puppet' King as he tried to lead Scotland against Cromwell's New Model

Army's republic in 1650–1. But, as in England, James went beyond governing with a 'firm hand' in his years as Charles' viceroy of Scotland in the early 1680s to ruling with a small clique and driving their opponents into exile – and he intensified this as King.

In foreign affairs, James appointed the pro-Jesuit Earl of Castlemaine (husband of Charles II's 1660s mistress Barbara Villiers) as his ambassador to Rome, an unfortunate choice given the Pope's attitude towards that Order which the Papacy currently regarded as being far too independent-minded and inclined to promote its own not the Pope's objectives. Either James was naively unware of the complexities of politics in Rome or he did not care, and possibly he was prompted (as in other matters) by his own, pro-Jesuit and pro-French Catholic chaplains. All this was clearly co-ordinated to boost the pro-French and pro-absolutist Catholic 'hard-liners', and equally importantly was careless of public opinion – with James probably thinking that his subjects should just 'obey orders' as their duty and that any quibbling was a sign of 1640s-style subversion. He had shared his family's traumatic experiences then, though not on the battlefield except for one trip to observe the battle of Edgehill as a nine-year-old in 1642 (he had been at the Royalist HQ in Oxford in 1642–6 and then interned by Parliament in London in 1646–8), but unlike his elder brother he had not learnt to be politically subtle and to plan his course carefully. The more people who used the opportunity of his toleration to convert to Catholicism the better, seems to have been his reasoning. But the evidence indicates that the number of people who took advantage of the revival in Catholic evangelism to convert was small. It was the perception of a 'wave' of conversions that mattered, and – as in the 1630s – the conversions at Court assumed an importance out of proportion to their numbers as did diplomatic relations with Rome. The revival of a church legal apparatus – the Court of High Commission – to enforce Royal policies on the Anglican clergy in 1686 caused complaints that Charles I's pre-1641 religio-legal powers were being illegally restored. This time, moreover, it was the majority religion not the minority 'sects' that was the target. The Court's 1686 prosecution of the obstinate Bishop Henry Compton, no doubt regarded by James as a bigot who needed to be made an example of, was particularly unfortunate in backfiring on the King. Compton's cause was seen as being that of the national church, under siege from Catholic proselytizing; and he even had substantial Dissenter support.[48] James made matters worse by this 'high-profile' reaction, as the Court did again in 1687 by prosecuting and expelling the Fellows of Magdalen College, Oxford for refusing to elect a Catholic President. The victims, legally at fault or not, were hailed as martyrs,[49] the Anglican Church rallied to them, and reportedly messages were sent to William in Holland requesting his urgent aid to save Protestantism from the King.[50] Nor was there merely 'paranoid' over-reaction to a few important but marginal cases. The impression of rising Catholic predominance in 'state institutions' was borne out by the fact that the percentage of Catholics in James' army was at least twice their percentage in the population and he actively introduced them into his Treasury Commission, the customs service, and the Inns of Court.[51] In modern Marxist terms, this was a classic 'march through the institutions' to secure control – or at least an aggressive and politically dangerous promotion of a feared minority.

Ireland was under the control of a Catholic Lord Lieutenant (Lord Tyrconnell, from a leading 1640s Royalist Catholic family) who was actively taking measures against the civic and legal predominance of the Protestant minority and creating a large Catholic army that could be used in England, ominously removing Protestant officers in 1687. It seemed that that nation was a warning of what James had in prospect for England. The 'high-profile' cases of legal action to promote Catholics to key roles in Oxford and Cambridge added to this. James now organised ruthless 'packing' of selection for the next Parliament by the King's electoral agents. This was led by Sunderland and headed by the Catholic lawyer Robert Brent. In retaliation to this danger of a Dissenter-Catholic alliance, Lord Halifax in his *Letter to a Dissenter* pointed out the unlikely incongruity of the Dissenters being able to trust the authoritarian, persecuting Church of Rome for long-term toleration and the threat of a political backlash from a resurgent Anglicanism to them on account of their alliance with the Catholics, warning the Dissenters that toleration from the Anglicans was a better long-term bet.[52]

The Dissenters had been recruited as Royal allies and arguments presented that the King was intending general toleration, and the political skills developed by the Whigs for their anti-James campaigns of 1679–81 were now being used on his behalf in alliance with the administrative and judicial structure erected by Charles after the Whigs' defeat. The 'threat' to the local powers and influence of the natural leaders of county society by the King's electoral agents in 1687–8 was particularly obvious. Resistance to the Royal interference in traditionally autonomous institutions, as most notably in the attempt to impose a Catholic Fellow on Magdalen College Oxford in 1687, was met with unhesitating use of judicial authority and evidence of popular support for the King's 'victims' was ignored. The King's tactics at Magdalen were typically crass and likely to stir up resentment; even if the Fellows were defying their legal sovereign's express wishes, it was provocative to choose the ultra-royalist Bishop of Chester to descend on the college on a 'visitation' and lecture the culprits on their 'semi-treasonous' insolence, and ambassador Barillon recalled that James boiled over with rage while telling him about the incident. It was not so much the anti-Catholic obstinacy that seemed to concern James as the personal insult to him; he saw rebels everywhere, though after witnessing the Civil War and having his father executed that was understandable. Moreover, once James had had his way and assorted obstructive Fellows had resigned and been replaced by Catholics he ordered the church's 'Court of High Commission' to investigate other colleges too, pushing ahead grimly with his plans no matter what the political cost. It is clear that James was far too optimistic about the mood of the country, too reassured by the confidence of his lay and priestly advisers, and too keen to discount all protests as minor and controllable incidents stimulated and magnified by his enemies. He clearly lacked the political skills and instincts of his elder brother and his grandfather, sharing his father's ability to alienate leading figures in local and national society.

The king's legislative and judicial 'onslaught' on Anglican predominance does appear to have proceeded in several distinct stages through 1685–8, each going further than the last in its methods, as analysed by J.R. Jones in *The Revolution of 1688 in England*.[53] It is not clear whether or not this was a matter of *'ad hoc'* arrangements or of a plan whose later stages were always intended to be implemented if circumstances proved favourable. James himself had no past record of being administratively-minded enough to have a coherent political 'plan' (though he had been a capable administrator of the navy as 'Lord Admiral' in the 1660s and had a talent for picking capable assistants, e.g. Samuel Pepys). So did he rely on a secret 'planner', and if so who was it – one of his priests, or the clever and devious 'backroom boy' ultra-Royalist politician Robert Spencer, earl of Sunderland? If there was a plan as such, notably it did not halt as opposition to James' new pro-Catholic activities rose – which shows that James, if not Sunderland, was concerned with 'doing his duty' (as he saw it) to aid his religion not with practical politics. Rising alarm at the evidence of the King's intentions was such that both the 'Tory' county grandees and gentry who had led or assisted Charles' assertion of royal power in the localities were mostly hostile to the King's plans by 1688.

Significantly, despite the long tradition of King and leaders of county Anglican society working together the answers to the King's electoral agents' 'Three Questions' of 1688 indicated that James would have to rely on Dissenters and pro-toleration 'Whigs' for support in enforcing his intended legislation. The government, using a network of legally expert and loyal treasury solicitors and other lawyers to investigate how best to 'pack' the next parliament with 'ground-level' visits to useful boroughs whose charters could be rigged and non-Anglican residents mobilised, showed a degree of skill which was similar to that (for an opposite political cause) of Shaftesbury's Whigs in 1679–81, but in vain. Halifax wrote that the only result of the King's campaign was to unite the disparate strands of local Tory/Anglican and Whig/Dissenter opposition against him, and ex-treasurer Lord Danby wrote that the government came to realise that it could only prevail against the majority of local opinion by force.[54]

Barillon and special French envoy Bonrepaus agreed that James had far too few supporters in the counties – none in some of them – to produce a compliant Parliament.[55] The King could not rely on his traditional local support to vote in favour of repealing the Test Acts and allied legislation, or to back the election of candidates pledged to do so. Though his new administrative agents were able to use local inter-factional feuds, offers to ambitious politicians, and a mixture of flattery and intimidation to secure enough 'loyalist', Whig, and Dissenter support to expect over 100 sympathetic new MPs' election in autumn 1688, this had been achieved by abandoning usual Royal supporters. It had also alienated the alarmed local 'power-brokers', Anglicans in particular and including powerful peers, and their anger added to existing alarm that the 'packed' Parliament would pass whatever legislation for arbitrary rule that the King intended. The contemporary measures in favour of Catholic political predominance in Ireland – which in fact restored influence to most of the population – and Louis XIV's 'dragonnades' actions against the Huguenots inflamed alarm at what that might imply. Similarly, though the leadership of the Anglican Church had not resisted the Declaration of Toleration in 1687 their reaction to that of 1688 was bolder – though James raised the stakes by requiring all the clergy to read it out in church in public. The latter now had to choose between obeying the King and standing up for doubts they might have as to the legality of his power to dispense with the legal framework prohibiting toleration. James' requirement for public reading of the document was a miscalculation of the amount of resistance he could expect. He ignored senior clerical appeals to be excused the onerous duty, and the amount of defiance, led by Archbishop Sancroft, did not cause him to back down. His personal meeting with the defiant bishops on 18 May 1688 led not to a politic Royal withdrawal of the orders but to angry accusations by him of rebellion.[56] Typically, James asserted that the bishops' defiance was worse than that of 'Puritan' preachers in 1640, bringing up the association of resistance to his authority and Civil War rebellion again. He seems to have believed that the Anglican clergy's persecution (at least to the extent of losing benefices and income, and in many cases their homes) by the victorious Parliamentarians in 1642–60, and the 'martyrdom' of Archbishop Laud, should have taught them to obey their King at all times, and that any failure in that regard was both ungrateful and treasonous.

The 'Seven Bishops' who had led defiance were charged with seditious libel, put in the Tower of London, and prosecuted in Westminster Hall with the full rigour of the law, enabling them to appear as martyrs for the national Church and make their case that the dispensing power was illegal. The strength of popular support for the Bishops and their stand,[57] testified to in contemporary diaries all over the country, should have given James a major warning, but he was intent on coercion. The judges failed to act as firmly on the side of the prosecution as could have been expected from precedent, attempting to arrange an acquittal on the less controversial grounds of legal technicality, and despite the evidence of popular support for the accused James ignored Sunderland's request to concede defeat and issue a pardon. (Even the subsequent Jacobite 'editor' and co-author of James' official *Memoirs* admitted that the King should have been more cautious in forcing the issue, though he wrongly blamed Sunderland for inciting him in order to ruin him.)[58] The jury's decision for an acquittal on 29 June was a public snub to James. The evident doubts of the judges – a category of officials usually Royal 'yes-men' – were serious to James' position and power, given the acquiescence that the judiciary had showed to the sovereign during the 1680s, and a sign of the intensity and scope of unease about his actions in the highest levels of society. With public opinion in the capital rejoicing at the verdict, the King could no longer doubt the extent of opposition to his supposedly innocuous attempt to enforce greater legal protection and public roles for the minority religions. Worse, there had been substantial Whig and Dissenter support for the Bishops[59] rather than their rallying to the King in support of toleration; the threat of arbitrary governance was clearly seen as more dangerous than that of Anglican intolerance. In retrospect the Whig pamphleteer Defoe reckoned that most Dissenters were repenting of their initial enthusiasm for James by 1688, and the writings of Richard Baxter and of less-well-known figures (e.g. Roger Morrice) show that they were uneasy at what the King intended.[60] Some refused to join in messages of public thanks to the King for his Declarations of Indulgence, and both the immanent rebel (and Tory ex-royal treasurer) Danby and later Jacobites reckoned the trial as having emboldened and united Protestant opposition to the King to think of revolution. Those Dissenters who had assisted James, e.g. Penn, were now snubbed by most of their co-religionists – which argues against the 'James the tolerant was a natural Dissenter ally' theory.

Greater caution was never that likely, owing to James' stubborn character and lack of his brother's political flexibility. As seen above, he deliberately relied on the advice of 'committed', contentious, zealous, politically isolated advisers from his accession. He marginalised some long-term associates whose attitude towards Catholic proselytization was unpalatable, e.g. his brothers-in-law Clarendon and Rochester (brothers of his late first wife Anne Hyde), and soon dismissed the staunchly monarchist but politically too moderate earl of Halifax, a subtle and skilful politician nicknamed the 'Trimmer' from his habit of shifting position to ally with the current dominant governing faction. Halifax was the arch-exponent of what would later become known as 'politics as the art of the possible' ; this was totally antithetic to the honest but domineering and inflexible James. Unlike Charles pre-1681, he did not bother to 'reach out' to as broad a base of political support as possible or to balance factions. Charles long tolerated powerful men whose advice he privately disliked, putting on a public 'face' of feigned interest, and was regarded as untrustworthy. The political question for James in appointments was whether someone was reliable – i.e., dedicated to assisting Catholicism and obeying controversial orders unhesitatingly. He preferred to rely on a narrow rather than a broad base of support – to him a circle of godly idealists committed to the Faith, to others a sinister cabal of Popish fanatics. Even within the narrow circle of the 'old' Catholic nobility, he sidelined some important but cautious (and anti-French) figures such as Cardinal Philip Howard, grandson of the Royalist Earl of Arundel (d. 1646), a former chaplain to Charles II's Queen and Grand Almoner of England, and a crucial 'go-between' in James' marriage to Mary of Modena. Indeed, the Cardinal had saved the proxy nuptials in Modena from collapse when a Papal dispensation failed to arrive. Howard, a senior adviser to Pope Innocent and resident in Rome, would have advised James to proceed more slowly had his advice been asked. Instead James relied on the less worldly or shrewd Father Petre, plus 'Tory' centraliser Sunderland who preferred to reassure the King than to tell him unpalatable truths. But the trajectory of Continental events – the revocation of the Edict of Nantes and then Franco-Dutch/German tensions – revived English fears of Louis and Catholics inopportunely for James. This was bound to revive fears of any English Catholic King, but James was safe as long as he maintained the support of the early-mid 1680s 'High Anglican' Royalists – which he threw away needlessly.

A toxic combination – the 'Seven Bishops' on trial plus the birth of a son to the King and Queen. But was this the 'final straw' for the opposition, or was revolt already intended?

The tension and sense of crisis in England was now ramped up to a new level by the mixture of politico-religious and dynastic crisis. Indeed, standing back to look at the events of June 1688 shows how bizarre the situation appears, and what a reversal of fortune it was from the 'High Tory' regime's stability under Charles II – the leadership of the Anglican Church on trial at the behest of a furious King, and the latter and his wife accused of passing off a changeling as their 'supposed' new son as organised by a sinister power-grabbing cabal of Catholics. The first event showed the King's lack of political commonsense; the second showed a situation of paranoia by his enemies plus an accusation of royal fraud that may have been deliberate 'fake news' but was believed by many of his subjects. Whoever invented the story of the King's 'son' being a fraud, they evidently gambled that it would be believed, possibly encouraged by existing rumours that Spring that the Queen was not really pregnant – and their story was duly taken up by many in the elite, even if 'believing' it publicly was one way of undermining a resented sovereign and helping to remove him. The trial of the 'Seven Bishops' coincided with the birth of a son and heir at St James' Palace on 10 June 1688, which presented the probability that James would be succeeded by a Catholic son, not by one of his Protestant daughters so those who were already alarmed by his manoeuvres would think that his regime would last into a second generation. Hence, plans to overthrow it received more support. The news that the Queen was pregnant had added a previously absent urgency to the fears of James' opponents since the previous November, as well as giving heart to Catholic proselytisers that they could have a second generation of Catholic kings and thus be able to alter English politico-religious policy permanently. But the pregnancy was not the 'surprise' start of a threat that the King would ensure that he had a Catholic heir. The danger of a Catholic heir (hence boosting sedition in an effort to prevent this happening by removing James) had already appeared and may have been due to James – in 1686 a document had emerged concerning a plan to persuade his younger daughter Anne to convert, though James insisted it was a forgery, and French Ambassador Barillon wrote that hope had not been abandoned of finding a Catholic heir.[61] Anne assured her sister Mary that she would never convert, so that might indicate a move by James in favour of the Catholic, half-French daughters of James' late sister Henriette-Louise, Duchess of Orleans and nieces of Louis XIV. The elder, Marie Louise (b. 1662), was married to the invalid King of Spain; the second, Anne Louise (b. 1669), to the French King's cousin and client the Duke of Savoy.

If Barillon was correct, the Queen's pregnancy and birth of a male heir may not have been as crucial to the downfall of James as they seemed in retrospect. Louis could not afford to see England and its resources pass to a hostile William (as Mary's 'Prince Consort or as King) when James died or was overthrown; he had every reason to press James to name a Catholic heir in place of his 'heretic' daughters. One of Louis' and James' mutual nieces, the daughters of the late Duchess d'Orleans, was a safer Queen of England for Louis than was Mary – and James' Catholic priests could be used to persuade him that his co-religionists would suffer if Mary became Queen. But the birth of a Catholic heir gave William a heightened role in England apart from his current long-term position as the political leader of the 'reversionary interest', the husband of the current heiress. The birth of a Prince would ruin his position of being able to count on English military aid against Louis once his father-in-law died. William continued to harbour Whig and Covenanter exiles, among them the talented propagandist Gilbert Burnet, and at the end of 1687 James ordered the English regiments in Dutch service to leave. (It was probably intended to shore up James' army in the event of a rebellion or his early death, as analysed by Maurice Ashley in his biography of the King.)[62] This would weaken William's army in the event of another war with France, though James had stayed scrupulously clear of diplomatic support for Louis and evaded French attempts to entangle him in an alliance ahead of the expected next conflict in Europe. Instead, James was doing his best to mediate in Louis' current dispute with Pope Innocent – and had apologised to Louis for the politically necessary official protests at the persecution of the Huguenots. It was in William's interests to exploit the anxieties that James' actions were causing and to make use of his existing political contacts in England. Much had been made of his earlier missions to England by his agents Bentinck and Dijkvelt as aimed at sounding out and encouraging dissent from 1685–7, but it is more likely that these careful examinations of senior aristocratic, church, and military/naval opinion had been mainly aimed at preserving William's wife's position ahead of her accession.[63] The future defector and later Duke of Marlborough, army officer John Churchill, used Dijkvelt's 1687 mission (which James feared was intended to stir up Parliament so he adjourned it quickly) to reassure William that Mary' s sister Anne would not accept any offers to convert to Catholicism in return for the succession. William was also encouraged against James long-term by hostile private correspondents such as his future courtier Henry Sidney (brother of the executed 1670s republican Algernon Sidney) and ex-Monmouth supporters, but he was too shrewd to accept the opinions of men who might have their own agenda and he used a wide variety of sources. Accordingly he now utilised the defecting naval officers Arthur Herbert and Edward Russell (both from major elite families) to contact old and establish new friends in England and sound out important people about the possibility of armed intervention, with the current Royal electoral campaign to organise a 'packed' Parliament for autumn 1688 providing heightened English provincial anxieties. It was also symptomatic of military opinion that few officers or men in the English regiments in Dutch service took advantage of James' orders to leave for home in March 1688, indicating their loyalties. Louis now began to fear that Sunderland was not loyal to James either.

The absence of a 'pre-emptive' French military campaign in the Rhineland in spring 1688 to enforce their claims to the Lower Palatinate (whose late ruler Charles had left his sister – Louis' sister-in-law – as presumed heiress) gave William the opportunity to plan an expedition to England that year. The expected crisis once the Episcopal Elector of Cologne died would also be likely to escalate into a French invasion, giving William the military excuse to intervene in England and secure its armed forces for his cause before this occurred. The date at which William decided on invasion is unclear, but seems to have preceded the birth of the Prince. S. R. Baxter in his biography of

William III (1966) dates the decision plausibly as having been taken in April, once William could be sure that the French were not going to attack the Rhineland that year.[64] William told Edward Russell in April of his intentions to invade in September 1688, if he was invited by men of sufficient standing – though these could only be provisional given the possibility of a distracting European crisis.[65] Indeed, the embassy he sent to London to congratulate the King on the birth of his son, led by Zuylestein, used the opportunity to contact William's potential supporters and co-ordinate the plan for an official letter to William from senior lay and religious figures – both Whigs and Tories – inviting him to intervene in England on his wife's behalf.[66] This was the necessary pretext for an invasion, as presenting him with a legal 'cover' and forcing senior figures among James' critics into a written commitment to the invasion which they could not back out of.

In the meantime, Mary sent a detailed list of questions to her sister Anne, as a witness of the Prince of Wales' birth, to find out if the Queen had definitely been seen to give birth and if a changeling could have brought into the birth-chamber. The answers indicated that fraud was extremely unlikely,[67] but this did not alter the political will to declare the baby an impostor. From the above evidence, it would seem that James had given enough indication of his plans to both parts of his alarmed Anglican elite and to William by June 1688 to trigger off plans for an invasion, even if the birth of a Prince was the 'last straw'. In a sense, the birth of James Francis Edward was an irrelevance as the decision to invade had already been taken. It was also supposed by opponents that if the Queen gave birth to a daughter or had a baby that died at birth (as on several previous occasions) the 'Jesuit plotters' at Court would quickly bring a changeling boy to the birth-chamber and claim that he was the King's son. Indeed, some doubted if the Queen was pregnant at all, and bizarre scenes took place as Princess Anne among others attempted to check that the Queen's swollen belly was real. Anne certainly chose to doubt the reality of the birth, and referred to mother and baby thereafter in abusive terms.[68] The chaotic scene at the traditionally public royal childbed enabled the 'opposition' to claim that the Prince was a fake smuggled into the room in a warming-pan, a fiction that many readily believed for political reasons in order to justify driving the baby out of the line of succession and making sure that in the coming coup Mary could be presented as the rightful heiress. An enterprising pamphleteer even drew up a plan of the Palace of St James' with a route from a side-door to the Queen's bedchamber helpfully inked in so that readers could see how the 'Catholic plotters' had smuggled the baby into the Queen's bed. Typically, James did not have the subtlety to insist that as many as possible Protestant peers and clergy (or even the bishops who were in the Tower) were brought to the Court to attend the 'lying-in' and birth, an event that usually took place in public in a large royal bedchamber, so that they were forced to admit that the birth had been genuine and the baby was the Queen's child – though they could still have gone back on this later.

The birth was duly followed by an escalating crisis as the appeal for intervention was made to William and his supporters launched a propaganda campaign urging members of the armed forces not to resist an invasion as if James was allowed to continue his present course and call a subservient Parliament he would enslave the nation to 'Popery'. At this point the Elector of Cologne died (24 May), meaning that a Continental crisis could be expected over his successor within months with his coadjutor and expected successor a French agent.[69] Following this, William recruited an exiled French Huguenot general (Count Schomberg) from service in Brandenburg, giving him a commission to command an invasion in mid-July. A force started to assemble in Holland. In September Louis sent an ultimatum to Emperor Leopold about evacuating Habsburg fortresses in the Palatinate which France required, and quickly launched an attack on the Palatinate fortress of Philippsburg on the middle Rhine – which reassured William that he would not be able to assist James that year.[70] But James' sluggish response to Louis' warnings about Dutch intentions gives rise to the seeming mystery of how and why he was caught unprepared. It led to French allegations that the reports were being suppressed and the King lulled into a false sense of security by the would-be traitor Sunderland – who seems to have expected invasion but not desertions, boasting that the Dissenters were loyal and the Anglicans would grumble but not act. The known political 'swings' of allegiance by Sunderland, who had started his career as one of the younger 'up and coming' Royal ministers under the pro-'Exclusionist' regime of 1679–81 before shifting tack to support Charles II's restoration of full Royal power in 1681–5 and was now a pro-Catholic enthusiast, were already a subject of hostile comment – and later he was shamelessly to work for James' replacements William and Mary too. Both pre-1689 and in the 1690s people had the worst interpretation of his motives – but his skill in self-preservation does not mean that he was so convinced of James' immanent fall that he was assisting this process. More likely he was caught unawares by the scale of defections in autumn 1688, even if he was already starting to distance himself from the obstinate King in case the latter was overthrown. The complaisant ambassador to Holland, D'Albeville, was also to blame – he believed William would attack France not Britain, and was then absent from his post on holiday during August. Only on 30 September did he warn the King that he was William's target.[71] The false rumours in Holland of a secret Anglo-French treaty to attack the Dutch (as in 1670) pushed the States-General into voting to back William's expedition, which would have been dubious had James managed to publicly distance himself from France

– another blunder by him. The French ambassador to the Dutch, D'Avaux, was warning London of a Dutch attack earlier; but James was annoyed at his boastful and inaccurate claim that an Anglo-French alliance existed so the King was unusually reluctant to follow D'Avaux's advice for these few weeks[72] – he feared D'Avaux was trying to 'railroad' him as an obedient ally. The same applied to D'Avaux's main English ally in The Hague, the pro-French Bevil Skelton. Indeed, D'Avaux was foolishly pretending to the Dutch that an alliance with James had been signed already – thus heightening their alarm.

At the same time, the warnings to James of 'leaks' by treacherous courtiers to William all came to him from French sources, so he could dismiss them as aimed at panicking him into falling into line with French policy; and they came through ambassador Barillon who was an ally of James' hard-line Scots Catholic minister Melfort and foe of Shrewsbury and Sunderland (who he reported to James, truthfully or not, for 'leaking' information to William). The first mention of a specific Dutch invasion was not made in official English documents until Admiral Lord Dartmouth's instructions of 1 (Old Style)/ 11 (New Style) October,[73] though it was already rumoured to be underway when diarist John Evelyn visited London on 18 (Old Style)/ 28 (New Style) September and James rushed back there from Windsor. Unknown to James, William was sent large sums of money from England before he landed to fund his invasion, amounting to some £200,000 in four to six weeks (a tenth of the kingdom's annual tax-revenues according to observer Daniel Petit in Holland).[74] Major contributors were rumoured to include the earl of Shrewsbury, a future secretary of state, and the ex-treasurer Danby (both among the famous seven elite signatories of the 'official' opposition invitation letter to William to invade), and John Churchill, along with Welsh magnate Sir Hugh Owen who apparently smuggled two chests of silver to Holland. James remained confident until the end of September that his son-in-law would never dare invade and took no steps against him or to investigate the possible disaffection among military and naval officers (currently being sounded out by William's agents). The most he would do is to stop Catholic officers in the fleet provocatively celebrating Mass on their ships to assuage naval discontent. Louis' warning to the States-General at the end of August that an invasion of England would be taken as a declaration of war on France only assisted rumours of a secret Anglo-French alliance. Meanwhile James told the French ambassador Barillon that he believed William's naval preparations were aimed against France and that the Dutch would not fight two enemies at once.[75]

Only on 30 September did ambassador D'Albeville specifically warn James that the naval descent was intended for England, although rumours of that were already sweeping through Whitehall as reported by Evelyn. Now James belatedly sought to win back support by issuing a general pardon and cancelling his intention to call the carefully selected Parliament. (The day that he issued these orders, 28 September, was nine days after William had heard of the attack on Philippsburg which enabled him to invade England.) A proclamation declared that he had no intentions against his subjects' religion or liberties and that William would submit Britain to foreign rule and prove a worse tyrant than Cromwell.[76] Sunderland's campaign of electoral intimidation was abandoned, talks were held with the alienated bishops, and efforts made to call up more troops and increase the army (which stood at about 40,000 men by late October). London was given its confiscated City Charter back,[77] in person by the humiliated Jeffreys. But all this was a case of 'too little, too late' though James did have a viable army of around 40,000 ready if it stayed loyal, and as William finally sailed for England at the end of October a series of events unfolded to unravel James' regime. The westerly wind presented William with some anxious moments as he sailed down the Channel, but an opportune shift in the wind to southwards enabled him to turn in towards the coast at Torbay. James arrived at Salisbury to be with his troops and ready to fight, but was famously unnerved and depressed by a series of nosebleeds.

Once William had landed safely at undefended Torbay on 5 November and got his troops, horses, and artillery ashore, the locals were still nervous of Royal reprisals as in 1685 and no important gentry or nobles joined him for several days. He was received by the Courtenays and was able to occupy Exeter, though its Bishop withdrew rather than stay to welcome him and he was short of money to pay his men or local recruits until the Earl of Shrewsbury seized Bristol at the beginning of December. By the time that the first major political figure, the veteran (pro-Monmouth) 'Exclusionist' Whig Sir Edward Seymour, arrived at William's headquarters the Prince was becoming impatient with English caution. Others followed and the Earl of Bath defected to him, securing his rear, but he told the new arrivals that they should have come sooner.[78] More rebellions now broke out, giving William an indication of widespread support that Monmouth had lacked. Danby, an important political player as chief minister in 1673–8 and the main Tory signatory of the invitation to William to intervene, secured York, Lord Delamere rose in Cheshire, and a coterie of nobles assisted the Earl of Devonshire in the East Midlands. Significantly the King was not attended by the local gentry in Salisbury and his new Secretary of State Middleton believed the gentry to be boycotting the King's camp and the common people to be antagonistic, which would have been the same even if James had been physically fit (instead of prostrated by nosebleeds) and willing to advance quickly. The King's only reliable supporter with a body of devoted Catholic troops, Tyrconnel, was in Ireland and no aid sent by him, via Liverpool, could reach the Royal army in time. With William advancing to Chard and his advance-guard as close as Sherborne, James accepted Feversham's advice to withdraw to a defensive line in the Thames valley rather than Churchill's to move forwards. Churchill may have been intending to defect anyway, and was rumoured to have planned to seize the King if he ventured away from his headquarters. James left for London on 26 November, and the main burst of desertions followed including Churchill, the King's nephew the Duke of Grafton, and his son-in-law Prince George of Denmark. The actual number of military desertions was quite small (around 2000?), but it was the identities of the deserters that mattered plus the perception that more could follow. By now Princess Anne had left Whitehall for Nottingham, and the King lost whatever coherence his cause still possessed and the military will to affect the outcome of events.

But the defeat of his cause did not entail his deposition, not least as William had found it politic to claim that he had come to save the Protestant religion and the nation's liberties not to remove the King. The summoning of a free Parliament was the centrepiece of his propaganda, and served to reassure the supporters of dynastic legitimacy that this was not a revolution aimed at usurping the throne. James, urged to summon this by the Church leadership in October to reassure the country, had temporised that he would consider it after the crisis was over although he did issue orders cancelling his planned 'packed' Parliament (27 September), banning Catholics from the next Parliament (21 September), closing down the controversial restored 'Court of High Commission' (5 October), restoring the cancelled City Charter of London (6 October), authorising the relevant bishop to restore the old Fellows to Magdalen College Oxford (11 October), and restoring the old cancelled corporation charters provided the replacements had not been fully legalised, i.e. 'enrolled', yet (17 October). He had thus shown his flexibility, albeit under pressure so presumably not convincing anyone that he was sincere. William's proclamation also promised the investigation of the legitimacy of the new Prince of Wales – though its outcome was politically inevitable, with Mary reinstated as heiress and so no Catholic to be the next king. William claimed that most of the nation's great men believed that the Prince was a changeling, showing the way in which anti-Catholic paranoia and mistrust of the King's motives had coalesced since the King had failed to deal firmly with the danger of this by 'managing' the Royal birth adequately. But despite the collapse of James' military and political position and loss of the initiative during November, the loss of his throne was still not an inevitability – and why he fled is an illustration of the priority of religion over commonsense that had ruined his strong position since 1685. Like his father in 1646–8, he had the opportunity to come to terms with his political neutralisation and serve as a figurehead for the coming government. Once he had returned demoralised to London he summoned an assembly of around fifty leading nobles and clerics on 27 November and was advised by his brother-in-law Rochester to call a free Parliament. On the 28th James issued writs for Parliament to meet in the New Year and a pardon to all defectors; he then sent an embassy (lords Halifax, Nottingham, and Godolphin) to William to learn the latter's terms. At Hungerford, William proposed what amounted to a mutual 'stand-off' by himself and James which left the initiative to the next Parliament. All proclamations against deserters were to be withdrawn and those arrested released; the City was to garrison the Tower and an appointee of William's take over Portsmouth (so the French could not land), and James and William were to withdraw thirty miles from London to wait for Parliament. When the latter met, the two were either to attend with equal numbers of guards or come unaccompanied. These terms were taken back to James on 11 December. But by this point the Lord Delamere's rebels had taken over control of Cheshire (the only provincial revolt to start before William had even left Exeter and so more risky), the Earl of Devonshire's rebels had seized Nottingham, and Danby's rebels had seized York while other lesser groups had seized most of the Midlands urban centres. The only coherent force likely to hold out – as closest to help from France – was at Portsmouth. In addition, the divided religious nature of the garrisons meant that the advancing rebels could usually appeal successfully to the Protestant officers to desert the unpopular (usually Irish) Catholic ones and come over to William – as Danby did with the officers at Hull.

William's main hope was, as Burnet told the Royal negotiator Halifax, that James would voluntarily leave the country.[79] By doing this, James would enable his son-in-law or his allied Parliament to declare that he had abdicated and justify removing him. As a final sign of his political ineptitude and lack of flexibility in an attempt to save his throne, James played into his hands. Given the national mood, the number of Royalist Tories who had abandoned the King at the first opportunity, and the near-universal dislike of the King's recent legislation, Parliament could be expected to take firm measures to secure the Protestant ascendancy and disinherit the new Prince of Wales, and William would have insisted on the latter. James decided to evacuate the child and his mother to the safety of France. On Sunday 2 December James duly told his queen's (Italian) Master of the Robes that the Prince was to leave London for France via Portsmouth on the 4th, which was duly done; the only other person to be told in advance was the French envoy Lauzun. The boy and his mother were in France before the invaders approached London and serious negotiations began. But giving way on the terms on offer in December 1688 would at best reduce James to a powerless figurehead of a regime headed by his son-in-law's nominees, on the lines of the 'regency' of William and Mary proposed as an option for 'Exclusion' in 1680–1. In fact he had already told Barillon that he was only negotiating to give his wife and son time to leave the country, and that he intended to follow them to France or go to Ireland. The Royal decision thus pre-dated the return of his commissioners from William's headquarters. There was no danger for William that James would stay in England and 'sit it out' to await a shift of popular opinion in his favour as the legitimate King. Unlike Charles I in 1648, the King was determined to leave his country rather than surrender to unwelcome political terms – a decision not only due to James' obstinacy but to the existence of a militarily strong government in France which was able to come to his aid, a factor absent in 1648. He duly set out for Louis' court and as he crossed the Thames from Whitehall threw the Great Seal (the royal 'stamp' authenticating his written legal actions) in the river, thus denying that sign of legality to his replacement. Unfortunately fate intervened in his escape-plans, denying him a grand exit as a 'martyr king' and landing him with a farcical one instead. He had fled London disguised as a girl in 1648; now he did so disguised as a sailor. Humiliatingly captured by local vigilantes looking for fleeing Catholics at Faversham, searched roughly by the locals who thought he was a priest, and placed under arrest at an inn, his spirits temporarily revived at his better-than-expected public reception on his return to Whitehall. Although his troops there were now declaring for William and Dutch guardsmen were arriving, making him a prisoner, he now considered staying to negotiate with William. Instead the Prince required him to leave London for his own safety as anti-Catholic rioting spread, and instead of going to the suggested Ham House (upstream near Richmond) he chose Rochester – a sign that he was now in favour of fleeing to France again. Anxious to be rid of him, William did not object or set strict guards on James' residence at Rochester and on the 23rd he was able to sail for France. It was typical of James' misfortunes that his three attempted or real departures from England in 1648 and 1688 were all devoid of dignity – the third time he only escaped because the son-in-law who coveted his throne allowed it.

Chapter 6

Early Hanoverian Royal Murders and Bastards

George I and his wife Sophia Dorothea: the strange disappearance of the Queen that never was

The quirks and unexpected dramas of Stuart dynastic history were never more evident than in the case of how the British ended up with the House of Hanover in 1714, as of the 1690s there were several remaining Stuart lines none of which were seemingly likely to keep them out. (Whether this would be the incumbent Protestant or another, Catholic branch of the family would depend on the fortunes of war as much as politics and genealogical accident.)

A most pressing political campaign at the end of William III's reign in 1700–02 was to ensure that the Stuart throne did not pass after him and his sister-in-law Anne, to a Catholic, be it his late wife Mary's half-brother James Francis Edward Stuart, the supposed 'warming-pan baby' of June 1688, or a more remote relative. James', Mary's, and Anne 's deposed father James II and VII had failed to restore himself to his British thrones by invasion from France in the years 1689–1701 and died in September 1701, though he had secured most of Ireland with a French army in 1689–91 and had also been recognised in parts of Scotland. William had forced Louis to recognise him as King of Great Britain in the 1697 Treaty of Ryswick, but the threat of an invasion led by France to restore the absolutist Stuart line expelled in 1688 had not gone away. William had never been popular in Great Britain, his far more acceptable wife Mary II (James II and VII's legal heiress if her half-brother was accepted as an impostor) had died young in December 1694, and English national opinion was sporadically active against the abrupt, asthmatic, and morose half-Dutch William throughout his reign. Nor was it clear how many members of the elite had kept in touch with the exiled Stuart court in France just as an 'insurance policy' in case they returned as opposed to actively plotting treachery; the ruthlessly flexible John Churchill (later Duke of Marlborough), William's best general but still mistrusted, was the most notorious of those who kept in touch with the exiled court. Once William III's nephew, Anne's son William, Duke of Gloucester, died aged eleven in 1700 the English political elite turned their attention to finding a Protestant heir to follow Anne – with the problem that most of her Stuart relatives were Catholics and/or connected to France.

The Act of Settlement of 1701, which came into operation as the Hanoverian Succession when Anne died on 1 August 1714, arranged contingency plans for the likely event of Anne, now thirty-six, not conceiving again following the recent death of her son, William, Duke of Gloucester, aged eleven. It transferred the throne of Great Britain and Ireland to the line of the youngest daughter of Charles I's sister Elizabeth of Bohemia and the Palatinate (1596–1662), excluding closer personnel who were all Catholics to prevent a repetition of James II's reign. Legally the next heir after James' excluded son by his second marriage, the supposed 'warming-pan-baby' fake Prince James Francis Edward was Anne Marie, the surviving younger daughter of the King's late sister Henriette Anne ('Minette'), Duchess of Orleans (1644–1670). She was however both a Catholic and married to a Catholic, the French King's cousin and client-ruler Duke Victor Amadeus of Savoy. Louis XIV, her ineffective father Philippe's dominant elder brother, had arranged this marriage to help tie Savoy to a close French alliance. The 'Winter Queen' Elizabeth of Bohemia, who easily outlived her two brothers Prince Henry (d. 1612) and King Charles I (executed 1649) and died at sixty-five early in 1662, had married Elector Frederick of the German Palatinate (Lower and Upper) in 1613, shortly after the surprise death of Prince Henry. The Palatinate family were the younger – Protestant – line of the House of Wittelsbach, Catholic sovereigns of Bavaria. In 1619 the rebellious Protestant population of Bohemia deposed their Catholic Habsburg sovereigns and invited them in as the new rulers. Frederick thus acquired a second Electoral vote in the college of seven Electors that chose future Holy Roman Emperors, increasing the number of Protestant votes and the chances of a Protestant replacing the long line of Catholics and ending the Habsburg grip on the title since 1452. They ruled but for one winter, hence the nickname, and were expelled by Habsburg troops the following year after the battle of the White Mountain; the Habsburgs' Bavarian allies then overran the Palatinate too. This crisis opened the Thirty Years' War, and there was fervent enthusiasm (if less financial generosity) in James I's final Parliaments in 1621–4 for organizing the reconquest.

Elizabeth, popular with the English as a Protestant heroine, mostly lived in Holland at The Hague and finally returned to England in 1660. Her second and third sons, Rupert and Maurice, had been active in their uncle's cause in the Civil War, following which they had to go into exile and Maurice ended up drowned in a Caribbean hurricane while serving with the Cavalier fleet. Her eldest son Charles Louis regained the Lower Palatinate on the Rhine in 1648 at the Peace of Westphalia as the Thirty Years' War ended, but Bavaria kept the Upper Palatinate on the Danube. He died in 1680, having broken up with his first wife (Charlotte of Hesse-Cassel) and remarried to his mistress Louise von Degenfeld, her lady-in-waiting. Their divorce would normally have been legal by Lutheran law as applied in the Palatinate, but Charlotte refused to agree to or recognise it so the legal status of his remarriage to Louise and of their surviving children (four sons) remained unclear. The status of the boys, though Protestant, was thus too shaky for the British government and elite to consider them as heirs in 1700–01. Charles Louis' only legally acceptable son was his offspring by Charlotte, Charles, who succeeded to the Palatinate in 1680 but died without male heirs in 1685; this led to Louis XIV's attempt to seize the state in the name of Charles Louis' daughter Elizabeth Charlotte ('Liselotte'), second wife of his homosexual brother Philippe of Orleans who was the widower of Charles II of England's sister Henriette Anne.

Elizabeth's second surviving son, the famous Royalist cavalry commander Prince Rupert (1619–82), had been next in line for the succession after Charles Louis and his eldest son. He had avoided marrying until his late middle age, although he was too busy campaigning in firstly the Thirty Years' War in Germany (where he was captured and spent two years in prison) and then in the English Civil War in his early adulthood when a marriage would normally have been arranged. Nor was he popular in England then, his depredations of Parliamentary towns in the manner of German warfare having won him the nickname of 'Prince Robber'. After his English service ended in 1645 with the fall of Bristol to the Parliamentarians he was a landless exile associated with a deposed royal dynasty and so he was no 'catch' for any ambitious European royal family, but after the Restoration in 1660 he returned to Britain aged forty and could have married had he so wished. He set up house as constable of Windsor Castle with two successive mistresses and eventually married the latter, the pioneering actress Margaret 'Peg' Hughes; she was an Irish Catholic and far his social inferior so he married her in secret to avoid political repercussions. Their daughter Ruperta was born illegitimate and so unable to succeed to the throne.

Elizabeth's younger sons were also dead by 1700, with Maurice having been drowned in 1652 and the impetuous Edward (1625–63) having married a rich Catholic Italian-French princess of the Gonzaga dynasty (dukes of Mantua) in 1645 and converted to Catholicism to please her family. Her parents had been based in France until her father inherited Mantua in 1630, and remained French in cultural and political orientation. Given the lack of prospects of the soon-to-be-defeated Stuarts in Protestant England and Scotland in 1645, the impoverished and landless Edward's decision to convert to Catholicism and settle at the aggressively Catholicizing French court is understandable, though it appalled his firmly Protestant mother and doomed any chances he had of a role in England after the Restoration. Edward's daughters then grew up in the staunchly Catholic orbit of Louis XIV's court and married Catholics too, and after the Restoration neither they nor their parents bothered with their English links. Sophia (born 1630), the youngest of the 'Winter Queen's' four daughters, was the only one still alive and Protestant in 1700 – two older sisters, the multi-talented linguist and philosopher Elizabeth (a correspondent of Descartes) and the artist Louise, were abbesses. Like Edward, Louise (abbess of Maubuisson in France) was a potential Stuart heir who had unexpectedly defied her Protestant mother and ignored the family's victimisation by the international Catholic royal elite by running off from their Dutch home in The Hague to become a Catholic under the influence of the French. Only Sophia had kept to her mother's Protestant links, and had married Ernest Augustus (born 1622), one of the contending princes of a minor branch of the ancient House of Brunswick in northern Germany who by a mixture of luck and shrewdness consolidated enough of his family's property into one state to have it raised to an Electorate (as 'Hanover') in 1692. (The House of Brunswick had once ruled Bavaria in the twelfth century before being dispossessed and fobbed off with northern German lands, so they had higher social pretensions than their amount of landholdership would normally entail – and they had been marital connections of the twelfth-century English kings.) Sophia's mother had first been approached for her marriage by Adolf Johann of Zweibrucken in south-western Germany, younger brother of and regent for Prince Charles who had inherited the kingdom of Sweden from his abdicating cousin Queen Christina and moved there in 1654. With him engaged in fighting across the Baltic world and trying to conquer and Protestantise Poland, Adolf Johann was ruling Zweibrucken for him and sought to marry Sophia in 1656 to link the principality to the larger regional 'power' of the Palatinate. But Sophia found him unattractive and only considered him reluctantly as she was ambitious to marry a ruling prince, and she soon changed her mind and persuaded her mother to call off the arrangements after a visit to the Palatinate court by George William (born 1624), one of the junior princes of the House of Brunswick, and his elder brother Ernest Augustus (born 1622).

At that point George William, third of the four sons of the late duke George of Calenberg (died 1641), a part of the sprawling north German complex of Brunswick principalities who was himself a younger son of Duke William of Luneburg (died 1592), was heir to the duchy of Calenberg after its current incumbent, his brother John Frederick (died 1665). Ernest Augustus was lined up to inherit the lesser title of (secular) prince-bishop of nearby Osnabruck, an episcopal principality within the Holy Roman Empire ruled successively since the Reformation by secular Protestant princes nominated by the Emperor; the 'bishopric' was only a legal title now that the principality was Lutheran not Catholic in religion, and did not entail any episcopal duties. He would only succeed to the more prestigious Calenberg if George William was transferred to another of the family's duchies (which he was to do in 1679 when he inherited the duchy of Celle).

George William was a better prospect than his brother, and Sophia duly fell for him and persuaded her parents into accepting an engagement. On a tour of Italy, the bridegroom had second thoughts and decided that he preferred the lifestyle of his bachelor status. He then persuaded Ernest Augustus to take his place and apply to marry Sophia in his stead, and agreed a formal document with him to be shown to her mother and eldest brother promising that he would never marry so either his own Calenberg (usually known as Hanover from the main family residence in that town from 1636) or the other family duchy of Brunswick-Grubenhagen would pass to Ernest Augustus and his heirs after him – assuming that their other two brothers did not have male heirs either. (This did in fact happen, consolidating the family lands in the hands of George William and Ernest Augustus, but as of 1658 it was a risk to assume this.) That improved his brother's landed and princely prospects, and Sophia and her family duly agreed the new arrangement; the various sub-states of the Brunswick conglomerate were smallish and divided but the family were descended from the major medieval dynasty of the dukes of Saxony, as evicted by Emperor Frederick 'Barbarossa' in the mid-twelfth century. The marriage took place in September 1658, though the bride's ex-fiance George William kept away as it would look bad taste for him to be there after he had jilted her and his brother John Frederick boycotted it, presumably annoyed at having the destination of the family duchies signed away behind his back.[1]

The marriage of Sophia and Ernest Augustus was reasonably affectionate and settled by the standards of the day in Germany, when princely marriages were usually arranged for diplomatic reasons of alliance and nobody expected anything more than a practical arrangement let alone any romance, and it duly produced six sons (all of whom survived to adulthood) and one daughter so it was successful in the matters that counted in that era. Ernest Augustus inherited Osnabruck in 1661 as arranged so they had appropriate social status in the status-obsessed world of petty German royalty, though by the mid-1670s Ernest was having an affair with the married Clara Elizabeth von Meysenbug (eighteen years younger than Sophia), wife of his eldest son's tutor/ 'governor' Count von Platen, whose daughter, born in 1675, was generally accepted as his.[2] The affair apparently distressed Sophia but as was usual she kept her mouth shut and did her best to be pleasant to the new '*maitresse en titre*', who at first extorted large amounts of presents from her lover and showed them off in public but eventually lost her grip on him as his energy and health declined and he came to appreciate his wife more.

Sophia and Ernest's eldest son George Louis, the later King George I of Great Britain, was born on 28 May 1660 – ironically, coincidental to his mother's cousin Charles II's restoration to the throne which he would inherit. The machinations of the large Brunswick family to constantly rearrange the succession to its various territories and try to consolidate them in one branch or the other, combined with the vagaries of its dukes and princes ending up with morganatic marriages (i.e. ones that were not of sufficiently acceptable social status to enable their male offspring to inherit the father's territories by German laws) or without sons, made it probable that George would be married off within the family to advance his parents' dynastic ambitions to consolidate their own territory. A marriage to another royal German candidate, or even one further afield, was however possible – and in any case a marriage of incompatible and strong-willed people could lead to disaster, as was to happen to him in the event, though the spectacular and apparently violent outcome to it was unusual for an era and social milieu more used to private pain and public 'cover-ups'. The pieces started to fall into place ahead of Sophia's visit to Italy with her husband and his brother John Frederick in winter 1664–5, when her husband arranged for her to take along in her suite a new, French Huguenot lady-in-waiting, Mademoiselle Eleanor d'Olbreuse. This beauty had previously been in the suite of the Italian Princesse de Tarente when the latter visited Hesse-Cassel in central Germany and met Ernest's other brother George William, who apparently fell for her. Ernest had Eleanor invited on the Italian tour, possibly in order to keep her apart from his brother and so diminish the danger of him marrying her and providing an heir who could inherit his lands, but instead Mlle d'Olbreuse turned down the invitation and went to the Dutch United Provinces for the winter instead – where her lover appears to have joined her. Their affair became serious, George William was determined on marriage despite the gulf in their respective social status that meant that his family and other social equals might not recognise their marriage, and when his and Ernest's brother Christian Louis, duke of Celle, fell dangerously ill both George William (who did not bother to reply to his sick brother's request for him to come and see him) and John Frederick claimed Celle after him.

John Frederick arrived to find that Christian had just died and tried to seize Celle though their father's will had proposed that George William, as the elder, have the free choice of Celle or Calenberg/Hanover after Christian. A war was threatened and Ernest put troops at George William's disposal; in the end John Frederick agreed to take Calenberg/ Hanover, plus Grubenhagen which George William detached from Celle and gave to him as compensation. The latter paid off Ernest for his help with the lordship of Diepholz, but he also persuaded his brother to agree to him marrying Eleanor d'Olbreuse – provided that it was made clear that this was a morganatic marriage so any son of theirs could not inherit George William's lands. These would now pass to Ernest Augustus – and as in the event George William inherited Celle in 1679 and passed Calenberg/ Hanover to Ernest, when George William died in 1705 his lands all passed to Ernest and Sophia's son George.

The marriage of George William and Eleanor only produced one child, daughter Sophia Dorothea in 1666, and the latter was to be married off to Ernest and Sophia's son George – with the engagement keeping the potentially tricky George William 'on side' to stay allied to Ernest's branch of the family. (It was still possible that the latter might overturn the morganatic status of the marriage and try to make it fully legal if he had a son, in order to pass on his lands to the latter.) This provided the future George I with his disastrously unsuitable wife, but also had the problem that his mother and no doubt many of the courtiers regarded the offspring of a scandalous morganatic marriage to a 'social climbing' ex-lady-in-waiting as beneath her husband's dignity as a rising North German prince of an ancient family and they were ready to treat the bride with hostility.[3] George William also made one abortive attempt to marry off Sophia Dorothea outside the immediate family, namely to the heir of the head of the senior Brunswick-Wolfenbuttel branch, but he died at a siege in 1676 before this was finalised. There was an ongoing risk that George William's provocative church marriage to Eleanor in 1675, which he had persuaded the Emperor Leopold (fount of dynastic law in the Empire) to approve, meant that he could now claim that any sons they had were fully legal – and pass on his lands to them, accepted by the Emperor, whatever he had promised Ernest and Sophia. In that sense Ernest's inheritance of Calenberg/Hanover from his brother John Frederick, who died suddenly at Ulm in Bavaria en route to Italy in December 1679, at least gave him and his family a stronger position from which to influence or bully George William into keeping his promises.

The Prussian ambassador to Calenberg/Hanover, Sponheim, now endeavoured to suggest a marriage between Sophia's eldest son George Ludwig and the English James, Duke of York's second daughter Anne (four and a half years younger) in 1679–80, at a time when it was not certain that Anne's elder sister Mary would be childless. The suggestion may have originated with James' cousin, Sophia's brother Prince Rupert. Sophia sniffed that Anne's late mother Anne Hyde, daughter of Charles II's minister Lord Clarendon (previously Sir Edward Hyde) was too low-born for such a marriage, but George did visit London during a tour in late 1680 after the Estates of Calenberg/Hanover had sworn formal allegiance to his father. He met Anne, apparently backed by her sister's husband William of Orange (who presumably wanted his sister-in-law tied to a fellow-Protestant to decrease her Catholic father's influence). He suggested palming Sophia Dorothea off on George's next brother, Frederick Augustus (1661–1690), to be sure of keeping Celle in the family.[4] The envoy from Anne's stepmother Mary of Modena's homeland heard that Anne was in love with George, but the plan was not followed up; possibly a veto from

Charles II was why it was abandoned.[5] It was supposed by later writers that either Anne rebuffed George and he had a dislike for her family and her country ever afterwards, or that conversely George rejected Anne and that was why she would not have any members of his family in her country even when they were her definite heirs (after she passed the age for child-bearing with no living children) and preparations for the future would have been logical.[6] There was some contemporary gossip to that effect about a distinct coldness between them dateable to their encounter in 1680, e.g. Bishop Burnet's account – but no agreement on who had been rebuffed and was most hostile or why. These seem to be searching for a personal and romantic explanation for perfectly explicable attitudes – George was cautious, wary, and undemonstrative by nature but not necessarily consumed with grudges towards Anne or England, and Anne (like Elizabeth I) did not want to be side-lined in her lifetime by people flocking tastelessly to court her heirs. It is also possible that the marriage was not seriously discussed during the visit, as he was empowered to listen to any suggestions but not to make any formal reply, and that doing this was left to his parents who chose not to pursue it as his Celle cousin was a more useful 'catch'. He later wrote to Prince Rupert's wife Peg Hughes in 1682 that he would have been honoured if Anne had chosen him but no proposal was made while he was in London.[7] A subsequent visit by George and his parents to the capital of Brandenburg, Berlin, saw talk that their target was the 'Great Elector' Frederick William's daughter Martha, but nothing came of this – probably due to her ill-health and unlikelihood of having healthy children. Instead George's clever and cultivated sister Sophia Charlotte (born 1668), 'Figuelotte' in her admiring mother's letters and later a famous patron and correspondent of the philosopher Leibnitz, was married off in 1684 to the Elector's son and heir, Frederick (later King Frederick I of Prussia so she acquired a crown too).

It was arranged in September 1682 that George would marry his paternal first cousin Sophia Dorothea, daughter of his uncle George William, in order to strengthen his claim to succeed her son-less father in his part of the Hanoverian family dominions (the duchy of Celle), as part of his parents' plan to consolidate all of the latter in their own immediate family. Given his father Ernest's obsessive desire to consolidate the family's domains and increase their status (soon to be rewarded with an Electorship in 1692, putting them in the front rank of Imperial princes), marrying George to Anne in 1680–1 would have meant abandoning the means chosen to fulfil the Celle annexation plan. This was possible and arguably would have saved George from a horrendous marriage to a wayward and impulsive girl alien to his dour character, but was unlikely as then Sophia Dorothea would have had another husband who might claim Celle backed by her devious father. At the time, indeed, there was no sign of disaster to come as George was reportedly very pleased with his bride and fancied himself in love with her, though he was a dutiful son and close to his mother and this would have been expected of him. Sophia certainly thought her son in love, or so she chose to put out in her (generally accurate and honest) private letters as assessed by George's modern biographer Ragnhild Hatton.[8] The marriage took place on 22 November 1682, and both George's parents and his younger brothers seem to have been pleased with Sophia Dorothea with his brother Charles Philip (1669–90) professing himself to adore her – and ending up accidentally introducing her to her future lover Count Konigsmarck, the man at the centre of the first royal Georgian murder mystery.

The supposedly happy couple had the expected son and heir, George Augustus (later King George II of Great Britain), in December 1683, shortly after the baby's father's return from the epochal Imperial campaign that saw the Ottoman Turks pushed back from the gates of Vienna for the final time. A daughter, Sophia Dorothea, followed in 1687. But Ernest now set the cat among the family pigeons by announcing that instead of dividing the lands he had accumulated among all his sons, as was the Brunswick family tradition, he intended to keep them in the hands of his eldest son and the younger ones would be paid to renounce all their claims, in writing and legally binding. This was only sensible as it had taken great efforts plus much luck in the form of elder brothers dying without sons to form the new 'state' of Hanover, which was to be recognised as an Electorate by the Emperor in 1692 and so enter the first rank of Imperial vassals; Brunswick had long been kept weak by its large dynasty and regular divisions of lands among many heirs. The larger and more successful German states, e.g. Bavaria and Saxony plus now Brandenburg, were those who had either stopped or minimalised the practice of joint inheritance by several sons and had gone over to primogeniture. Now Ernest's second son, Frederick Augustus, who had the best hopes of a substantial landed share of the family lands after his elder brother under the old dispensation, was to be bought off with a large sum of money – but he refused to co-operate, tried and failed to persuade his mother to help him, and then went off to seek the aid of the head of the elder branch of the dynasty in Wolfenbuttel, duke Anthony Ulrich. The latter did not want his junior cousin Ernest establishing a larger principality than himself plus an electoral title and backed Frederick, and Frederick went off to join the Imperial army in the ongoing war to reconquer Hungary from the Turks and to earn the Emperor's goodwill too. A breach with George followed, and when Frederick died on campaign in 1690 his next brother Maximilian (born 1669), who would now be in line to succeed to whatever lands Frederick had expected to gain under the old arrangements, withdrew his previous acceptance of the 'primogeniture' plan and defied his father and elder brother too. Maximilian also dabbled with other German courts, especially Wolfenbuttel, to stir up sympathy and had more backing from his mother than Frederick had had; and in February 1692 his father put him under house-arrest.

This was the unpromising background of family tension to the breakdown of George and Sophia Dorothea's marriage, and by 1686 Sophia Dorothea (who had accompanied her husband for the first part of the 1683 campaign which was a sign of a good relationship) was said by her lady-in-waiting to have tired of her husband.[9] Possibly she found the domestic routine of the court boring when her husband was away fighting the Turks for the better part of every summer in the mid-late 1680s and she had to play second fiddle to her powerful mother-in-law. Though George was dutiful and probably not as dull as legend had it, he was never the sort of character to appeal to a restless young woman used to attention and stimulation, and his later manner of life suggests that he preferred a quieter domestic lifestyle than she did. George was probably also the first of the pair to take a lover, namely his future long-term mistress and probable morganatic second wife Melusine von der Schulenberg, a lady-in-waiting to his mother – and tall and thin enough to be nicknamed 'the Scarecrow' by Sophia in her correspondence and later to be known as 'the Maypole' when she accompanied George to England. Their first child was born in January 1692 so the affair was underway by spring 1691, and by this time Sophia Dorothea was having a secret correspondence with a dashing Swedish officer in the Hanoverian army, count Philipp Christoff von Konigsmarck. He had been introduced to her, innocently enough, by his fellow-officer Charles Philip, George's younger brother, in 1689; but the latter had since been killed in action in Hungary and Sophia Dorothea had kept up the correspondence. There was a connection through Konigsmarck's family with his admirer's family, as his sister was married to another Swedish officer serving her father George William and Sophia Dorothea knew her. Presumably a mixture of boredom and a desire to be daring and do something that her husband's disliked parents would find horrifying inspired her, along with his charm and flattery, but it was not until 1692 that they were known to be having an affair – and she was also having rows with her husband in public and then staging petulant sulks. Possibly, as in other more recent failed royal marriages, she was hoping initially to win her husband round to taking more notice of her by playing 'hard to get' and misjudged his reaction; he was embarrassed at the scenes and retreated to his far more placid and agreeable mistress, to whom he would be faithful for over thirty years. Ironically, George and Sophia Dorothea's son George (II of England) was also to stray from the marital bed but in a similar manner, to only one woman at a time – and his wife Caroline was to handle this more cleverly than her mother-in-law did and keep her marriage viable. The English gossips thought later that George (I)'s other close companion, Sophia Charlotte von Kielmansegg, later Countess of Darlington and nicknamed 'the Elephant' from her size, was also a mistress but in fact she was his half-sister, Ernest's illegitimate daughter.[10] The affair between Sophia Dorothea and Konigsmarck proceeded from her giving him permission to write to her from campaign but her not replying in (probably) July 1690 to clandestine meetings, probably not yet adulterous, when he came to Hanover at the end of that year's campaign. Most of their letters, which they sent for safe-keeping every six months to his sister Aurora von Konigsmarck, have survived and George's biographer Ragnhild Hatton reckons that there is no sign in their flirtatious tone of actual physical relations until March 1692. Sophia Dorothea was however to insist throughout her life that she had not been unfaithful, though she might have 'offended' her husband – and she sought to make her admirer write to her more often by telling him that George was writing more frequently than him. At the least she and her admirer were soon fantasizing about a future life together in ardent tones and anticipating this, whether or not it was initially a fantasy; as the contemporary social 'mores' of German high society valued discretion above all else a secret lover who was not generally known was a different matter for a royal princess to planning to run off with her admirer and so humiliate her husband and his family.

The main problem with Sophia Dorothea's affair to George's ruthlessly worldly parents and their advisers was that the evident attraction and strong flirtation (if not worse) between the pair was seen in public in 1692–3 and increasingly talked about, and for a newly-appointed Elector who had just climbed to this much-coveted post and was no doubt still resented by his rivals as an 'arriviste' this would be even more insufferable than usual. Apparently Sophia Dorothea was warned to at least show more discretion by both Sophia and Ernest, plus George's sister on her visits from Berlin, and Konigsmarck was warned by George's surviving brothers, his fellow-officers. Marshal Podevils warned him that he was being watched. The presumed lovers ignored them, and Konigsmarck turned down potentially invaluable offers of marriage from local nobles on behalf of their daughters – one from his lover's future nemesis, Ernest's senior aide Count Platen. He then proceeded to blame the latter's wife, Ernest's mistress, for hindering his career and his access to Sophia Dorothea in revenge for his turning down her daughter – and it is logical that the Platens were indeed stirring up Ernest and George in revenge, though Konigsmarck's conduct was already legally treason by committing adultery with a royal. When George was away on campaign Sophia Dorothea made excuses to leave the Hanoverian royals' main palace at Herrenhausen and her in-laws' surveillance, either (supposedly) because her admiring brother-in-law Maximilian was lodged too near her apartments for propriety in her husband's absence or because her parents needed her back in Celle. These were just excuses, as George warned her he was aware in a letter that has survived.

But the pair had their own problems, as their letters show that Konigsmarck was from time to time madly jealous of the attentions that Sophia Dorothea showed to other male admirers (was she trying to make him feel insecure?) and she did not have any money independently of her parents for them to live on if they did run away together. Konigsmarck, extravagant and heedless of financial caution, was up to his ears in debt and expected her to finance their new life, but she could not get money out of her parents in a hurry as he wished and they disapproved of her affair and would not help her. Her mother refused to sell off her jewellery to fund the lovers and clearly wanted the embarrassing business to end.

The prospect of some income to live off however finally appeared in late spring 1694, as Konigsmarck's old commander in the Netherlands campaign in 1691, Augustus of Saxony, succeeded his brother as Elector there and the Swedish count went there to reclaim his substantial (gambling) debts from Augustus to be offered a regimental command instead. He accepted, and the couple made plans for their elopement with Konigsmarck resigning his military post in Hanover to take up his new command. The visit to Saxony is also supposed to have included Konigsmarck, over-confident and indiscreet, sneering about his foe Countess Platen (apparently repeating gossip that she was a spendthrift who bathed in milk) and about the unattractiveness of George's gangling mistress Melusine von der Schulenberg, and these and/or other stories found their way back to Hanover and enraged Ernest and George. The latter was alleged to have confronted his wife about her affair and had to be pulled off her by the servants. Somehow the couple's plans to elope seem to have reached the ears of George's parents, and drastic action was duly planned at the end of June 1694 as the count returned to Hanover to wind up his affairs there before leaving for good. What is not clear is if George knew what was going on and if his departure for Berlin, apparently to discuss the embarrassing crisis with his sister and brother-in-law, just before the resulting showdown was a sign that he did not know the crisis was about to come to a head or whether his parents 'got him out of the way' so as not to involve him. It is still not clear if he knew what was going to happen, or suspected it and was content to be able to claim ignorance if it came out; either way, he showed no objection to the subsequent plan for his divorce that followed his wife's entrapment.[10] Sophia wrote to a friend after the dramatic denouement of the crisis that George was still in Berlin and had no idea of what had just happened, but this may have been a 'cover-up' to protect his reputation.[11] Was it his idea to get his wife's lover out of the way permanently, or that of his parents? Did the latter (or George) not have any clear idea if Sophia Dorothea would have the 'impudence' to cause a scandal by running away with her lover, and so 'set up' a scenario where they could see if she intended to do this on Konigsmarck's return to wind up his affairs in Hanover – and then catch her out?

On the night of 1/11 July 1694, Konigsmarck disappeared – apparently during a late-night assignation at the 'town palace' of the Hanoverian royals, the 'Leine Schloss' in Hanover. It was unusual for any of the royal family to be there in the summer as they usually preferred Herrenhausen with its gardens, so was the fact that Sophia Dorothea had refused to join her mother-in-law out at Herrenhausen as planned and stayed at her apartments in the Leine Schloss in town a warning sign to Sophia and Ernest of an impending elopement? In fact Konigsmarck had arranged his affairs with his household in Hanover for his departure for his new regiment in Saxony (currently stationed in the Rhineland for the current Anglo-Dutch-German war with Louis XIV) on the 5th (Old Style)/ 15th (New Style), so he was not planning to 'bolt' with his lover that night. But he had not started putting his affairs in order or even paying farewell calls on his fellow officers in Hanover by the time he disappeared, contrary to his usual sociable nature, so this would have warned George's parents that he was up to something. Ernest arrived at the Leine Schloss contrary to his usual practice of joining his wife for the hotter weather at Herrenhasuen, and was supposedly sick in bed when the drama occurred. The story that got out to the Danish envoy Otto Mencken, accurate or not, had it that the interception was the work of the revenge-seeking Countess Platen, who had planted spies outside the palace to see if the adulterous count turned up and who duly informed Ernest when he did. On the night of 1/11 July Konigsmarck was seen entering the palace and making his way to Sophia Dorothea's apartments where she was in residence. According to her lady-in-waiting Eleonore von dem Knesebeck, who had acted as 'go-between' and put her mistress' letters secretly in Konigsmarck's hat and gloves for him to find, he did not reach the princess – and she was interrogated harshly by Ernest's aide Count Platen (complaisant husband of the Elector's mistress the Countess, so one of the trusted inner circle) and threatened with torture to make her confess the truth about the affair.[12] It is apparent that Konigsmarck was intercepted, and as he was never seen again it is virtually certain that he was killed – but whether this was a deliberate assassination planned beforehand to punish and silence him and 'cover up' the disgraceful affair is unclear. The intention may have been to capture and imprison him in secret on 'state security' charges, as was within the Elector's legal rights, but he resisted and was killed trying to escape – or this may have been a convenient excuse for a 'hit'. The head of the elder branch of the Brunswick dynasty, Duke Anthony Ulrich of Brunswick-Wolfenbuttel (his court being a possible destination for the lovers if Sophia Dorothea sought his aid as Ernest's disinherited second son had done), heard from Danish diplomat Otto Mencken that four armed courtiers had intercepted and stabbed Konigsmarck to death and one 'Montalban' had been the killer. This was probably derived from court gossip in Hanover that reached the Danish embassy and some historians have doubted it, but it has been discovered that an Italian courtier called Don Nicolo Montalbano, usually known as Montalban, who had been with the court since 1672, was given an unusually large grant of 150,000 thalers by Ernest a few weeks after the disappearance. This was ten times the annual salary of a highly-placed courtier, so a 'pay-off' for doing some secret great service to the dynasty would seem probable and the date implies that this is likely to have been connected to the Konigsmarck affair; it was also to be paid by quarterly instalments which implies both a need to keep its huge size carefully hidden and an incentive for Montalbano to keep his side of the bargain so he would continue to be paid. The other courtiers involved according to Mencken's source or sources were one Von Subenvol, a member of Ernest's equivalent of the English royal 'Privy Chamber' and married to his illegitimate daughter; Von Klencke, a senior member of the 'Chamber'; and the head of the household of George's son George Augustus, Freiherr von Elz. All were senior courtiers on intimate terms with the dynasty's males, and ideal for a 'hit squad' – be it murderers or kidnappers – brought in to protect the family's reputation by eliminating a 'loose cannon' who had betrayed and could disgrace his employer. According to Mencken, Konigsmarck's body was weighted down and thrown into the nearby river in a sack; in any case, it was never found. After George moved to England in 1714 courtier Horace Walpole (son of the 'prime minister' from 1721–42, Sir Robert Walpole) heard that Konigsmarck was secretly buried within the palace grounds; but his source and its reliability are unknown.[13]

With Konigsmarck disposed of, Sophia Dorothea was confined to her apartments and persuaded her panicking lady-in-waiting Eleonore von dem Knesebeck not to flee as that would be taken as a sign of guilt. She may have hoped to brazen it out, but a search of her apartments discovered compromising letters from Konigsmarck and both were interrogated, Eleonore by the ruthless royal aide Count Platen. Ernest and his brother George William, Sophia Dorothea's father, agreed that a divorce was necessary rather than trying to carry on with the marriage as if nothing had happened and forcing the miscreant wife to put up with it, a more normal course for the dignity-conscious world of the small German courts. Covering up the affair and pretending that the marriage was rescuable would have made gossip less so it was more advantageous, but evidently they – and George – could and would not trust Sophia Dorothea again. The divorce – allowed under Lutheran law, though for future reference this was not so easy in English law so George's divorce would be legally questionable for a future Supreme Governor of the Church of England – was to be on the grounds of Sophia Dorothea's unreasonable behaviour, i.e., refusal to cohabit with George. The two rulers, Ernest and George William, acting as heads of the family and as fathers of the two parties involved, agreed that Sophia Dorothea would be confined by her father in his territory, her children would be removed from her permanently and put in their father's sole care (much criticised by modern writers as cruel and spiteful but normal for the era as the father was the legal head of the family household), and Sophia Dorothea would be given a small annual income of 8,000 thaler for her expenses until her father died. (This then rose to 12,000 thaler per annum thereafter.) Sophia Dorothea was removed under armed guard to the remote country town of Ahlden in her father's territory and shut up in the local '*schloss*' – technically a castle, but in fact a country estate with extensive grounds so she was not that harshly treated or imprisoned in a gloomy medieval stone prison as some English writers later assumed. George also promised her father in writing not to make her imprisonment harsher once the latter was dead, which he kept to, and he allowed her to keep the income from various estates which came to her on her father's death in 1705. He was scrupulous and only vindictive in terms of her separation from her children, and by contemporary 'mores' a woman 'tainted' with adultery and trying to run off with her lover was morally polluted and not fit to be given access to children who she might influence to the detriment of their morals. She was allowed out for hunting expeditions under guard, but not allowed visitors without her father's and later her ex-husband's permission. Indeed, she was not told the terms of her divorce and subsequent treatment until it had all been agreed (in legal documents drawn up by her father and uncle in Hanover); then she was presented with a '*fait accompli*'.[14] Nor was she ever allowed to see her children again, and it is well known that George had all portraits of her removed from his homes and did not wish her ever to be mentioned in his presence.[15] The psychological effect of this on his children was not something that would occur to or bother a conventional ruling prince of that era, though it probably accounts for some of his son George II's peculiarities of character and must have added to the resentment of his father's strict control of him which was to break out into a political as well as personal breach in England in 1717. But although George II apparently ordered his mother's portrait to be put up again once he was king and able to do what he liked, he seemingly changed his mind about his mother's innocence shortly afterwards – allegedly after reading 'closed' letters in the royal archives at Hanover attesting to her adultery. A few years later George's notoriously gossipy court memorialist John Hervey testified that George, like his father, never mentioned Sophia Dorothea.[16]

The disappearance of Konigsmarck caused a great scandal at the time and as would be expected both his employer-to-be and old commander Elector Augustus of Saxony and his well-connected sister Aurora von Konigsmarck made extensive and futile enquiries at the Hanoverian court. This embarrassment for the Hanoverian royals might be used to argue in favour of any killing being by accident, as it was potentially as damaging for them to have rumours circulating of a secret murder and 'cover-up' as it would be to have a live and angry Konigsmarck free back in Saxony trying to get his ex-lover released from custody and possibly revealing the details of their affair to embarrass her captors. (It would also embarrass Sophia Dorothea who would be exposed as a 'slut' to the censorious world of the European nobility and royals – but it would humiliate George too.) But in terms of strict political reality, nothing could be proved of the adulterous affair if both guilty parties and the victim stayed silent, and with George keeping quiet about the background to his divorce and Sophia Dorothea – unstable and capricious so capable of embarrassing outbursts – locked up out of public sight, silencing Konigsmarck meant that only rumours could emerge. The Hanoverian court maintained a wall of silence though it led to stories that the new Elector and his son were thugs who resorted to murder like uncivilised medieval barons, Sophia did not write to her usual correspondents for some weeks (presumably to let gossip die down) and then blandly claimed that she had no idea what had happened to Konigsmarck, and the potential witness Eleonore von dem Knesebeck was shut up in the fortress of Scharzfels (for alienating George's wife from him, which was a reasonable charge given her past role) to keep her quiet. Eventually the scandal was largely forgotten, beyond a general air of unsavouriness that followed George's reputation for the rest of his life as he was assumed to have been more of a major active participant in events (murder included) than may have been the case.

The incident was however useful propaganda for his foes, and given the bad feeling between Wolfenbuttel and Hanover over Anthony Ulrich's opposition to the creation of the Electorate of Hanover and Augustus of Saxony's patronage of Konigsmarck these two were able and willing to use the episode to stir up anti-Hanover intrigue. Once Elector Ernest died in 1698 and George was Elector intrigue and resentment centred on him, as the man who had had his wife locked up and her lover murdered, although luckily for him the requirements of international diplomacy meant that once the 'Great Northern War' (Sweden vs Denmark, Russia, Poland, Saxony, and Brandenburg) broke out in 1700 Denmark needed Hanover as an ally and ceased its hostility and in 1706 Saxony did likewise. As from 1701 Sophia and her son were heirs to the British thrones so the Hanoverian royals had 'great expectations' in international power politics and those keen to win their goodwill could not afford to annoy them, especially foes of Louis XIV with whom Britain, the Dutch and much of Germany was at war. The efforts of Sophia Dorothea's mother Eleanor d'Olbreuse to defy her husband and brother-in-law and win backing for the disgraced princess' release, e.g. from Queen Anne who was now at odds with her unwanted Hanoverian heirs, had no useful results. Nor was Louis, obsessed with French and Catholic priorities, prepared to help Sophia Dorothea escape and seek refuge in France as her friends suggested to him – and he would only receive her if she converted to Catholicism first. To make matters worse, although the 'loose cannon' Eleonore von dem Knesebeck, her ex-lady-in-waiting and confidante, managed to escape from her prison at Scharzfels and went 'on the run' across Europe she did not help her ex-mistress but accused her of using her, spending her money on clothes, not giving her faithful assistant enough to live on, and causing her ruin. She even tried to offer her goodwill and services to George and his mistress Melusine von der Schulenberg with flattering (not to mention grovelling) letters, no doubt hoping for hard cash, but was ruthlessly ignored.[17]

But George's past life was to assume a new importance after he came to the thrones of Great Britain in August 1714 and people began to wonder what had happened to his wife, and visitors to court noted that she was never referred to. Contemporary gossip, made the most of by George's Jacobite enemies, made the most of the rumours about the collapse of his marriage and the fates of Sophia Dorothea and Konigsmarck, and as a major Jacobite invasion and rebellion was unsuccessfully launched in 1715 the scandal of George locking up his adulterous wife was a useful weapon to use against him. Some Jacobites even referred to Sophia Dorothea as 'Queen of Great Britain' to embarrass her ex-husband and a party of Scots even tried to gain admittance to the *'schloss'* at Ahlden to see her in a surprise visit in 1718. On a more practical level, the possibility arose of foes of the House of Hanover like Charles XII of Sweden, a noted adventurer and military gambler, trying to rescue her; and when her daughter, the Queen of Prussia, tried to negotiate her release in 1725 via the mediation of Count of Bar it was Sophia Dorothea who refused to co-operate as she expected any settlement to vindicate her conduct in 1694 and so cancel the divorce. This was unacceptable to George, and the 'Queen that never was' stayed in custody until her death in 1726.

Rumours of princesses' royal bastards – and the unsavoury case of the death of the Duke of Cumberland's valet. George I's son Prince Frederick – illegitimate? Or was this just a case of exaggerated parental alienation?

George II has often been written off down the centuries as if not exactly a figure of fun at any rate a man of limited intellect and even more limited political ability – although it cannot be denied that he was also honest, honourable, and unpretentious. He had a sense of duty, he led his troops in battle in person

(Dettingen, 1743) as the last British monarch to date to do so, and he was usually content to leave political matters in the hands of his more capable ministers whom he learnt to trust (especially Walpole in 1727–42). Famously, when he unexpectedly came to the throne after his father George I – normally in good health and only sixty-seven, his mother having lived to eighty-four – died suddenly on a trip to Hanover and his first reaction on being told (in bed at Ormonde Lodge, Richmond) was to think it was a ruse by his father to test his reactions.

When he believed the story he told his informant Sir Robert Walpole, his father's chief minister since 1721 – who had abandoned the Prince's own Whig faction for the chance of resuming office under the then King in 1720 – to take his orders from George's own favoured candidate to be First Lord of the Treasury, the more loyal but less able or inspiring Spencer Compton (Earl of Wilmington). This was the latter's chance to show what he could do and cement his role permanently, but he did not live up to the occasion and could not even put a suitable accession Privy Council meeting address together. He had to ask Walpole for help, and the latter was able to show the new King that he was a more reliable and assertive chief minister. After the King's initial snub to Walpole he repented of it and let his wife Caroline of Ansbach (a junior branch of the House of Hohenzollern of Brandenburg/ Prussia), who had a better instinct for politics and appreciated the 'first minister's ability, talk him into keeping Walpole on. But this has seemed an early and typical instance of George being a blustering, 'hasty' buffoon lacking in brains or political intelligence and his wife really ruling from behind the scenes.

The mystery and misunderstandings over whether it was George II rather than George I who really gave the crucial boost to the growth of a system of 'Cabinet government' headed by the 'Prime Minister' (then only a nickname, not an actual part of the political or legal terminology) by withdrawing from politics after 1727 has now been explained by more careful examination of contemporary official papers to add to the gossip (much of it from hostile, pro-Jacobite sources) on which earlier dismissals of the first two Hanoverian kings were based. George II was more flexible in politics than he appeared, and his boorish remarks to and snubs of his long-suffering wife plus his unapologetic suspicion of the liberal arts have won him few modern admirers, but this was more of a matter of personal 'style' than serious policy. These were after all semi-private remarks made in the intimacy of his family plus a few trusted senior courtiers, not official 'policy' – and George II's Anglicised household had more surviving (English) memorialists than his father's German one. It was clearly important to him to be seen to be master in his own house, and this and embarrassment at his own intellectual and cultural limitations no doubt led to prickly assertions of his power and snubs to his wife. But he was not a complete philistine despite his preferring stirring military music and straightforward portraits to anything complex, and he was after all the patron of Handel if not at all well-read like his wife (a regular correspondent of the philosopher Leibnitz) or as musical as his elder son and his daughters (who played musical instruments for pleasure, as shown in a famous portrait). The tradition post-1660 of royal patronage of major musical figures based at Court, usually centred on the Chapel Royal with its organists, continued – though the post-1714 monarchs lacked a major English-born musical genius of the stature of Henry Purcell or John Blow under the last Stuarts, this was hardly his fault.

The worst that can be said was that George lacked the aesthetic appreciation of other North German royal figures such as his sister's son Frederick 'the Great' of Prussia – but the latter's father Frederick William, the 'Sergeant-Major King', was far more brusque, petty-minded, and officious than him (and treated his son worse). George's 'bark was worse than his bite' and despite his authoritarian private behaviour to his family and his façade of bad temper and pomposity he had the sense to recognise and rely on Caroline's brains. Due to this he accepted her judgement of trusting in Walpole. Thus despite his greater knowledge of and potential for involvement in British politics than his father – and his aggressive character – his accession did not see him reversing George I's '*laissez faire*' attitude to British political life.

This was the era when the King was ceasing to attend Cabinet meetings and was leaving the day-to-day business of politics and administration to his ministers, though they still remained 'his' ministers, chosen and replaced by him at will and not usually being appointed or dismissed (or resigning) '*en bloc*' as a 'government' headed by or seeing themselves as solely responsible to the First Lord of the Treasury. A complete 'clear-out' of a ministry when its leader died or was sacked was the exception rather than the norm, with the sharpest breaks in continuity coming at a monarch's decease when their successor wanted to put their own people in charge as in 1714 – but not in 1727. The old assumption that the first king to cease regularly chairing Cabinet meetings or taking a close interest in governing was George I and that he did this as he could not speak English is a myth. His modern biographer Ragnhild Hatton has shown that George could speak a little English, though he preferred to speak or write French, and most of his senior ministers could do the latter so there was no new 'communications problem' in Cabinet and George also continued to chair some, if not all, Cabinet meetings during the mid-late 1710s.[18] It was George II who ceased to attend Cabinet meetings, which he had been doing as Prince of Wales while on good terms with his father in 1714–17, after he had a major row with his father, left Court and was forbidden to return for three years, and went into political 'opposition' as patron of a faction of Whigs opposed to the ministry in 1717. The Prince did not resume Cabinet attendance when he belatedly made up his quarrel with the King in 1720 and remained at odds with the then ministry and with that of Walpole until 1727, and for most of this period the King trusted Walpole to look after his interests in Cabinet and did not resume attending either. When George II came to the throne he usually left matters of government in Walpole's hands too, though he would very occasionally attend Cabinet meetings on matters in which he had an interest (foreign or military affairs). In any case, he was often away in Hanover. There was no 'convention' at this point that the King stayed out of politics as a matter of principle or of propriety, merely a lack of interest in it and general reliance by George on his successive 'chief ministers' to manage things for him. So it was as much Walpole's efficiency and trustworthiness as the legendary 'German kings who could not speak English' that led to the monarch leaving the Cabinet to run its own affairs. But George II still kept an effective veto on who was to be in office, such as William Pitt the Elder in the early 1740s after the latter had made his name opposing the subordination of British foreign policy to Hanoverian interests and the angry King kept him out of office for several years despite his potential use to the then government. It was difficult (but not impossible) to get George II to face political reality and accept an unwanted minister because of their political 'weight' in the Commons, as with Pitt who he finally accepted in 1746. Nor could he force a restoration of his trusted foreign policy 'fixer' Lord Carteret to office on the Pelham ministry in 1746; he was forced to stop taking even unofficial advice from him by their ultimatum as he could not do without them in office due to the number of MPs and peers supporting them.[19] This if anything marked the King having to 'take a step back' from front-line politics, if only temporarily until PM Henry Pelham died in 1754 and the King could arrange a new ministry on easier terms. It was quite within the (unwritten and fluid) 'constitution' of the time for the King to take a greater interest in politics or attend Cabinet meetings and put forward proposals should he so wish, though the consternation and criticism when his grandson and successor George III proposed to take this attitude and start to direct his ministers in the early 1760s, after a lapse of over forty years in this, shows that the mid-century political elite had become used to managing without Royal interference.

The fact that George II treated his heir Prince Frederick with as much suspicion and intolerance as his father had treated him could be put down to a mixture of heredity and an unconscious resentment of the person who would succeed him and so reminded him of his mortality, but it was probably made worse by the physical separation between them that followed George I's accession when the latter left Frederick in Hanover. (It was up to the King as head of the royal dynasty what happened to his grandchildren as well as his children, under English law; when George I quarrelled with his son he insisted that the latter's non-infant daughters lived with him, not with their parents.) The same applies to the fierce and at times vicious resentment that Caroline, normally a more open-minded person, showed to her elder son, who aroused her loathing in terms that were gleefully recorded by contemporary Court diarists. Some of Caroline's outbursts indeed even suggested that she regarded Frederick as so loathsome that he was unfit to be King, and one or two remarks plus other 'evidence' from the time of his birth implied that he might have been illegitimate, i.e., not the King's son – though this is extremely unlikely. Was this talk just her exercising a fantasy whereby she could have Frederick excluded from the throne, and releasing her private dislike of him this way? Modern psychologists could have a field day with analysing why she reacted to her son in this way, and it is possible that this reflects her own insecurity as a child – when she had lost her father early and (aged ten) been pitched into the embarrassing and even dangerous situation of her mother's failed second marriage to the unstable and potentially murderous Elector John George of Saxony. Also, the orders of George I to have Frederick left in Hanover in 1714 caused a thirteen-year separation between Caroline and her son, and she seems to have viewed her next boy, William (born 1721), as her favourite instead – making the best of a situation which she could not remedy? Personal trauma could lie behind this unusual behaviour.

Possibly the behaviour and failings of George and Caroline as parents have seemed worse mainly because their private outbursts were recorded and published, mostly by her close adviser Lord Hervey, an assiduous mischief-maker and gossip, unlike with the family quarrels of earlier generations of monarchs. Their eldest son Frederick's spendthrift habits and open populism probably also annoyed her as being feckless; she had had a very emotionally and financially insecure childhood, losing her father at a young age and being taken off by her mother to Saxony when the latter married its ruler John George (who was suspected of trying to poison her).[20] This danger ended with his death in 1694 and the accession of his brother Augustus – which as seen above also led to the final crisis in the relationship of George I's wife with Count von Konigsmarck and the latter's disappearance. Caroline then ended up as the protegee of George I's highly intelligent and competent sister, the Queen of Prussia, and was recommended by her to marry into the Hanoverian dynasty; her parental problems and hard lessons about human nature probably meant that her son's rakish insouciance made her angrier than if she had had a good experience of a louche court like Saxony. Frederick was born on 20 January 1707 by English reckoning, which was 1 February by the 'Gregorian' Calendar in use on the Continent which the English duly adopted in 1752. The private nature of the birth was unusual for courts of the era, where gossip about stillbirths and the placing of suppositious babies in beds to pretend that an heir had been safely delivered (with or without the use of warming-pans as with 'James III's' birth in 1688) was rife, and considering what had happened at St James' Palace in 1688 there was thus a chance that should a 'political' case appear later for Frederick's disinheritance this private birth and the resultant gossip that he was a 'fake' and a changeling (added to by jokes about his not resembling his parents and being 'dark-skinned' like his grandfather's Turkish attendants) could be used by his opponents.[21]

The latter would include his parents by the time he was adult, and their open preference for his younger brother William (born 1721), later Duke of Cumberland, opens the possibility that this scenario could actually have played out after the final rupture between parents and elder son in 1737. According to the memoirs of her confidante Lord Hervey (who was admittedly by this point an enemy of Frederick's), she once told the latter as she spotted Frederick outside her window that she wished the earth would swallow him up and send him to Hell; after his own theatre eclipsed his father's favourite one in the Haymarket she allegedly said his popularity made her vomit. Indeed, by the time that Caroline was dying she was apparently refusing to see her elder son again despite his frantic appeals, or at best refusing to do so as it would send the King, who did not want him there and accused him of intending to show off his insincere 'devotion' to the public, into a rage. She was recorded as saying that one advantage of dying was that she would never have to set eyes on him again[22] – which was extreme even for the era and a notoriously dysfunctional royal family.

Was Frederick's parents' loathing and the apparent gossip about his birth serious enough that George II could have taken up the cause of disinheriting Frederick as a posthumous tribute to his wife and her low opinion of him? He only officially declared him heir in 1747. The private nature of the birth in 1707 was however probably due to its being unexpectedly soon – Caroline apparently went into labour in the middle of dinner – and arrangements for senior Hanoverian courtiers to come to the birth-chamber and witness it not being in place or simply to the shy Caroline not wanting them there. At the time, the fact that Frederick did not physically resemble his parents was noted and gossiped about, and the boy was nicknamed 'the Griff' which was a West Indian term for a 'half-caste', which may have been a joke but was open to later claims that one of his grandfather's Turkish attendants was the real father. There was no sign of any antipathy towards the boy on the part of his parents in his early years, although as was usual for an eighteenth-century warrior Prince the new father took little interest in Frederick or indeed in his growing brood of daughters either. But when George I inherited the British thrones in August 1714 he chose to invite his son and daughter-in-law plus grand-daughters to come to live in England, while insisting that the seven-year-old Frederick should stay behind in Hanover and be educated there.[23] This reassured the citizens of Hanover that they had not been abandoned and kept a family 'presence' at the late Electress Sophia's grand palace of Herrenhausen and the smaller, older 'Leine Schloss', but it meant that the new Prince of Wales and his wife saw nothing of Frederick for the next thirteen years although George I did meet him when he regularly visited Hanover. This presumably helped to create a barrier between the boy and his parents, and when his younger brother William was born in England in 1721 he was treated with notably more affection and enthusiasm and emerged as his parents' favourite. This raises the possibility that if George II and Caroline had been determined enough they could have planned to have William, the future 'Butcher Cumberland' of the 1746 Jacobite massacres, declared heir to the British thrones and kept Frederick in Germany to rule Hanover – but this potential royal drama never played out.

Royal bastards or just gossip?

Case 1, Princess Amelia

The case of the violent alienation between Frederick and his parents – extreme even for the notoriously feuding fathers and sons of the House of Hanover – seems more likely to owe its explanation to psychology and political 'choices' than to any serious chance of Frederick being illegitimate. The gossip about his appearance and possible father at the time of his birth in 1707 was probably no more than just that, and the same can be said for the equally unlikely rumours that met the patronage that his equally talented and artistic sister Princess Amelia (1711–86) showed to the prolific mid-Georgian composer Samuel Arnold. Born in London in August 1740 from an ordinary middle-class background, registered as the son of Thomas Arnold, this eminent and popular but now forgotten composer was musically educated as a chorister at the Chapel Royal (the main unofficial 'training school' for both singers and composers in the country and an invaluable source of future connections in a precarious career where patronage by the elite was essential for those not possessing independent means). Later the first English writer of operas (the era's dominant composer Handel being of German birth and background), Arnold was clearly a man of initiative and ability with new ideas and by the mid-1760s was the first resident composer at the capital's leading theatre for musical productions, Covent Garden. A pupil of the organist John Blow and due to his Chapel Royal background in a situation to be 'talent-spotted' by older musicians and well-heeled patrons at a young age, he was taken up as a protégé by Amelia. She was an unusual figure in the deeply conventional world of the rigidly traditional and hierarchical Georgian court and was clearly not afraid to risk censure, though no more so than her elder brother Frederick who had deeper musical interests and connections and indeed set up his own theatre in the West End. The chances of the oft-cited story of Amelia being Arnold's mother being genuine are extremely unlikely, and the contemporary gossip in London 'High Society' about why the socially insignificant Arnold was patronised by the Princess gave no specific details of who the father was supposed to be. Nor can it be traced to a definite or trustworthy source. It probably owed its origin to mystified and sometimes spiteful speculation about why the unmarried Princess – whose lack of a husband was unusual for the era, though shared by her shyer and less robust sister Caroline – was taking an interest in a man with no 'connections' young enough to be her son. Given the contemporary secrecy about what went on at the royal court and its restricted social 'milieu' with the King (and until she died in 1737 Queen Caroline) jealously guarding their daughters, rumours were bound to spread.

The most that can be said is that the bold and unconventional Amelia was the sort of young woman who would attract rumours, and her capability in performing music (in a small family 'ensemble' with her elder brother and sisters, as shown in paintings commissioned by Frederick) showed her to be something of a 'maverick'. She was also a first-class rider, unusual for princesses of the era, and was allowed to go hunting which became her passion; she rode astride rather than using the conventional and more decorous 'side-saddle' manner at times, which was seen at the time as scandalous and a sign of woefully 'forward' lack of feminine modesty (and potentially damaging to her reproductive ability). Worse, she even wore breeches rather than the usual long and cumbersome riding-habit dresses, and although her manner of riding was probably safer for her and helped her to keep up with the men in the hunting-field it no doubt led to spiteful remarks in her social circle about her being a 'hoyden' who lacked decorum and was capable of anything. By the late 1720s court memorialists were writing that she spent most of her time out hunting or in the stables grooming her horses. She was even said to turn up at church on Sundays in her riding-gear, another major breach of social convention, with a dog under each arm.

Her initial lack of a husband at the usual age for engagements was however not her doing, as her aunt Queen Sophia Dorothea of Prussia (George II's sister) wanted to secure Amelia for her own eldest son Frederick (1712–86), later 'the Great' of Prussia and the age's foremost warlord. As unconventional as Amelia and as fond of the tough and masculine world of cavalry officers (though based on warfare rather than hunting) and also artistic and a skilled flautist, Frederick would have made a challenging but possibly compatible husband for Amelia – and given that he was more fond of men than women, neglected his wife, and was probably homosexual he would have been unlikely to make many sexual demands of her. The second part of the planned Hanoverian/Prussian 'family compact' was to be for Britain's Prince Frederick to marry Sophia Dorothea's daughter, Wilhelmina. But at this point (around 1725–7) although George I was in favour, Sophia Dorothea's obsessive 'control freak' martinet husband King Frederick William (d 1740) was not, and he was a brutal and headstrong petty disciplinarian who made George II look reasonable. A highly capable ruler and the creator of Prussia's war-winning 'military machine' but also deeply eccentric and a collector of giant soldiers to enrol in his personal regiment of guards and drill happily on the parade-ground for hours on end, the King of Prussia was not in favour of his wife's plans and 'sat on' them. The same problem of a 'veto' occurred when the idea was revived in 1729 as an alternative to Frederick of Prussia's then planned engagement to Elizabeth of Brunswick-Bevern, the niece of the Holy Roman Emperor Charles VI's wife. This time the Imperial court in Vienna preferred to see Elizabeth married to Prince Frederick of Great Britain instead as part of an Anglo-Imperial alliance and so tried to insist that this occur and Frederick of Prussia marry Amelia; but Frederick William prevented this by rushing through the Frederick/Elizabeth marriage.[24]

After this several minor German princes offered for her hand, but she was uninterested in them and her parents let her turn them all down; she remained at her parents' court where she was rumoured to be having affairs with several of her male friends from the hunting 'field'. One of these was the powerful political 'fixer' and 'borough-monger' Thomas Pelham-Holles (born 1694), duke of Newcastle and secretary of state from 1724–54 – and then 'Prime Minister' (ie First Lord of the Treasury) after the death of his brother and political partner Henry Pelham. More serious stories, but still only by inference, linked her to Charles Fitzroy (born 1683), second duke of Grafton, grandson of Charles II and former (1724–7) Lord Lieutenant of Ireland, a socially 'grand' but politically minor figure who seems to have spent most of his time based away from 'High Society' on his family estates in Suffolk (where he was Lord Lieutenant of the county for over forty years). Both her alleged lovers were much older than her, so was she looking for a 'father figure' less curmudgeonly than her own father? She apparently disappeared for hours on end with Grafton during hunting, away from any chaperones, though this could be a natural desire for some privacy after life under minute observation at court. Once during a hunt at Windsor, with the King absent in Hanover so if any scandal resulted it would be 'old news' by the time he returned, Amelia and the Duke rode away from their attendants for hours and did not return until long after dark, and the row that resulted with Queen Caroline led to her threatening to inform the King. (She did not.) So it is not impossible that Amelia and the duke did have an affair, but it is unlikely that any pregnancy – or her absence from court to cover this up – would have gone unnoticed in the bitchy memoirs of the day. Lord Hervey was a particular critic of Amelia and would have been likely to note and stir up any gossip; he wrote that she was intensely dislikeable, evil-tongued and fond of disobliging gossip, though the shrewd Lady Pomfret reckoned her to be pleasant, thoughtful, and generally liked for her honesty and lack of arrogance.[25]

Cases 2 and 3: Princess Caroline of Brunswick and Princess Sophia of Great Britain, and the Duke of Cumberland's alleged murder of his valet. The family of George III.

The circumstances of court life made gossip about secret affairs and illegitimate children seem attractive and plausible, as people speculated about what went on behind closed doors in the lives of the great. Like modern tabloid journalism, much of it was sheer guesswork or lurid imaginings – and the situation became worse under George III after 1760. It should also be remembered that all this gossip also had a political context quite apart from the lack of knowledge of what actually went on at court, leading to wild speculation in an era of tabloid-like sensational cheap newspapers looking to attract readers. Unlike his grandfather George III took an active and moralistic interest in English politics after 1760, 'shaking up' the close world of a power-monopolizing 'establishment' by the faction-ridden Whig party who had held onto power since the early years of George I's reign (1715/16) due to George I and George II fearing the Tories as secret Jacobites. This 'closed circle' of job-sharing Whig magnates (led skilfully by Sir Robert Walpole until 1742 and thence the Pelham brothers) had been resented by both excluded minor Whig factions and the Tories as what became known as 'Old Corruption', and Prince Frederick had originally promised to end this when he became King but had ended up predeceasing his father, dying at forty-four in 1751. His supporters then transferred their allegiance to his widow Princess Augusta (of Saxe-Gotha) and his then teenage son, the later George III, and once George became King in October 1760 he duly put more non-elite figures into government and talked enthusiastically of cleaning out the Augean stable of Whig corruption as a responsible and 'inclusive' (as we would now call it) 'Patriot King'. The war-winning Whig government, technically led as First Lord by his grandfather's long-term minister (and his aunt Amelia's supposed ex-lover) Newcastle but dominated by the brilliant and maverick Secretary of State William Pitt (the Elder), was forced to admit George's Scots Tory ex-tutor, the Earl of Bute, as a minister and he later took over as first minister in 1762–3. This sort of 'opening' for politicians outside the inner circle of monopolistic Whigs was controversial with and resented by the latter, quite apart from the questions of the competence and new (peace-making) priorities of Bute who was seen as letting the defeated French and Spanish off too lightly in the Peace of Paris in 1762 and was subject to vicious anti-Scots prejudice. In the chaotic world of 1760s politics, power was 'up for grabs' amidst a confusing mixture of Whig and Tory factions and personal rivalries and no government lasted for long, and in addition there was criticism of the young King from 'Old Whig' circles for his having supposedly breached established constitutional practice by interfering in politics at all and nominating his personal friends and allies as ministers. Concepts of George as a dictatorial, rigidly 'controlling', and fumbling interferer in political life were rife in the 1760s well before the American crisis, and this duly fed into spiteful gossip about him and his family among his opponents in politics and feverishly 'judgmental' journalists such as the rabble-rousing democratic champion John Wilkes. Criticism of royal political interference and apparent misjudgements were to rise again as the American war was mishandled and lost after 1776, with the famous 'Dunning Resolution' that the power of the King had grown too far and should be cut back. Were all the sources of stories about secret scandals at court as 'unbiased' as they pretended?

At the time princesses were supposed to stay under the control of their parents as obedient attendants until such time as they married, the latter being arranged by their parents for reasons of political inter-dynastic links to suitable other royal families – given that the husband had to be Protestant for reasons of nationalist anti-Catholic politics and social attitudes in England, usually in Germany or Scandinavia. The bridegroom (or his parents if his father was a reigning sovereign) might well seek out a suitable princess on the grounds of favourable reports of her appearance, character and health from ambassadors at or visitors to her parents' court, with ability to produce an heir plus 'spares' for his dynasty at a premium. However, for a princess to be able to exercise any choice in the matter – or even be consulted – or allowed to see her bridegroom before the wedding – was unusual and entirely up to her parents, and if no suitable husband appeared (or in some cases if the bride was allowed to decline an offer of marriage) she would end up hanging around the court as an attendant on her mother for the latter's lifetime, probably bored and/or depressed. This was to be the fate of most of the obsessively watchful (though well-meaning) George III's daughters, as once the French Revolutionary wars broke out the usual supply of potential husbands from Germany dried up and the King and his equally status-obsessed wife Charlotte of Mecklenberg-Strelitz would not contemplate any daughter of theirs disgracing the dynasty by contracting a marriage with anyone of lower rank than a royal. Both parents seem to have preferred their daughters to remain 'frozen in time' as adults within the bounds of the family as they had been as girls, preserving the ideal of family life as an example to their subjects in an era of profound and violent political turbulence. Although contacts and marital arrangements with German states were now difficult, the fact that only one of the King's six daughters married in this period – the eldest,

Charlotte (born 1766), who would have been expected to marry first in any case as per the usual conventions of dynastic etiquette and who was married off to the corpulent ruling prince of Wurtemberg in 1797 – was remarked upon. The other girls remained at home under their father's authority into their twenties and thirties, accompanying their watchful and fiercely possessive mother around and subject to her increasingly obsessive petty demands in a world of constricting social etiquette and stifling boredom. Indeed they referred to their life semi-jokily as 'the Nunnery ' to their sympathetic but powerless eldest brother the Prince of Wales (later King George IV).[26] The suggestion that Charlotte's next (and more confident and outgoing) sister Elizabeth should marry the exiled heir of the French royal Duke Philippe of Orleans, Louis Philippe (later to be made king of France by another revolution in 1830), was sat upon by the Queen in the late 1790s as not only were his prospects of a throne then minimal but he was a Catholic and the idea of one of his daughters marrying one would upset the mentally fragile King.

Apart from the lack of the usual suitors after the European war broke out in 1793 the King and Queen were very much aware of the danger of overseas royal husbands turning out to be dissolute and immoral rakes who took mistresses, drank and gambled heavily, and ran up huge debts – as were most of their own sons – and were obsessively careful about suggestions about potential marriages. But it was seen as significant that the approach from the relatively innocuous Frederick of Wurtemberg for Princess Charlotte's hand was the only successful one and even she was thirty-one before she married, and as the King aged and slowly withdrew from his former obsessively dominant role in family life his eldest son tried to help his sisters escape the court by suggesting various potential husbands for them to Queen Charlotte but was repeatedly snubbed. The failure to agree or indeed encourage other offers for the girls was blamed on the obsessive protection and domination of these unfortunates by their eccentric, petty-minded and financially stingey parents (who were duly mocked in the era's savage cartoons as ugly, prudish misers), and in this context stories have emerged with some degree of credibility of secret love-affairs and at least one illegitimate child surrounding the princesses. The main scandal, real or imagined, surrounded the lively, good-looking and popular Princess Sophia (born 1777) and her admirer Captain Thomas Garth, who were said to have had a baby in 1800, and will be examined below. It has been reckoned by many modern analysts to be plausible, along with the rumours surrounding an affair by her youngest sister Amelia (1783–1810). At the time, alarmingly – and symptomatic of what people were ready to believe of certain members of the supposedly respectable royal family – it was even alleged that the father of Sophia's 'love-child' might be her own brother, the deeply unpopular and reactionary Ernest, Duke of Cumberland who at the time was fulfilling the requirements in popular imaginings of the resident 'bad boy' of the royal family. The spread of such rumours was probably made more likely by the increasingly and obsessively restricted lives that George III (never quite the same man after his first major breakdown and apparent 'madness' in 1788) and Queen Charlotte were imposing on their unmarried daughters, in a unglamorous and dowdy existence at Windsor Castle's Lower Lodge and the small royal 'palace' at Kew.

But the first major scandal did not surround one of the princesses but the Prince of Wales' wife (and first cousin) Caroline of Brunswick (born 1768), a brash, 'loud', untidy, careless, and deeply unconventional young woman to whom he had been married off unwillingly in 1795 as his parents insisted that he get married – legally this time – as a condition for having his huge debts paid off. The wayward and spendthrift Prince, the most notorious among a batch of selfish and extravagant brothers who their father despaired of, had in fact secretly 'married' the twice-widowed Catholic object of his extravagantly emotional devotions, Mrs Maria Fitzherbert (nee Smythe), privately in 1785 in defiance of the Royal Marriages Act of 1772, which required his father's written approval for this, and all legislation banning royals from marrying Catholics. But this was technically illegal, and by 1794–5 George had tired of Maria and was desperate enough for his debts to be paid off to agree to marry his cousin, the daughter of his father's elder sister Augusta (1737–1813) by the duke of Brunswick, as his parents wished. The pair were, as had been made much of ever since, totally incompatible and this match was a disaster that showed up the failures of the old royal 'arranged marriage' system – though the fault lay mainly with George, who was never one for self-restraint or putting the good of his family or the nation first.

Caroline was uncouth, poorly educated, badly-dressed, not too fond of washing as her detractors gleefully pointed out, bold and rather coarse in her conversation which was not seen as desirable in a princess at the peak of Society, and as passionate and thoughtless as her husband though well-meaning and good-natured. While the match was being negotiated by diplomat James Harris, earl of Malmesbury, Caroline's father the duke of Brunswick warned the earl that although Caroline was good-natured and 'natural' in her manners she was also headstrong and tactless. Given her would-be fiance's reputation for having mistresses and a wild social life, centred on his lavishly-rebuilt home at Carlton House (off the Mall in London) and the Brighton Pavilion (not yet an Oriental extravaganza but a modest classical villa), he feared that Caroline would soon be disillusioned and she was tactless enough to make her feelings known, loudly and publicly. After observing her behaviour in public at parties and dinners, Malmesbury agreed that she was gauche, forceful, too open in her gushing expressions of fondness for her friends, and totally unladylike. The king ignored this and pressed on, and Caroline did not take up the diplomat's friendly but firm hints that she should behave with tact, modesty, and decorum at the English court and not object to her husband having mistresses. Famously, Prince George was reported to have turned pale on first setting eyes on her at the formal introduction and asked for a glass of brandy. He then tried to back out of the marriage, was bullied into going on with it, and reportedly spent the wedding-night (8 April 1795) lying drunk in the fireplace of their bedchamber before belatedly climbing into bed and probably conceiving their daughter Princess Charlotte. Their cohabitation did not last more than a few weeks, and thereafter they were living apart and were noted for their mutual hostility – though George was probably being manipulated into acting on his distaste for his wife by his scheming mistress, Lady Jersey, who wanted to break them up for her own ambitions.[27] Once Charlotte was born and the King had his heir's heir safely delivered the Prince and Princess split up by mutual agreement, with the Prince making the first formal request for this to his dismayed and furious father who would never have put his emotions above his public duty. (Or would he? See next chapter.)

The prince was now vowing his renewed devotion to the previously abandoned Mrs Fitzherbert as the love of his life again, though at the time his love was probably more of a sentimental attachment and the latest of his successive romantic devotions to seemingly tender and understanding young women (from actress 'Perdita' Robinson onwards). The King, probably accurately, blamed the grip that the mischief-making Lady Jersey had on his son, and tried to demand that the Prince give her up and try to reconcile with his wife as the public expected. The public rows of this first 'War of the Waleses' and the torrent of gossip about them was mostly hostile to the Prince as a shameless adulterer, and with demonstrations in the Princess' favour as she attended the opera and her husband regarded as a selfish blackguard this also raised a political danger. The unpopular French monarchy had fallen to popular hatred and scheming republican politicians in a violent revolution and Louis XVI and Marie Antoinette had been guillotined; would the Prince's behaviour bring the British monarchy down next?

The King and Queen tried desperately to insist that they stayed together for the sake of appearances and delayed a separation for as long as possible. The Prince kept Lady Jersey and went back to Mrs Fitzherbert in Brighton part-time, Princess Charlotte was settled with her household at Warwick House a short distance from her father's Carlton House, and the restless Caroline lived firstly out of London (and away from close scrutiny, as her foes pointed out) at the Old Rectory in Charing, Kent and later on at Montague House in Blackheath, several miles out of the City and so (according to critics) far enough away to enable her to conduct her affairs in more privacy. Living off an income of £5000 a year with a moderately-sized household, the seemliness of her conduct and her relationships with various male admirers soon came under question – though as seen she had been noted for her lack of the usual socially seemly tact and modesty since before her arrival in England, so it was not new. As with earlier rumours of debauchery among the royal family, there was probably a mixture of exaggerated gossip and outright invention plus the meddling of interested parties, but in this case it was a figure generally seen as the 'victim' not the guilty party (i.e. Caroline) who was to be the accused and, unusually, her own conduct seemed to point to her guilt rather than the rumours all coming from hostile sources. But as seen above, her own tactless and shoulder-shrugging attitude to contemporary decorum and her insistence on going her own way made this understandable – and it is not inconceivable given her long history of public lack of care for her reputation that she had also developed a fondness for shocking people and rather enjoyed being the subject of (albeit scandalised) attention. Presiding over a large but reasonably well-run household, running up bills but within reason and nowhere as bad as her estranged husband did, Caroline was fond of entertaining at Montague House and had a large social circle but was criticised – and not just by partisans of the Prince out to make trouble for her – for her coarse and ribald conversation and lack of commonsense or restraint which spoiled the tone of her natural and witty repartee. Her new head of the Privy Purse (i.e. household expenditure), Miss Hayman, found when she arrived from her previous post as sub-governess to the Princess' daughter that Caroline had the socially unseemly habit of taking one of her gentlemen guests off away from the rest of company after dinner for a few hours on their own away from witnesses, of which much could be made by her detractors, and gave her a friendly warning that this was not the English custom and would be misinterpreted. Caroline was furious with her for interfering and did not take the hint though did not sack her either. She flirted openly with male guests as a matter of course and regarded what she did as her own business; these included the rising Scots writer Sir Walter Scott and the current Society 'beau' and future Prime Minister William Lamb (Lord Melbourne), who regarded her as little short of insane thanks to her unbalanced and shifting moods and reckless talk. The elegant and gentlemanly Whig society host Lord Holland, albeit not unbiased as he was from the Prince's party and was the nephew of George's boon companion Charles James Fox, regarded her as 'worthless'. Caroline also took up and spent time with rising young socialites and politicians 'on the make', who needed a prominent patron and were thrilled to be taken up by the heir to the throne's wife, and these included the future Foreign Secretary and (briefly) Prime Minister, George Canning, who despite his many talents lacked money and connections and was looked down on by many as the son of an actress. Canning and other confidantes who Caroline spent time with were rumoured to be her lovers and to be using her for social advancement, although such stories were inevitable and were probably largely jealousy from their rivals.

The Princess' habit of taking up and helping an assortment of young orphans, who she found suitable foster-parents around her home, was 'charity work' rather than anything more sinister, but this process was not handled with care to avoid any unpleasant rumours about where exactly the children came from and their real parentage. As with the reputed lovers, scandal might well have been avoided with more careful conduct but the evidently reckless or 'alienated' Princess could not be bothered to listen to advice. There were rumours that she was pregnant in the autumn of 1801 and again in 1802, and later the Prince told his confidante Lady Bessborough (younger sister of the great Whig beauty and hostess Georgiana, duchess of Devonshire) that he had heard that his wife had given birth to a child. This could be used as a political 'weapon' to discredit her as a slut and distract public obloquy from himself, and on a practical level could be used to get round his father's obstinate refusal to countenance a royal divorce by insisting that Caroline's behaviour was so shameful that something had to be done to rescue the Prince's honour. No action was taken for several years, possibly due to a lack of hard proof, but in summer 1805 Lady Douglas, wife of minor courtier Sir John Douglas (Groom of the Bedchamber to the Prince's younger brother the Duke of Sussex), came out with a bizarre and sensational new 'twist' to the story. The lady in question was as much of a 'social climber' of middle-class origins as Caroline's alleged lover Canning and was not of unblemished reputation herself, at least as regards ambition, showing off her connections via her husband's post, and when snubbed vindictiveness, and she was supposed to be having an affair with her husband's old commander in the Navy in the Mediterraean, the rackety socialite Admiral Sir Sydney Smith, who was their guest/lodger at their house near the Princess'. Apparently the Princess had banned her former guest Lady Douglas from Montague House after discovering that she had been spreading unpleasant gossip about what went on there, and was supposed to have sent both her and her husband malicious anonymous letters about and obscene drawings of Lady Douglas having sexual relations with Admiral Smith. The Douglases made equally vivid but less artistic complaints about the love-affairs of the Princess, who denied them, and then took their story to the Prince with a list of specific accusations in writing. According to lord chancellor Lord Erskine the embarrassed Prince tried to ignore it all at first as it would be too embarrassing to the Royal Family as a while if it became public (though Erskine was seeking to reassure the King of his son's worthy motives at the time of this assertion), but when he realised that the story would not die down he took it to firstly the Prime Minister, the younger William Pitt, and then to the ex-chancellor Lord Thurlow. Both agreed with him that it was impossible to 'hush up' and said that the King needed to be informed, so the increasingly fragile and ageing King George – who had been on good terms with Caroline and probably knew little if any of the gossip – was told and agreed to a formal but discreet enquiry if his ministers wished it.

As a result, in summer 1806 the new 'Government of all the Talents' (a shaky Whig-Tory coalition following Pitt's death) launched what was referred to as the 'Delicate Investigation', as quietly as was practicable, with the 'Prime Minister' Lord Grenville joined on the commission by Erskine, Home Secretary Lord Spencer, and another senior minister and lawyer, Lord Ellenborough, aided by the (Whig radical) Solicitor-General, Sir Samuel Romilly. This started its work with the detailed evidence of the vengeful Lady Douglas, who (whether truthfully or not) played up what she had heard from the indiscreet, boastful, and explicitly frank Caroline during their time as intimate friends. She alleged that Caroline had confessed to taking up a series of infant orphans as her proteges and having them around her house so that when she became pregnant and had an illegitimate child to look after nobody would think it special or realise that the baby was hers rather than another of her young foundlings. The Princess encouraged Lady Douglas to take up Sir Sydney Smith as her lover as she had found him to be worthwhile in bed herself, and it was quite likely that the promiscuous admiral was the father of the child that Lady Douglas believed the Princess had had. The spiteful Lady Douglas' husband then gave evidence for the Princess' frequent visits to his home to see Smith, as did other witnesses, and members of the Princess' household had evidence for his lengthy visits. Her ex-'Page of the Backstairs' Robert Bidgood testified that Smith had been at the house in the early morning, hours before the usual time for guests, i.e., that he had presumably stayed overnight, though he had been in the Prince's service for many years before joining his wife so he might have been helping him out by slandering his wife. Bidgood's wife then provided the juicy story that she had heard that a maid had found the Princess and Admiral in her bedchamber in a compromising situation and had been so shocked that after leaving the room in a hurry she had fainted. Frances Lloyd, the local coffee-house proprietor and a member of the Princess' household, said that a doctor who had come to attend her had asked if the Prince ever visited Blackheath as he knew that the Princess was pregnant, and she had once opened the curtains at six in the morning to get her mistress an unusually early breakfast to find her and a man walking in the garden. Bidgood also testified to a Captain Thomas Manby, RN, staying with the Princess on her visit to Southend in 1804 and apparently sharing her bedroom, and Admiral Smith admitted that he had once found the Princess flirtatiously nudging Manby's feet with hers under the table on a visit to Montague House and that after she invited the Captain upstairs he had gone home himself. (Manby himself was alleged later by his brother in his memoirs to have been offered £40, 000 by the Prince's secretary McMahon to testify in the Douglas' favour but had refused.) Another of the Princess' servants formerly employed by the Prince, 'Page of the Backstairs' William Cole, accused her of being too intimate with both Admiral Smith and George Canning, and said that he had been dismissed after finding her on the sofa in her private drawing-room with Smith. But other servants denied that they had seen any improprieties at all, beyond the fact that she spent time alone with assorted gentlemen or the unwisdom of having Captain Manby in her lodgings (probably overnight) during the 1804 trip, and her close attendant ('Page of the Presence') Thomas Stikerman said that he did not think that she had ever been pregnant while at Blackheath though she had not looked pregnant earlier while carrying Princess Charlotte. Two doctors who had attended her, one of them the man who had supposedly asked about the Prince's visits but who now denied this, insisted that they had not seen any evidence of a pregnancy, and her protégé the fashionable portrait-painter Thomas Lawrence admitted sleeping in the same house as her but denied that he had ever been alone with her behind a locked door or heard or done anything improper.

The extensive evidence of improper and unwise conduct by the era's standards could not be ruled as all gossip as it was too widespread and was alleged by witnesses who had no obvious reason to lie. The evidence of actual adultery was far harder to prove and relied on unsupported stories by servants who could have been bribed and in some cases had previously worked for the Prince, who wanted a divorce, or else on the stories of the unreliable and evidently bitter Douglases. (The allegations of offers of cash to people like Manby to testify did not come out.) Accordingly the commission had to accept that there was no proof of the Princess having any love-affairs as opposed to unwise flirting and intimacy with men she was not married to, and the same lack of proof applied to the allegations of an illegitimate child. These latter had centred on her latest and closest infant protégé, known as 'William Austin', and the commission agreed that the baby had been born as per the official records, on 11 July 1802 at Brownlow Street Hospital, London. His destitute mother Sophia Austin (his father had recently been made redundant as a docker) had taken him down to Blackheath to beg for help from the Princess who had a reputation for giving charity to poor mothers, and in conversation with the page Stikeman the latter had suggested that if Sophia could bear to part with her child the Princess might adopt it and find it a secure home. As agreed Sophia had returned one day when the Princess was at home and shown her baby to Caroline, and the latter had duly taken him in and referred to bringing him up herself as if he was a prince. Worried by suggestions from the coffee-room proprietor that there was no room for a baby in the house and he would probably be 'farmed out' to the steward's wife, Sophia had returned some days later to check up on her son and had found that Caroline was indeed looking after him in person, as promised. The latter also found Sophia's husband a new job, and she had nothing to complain of to the commission. (The baby was later educated at Caroline's expense at the Greenwich school run by Dr Charles Burney, brother of the author Fanny Burney.)

The commission concluded that 'Willie Austin', as the Princess called him, was not her son, though she had endeavoured to persuade Lady Douglas that she was with child. The historian Samuel Lysons and others were clear in their analyses of the case that Caroline had persuaded Lady Douglas that she was pregnant, for whatever motive, and the latter and her husband had given their evidence in good faith. But had she just been 'winding up' Lady Douglas to scandalise her as a joke, regardless of the consequences? There were other stories that she was pregnant, circulating in Greenwich in 1802, and a story from a believable source got to the Earl of Westmorland, formerly Lord Privy Seal to early 1806, who informed ex-PM Lord Addington of it, that a document proving this was testified to by a reliable lawyer. Richard Edwards of Crane Court, Fleet Street, printer of a book about the affair at the time, claimed to have written proof of it (but did not produce this), and recent Paymaster-General and well-known society gossip Lord Glenbervie (another Douglas) believed that the Austin boy was Caroline's son. Notably, whether to assist the reputation of the Royal Family by staging a 'cover-up' or not, the 1806 coalition government did not release the official report into the case of Caroline and her 'lovers' and 'baby', presumably fearing that she would be blackened by publication of her indiscreet and raunchy conduct; if so, the Prince's hopes of stirring up pressure for a divorce were stymied. The report was not published until 1813 – after the assassination of a leading government legal adviser in 1806–7 and the PM in 1809–12, Spencer Perceval, which may have removed a block on it. To add to the mystery, Caroline later claimed that the boy who she brought up was not the original 'Willie Austin', who she had taken on but soon sent away, but a 'lookalike' for whom 'Willie' had been chosen as resembling him to allay his mother's suspicions. The actual baby she looked after and later legally adopted, who had been substituted for Willie, was the illegitimate son of an admirer of hers, Prince Louis Ferdinand of Prussia, who she had agreed to look after for his father. Louis had been in love with her and had been killed at the battle of Jena in 1806, and she had been in love with him too so she had helped him out with the child.[28]

This story was as unlikely as others of the unreliable Princess and sounds more like a third-rate romance, and given her unstable character and increasing eccentricity it cannot be taken at face value. But she was attached enough to it to repeat it when she was dying in 1821 to a Dr Lushington, though by that point she might have lost touch with reality and believed it herself. Her conduct in her last years while touring Italy with her latest admirer, her 'major-domo' Benjamin Pergami, was increasingly bizarre and even more uninhibited than usual. Lushington also later claimed to have had it confirmed to him by other unidentified parties, in an 1858 statement to Caroline's long-term political ally Lord Brougham.[29] Perhaps typically, Caroline was not 'warned off' associating with Willie Austin in public by the investigation, however wise that might have been for her, but continued to live with and fuss over him and after the end of the Napoleonic Wars in 1815 took him abroad with the rest of her rackety household to tour the Continent. She then brought him back to England as she sought in vain to assert her right to be Queen, and named him as her residual heir in 1821. Her innocence of having an illegitimate child is likely, but for once the worst charges came about because of her own conduct – which was indiscreet and controversial long before she could claim to be a 'victim of the elite'.

In contrast to the tangled story of the 'Delicate Investigation' and the claims by and about Princess Caroline, the case of her sister-in-law Princess Sophia and her alleged lover seems more straightforward. Nor did it rely so heavily on the evidence of 'backstairs tittle-tattle' by royal household servants who may have had grudges or been bribed by the Prince of Wales; rather, there was discernible sympathy for this Princess who had been shut up in semi-seclusion for decades in the rigidly conventional world of the dull and tedious Hanoverian court and palaces by her 'controlling', selfish and obsessive mother. The moral and 'upright' but deeply conventional Queen Charlotte, no doubt to a degree traumatised by the sporadic and unpredictable descents of her husband into what was generally written off as 'madness' (and still has not been definitely established as a case of porphyria rather than a mainly psychological problem), was in a difficult position as her husband's decline passed on more of the duties of 'leadership' and establishing a direction for the gossip-riven court to her. She was faithful to and shared George III's rigid standards of conduct and propriety, with the public gossip about her wayward sons' debaucheries and huge debts humiliating her and her husband and showing that their ultra-careful training of their sons to be decorous, responsible and dutiful royal princes had totally failed to rein in their instincts. Their 'ideal' of family life in the 1760s to 1780s as a large and seemingly happy if obsessively well-ordered family unit, living with middle-class decorum and financial restraint in the quiet worlds of the Upper and Lower Lodges at Windsor (large Georgian houses next to the south side of the Upper Ward of the Castle) and the 'Dutch House' and adjoining buildings at Kew, had broken down as their sons grew up into (mostly) scandalous rakes associating with what George and Charlotte regarded as the worst dregs of 'High Society'. Indeed at the height of the King's worst attack of 'madness' in 1788 his own ravings had extended to obscene expressions of enthusiasm for other court ladies (he imagined he was married to Lady Pembroke) that showed what was going on in his mind and humiliated his wife. In response Charlotte clung to rigid rules of propriety, created a comforting (for herself) protective 'wall' around herself and her daughters, and sought to keep the latter away from court rakes and to ensure that no scandals affected them. The way that possibilities of their marrying were exhaustively examined and almost all rejected out of hand suggested then, and has ever since, that the Queen was selfishly using her daughters' attendance on her all year round, year after year, for her own mental wellbeing and had no real concern for their happiness or what would happen to them when she was gone – and her son the Prince of Wales was far more supportive of their needs. Despite the Queen's controls, she could not prevent assorted courtiers in attendance on her family (who were mostly middle-aged as handsome younger men were seen by her as a threat) having friendships with the Princesses, and rumours of more duly spread in a few cases of the livelier and less discreet girls. These, unlike the stories about Caroline, were not obviously fuelled by political or inter-dynastic motives.

The main rumours surrounded the charming, 'outgoing', and apparently flirtatious Sophia, second youngest of the five daughters left unmarried at Princess Charlotte's marriage to the Prince of Wurtemberg in 1797 and aged nineteen at the time. Passionate, moody, and delicate and not even considered for an offer of marriage unlike her elder sisters Augusta (who was said to have developed affections for two socially unacceptable men, firstly Dr Henry Vaughan and then royal equerry Major-General Sir Brent Spencer) and Elizabeth (who as mentioned above was considered for Louis Philippe of Orleans), Sophia was linked by gossip to another royal equerry, the much older Major-General Thomas Garth. Thirty-three years older than her, small, and disfigured by a large purple birthmark on his face, he could almost have been selected by the watchful King and Queen as the sort of man who a romantic and desperate daughter of theirs would not fall in love with, so safe to be in proximity to her. However, rumour had it that Sophia not only fell in love with him but became pregnant, and that a baby was duly born on the royal summer visit to Weymouth in August 1800. The royal party, consisting of the King, Queen, Princesses, and a smaller than usual 'inner household', usually lived a less closely controlled existence at Gloucester Lodge on Weymouth seafront than they did at Windsor or Kew, though the Princesses still had to attend their parents for daily walks on the promenade, the King's famous therapeutic sea-bathing (from a discreet bathing-machine on the beach, with a band nearby playing the national anthem as he entered the waves), the usual naval review at Portland, and local visits to the gentry and aristocracy. A princess, her figure discreetly covered by the era's voluminous dresses with the King's eyesight deteriorating by this point and the Queen preoccupied, might have managed to conceal her pregnancy if she was not too large and then give birth with servants' help while her parents were busy on social duties, pleading infirmity to stay in her room for a few days. Sophia's brother Edward, Duke of Kent (born 1767), later Queen Victoria's father, apparently believed and spread stories that Sophia had had a child by General Garth in 1800, and later Early Victorian gossip/diarist Charles Greville – well-connected socially and clerk to the Privy Council – was told about the episode by Lady Bath, quoting her knowledgeable and honest 'in-law', the Queen's then 'Mistress of the Robes' (i.e. close attendant) Lady Caroline Thynne. Apparently the affair – or at least the occasion when Sophia had become pregnant – had occurred at a time in late 1799 when General Garth was housed temporarily in the same royal residence as the Princesses at Windsor, i.e. Lower Lodge – with the King and Queen being next-door at Upper Lodge. The King was told that Sophia had a bad case of dropsy, which would cause her to swell up, and was too ailing or trustful to query it – or else chose to accept this excuse rather than give himself more mental strain. Her son was supposed to have been handed to and adopted by Major Herbert Taylor, the discreet secretary to the Princess' second oldest brother and close ally Frederick, Duke of York (born 1763) and later Private Secretary to the King as his deteriorating eyes prevented him doing his own correspondence any longer. Taylor's family at Weymouth brought 'Thomas Taylor' up there, and Sophia was able to see him on the family holidays there – and her increasing invalidism could be put down to the difficult birth. Garth apparently adopted the boy in 1804, but fell out with Sophia – possibly due to him complaining that she had stopped wanting to see 'Tommy', whereas her letters refer to how painful she found doing this when she could not acknowledge him. She might even have secretly married Garth, who continued to rise at court and later became a senior official in the heiress apparent Princess Charlotte of Wales' household.[30] Evidently no taint of any malevolent intrigue affected Sophia and Garth as it had Princess Caroline, and if the story is true there was general court sympathy for them and a desire to help not expose them – and rewards for being discreet? This might argue for the story being true.

Ironically, Weymouth was also a major setting for one of the other secret alleged affairs surrounding one of the frustrated younger daughters of George III and Charlotte, in this case the passionate and romantic – and determined – Princess Amelia (1783–1810), the King's adored youngest daughter. As indiscreet as Sophia at first in her enthusiasm for an older man, Amelia fell for another royal equerry in 1800 or 1801 – in this case the more handsome Charles Fitzroy, a protégé of Sophia's apparent lover General Garth and the younger son of the Earl of Southampton so more socially acceptable (but still unacceptable as a husband to the status-conscious King and Queen). The same age as the Prince of Wales so twenty-one years older than Amelia, Fitzroy was free enough from suspicion to be allowed to stay behind at Weymouth with the ailing Amelia in late summer 1801 after the rest of the Royal party left but she needed more healthy sea air; he escorted her on her recuperative rides and later did so again once she returned to Windsor with her governess, Miss Gomme. Letters were exchanged and hidden, quiet walks and rides were taken in secluded parts of Windsor Great Park, and by 1803 Miss Gomme had tumbled to the existence of a relationship; she demanded that Amelia end it and when she took no notice the governess went to the Queen. The furious Amelia failed to have her betrayer sacked, and the Queen wrote her a letter – remarkably restrained given her usual attitude – warning her not to go out with Fitzroy alone but not going beyond that. Probably the King's delicate state after his 1801 recurrence of his 'madness' was distracting or wearing her out, and she warned her daughter not to say anything to her father and make the family's problems worse. Amelia apparently replied that she was old enough (twenty) to run her own life and could not submit to being governed like a child, or so she told her equally frustrated sister Mary (who was eventually to be permitted to marry her cousin the Duke of Gloucester once the King was too frail to stop her). But she was more discreet, though her passionate references to Fitzroy in family letters and those to Fitzroy himself show her continuing devotion; and she was remarkably 'forward' for a princess in a rigidly genteel era and milieu in discussing her medical and even gynaecological problems with him. The eccentric Princess Caroline, her sister-in-law, even suggested that her delicate and soon declining health was due to her catching a venereal infection during a torrid relationship with the nephew of her doctor in 1798, but that was probably just another of her bizarre fantasies. The problems were, however, exacerbated by mischievous anonymous letters to Miss Gomme accusing her of deliberately ignoring the affair and so allowing the world to gossip about Amelia and Fitzroy, which if true would suggest that their affair was generally known at court though kept from the king. (The author was eventually revealed as wayward court gossip Lady Georgiana Bulkeley, to whom the king had been making erotic suggestions during his illness in 1804 to his wife's horror.) The panicking Miss Gomme went to the Queen's confidante and assistant, her daughter Princess Elizabeth, to excuse herself and demand that the Queen did something, but she was calmed down and told that the matter was in hand; the Queen wrote firmly and uncompromisingly to Amelia to insist that there was no question of a marriage to Fitzroy or anyone else while the king lived as it would disgrace and distress him. George III's well-being was put above his daughter's, and the furious Amelia failed to go through with an apparent threat to appeal to the Privy Council for the right to marry once she was old enough to legally use them to sidestep her father (i.e. once she was twenty-five, in August 1808).

Tragically, Amelia ended up dying of tuberculosis on 2 November 1810 so she never had a chance to marry – and her death probably tipped her distressed father's mind into his final attack of 'insanity' a few months later. The mystery in this case was not so much of whether there was an affair, albeit more likely a platonic one, but of why the Queen failed to stand up for her distressed and ailing daughter's rights once she was legally old enough to defy the Royal Marriages Act in 1808 – but probably she was too exhausted and too concerned for the King to care.

There was a darker side to the stories surrounding Princess Sophia and General Garth, whether they were accurate or just gossip and whether there was a link to the baby apparently born in 1800. One version of the story had it that the baby was the child not of General Garth but of the Princess' alleged improperly 'over-fond' brother Duke Ernest, of Cumberland (born 1771), a disreputable rake and figure of intense rumour and hostile stories in the decades after 1800. These may have arisen due to his unrepentantly conservative political views and intensely 'reactionary' attitude to any reform, which made him many enemies and led to genuine fears that this rumoured enthusiast for repression could end up as regent or even King after George III's grand-daughter and next-but-one heir Princess Charlotte unexpectedly died in childbirth in November 1817. Granted the ill-health and unlikelihood of remarriage and having a child for the former Prince of Wales, now King George IV, in 1820–30, and the lack of legitimate children for his next brothers (the Duke of York, d 1827, and William, Duke of Clarence, who was King in 1830–7), the unexpected death of their younger brother Edward, Duke of Kent in January 1820 left only his daughter Victoria in the way of Ernest's accession. As she would not be legally adult until May 1837, the death of her father's brothers Frederick and William without heirs would make her Queen but possibly let in Ernest as regent – so would he repress any attempt at constitutional reform by violence and/or provoke a revolution? This gave political 'clout' to sensational and increasingly unpleasant rumours about Ernest's intentions, and given his brusque, abrupt and bad-tempered character and his rackety private life these were seen as believable. This gossip extended in the turbulent 1820s to stories that he had committed incest with Sophia and was the real father of her child, and his close and 'unhealthy' attachment to her was cited as evidence. There was also the connected case of General Garth's son Captain Thomas Garth, presumably the baby of 1800, who in May 1829 lodged an affidavit with the Court of Chancery for the enforcement of a legal agreement he had apparently made earlier with Captain Herbert Taylor. As seen above, Taylor was the Duke of York's and the King's private secretary and the man who had allegedly initially adopted Sophia's illegitimate son. Taylor had apparently agreed to pay all the Captain's gambling debts and give him a £1,000 per annum 'pay-off' if he would hand over a box of his containing papers 'referring to his rank and situation in life' to the City banker John Dean Paul. This box would then be sealed up by Taylor with his official seal and not opened without his permission – but in the event Taylor had not paid up, allegedly due to Garth copying some of the papers before they were handed over and showing some of these to newspaper editors.

This seemed to be a classic case of a 'cover-up' by royal 'fixers', as with the similar case of Charles II, Lucy Walter, and the 'Black Box' in the 1650s, and also of the story leaking out as one of the parties sought to make money out of it. The Captain was rumoured at the time to be the son of Sophia by General Garth and said his ageing father had given him the box when ill, though when he attempted to use its contents to extort money from the Royal Family the General loyally tried to retrieve it. The troublemaking Captain was also said to have revealed unknown details connected to the Duke of Cumberland's misdemeanours in those papers he showed to anti-conservative editors – who would have been delighted to have any 'dirt' to throw at the reactionary Duke. This may have led to the stories that the 1800 baby's father was Cumberland not Garth and that he was an incestuous rake or a rapist, though the mischief-making wife of the Russian ambassador, society hostess Countess Lieven, was also suspected of being behind it. Or did the story originally come (pre-1821) from Princess Caroline, who had delighted in repeating lurid stories however unreliable they were? The well-connected gossip Charles Greville heard and wrote in his indiscreet memoirs that Sir Herbert Taylor had said that letters by Sophia had alleged that Cumberland had tried to assault her, and Greville believed that that was why Queen Charlotte had banned the Duke from unchaperoned visits to his sisters – but in fact that rule had applied to all the Royal Dukes and been set up to prevent gossip about them. The same could have applied to an alleged request by the then Prince Regent, now George IV, for his sisters not to see Cumberland unchaperoned. Also, in the fevered political atmosphere of 1829, the year when George IV finally gave in to liberal pressure and allowed 'Catholic Emancipation' as necessary to stave off serious crisis, Cumberland the arch-reactionary was so unpopular that his enemies would believe or use any scandal to ruin him and it was generally believed that he was behind some unknown but hideous scandal in the Royal Family that was being 'hushed up' to protect him.[31] The story about him and Sophia was probably part of this, though its timing was at least partly accidental if it was really a squabble over a 'pay-off' between Taylor and Captain Garth that led to the latter leaking details to the press. Arguably Garth, mercenary in his quest for money and/or genuinely in need and furious at having his real identity covered up, had realised that he had enough written 'proof' of his royal birth to be able to extort money from Captain Taylor, though he was betraying his own father, his foster-father Taylor, and his unfortunate mother in the process.

As for Cumberland, he had an unsavoury reputation for uninhibited sexual misdemeanours that did not just rest on this case, though it is worth noting that the worst stories were all circulating during the time of his greatest role as a political 'threat' to reform after the death of the Duke of York in 1827 and the failure of Prince William to have a surviving child placed him nearer the throne. In 1829 he was said to have been caught by Lord Chancellor Lord Lyndhurst (a Tory so not a political foe out to embarrass him) trying to rape his wife, though it is more likely that the apparent violent confrontation between Cumberland and Lady Lyndhurst that her husband interrupted involved him abusing her husband for abandoning his conservative principles by voting for his bugbear, Catholic Emancipation. Later one of his mistresses was allegedly caught in bed with him by her husband who then 'committed suicide' (like his valet Sellis, see below?)

The sensational nature of them may also owe something to the existence of an earlier murky scandal and lurid rumours about the Duke arising from the strange and violent death of his valet Joseph Sellis after an apparent attack (by him?) on the Duke at the Duke's apartments at St James' Palace on the night of 30–31 May 1810. According to the Duke's account, a few hours after he had returned to his rooms at the palace from a concert he was woken up by being struck two blows on the head with a sharp weapon, later identified as his regimental sword, but could not see his assailant in the dark. He was hit twice more before he could get up and his attacker fled. He called out to his valets, Messrs Sellis and Neale, in their bedrooms next-door for help, but only Neale rushed in and the assailant managed to make his escape in the dark in the confusion. Once Neale had seen to the injured Duke he went to alert Sellis, but found his door locked and could not get a response; the Duke then told him to arouse the other servants and make sure that nobody left the palace. He did so, but they found the supposedly locked-up state apartments on the far side of Sellis' room unlocked – and if Sellis was to enter the Duke's room without going through Neale's intervening bedroom he would have had to go through these rooms. The Duke subsequently said that the attacker had disappeared through a door into these state apartments, and servants testified to having heard noises from the Duke's bedroom's annex/closet late the previous evening which (combined with Sellis' slippers and a lantern being found there) implied that he had hidden there before the Duke returned from the concert. The door from the state apartments to Sellis' room was unlocked, and at a strange gurgling sound from inside the palace porter ran in and found that Sellis had apparently cut his throat on being cornered; he was lying on his bed, his razor was lying by the basin, and he died shortly afterwards. It was reckoned and was accepted at the official inquest that Sellis had tried to murder the Duke and on being interrupted by Neale had fled and killed himself, but the motive for the murder was unclear and it was soon being alleged across London that the Duke had been having an affair with Mrs Sellis and might be the father of her latest child (to whom he and Princess Augusta were godparents). Had he been discovered in bed with Mrs Sellis by her husband and nearly killed in a 'crime of passion'?

The unanimous evidence of the servants as to Sellis' movements and what the chain of events had been was dismissed as a 'cover-up', though the jury at the inquest had been full of hard-headed and in some cases politically radical local shopkeepers (i.e. likely political critics of the Duke) and been headed by the well-known radical agitator and parliamentary reformist Francis Place. The latter, lieutenant of current reformist leader Sir Francis Burdett, was hardly a man to assist the Duke in a 'cover-up'. The attack had clearly not been a sham as the Duke had been seriously injured with deep slashes to his face, but to the London cynics it was suspicious that he had not died if Sellis had been able to hit him in the face several times with a sharp cavalry sabre. There was also the question of how he had got a wound on his thigh if Sellis had been aiming at his head and had fled as soon as the Duke roused, what Sellis' slippers and a lantern were doing when they were conveniently found in the bedroom annex/closet (would the attacker not need to keep his shoes on as he attacked the Duke?), and whether all Sellis' injuries could be accounted for by his suicidal throat-slashing. And why was only one of the doctors who examined Sellis called to give evidence? As to motives, the fact that Sellis was a foreign (Corsican) Catholic and the Duke a blusteringly offensive 'hard-line' Protestant hater of Catholics did not explain why the valet had suddenly – or after some botched basic planning? – gone berserk and tried to kill him. Sellis had once been in trouble for thieving when living in the US and had left there after a complaint to the New York magistrates, but his fellow-valet Neale was on very bad terms with him. The reason he had been sleeping in a room next to the Duke rather than at his own apartment with his wife – only one valet was on duty at a time, and on the night in question that had been Neale – was due to one of his children being ill, not a 'plot' by him. The tone of the conservative press, eg the *Morning Post*, about him after the incident was also highly aggressive on inadequate evidence and lambasted excitable Italians in general.

Later even stories about a sordid homosexual affair that had gone wrong were circulated, possibly involving Cumberland having a relationship with his other valet, Neale (Sellis being married with four children so an unlikely culprit) and being caught in bed with him by Sellis who he then threatened. The official – and rather hurried – inquest on 1 June did have its problems, though the rather casual way in which foreman-designate Place was apparently asked to nominate some assistant members rather than them being chosen at random from householders need not reflect a 'fit-up job' as was alleged in later radical newspapers. The same applies to the quick and unanimous account of events provided by the Royal Household to assorted newspapers. As a serially unpopular reactionary the Duke was still being accused of a 'cover-up' and lies by the radical *Satirist* magazine twenty years later, and sued its editor successfully for libel. It was apparent that the long series of scandals about the sons of George III – and the prevailing tendency for the cynical public to believe the worst about them – had reached a climax.[32] More prosaically, it is probable that the mixture of loud and scornful ducal resistance to reform throughout the period 1810–32 made Cumberland a 'sitting duck' for the worst type of gossip and for stories based on the flimsiest evidence. Even when someone tried to murder him he was soon seen as the guilty party. The truth of the Cumberland/Sellis episode is probably unprovable, though the elements of 'damage control' (e.g. at the inquest) added to fevered contemporary suspicion of the official story, and it is best seen as hard evidence of how the most lurid rumours about the 'great' being believed by many people is hardly a new phenomenon.

One thing to be noted regarding all these lurid scandals was that their focus was now on personal sexual misconduct by individual Royals rather than stories with any political implication, beyond the lurking possibility that controversial figures such as Ernest Augustus, Duke of Cumberland were disliked (and 'smeared' by the press?) partly out of fear of their potential for repression should they ever sit on or dominate the throne. The open politico-religious element of a scandal, such as the long-term implications of the 'Secret Treaty of Dover', the legitimacy of the Duke of Monmouth as a potential Protestant heir, or the birth of James VII and II's son in 1688, were usually missing. The Hanoverian Succession, as the follow-up to the expulsion of the 'tyrannical Catholic menace' James from the throne, had stabilised the political system and the creation of the long-term 'Whig Supremacy' of one-party rule after 1714 added to this, though the personal character and role of the monarch was still important. But now scandal was more a matter of gossip and personal or factional clashes at Court, though it could still escalate into a major issue.

Chapter 7

George III and his 'Marriage' to Hannah Lightfoot. The Fair Quaker and Royal Bigamy?

The assertion that George III, as well as his eldest son, married secretly rests on flimsy evidence. The other party was supposed to have been the 'Fair Quaker', Hannah Lightfoot, a mysterious figure who some nineteenth-century writers even declared had never existed; the date Spring 1759, when George was heir to his grandfather George II's throne and aged twenty. He was living at his widowed mother Princess Augusta's London residence, Leicester House, acquired by his father Prince Frederick Louis (d. 1751) after he broke with the King in 1737, and by all accounts was under close supervision – not least from his manipulative and ambitious tutor, Augusta's confidante John Stuart, Lord Bute. The latter, a Scots peer of few political connections (and even less support among the inter-connected elite of either kingdom) who had been taken on by the late Prince Frederick as a courtier and boon companion in the 1740s, would intrigue his way to becoming first Secretary of State and later Prime Minister once young and idealistic George was King. But arguably he did not have a great deal of ambition and his sudden rise owed more to George's enthusiasm for it than his own as the idealistic young King saw him as honest and reliable unlike the 'self-serving' and 'renowned' for 'nest-feathering' elite of the dominant 'Whig' oligarchy who had inter-linked politics since the Hanoverian succession in August 1714. Bute himself had no political experience or skill, never having stood for election or having a group of 'political' friends, and was said by the shrewd Frederick to have been more suited to be an ambassador than a politician as he was 'showy' and fond of striking a pose at formal occasions with a grand display; contemporaries such as Secretary of State (and 1782–3 'Prime Minister') Lord Shelburne and George III's 'governor' Lord Waldegrave called him well-read, knowledgeable on a limited range of intellectually fashionable subjects (eg science), and capable of making himself agreeable (especially to women) but pompous, timid about taking action in between bursts of rashness, lacking common sense, and very much on his dignity.[1] Neither Bute nor the highly moral Augusta, a politically inexperienced princess from a respectable and tradition-bound minor German court (Saxe-Gotha, a junior branch of the large royal line ruling the Electorate of Saxony and its minor dependencies) would have looked favourably on the Prince embarrassing the Royal Family with a private, 'hole in the corner' marriage of unequal status. By contemporary reckoning, a Prince was supposed to marry a fellow-royal – and as the Act of Settlement of 1701 in England (applying to Scotland too after the Union of 1707) had banned English kings from being or marrying Catholics this meant in practice a German or Scandinavian princess. The whole point of the untried Prince's political appeal as his grandfather George II's heir in the mid-late 1750s was to present a 'clean sheet' of non-corrupt, honest government after the squalid compromises and partisanship of the 'Old System' of one-party Whig government by a clique of well-connected, 'nest-feathering' politicians since 1714, whether or not this meant bringing the disgraced Tory 'party' (who the Whigs had 'smeared' as treasonable Jacobites) back into power.

The appeal of an honest 'Patriot King' untainted by association with George II's Whig regime had been the basis of the late Prince Frederick Louis' political 'programme', as crafted for him by side-lined Tory ex-minister Lord Bolingbroke (Henry St John), and George had inherited this role when Frederick died suddenly aged forty-four in 1751. A marriage to a woman of low rank, presumed to be the result of youthful lust and naivety if not falling victim to a social climber, would ruin all that; and George had been carefully educated by Bute to realise his responsibilities and need for self-control.[1] Unlike his eldest son at the time of his first marital excursion in 1785, he was not in possession of his own Household and residence and able to come and go as he pleased. He was being taught by Bute to set a good moral example as the exemplar of the ideal of a 'Patriot King', which involved distancing himself from the corrupt and amoral behaviour of the ruling 'Whig' establishment[2] – and when he came to the throne in October 1760 he was quick to endeavour to put this into practice although the existing Whig government had recently brought the country great glory and success in the Seven Years' War with an 'Annus Mirabilis' in 1759 (headed by the conquest of Quebec from France). Indeed, Bute's papers concerning Royal history which the Prince studied for guidance attacked assorted princes who had set a bad example by indulging in the sins of the flesh with mistresses, such as William I's eldest son Robert, and even criticised Prince Frederick Louis for submitting to female influence – and accused George II of listening to his mistress Lady Yarmouth in making appointments and deciding policy.[3] Bute was therefore not likely to want the young Prince to indulge in female entanglements like his father and grandfather, and indeed was meant to set a new and high standard of moral behaviour – and the timid and admiring George was not the sort of youth to rebel against these strictures. Bute, from the Tory nobility who the Whigs and their Hanoverian masters George I and II had excluded from office for three-and-a-half decades and a former friend of

Prince Frederick Louis, was an 'outsider' in London politics and had no flair for making allies among the English nobility either. He had neither estates in England nor money, major drawbacks for a Scots noble 'on the make', lacked important family connections among the 'cousinhood' that dominated high Whig politics, and was entirely dependent on the goodwill of his Royal patrons Frederick Louis and Augusta. Nor did he have the political agility of those 'outsiders' who did make it, like William Pitt. He was forced into senior office by eager George III in 1761 as one of the Secretaries of State against the will of the current government under the 'First Lord of the Treasury' since 1757, the Duke of Newcastle, and the other Secretary of State William Pitt (the Elder). He soon became First Lord of the Treasury i.e. 'Prime Minister' (in practice as the office did not formally exist) at the King's express will in order to 'clean out' the 'Old System' of Whig factional monopoly of power, and both Pitt (himself an 'outsider' to the main Whig political elite who had risen to prominence by attacking its subservience to George II over backing Hanover's rather than Britain's priorities in Continental policy) and Newcastle's 'Old Whig' clique were side-lined.[4] George's determination to assert his ideals and rule as well as reign presented him with major political problems. His insistence in pressing on with this and championing Bute against the Whig 'ruling class' showed his stubbornness in a cause he felt was right; but could this be a likely course for his private life too?

George had a high sense of his dignity and an obsession with seemliness, in contrast to the rakish behaviour of his father Frederick and his sons as young men. His mother had kept him clear of the sort of rakish young noblemen who had influenced his father as a young man, and unlike Frederick Louis and George II there is no sign of the young Prince ever reacting badly against the older generation (represented in this case by his grandfather as his father had died when he was thirteen). He was a keenly believing Churchman with a mixture of idealism and a legalistic mindset, whose determination to keep his Coronation Oath and prohibit Catholic Emancipation was to lose him his Prime Minister (the younger Pitt) in 1801. All the indications are that he took notions of adultery very seriously and deplored it in his youth, when his brothers' conduct was notorious, as well as in later decades. He was particularly embarrassed by the behaviour of his youngest brother Henry, Duke of Cumberland (1745–90) in living openly with first a reputed prostitute, Polly Jones, and then his mistress Lady Grosvenor, who he had lured away from her husband.[5] The latter then resorted to a succession of prostitutes and he and his wife sued each other for adultery in a messy divorce-case in 1770, followed gleefully by the press – in which Prince Henry's selfish financial meanness to Lady Grosvenor was fully revealed. Having abandoned both Polly and Lady Grosvenor in turn when he became bored and violated contemporary 'mores' for decent behaviour by not paying any money to either to keep them solvent after the affairs ended, he informed the King suddenly in November 1771 that he had married – to a socially insignificant and impoverished widow, Anne Horton, who was the daughter of Lord Irnham and much his social junior.[6] The King's next brother Edward, Duke of York, had already died young, aged twenty-eight in 1768, of a chill or malaria on an expensive tour of France and Italy at Monaco after running through his allowance on gambling, women, and buying and running his own theatre – possibly weakened by his well-known dissipation.[7]

Technically, the requirements of the 1754 Marriages Act that any marriage in England had to be advertised in church in advance (hence the ceremony of 'calling the banns' for forthcoming marriages in each parish) and open to the public, with witnesses in attendance, did not apply to Royalty – so Henry had not broken the law and neither would the King have done had he conducted a private marriage. But George was highly sensible of the disgrace his brothers' conduct had brought upon the Royal Family, which he (in advance of the similarly-minded Queen Victoria) regarded as a suitable moral example to the nation. He even wrote to his other surviving brother Prince William, Duke of Gloucester, in a fury that this sort of underhand behaviour and acquisition of socially junior subjects as Royal 'in-laws' could lead to civil war as witnessed by the Wars of the Roses – presumably a reference to Edward IV and Elizabeth Woodville.[8] The Royal Marriages Act of 1772 was one result of this, as he sought to end the threat of unsuitable women entangling his brothers – and later on his sons – in marriage to the detriment of the family's reputation by making every descendant of George II under twenty-five seek Privy Council permission to marry.[9]

But would George really have committed the same sort of offence himself in 1759 or 1760, even as a youth of twenty or twenty-one? Hannah Lightfoot, his supposed inamorata or 'wife', was explicitly identified as a Quaker; the Prince therefore could not marry her publicly due to the difference in religion as well as in rank. The last British sovereign to marry a commoner had been James II, who had (secretly) married his brother's Lord Chancellor's daughter Anne Hyde when he was heir to the throne in 1660. The last sovereign to marry a commoner openly had been Henry VIII, who had married Katherine Parr in 1543. If any secret marriage came out it would thus cause a major scandal. But technically such an act would still be legal as of 1759; the Royal Marriages Act was not passed until 1772. Marriage for Anglicans in England was supposed to be conducted by a Church of England clergyman in a church as of the Act introduced by Lord Chancellor Hardwicke in 1754, though rules were laxer in Scotland – hence the rush of aspiring couples across the Border to be married on secular premises at Gretna Green. Marrying Hannah would have been legal – so if this did occur any public marriage to a foreign princess later would be bigamy and the offspring of it debarred from the throne. Was George, a Prince brought up to set a good moral example as an Anglican King of impeccable virtue, expecting to pretend that he wanted to stay unmarried to any foreign princess and so avoid bigamy? That would make his next brother, the rakish and irresponsible Edward, Duke of York (d. 1767), his heir unless George confessed to his secret and presented any children he had by Hannah to the world.

The notion of George contracting a secret marriage in spring 1759 thus does not make personal or political sense. His moralistic, even naïve character at this point was confirmed by his published correspondence with Bute of the late 1750s. Similarly, there is no mention of any rumours of his connection to a Quakeress among the accounts of the well-informed 'High Society' gossips of the late 1750s. These scions of the nobility, male and female, were keeping a close eye on the current events at Leicester House and the intentions of their future King, with his grandfather aged in his mid-seventies and not likely to last much longer. The only rumoured romance George had in 1759–60 was with Lady Sarah Lennox (born 1745 so six years his junior), daughter of the second Duke of Richmond (d. 1750) and of far more suitable (though still inferior) social status. They apparently first met in November 1759 when fourteen-year-old Sarah, newly arrived from Ireland and living with her elder sister Caroline and brother-in-law Henry Fox, Lord Holland (a leading Whig politician) at Holland House in Kensington, was presented at Court to the King.[10] The Prince was at this ceremony at St James' Palace and fell in love at first sight, and he proceeded to pay court to her – in an awkward and unpolished manner showing his lack of experience – at Court 'drawing-rooms' into the New Year. Indeed, the contemporary accounts of the affair speak of him having claimed this was his first romance, which his awkward behaviour confirmed. Having admired her intensely at their first meeting but done little except chat awkwardly at subsequent Court events, his letters to Bute (in whom he confided as the nearest thing he had to a male mentor) show that he was torn between desire to consider her as a wife and fears that it would be imprudent. He was aware that Bute would disapprove of her as a consort – she was not only a commoner but closely connected to the ruling Whigs, as her sister was married to the Paymaster-General (and rake) Henry Fox. Fox could be accused by suspicious political foes like Bute of using Sarah to lure George into the Whig 'camp', and George duly hesitated about confessing his feelings to Bute but dropped some hints of his having fallen in love in a letter some time in autumn 1759.[11] He continued to pursue and spend time with Sarah, notably at a Twelfth Night ball on 6 January 1760 where he asked about her family – possibly to gauge their reactions to an engagement. He finally confessed the extent of his feelings and for whom they were intended in a later letter to Bute some time that winter, and admitted 'I don't deny that I have flattered myself with hopes that one day or another you would consent to my raising her to a Throne'.[12] He also assured that he had never had any improper thoughts, i.e.. about making Sarah his mistress – and it would have been totally out of his unworldly and 'moral' character to have concealed such plans (or any earlier relationship with a Miss Lightfoot?) from Bute given that he always treated the latter as his 'confessor'. His hesitation about admitting the Lennox attachment was clearly out of embarrassment at letting Bute and his own mother's standards down and a fear that Bute would oppose a marriage, not out of deviousness. But he was prepared to accept his tutor's advice – and his veto as a wise 'expert' whose judgement he trusted, which implies that he would have done the same with any other love-affair about which he was serious. He would rather give up Sarah than Bute's friendship, which shows his priorities.

Bute affirmed firmly in his reply that any marriage was impossible and George owed it to his 'birthright and what you wish to be' to abandon any such thoughts.[13] By implication, he could not be a moral 'Patriot King' and a shining example to his subjects and marry a commoner. George accepted this[14] but continued to pay Lady Sarah marked attention through 1760 and into spring 1761 as was noticed at soirees.[15] Having become King in October 1760, he could technically marry who he liked and defy his advisers if he saw fit but he remained hesitant. There was no indication that this affair was anything but chaste, even when George became King and could have had the political and social power to assert his right to make her his mistress if not his wife (although she was only fourteen and it would have ruined her for the 'marriage-market'). He also mentioned the idea of having an English Queen to Sarah's friend Susan Fox-Strangeways at a reception, and asked Sarah later if Susan had told her this – so possibly he was gaining in confidence and considering ignoring Bute's opinion after all, or at least mulling it over wistfully.[16] The shameless Henry Fox indeed encouraged Sarah to put herself in the King's way in late spring 1761 in the hope of an entanglement, using the proximity of Holland House to the King's route from Kew or Kensington Palace to State ceremonies at St James' to allegedly arrange for her to hang around the probable royal itinerary and intercept George. Court gossip Horace Walpole believed this claim and even wrote that Fox left Sarah unchaperoned in Holland House and sent her out to rake hay on the King's route wearing a skimpy dress like a farm-girl to inflame him.[17] A contemporary print of the pair as courting couple 'Palemon and Lavinia' (a reference to an illicit courtly love-affair in Chaucer's *Knight's Tale*) arm-in-arm in the grounds of Holland House was also in existence. But if there was any flirting it went no further, and the King's last-known, public contact with Sarah was a brief exchange at Court on 18 June; on 4 July his engagement to Princess Charlotte of Meckenberg-Strelitz was announced.[18] The search for a German Protestant bride had been going on since late in 1760 by the King's wish, with only Bute among his advisers knowing about it; Baron von Munchhausen, the Hanoverian minister in London, was asked to draw up a shortlist and this was duly narrowed down.[19] George may have been thinking about the chances of his 'bucking the system' and marrying in England after all into spring 1761 if the exchange with Lady Susan was recorded accurately, but he was shown as not being the sort of man to put his duty last even when he had full Royal powers – which affects the question of Hannah Lightfoot too. His eldest son would have behaved very differently in similar circumstances.

George III always acted with propriety and consideration for his duty to his mentor Bute, his self-respect, and Sarah's reputation. The surviving correspondence makes his behaviour – and his priorities – clear. His attitude to a girl of lower social rank might have been such as to take her briefly for a mistress (though it is unlikely that his Anglican moral scruples would mean that he would feel obliged to 'marry' her to make their sexual relations acceptable), but the letters exchanged with Bute over the issue of Lady Sarah suggest strongly that this was his first romance and he did not know how to proceed but was in control of his feelings and put his duty first throughout. By this reckoning, he had not had any passionate feelings for a girl before. Also, by all accounts Hannah (born in or near 1730 and eight years or so his senior, the daughter of London shoemaker Matthew Lightfoot) was already married to a Mr Isaac Axford at the time when later stories claimed she and George became involved – the date of Axford's marriage to Hannah was recorded in a marriage certificate as 11 December 1753 and Hannah was allegedly abducted by George immediately after that or a few weeks later. (But the putative 'George/Hannah' marriage certificate from St Anne's church, Kew, a copy of which was preserved in the Public Records Office, was dated April 1759.) Might George have considered the Axford marriage 'forced' – supposedly by his anxious family – and so illegal in the eyes of God?

Mr Axford had apparently remarried into the Bartlett family in 1759 in his native Wiltshire, so he presumably assumed Hannah dead or his previous marriage a fraud. (To add to the difficulties facing later researchers there were two separate Isaac Axfords from the district, one born in 1730 and one born in 1734.) There was also the mystery of the alleged theft of a chest containing the Kew parish church records on 22 February 1845, allegedly organised by the Royal Family (who else?) to cover up the embarrassing truth – with similarities to the alleged theft of Lucy Walter's papers by Charles II's agents.[20] The later stories blamed George's mother and his tutor Lord Bute, with or without the assistance of William Pitt (who was a minor political figure unlikely to have been involved as of 1753, but in 1759 the real leader of the government), for persuading Hannah to marry her admirer Mr Axford in the vain hope of dissuading George from pursuing her. The 'go-between' who offered money to Hannah to marry Mr Axford was named in 1820s stories as Elizabeth (nee Chudleigh), Duchess of Kingston – a 'racy' character well-known to 1750s 'High Society' as having appeared topless in theatricals at a public ball in her youth, and later accused of bigamy. Was this just a case of gossip picking up the name of a known 'dodgy' character to add to the drama, or was Elizabeth an 'unshockable' and hard-headed intermediary who it was logical for the Princess of Wales or her friend Lord Bute to choose to help 'shut up' Hannah? Hannah was agreed in accounts originating from the Axford family to have married Mr Axford before she 'disappeared', allegedly to a 'love-nest' with George who had presumably tracked her down. If an apparent 'marriage certificate' for her and 'George Guelph' (the Hanoverian family surname) at Peckham was genuine he had set her up there, though another story has her 'hideout' as being a farm in Lambeth – with the Prince visiting her while taking his horse out for exercise from his mother's residence on the other side of the Thames at Carlton House.

But the Prince would have been knowingly committing adultery given the existence of records proving the Lightfoot-Axford marriage and her 'rescue' from her husband's house. Is it really likely that a strictly-tutored and earnest young Anglican known for his morals would have been prepared to commit sin so blatantly, or could he have regarded the Axford marriage as a fraud as Hannah had been tricked or intimidated into it ? If – as alleged in a supposed 'will' of Hannah dated 1762 – he had been involved enough to have at least one if not three children by Hannah, it is unlikely that he would have been so awkward and inexperienced in matters of love as he was clearly to be with Sarah Lennox in his better-recorded relationship dated at 1759–60. This was an inexperienced and honourable young man, uncertain of how to proceed and wary of the wisdom of marrying an English girl – albeit an aristocrat descended from Charles II – rather than the expected foreign princess. Indeed, the outcome showed that although George was fond of Lady Sarah he was not prepared to run the risk of such a connection, whether or not his mother and Lord Bute asked him to withdraw. This was not the behaviour of an accomplished and reckless lover prepared to marry in secret, like two of his brothers and two of his sons. He was not the sort of young man who would be likely to contract a secret marriage with a person of lower rank like Hannah who was not even from the nobility, and if he had been involved with Hannah in a regular secret liaison involving several children by 1759–60 he would hardly have been so awkward and apparently inexperienced with Sarah.

George IV's illegal secret marriage to the Catholic widow Maria Anne Fitzherbert (Smythe) in 1785 was an established fact with contemporary witnesses and was not denied by the participants, but this is not the case with the story of his father and Hannah Lightfoot. As we have seen, nor was it in character and George as of 1760 was not a person experienced in relationships with the opposite sex. It is highly unlikely given his shy character and his moral earnestness that he had ever had a mistress, let alone at the age of fifteen or sixteen or so c. 1753–5. The most that might be possible was that Hannah was briefly George's mistress in spring 1761, once he was King, with it being made clear to all parties that it was not going to end in marriage. That sort of Royal relationship with a commoner was regarded as acceptable, though any 'serious' and long-standing connection in the eighteenth century tended to be with a member of the nobility. George I, divorced under Lutheran law before he came to England.in 1714, had at least one open and acknowledged mistress of high social rank, the German-born Melusine von der Schulenberg, Duchess of Kendal; Sophie von Kielmansegg, Countess of Darlington, his other female companion who was assumed by the public to be his mistress, was in fact his half-sister. George II had a noble English mistress, Henrietta Howard, Countess of Suffolk, during his wife's lifetime, out of habit rather than passion; as a widower his mistress was Amelia Sophia, Baroness von Walmoden, Countess of Yarmouth. George's father Frederick, Prince of Wales, had more low-born and ephemeral mistresses and no such '*maitresse en titre*'. The depth of coverage of Royal Family characters and love-lives in contemporary memoirs is extensive, and it is clear that George's character bore little similarity to that of his profligate father and his younger brothers let alone his rakish older sons. He was also isolated from other Princes of the family who could have set him a rakish example – unlike his sons were to be in the 1780s. He was in fact under the guardianship of a strict mother alienated from such 'high-living' Royal princes as her late husband's brother, William Augustus, Duke of Cumberland – who she and her circle feared as likely to claim the regency if George II died while Prince George was under-age. (They and the Prince even believed Cumberland capable of murdering him to seize the throne.)

The most that could be expected is that a restless George, aged twenty-one in June 1758, might have had one or more secret mistresses, tolerated by his mother's watchful courtiers such as Bute, to 'initiate' him into love as a preparation for his marriage – a common Royal practice. It would have been made clear that he could not marry the woman in question. This date is more realistic for any affair than 1753/5, though the Lennox courtship shows that he was still naïve and awkward even aged twenty. Given Bute's views on past royal indiscretions as seen above, the latter would have been reluctant to provide a mistress and so risk George becoming a rake like his father – though allowing one secret mistress if George insisted on it might have been possible. It is in this light that the first and only strictly contemporary mention of a Quaker mistress of George's first appears, in a letter from Lady Sophia Egerton to her uncle Count William Bentinck on 10 December 1759 which was preserved in the family's Egerton Papers. She wrote that it was said that George had kept a beautiful Quaker as a mistress for some years; she was now dead and they had had a child.[21] There is no mention of marriage, and this is well before the date of Hannah's supposed will of 1762. It has been suggested that Sophia might have picked up the story as gossip from her close relative Lady Caroline Egerton, who had had land-dealings at Harrow in Middlesex with a Mr John Lightfoot. The story was revived in a reference in the *Public Advertiser* newspaper of 7 September 1770, at the time of scandalous stories about the affairs of George's oldest surviving brother Henry Frederick, Duke of Cumberland, currently connected to the lower-ranking adventuress Ann Horton who, it was to turn out, he had secretly married. A sly and 'knowing' hint is given of a connection between the Duke's older brother, unnamed but obviously the King, and a 'Fair Quaker'[22] – but not that he had married her (which would have made the King's children by Queen Charlotte illegitimate if the 'wife' had been alive when George married her in 1761). The writer may have feared a libel-suit, or not have intended the hint at a secret marriage – which was made by readers once it had been revealed that Cumberland and Ann Horton, the other Royal pair cited, had married. There was also a reference to a 'Fair Quaker of St. James' market' as an anonymous mistress of a Royal personage in the *Reading Mercury* in 1771 – again, not naming the King (for fear of prosecution?). In an edition of *The Citizen* on 26 February 1776 Hannah is referred to by name (as 'Miss L…htf…t') as the Quaker in question.[23]

More details had to wait for decades, with the obvious risk that non-contemporary stories by non-witnesses were embellishing the truth. The unpopularity of George III's attempts to restore Royal influence over the political process among the domineering Whig factions of the 1760s, who had long been used to the monarchy letting them run politics under George II, could also imply a motive for a 'smear' aimed at the King. The latter was falsely accused of attempting to restore the autocratic rule of the Stuarts, as opposed to what George actually *intended* – i.e. to rule as political leader of all his subjects, marginalised Tories and non-partisans included, rather than as the 'front-man' of a group of tightly-knit Whig factions based around a few important families. The examples of illegal private marriages set by George's sons, especially George IV, after the mid-1780s could lead to people reading the same sort of behaviour back into his father's conduct in this period and assuming that the King was just as bad as his sons. Lurid scandal about Royals was the order of the day, with the current Duke of Cumberland (George IV's brother Ernest Augustus) being accused of murdering his valet and having a child by his sister, and George IV's relationship with Mrs Fitzherbert, was well-known. The profligate behaviour of George III's sons was taken as the 'norm', and George III's upright character and close control by his mother as a young man were not generally known; from 1811 to 1820 he was a blind and insane invalid living like a hermit in Windsor Castle. It was not seen as impossible that his Royal Marriages Act of 1772 had been designed to prevent repetition of his own youthful follies as well as those of his sons. But it is notable that the 'marriage' story was slow to emerge, and did not do so in the lifetimes of anyone involved. In 1815 Nathaniel Wraxall referred to George III and an unnamed Quaker in his *Historical Memoirs of My Own Time*, and notes by Hester Piozzi in the 1836 edition said that a son was still alive as of that date.[24] That might be a reference to a 'General John Macketeer' (died c. 1820) whose family later claimed he had admitted he was the son of the King and Hannah. There was also the case of the mysterious portrait of a demure young lady by Sir Joshua Reynolds, said to be of Hannah, that was hanging at Knole House (home of the Sackville dynasty) by 1817 when it was cited in a guidebook as being of the 'Fair Quaker', but not on what evidence. Another painting of the 'Fair Quaker' was said to have been done by the famous mid-eighteenth-century London engraver William Hogarth, and to be included in a group of contemporary paintings put up for auction in June 1806, as per an article of 3 June in the *Morning Post*. The nickname of 'Fair Quaker' for Hannah would appear to have come from a 1710 romantic play by Charles Shadwell entitled *The Fair Quaker of Deal*, which was revived at the Theatre Royal in Drury Lane in 1737 – and which London gossips of the 1750s may well have seen and judged to be appropriate for 'Hannah's situation. The precise career and later life of the woman in question was however such a mystery that though she was (conveniently?) said to have died around 1761–2 nobody was certain about when or where this had happened, or if she had outlived her mother or not. In the nineteenth century a tradition grew up that she had been buried unobtrusively at Islington.

In April 1821 – a year after George III's death – the *Monthly Magazine* started a correspondence among its readers concerning the case, months after the major Royal scandal of the current King's attempt to divorce his adulterous wife Queen Caroline by Act of Parliament (which gripped the nation). The Queen's trial for adultery in the House of Lords failed to secure a 'guilty' verdict but dragged the reputation of the Royal Family through the mud, with accusations being flung by Caroline's defenders at the equally immoral King, and in this atmosphere anything could be believed of them. The notion that the upright George III had also had a guilty secret was thus believable, and in commercial reality helped to sell the paper. But there was no suggestion of a marriage to Hannah Lightfoot, which would have risked libel proceedings by hinting that if she had not died before George IV was born in August 1762 he was not legally King. He was about to be crowned, and the embittered

Queen's supporters would have been able to make major use of this story. But was it omitted as too hot to handle, or because nobody had thought of it yet? Instead, testimony was provided by Hannah's stepson, a Mr Axford – son by a second marriage of the Isaac Axford – who subsequent investigations that he had married Hannah at a chapel on Curzon Street, Mayfair, on 11 December 1753.[25] Hannah had 'disappeared' before Mr Axford's father Isaac married his mother (Miss Bartlett) in 1759 and had been presumed dead, which story agrees with extant records of Hannah's local Quaker 'Meeting' for 1756–7 that she had ceased attending and her address was not known. Mr Axford now claimed that a few weeks after his father's first marriage a coach and-four had driven up to their door and Hannah had climbed aboard and left. She had never returned or been heard of again, though he had made enquiries of her at Richmond and Kew (i.e. around the main Royal 'country' residences, then in Kew Gardens).[26]

Later stories, probably invented, alleged that Mr Axford had chased after his wife on horseback but had had to stop at a toll-gate to pay his toll while the Prince or his coachman shouted to the tollkeeper who they were and the coach was let through – which sounds more like some rake's ingenious ploy to get through the tollgate (or a courtier borrowing a Royal coach and coachman for his own use?) than any realistic sort of conduct for the shy and withdrawn Prince George in 1753/4. The implication was that Isaac had blamed Prince George or his relatives for abducting Hannah – but if he had heard the story accurately George had only been fifteen at the time and was too young to have been an accomplished rake capable of abducting people while his ruthless and potentially unscrupulous uncle William, Duke of Cumberland (the 'Butcher' of the Highlanders in 1746) was feared by George as a potential murderer and would not have been approached for help. There was also a muddle over whether the date was 1753 or 1759, with the Axford family clearly believing the former but the two 'marriage certificates' (one for Kew and one for Peckham) that later surfaced for 'George Guelph and Hannah Lightfoot' dated 1759.

Subsequent stories alleged that Hannah's shoemaker father Matthew had died when she was a child (c. 1733) and she had been brought up in her mother's brother Henry Wheeler's linendraper's shop at St James' Market, not extant but once situated near the Haymarket and Pall Mall – close to Princess Augusta's home at Carlton House where George lived until 1760. A restless and impoverished Hannah might have been rash enough to go off with some lover from Court and abandon her husband, but this did not mean the Prince of Wales – did Mr Axford or his friends assume in the 1780s that George III must be to blame because his eldest son now had a reputation for a secret marriage? According to Hannah's mother's will, she was still missing when this document was drawn up in 1760 and her mother did not know if she was still alive – though it may well have been that Hannah, as a Court noble's lover, had broken off contact with her family sooner than be denounced for disgracing her parents. The same applies to the London Society of Friends' records in 1756–7 that Hannah, a former attender of their meetings, had been expelled in her absence for marrying a non-member and was currently uncontactable.

The story of the marriage only appeared in an anonymous work by a supporter of Queen Caroline, published after her death (1821) in 1824. The author of *An Historical Fragment Relative* to *Her Late Majesty Queen* was apparently Olivia Serres, a miniature-painter with distant Court connections. who believed she was the daughter of George III's brother the Duke of Cumberland. Apparently she had been living at the then Prince of Wales' summer 'Court' residence, Brighton, as a portrait-painter in 1805–6, but had she heard any genuine rumours about Hannah (or her own origins) there, or was she a fantasist or an ambitious money-maker? Arguably her self-proclaimed connection to Cumberland meant that she would have a grudge against that man's elder brother for opposing his marriage to a non-royal (and so preventing her from being accepted publicly as Cumberland's daughter by the Court and given a Royal financial grant?). Had she been told or assumed that status-obsessed George III, who wanted Cumberland to abandon his 'low-class' female partner, was to blame for her being ignored by her 'father'? She made the accusation that the Prince of Wales' wife Princess Caroline had believed George and Hannah Lightfoot to have been married, but gave no further details.[27] Even if Caroline had said this at one point, she was a notoriously unreliable and verbally mischievous woman who had also claimed that a young male 'ward' who appeared mysteriously at her post-separation residence at Blackheath c.1800, 'William Smith/Austin', was her illegitimate son. Admiral Sir Sydney Smith, a well-known admirer of Caroline's, was alleged to be the father. A subsequent enquiry launched at the behest of her estranged husband Prince George, the 'Delicate Investigation', never proved this, and the father of this boy was never identified – so was she making up stories about her father-in-law George III too? It was also alleged in 1820s newspaper correspondence that Queen Charlotte had regarded her eldest son George IV as not legitimately King as he had been born while Hannah was still alive, and that she had 're-married' George III privately at Kew c. 1765 after hearing that Hannah was dead – but this was unproveable and was at a time when George IV was believed to be capable of anything by his detractors so declaring him not legally King was politically useful. Other stories had Hannah as still being alive into the 1820s but living under an assumed name in Warminster, Wiltshire, but the locally-based Marquis of Bath was said to have found out that she was by now dead. Mr. Axford was remembered by his customers as a secretive butcher with a shop in the City of London, implying that he might have been 'bought off' to keep him quiet.

Given that the 1821 newspaper correspondence had provided relatively reliable evidence that the elusive Hannah had disappeared after 1756, her date of death could not be known – so not only George IV but his younger brothers might all be illegitimate if Hannah had married the late King. In that case, it would be unclear who was the legitimate King and the entire current generation of the Hanoverian dynasty – and their children, of whom Victoria was the only legitimate one – could be illegally claiming rights to the throne. Unless Hannah's date of death could be verified, the rightful King would be the only son of any of George's brothers – William, Duke of Gloucester (1776 – 1834). The political implications thus threatened Queen Victoria's right to be Queen after William IV too, giving a reason for the story to remain out of sight – or so Hannah's later supporters were to claim.

Later claims and alleged children. All very unlikely?

It was not until the 1860s that the story produced further sensational claims and the first alleged documentation, provided by Olivia Serres' daughter Olivia Ryves. During a court-case which she launched in 1866 to establish her mother's claims as the Duke of Cumberland's daughter, she produced two alleged 'marriage certificates', dated 17 April and 27 May 1759, which said that George and Hannah had been married privately in Kew by a clergyman called 'James Wilmot' on that date.[28] The clergyman had also written a separate confirmation that the marriage had occurred and had been legal. The 'witness' to the ceremony was William Pitt, Secretary of State for the South and the principal figure in the government of Lord Newcastle – although a Government legal officer or a reliable Court chaplain would have been more logical and in fact Pitt was not close to Prince George at the time. He had been a political ally of George's mother Augusta and Bute in 1754–7 as the most talented and ambitious young 'Whig' politician alienated from the then governments, run by firstly Henry Pelham (d. 1754) and then his brother the Duke of Newcastle.

Their governments, the epitome of the 'Old System' of a closely-knit, corrupt and nepotistic group of factions, had been seen by critics as promoting the interests of George II's beloved Electorate of Hanover over those of Great Britain in foreign policy, and skilful orator Pitt had denounced this on behalf of the 'patriotic interest'. Pitt had thus acted as a spokesman for the 'opposition' based at Leicester House, promoting the notion that the Prince's coming to power would mean a return to honest, patriotic government. But he had then accepted senior office as 'Secretary of State for the South' in a new government formed to manage the Seven Years' War in 1757, in a surprise alliance with Newcastle who retained the office of First Lord of the Treasury and effective

'Prime Minister'; the war was run by a duopoly of Newcastle (in charge of domestic governance and finance) and Pitt (as strategist and 'cheerleader' for foreign policy). This amounted to a 'betrayal' as seen by the Prince's faction at Leicester House. Also, Prince George had refused an offer from the King for him to move out of Leicester House and away from his mother and Bute to set up his own household at St. James' Palace in 1756, which would have given him the 'space' and independence to pursue a private love-life if he so desired. He was thus not interested in having a more autonomous lifestyle at this point, and did not chafe at his mother's or Bute's control.

As effective co-leader of the Whig government disliked by George and Lord Bute and implementer of an expensive war against France of which they disapproved, Pitt was the subject of their machinations once George became King in October 1760 and was eventually driven to resign. He was not George's confidante at any date, and his loyalties in 1757–60 lay with the elderly King who would have wanted to halt any marriage between Prince George and a non-royal or to declare it illegal. Why would the Prince have approached someone who he scarcely knew and did not trust for help with his affair? Pitt was not a logical or credible choice for a witness to the alleged marriage, the use of his name suggesting that it had been inserted by a person who had little idea of the real political situation at the Royal Court in 1757–60. The case attracted a lot of interest in less deferential sections of the media, mainly in Ireland (where the British 'establishment' and by extension the Royal Family were unpopular with much of the poorer and 'political' sections of the public after the Great Famine of the 1840s and George III was a particular *bete noire* for approving the Act of Union that had closed down the Irish Parliament in 1801). Given the current seclusion of Queen Victoria from public life after the death of Prince Albert, criticism of her for failing to carry out the Royal duties that she was paid for, and attacks on the Prince of Wales' playboy life, alleging that the Queen's grandfather had been a bigamist – and that she might not even be the legal sovereign – was a potential weapon for her republican and Irish opponents to use. By the same definition, 'closing down' the story quickly as malicious rubbish was an imperative for the government – and even if its 'experts' were correct in 'rubbishing' the supposed marriage certificate their political enemies would not believe it. The judicial enquiry duly decided that despite the sworn oath of a 'handwriting expert' that the signatures of the participants were genuine the documents were all fakes. The same was decided of Hannah's alleged 'will' (dated 7 July 1762), produced by Lavinia Ryves, which referred to her as 'Hannah Regina' and entrusted Hannah's son and two daughters to their father George III. (The only contemporary reference to Hannah having childen by George, as seen, referred to one child being alive in 1759.) Lavinia Ryves also failed to prove that her mother had been Cumberland's daughter –

although her supporters inevitably claimed that she was victimised to protect Queen Victoria's rights to the throne.

After Lavinia's legal defeat the sceptics went on the offensive as the case revived interest in Hannah, with the extra complication that this was not only a time of rising republicanism but conservative fears about the implications of current radical demands for a new Reform Act to extend the (already controversial) voting reforms of 1832 further. Would the demands for a much wider franchise extend to the working-classes (as backed by rowdy popular demonstrations in London) and lead to 'mob rule' and/or a seizure of power by radicals and republicans? In this charged atmosphere, the governing elite could scare 'sensible' newspapers into staying silent about a case that could encourage republicanism – but did they? In 1867 William John Thomas, founder of *Notes and Queries* magazine (which acted as a 'sorting-office' for correspondents to exchange details of private research), endeavoured to prove that Hannah had never existed. His assertion was disproved by John Heneage Jesse and Horace Bleakely, though it was still not clear what had happened to her after her abandonment (voluntary or not) of Isaac Axford. The political 'outsider' Charles Bradlaugh, a well-known mid-Victorian atheist and controversialist, made a habit of annoying the 'Establishment', asking awkward questions and refusing to be intimidated – as shown by his long campaign to be allowed to 'affirm' rather than take the oath as a Christian in order to sit in the Commons. The 1870s' equivalent of George III's political bugbear John Wilkes at the time of Hannah's alleged relationship, he boldly claimed that the 'marriage' was genuine and that Queen Victoria had no right to the throne. His provocative book on the Lightfoot case, *The Impeachment of The House of Brunswick* (1872), produced the requisite outrage and volley of denials.[29] In fact, he was over-stating the case – even if George had been legally married to Hannah and Miss Ryves' documents were genuine, the will she had produced implied that Hannah had died well before George III's fourth son, Victoria' s father Prince Edward, had been born (1767). Even if George IV, born 1762 – and possibly his next two brothers (born 1763 and 1765) – were bastards, George III had had time to re-marry Queen Charlotte after Hannah's death and legitimize any subsequent children.

The allegation made in an anonymous pamphlet in 1824 and again in the 1860s that George IV's wife Caroline of Brunswick had believed in the marriage being legal might indicate that she had heard rumours at Court or among her 'in-laws' in her years of dealing with the Royal Family, but she was not exactly a reliable source. Bitter after her treatment by George IV and estranged from him within months of their marriage, she lived apart fom him in Greenwich Park until the end of the Napoleonic Wars enabled her to travel abroad – when her odd and indecorous behaviour, vulgarity, public semi-nudity, and relationship with her ' major-domo' Bartolomeo Pergami made her an object of ridicule. She returned to England on becoming Queen in 1820 but was denied her proper status by her husband's orders and put on trial for adultery in the House of Lords in an attempt to secure a Parliamentary Bill to divorce her. That failed, but she was barred from attending the coronation by prize-fighters physically keeping her out of Westminster Abbey and died (suspiciously?) suddenly a few months later. She was quite capable of wanting to embarrass her husband by proclaiming him illegitimate and as their daughter Charlotte had died in November 1817 such an act would not affect the Royal status of any children of theirs. Moreover, if George and his siblings were all disinherited the throne would pass to the nearest heir of George III's elder sister, Princess Augusta (d. 1813), Caroline's own mother – i.e her brother's son the Duke of Brunswick. Her motives in believing that her husband's generation of Hanoverians were illegitimate were not exactly disinterested.

The advocacy of Bradlaugh for Hannah's case only served to make it seem more implausible, but the contemporary strength of anti-monarchic feeling made refutation of his claims essential. 1872 was a time of well-attended republican rallies amidst serious complaints (some in Parliament) about Victoria's long withdrawal from public life following Prince Albert's death and near-invisibility at Balmoral, with cartoons about her abandonment of her duties and implications that she was a waste of public money. In recent years someone had put up a 'To Let' notice on the gates of the deserted Buckingham Palace, and stories were starting to emerge about her suspiciously close relationship with her 'Highland Servant' John Brown. They were to be accused of marrying in secret, like George III and Hannah – again, the public reputation of the monarch for prudishness and high morals seemed only to stir up malicious stories of what was really going on in private. Her eldest son Albert Edward was known as an adulterous rake like George IV, although his recovery from a dangerous bout of typhoid in December 1871 was turned into an excuse for a public service of thanksgiving at St Paul's Cathedral where the Queen could show herself in public. 1872 was a dangerous time to be making allegations about the legitimacy of the current monarch's seat on the throne, and the case still had serious political overtones. It could not be considered on its merits, though even without a political need to deny the marriage it would have rested on flimsy foundations. Some serious documentary research did follow among early twentieth-century biographers – at a time when the atmosphere surrounding the Royal Family was also less heated.

Mary Penderel was the first intensive investigator of the case; her book *The Fair Quaker* (1910) was followed by a second in collaboration with Justinian Mallett, *Princess or Pretender?* (1939). They claimed that Olivia Serres had exaggerated the extent of the affair but Hannah and George had had some form of relationship.[30] The Prince's relationship with Lady Sarah Lennox had, however, been his first serious consideration of marriage, as seen by his correspondence with Bute. Any genuine relationship between George and Hannah would make more logic after his marriage (when the Queen was 'out of action' pregnant?) but in any case any 'marriage documents' would be fake and the possibility must arise that Hannah's husband Mr Axford was incorrect in assuming the mystery lover to be the Prince/King. Did some courtier pass himself off as George?

The issue of George's and Hannah's children was also subject to conflicting opinions, with the most sensational claim being the easiest to disprove. Their 'son' was once identified with a mysterious man called, appropriately, 'George Rex', born 1765, who had emigrated to the infant colony of Cape Province (South Africa) in 1797 and had received a huge estate at Knynsa (24,000 acres) and the lucrative honorific offices of Marshal and Sergeant-at-Mace to the colony's Vice-Admiralty Court.[30] Had these grants been a 'pay-off' from his father in return for his leaving England for good? Possibly the name 'Rex' suggested the 'cover-up', though it was a rather obvious 'clue' to his 'real identity' as seen by his excited partisans. There were also claims by alleged relatives on the internet as late as the 2000s that George Rex had been George III's son according to the ubiquitous and unproveable 'family legend' and had been sent off to the North American colonies with his mother Hannah, presumably around 1760 to get him out of the way of any investigation by anti-Royal mischief-makers. George III had known about their location and had sent his son a present when the man's child, his first grandson, was born (c. 1780), but after the American Revolution the family had found it prudent to relocate to the new British colony at Cape Town in South Africa (actually acquired in 1795). An alternative version linked George's 'wife' and her children to Nova Scotia – still in British hands after 1783 so they would not have needed to leave. The George Rex story and its possibilities for George III's marriage to Charlotte of Mecklenberg-Strelitz being bigamy was still being brought up in the 1990s, at a time of renewed scepticism about the Royal Family's behaviour as the marriages of the Prince of Wales and Duke of York collapsed – as seen in a *Sunday Express* article of 18 June 1995.

The alleged date of George Rex's birth, 1765, was rather late considering that the 'will' of Hannah Lightfoot mentioning her children produced by Lavinia Ryves – the only documentary 'evidence' of a 'son' existing – was dated 1762. Conspiracy theorists, of course, could argue that the date '1765' was a fake, introduced to throw people off the scent. In fact a full scholarly investigation in South Africa by Patricia Storror (*George Rex; Death of a Legend.* 1974), had shown that George Rex was in fact registered as the son of respectable distiller, John Rex of London, hence the surname. Ian Christie discovered his birth records, stating that he was born on 29 August 1765 and baptised at Whitechapel on 2 September; John Rex (1725 – 92) and his wife Sarah (1730 – 1802) are fully recorded too and neither had any connection to Court.[31] The identification of the 'son' of George and Hannah as Mr Rex was therefore disproved, and in any case was an issue without direct bearing on the question of Hannah's marriage. A subsequent TV programme tested members of the Rex family who claimed descent from George Rex for DNA to match the Royal Family's and found none, so that seemed to have settled the matter. But a question-mark still hangs over the possibility that George and Hannah did have children, albeit illegitimate ones. Though the Prince's correspondence turned up no trace of them, enthusiasts could claim that he or decorous Victorian archivists had 'weeded' it to remove all trace of scandal. In December 2000 *British Archaeology* magazine reported on the possible discovery of the tomb of a daughter of George and Hannah at St Peter's Church, Carmarthen. The *Monthly Magazine* correspondence on the issue in 1821 had turned up the story that a 'gentleman of the name of Dalton' had married a daughter of George and Hannah; this woman was now suggested as the 'Charlotte Augusta Dalton' buried at Carmarthen in 1823. (Charlotte and Augusta were the names of two of George III's older daughters by Queen Charlotte, born in the mid-late 1760s). It was suggested that King George IV's apparent gift of an organ to the church might be connected to gratitude for its use as a burial site for his half-sister; but this could well be coincidence. Charlotte Dalton's mother was called 'Ritzau' not 'Lightfoot' or 'Axford' according to Mary Pendered's research – which does not rule out the possibility that as a German she had a Court connection, hence the Royal gift.[32]

The story of George III and Hannah Lightfoot thus relies on substantially less evidence than the cases of Edward IV or Charles II's secret marriages, and is highly improbable. It is more likely that if Hannah's abandoned husband believed her 'seducer' to be the then Prince of Wales, he was mistaken and some courtier was (jokily?) using the Prince's identity. Perhaps the long history of believers in this claim tells us more about what the sceptical public was prepared to believe of Royalty in the late eighteenth century and the nineteenth century – and in the 1990s – than about George III. Is this a warning about the illogical lengths to which disbelief in official 'spin' will go?

Notes

Chapter 1: James VI and I and the Gowrie House Conspiracy, 1600. Royal Kidnap Plot or Royal 'Honey-Trap'?

1. Alan Stewart, *The Cradle King: Life of James VI and I* (Chatto and Windus 2001) p. 64–9; David Calderwood, *History of the Kirk In Scotland* (ed Thomas Thomson, 8 vols, Woodrow Society Edinburgh 1842–9) vol 3 pp. 640–93.
2. Calderwood, p. 645; *Sir James Melville, Memoirs of His Own Life* (Bannatyne Club, Edinburgh 1827) pp. 110–11, 287.
3. Gilbert Burnet, *A History of My Own Time* (ed. Osmund Airy, 1897) vol 1 p. 26.
4. Stewart, pp, 135–6; Calderwood, vol 5 p. 296.
5. Stewart pp. 131–2; Calderwood, vol 5 pp. 140–5; Calendar of State Papers Scotland vol 10, pp. 633–6.
6. Calderwood, vol 5 p. 256; Thomson, *The History and Life of James the Sixth* p. 270–2.
7. CSP Scotland 1593–5, p. 193.
8. Ibid, pp. 304 and 327–8.
9. Robert Pitcairn, *Criminal Trials in Scotland,* Edinburgh 1833) vol 2 p. 207.
10. Ibid, p. 207; Sir Walter Scott, *Secret History of the Court of James I* (Edinburgh 1811) p. 146.
11. Pitcairn, vol 2 pp. 237–8.
12. John D. Davies, *Blood of Kings: the Stuarts, the Ruthvens and the Gowrie Conspiracy* (Ian Allan and Co, 2010) pp. 143–4.
13. Calendar of State Papers, Elizabeth I 1598–1601, ed Mary Everett Green (HMSO 1869), pp. 465 ff.
14. Pitcairn, vol 2 pp. 156–7 and 249–50.
15. CSP Scotland 1597–1603, p. 702; Andrew Lang, *James Vi and the Gowrie Conspiracy* (1902).
16. CSP Scotland 1597–1603, p. 694; Lang pp. 13 and 48–9.
17. Maidstone Centre for Kentish Studies: Dering Mss. U 275, C 1/17; for analysis of the official account, see Davies pp. 219–24.
18. CSP Scotland 1597–1603, p. 723.
19. E. Peyton, *The Divine Catastrophe of the Kingly House of Stuart* (1652) p. 339; G. P. R. Jones, *An Investigation into the Circumstances surrounding the Murder of John, Earl of Gowrie* (1849).
20. Calderwood, vol 6 p. 46; Davies, pp. 202–3.
21. Davies, pp. 189–90.
22. Ibid; BL Additional Mss. 31022, f. 107; Historical Manuscripts Commission: Cecil Papers, vol x, p. 365.
23. Davies, ibid.
24. Ibid, pp. 182–3; *Sprott Confessions*, pp. 39–40.

Chapter 2: James I's Bisexual Favourite, His Mistress, and the Poisoning in the Tower: The Overbury Scandal

1. David Starkey, ed, *The English Court from the Wars of the Roses to the English Civil War* (Longmans 1987), article by Neil Cuddy, 'The revival of the entourage: the Bedchamber of James I, 1603–1625', pp. 173–225, at pp. 184–7.
2. Ibid pp. 189–90; F. H. Mares, ed, *Memoirs of Sir Robert Carey* (Oxford UP 1972) p. 66.
3. Calendar of State Papers Domestic 1603–1610, p. 147; BL Additional Mss. 15,476 f. 92v.
4. CSP Domestic 1637–8, p. 216.
5. Cuddy, p. 193.
6. H. M. Colvin, ed, *History of the King's Works* (6 vols, HMSO 1963–82), vol 4 pp. 32, 175, 237; N A E 351/3369.

7. H. Harington, ed, *Nugae Antiquae* (2 vols, 1804) vol 1 p. 345.
8. Cuddy, p. 197; Mares, *Memoirs of Sir Carey*, p. 66; Edward Hyde, *History of the Great Rebellion and Civil Wars in England,* ed W. D. Macray (Oxford 1888) vol 1 p. 74; G. Goodman, *The Court of King James.* ed. Brewer, 1839) vol 1 p. 40.
9. Cuddy, pp. 188–9 and 197–8.
10. Lee, *Government by Pen: Scotland under King James VI and I,* (Urbana University Press, Illinois, 1980) pp. 36–7.
11. J. Harington, *Letters and Epigrams of Sir John Harringtion together with Prayse of Private Life*, ed Norman McClure (University of Pennsylvania Press, Philadelphia 1930) pp. 19–21. Goodman, vol 1 pp. 39–40; Ralph Weldon in *Sir Walter Scott,* Secret History of the Court of James I (Edinburgh 1811) vol ii pp. 332–3.
12. Anne Somerset, *Unnatural Murder: Poison at the Court of James I* (Weidenfeld and Nicolson 1997) p. 54.
13. Comte Leveneur de Tillieres, *Memoirs*, ed M.C. Hippeau (Paris 1863) p. 2.
14. Scott, vol 1 pp. 374–5; Harington vol I p. 398; Arthur Wilson, *The history of Great Britain, during the Life of King James I (1603)* (1653) p. 54.
15. CSP Domestic 1603–10, p. 385; Historical Manuscripts Commission: Salisbury Mss. vol xix, p. 456; Cuddy, p. 187.
16. HMC Salisbury, vol xix p. 269n; S. R. Gardiner, *History of England 1603–42* (1900), vol 2 p. 46.
17. Sir John Oglander, *A Royalist's Notebook*, ed Frank Bamford (1936) p. 196; R. Coke, *A Detection of the Court and State of England* (1719) p. 87; Goodman, vol 1 p. 18.
18. Elizabeth Bourcier, ed, *The Diary of Sir Simonds D'Ewes 1622–1624* (Paris 1974) pp. 92–3.
19. Anne Somerset, p. 29.
20. Wilson, p. 56; *Letters of John Chamberlain,* ed N McClure (Philadelphia 1939) vol 1 pp. 300, 302.
21. Goodman, vol 1 p. 215; Scott, vol I p. 376.
22. *Letters of John Holles,* ed P. R. Seddon (Thoroton Record Society Series, Nottingham 1975–86) vol I pp. 72–3.
23. R. F. Patterson, *Ben Johnson: Conversations with William Drummond of Hawthornden* (1933) p. 20; BL Additional Mss. 15476 f. 93.
24. Scott, vol 1 p. 374; Goodman, vol I pp. 215–16; John Aubrey, *Brief Lives* (ed Oliver Lawson Dick, 1978) p. 417.
25. S. R. Gardiner, *Parliamentary Debates in 1610*10 (Camden Society 1862) pp. 144–5; HMC Salisbury Mss. vol xxi, pp. 264–5; Goodman, vol 1 p. 41; Wallace Notestein, *The House of Commons 1604–1610* 1971) p. 433.
26. Wilson, p. 79; Goodman, vol I p. 216 and vol 2 p. 145; HMC Downshire Mss. vol 3, pp. 83 and 138–9.
27. Somerset, p.96.
28. Chester City Record Office, CR 63/2/19, f. 10.
29. Ralph Winwood, *Memorials of Affairs of State in the Reigns of Queen Elizabeth and James I: Great Order of Poisoning (*1846) p. 128; McClure, vol 1 p. 442; *Life and Letters of Henry Wooten ed* (Oxford 1907) vl 2 p. 19.
30. Cambridge University Library: Dd 3 63, ff. 31, 37, 44, 53.
31. NA: SP 14/82/ 47, ff. 60–60v.
32. Winwood, vol 3 p. 447; Wotton, vol 2 pp. 19–20; NA: SP 14/72/146; BL Harleian Mss 7002, f. 286v.
33. William Cobbett, *State Trials,* vol 2 pp. 787, 807, 816; Halliwell, *Secret History of the Reign of King James I* (1845) vol 2 p. 357; Scott, vol 1 pp. 388–89; BL Harleian Mss. 39, ff. 420v and 431v.
34. Cobbett, vol 2 p. 807, 810.
35. Ibid, pp. 811–12.
36. Ibid, p. 802.
37. Ibid pp. 813–14; Thomas Birch, *The Court and Times of James I* (1848) vol 1 , p. 269.
38. Cobbett, pp. 821, 826–7; The Case of Insufficiency Discussed, touching the Divorce Between the Lady Frances Howard and Robert earl of Essex (1711) pp. 31–2.
39. Somerset, pp. 167–8.
40. Cobbett, vol 2 p. 83; Bodleian Library: Tanner Mss. 299, f. 198.

41. Bodleian Library: Tanner Mss. 199, f. 198v; NA: SP 14/82/30, f. 40; SP 14/82/ 20, f. 24; SP 14/81/ 118, f. 202; SP 14/82/3, f. 3; SP 14/82/19, f. 23; Cobbett, vol 2 pp. 916–17.
42. Bodleian Library: Willis Mss. 58, f. 228v; Tanner Mss. 299, ff. 195 and 199; NA: SP 14/82/3, f. 3; Historical Manuscripts Commission: Buccleuch Mss. vol 1 p. 160.
43. Bodleian Library: Tanner Mss. 299, ff. 195, 199; Amos pp. 215–16.
44. NA: SP 14/83/70, f. 129; SP 14/83/73; SP 14/82/3, f. 3v; Amos p. 388.
45. Winwood, vol 3 p. 475; Wotton, vol 2 p. 22; BL Harleian Mss. 7002, ff. 281v, 286, 291; Cambridge University Library: Dd 3 63, f. 44; NA: SP 14/82/3, f.3.
46. NA: SP 14/82/19, f. 23; SP 14/82/20, f. 24; SP 14/82/30, f. 40; SP 14/83/32, f.43.
47. SP 14/86/ 6, f. 13.
48. Bodleian Library: Wilis Mss. 58, f. 234.
49. BL Harleian Mss. 7002, ff. 286v, 287, 288; NA: SP 14/81/111, f. 207; SP 14/82/5, f.6; SP 14/82/23, f. 28; HMCBuccleuch Mss. vol 1 p. 139.
50. Cobbett, vol 2 p. 922; BL Harleian Mss. 7002, f. 288v; Francis Anthony, *Collectanea Cymica*, pp. 73–8.
51. Somerset, pp. 208–9.
52. NA: SP 14/72/145, f. 257; SP 14/82/46, f. 59; BL Additional Mss. 15476, f. 93.
53. Cambridge University Library: Dd 3 63, ff. 44 and 49.
54. BL Harleian Mss. 7002, f. 290 and 290v; Cambridge University Library: Dd 3 63, f. 49.
55. Bodleian Library: Willis Mss. 58, f. 231v-232; BL Cotton Library: Titus B VII, f. 486; NA: SP 14/82/39, f. 51.
56. NA: SP 14/82/26, f. 35; BL Harleian Mss. 7002, f. 29.
57. Cambridge University Library: Dd 3 63, f. 53v.
58. HMC Buccleuch Mss vol 1 p. 160.
59. Scott, vol 1 pp. 385–6 and 404–5; NA: SP 14/82/ 71, f. 88v.
60. Somerset, pp. 244–8.
61. Goodman, vol I p. 257; Halliwell, vol I p. 70.
62. W. Sanderson, *A Complete History of the Lives and Reigns of Mary Queen of Scotland and Her Son and Successor James* VI *King of Scotland and King of Scotland and Great Britain and France and Ireland* (1656) p. 456; Halliwell, vol 1 p. 86.
63. G.P.V. Akrigg, *Letters of King James VI and I* (University of California Press 1984) p. 335–41.
64. Holles, vol I p. 68.
65. BL Additional Mss. 35832, f. 6; NA: SP 14/82/3, ff. 3v, 4v; Bodleian Library: Willis Mss. 58, f. 229; Tanner Mss. 299, f. 200.
66. Scott, vol 1 pp. 403–5, 407; Sanderson p. 414.
67. Bodleian Library: Tanner Mss. 299, f. 194; HMC Downshire Mss. vol 5 p. 319; HMC Buccleuch Mss. vol 1 pp. 160–1; Halliwell, vol I p. 69; NA: SP 14/81/86.
68. NA: SP 14/81/ 88, ff. 149–149v; Bodleian Mss: Smith Mss. 17, f. 30.
69. HMC Salisbury manuscripts, vol 22 p. 29; NA: SP 14/83/70, f. 129v; Cobbett, vol 2 p. 99.
70. Cobbett, vol 2 pp. 930, 1031; NA: SP 14/81/90, f. 151; SP 14/83/74.
71. NA: SP 14/82/23, ff. 28 and 35; Scott, vol 1 pp. 411–12.
72. BL Additional Mss. 35832, f. 5; Cobbett, vol 2 p. 915.
73. Ibid p. 933; Halliwell, vol I p. 87.
74. Bodleian: Tanner Mss. 299, ff. 19607; Willis Mss. 58, ff. 227v and 229.
75. Bodleian Library: Tanner Mss. 299, ff. 198v, 199, 199v; Willis Mss. 58, f. 235v; Cobbett, vol 2 pp. 939–40.
76. Amos pp. 215–16; Cobbett, vol 2 pp. 943–4, 947; Birch, vol I p. 380.
77. Cobbett, vol 2 p. 950; NA: SP 14/34/ 11, f. 24; SP 14/83/85; Birch, vol I p. 384.
78. James Spedding, The Works of Francis Bacon (1857–74), vol 12 pp.287–9.
79. Bodleian Library: Willis Mss. 58, f. 212; Spedding, vol 12 pp. 313–14.
80. HMC Downshire Mss. vol 5, pp. 510–11; Cobbett, vol 2 p. 917.

Chapter 3. Charles II and the Secret Treaty of Dover: Did he Really Intend to Convert to Catholicism?

1. Ronald Hutton, *Charles II*, pp. 184–5; Acts of the Privy Council of Scotland, vol 7, pp. 415–29; Bodleian Library: Carte Mss. 32, ff, 68–9.

2. Acts of Privy Council of Scotland, vol 7, p. 448–51 and 459–61; Gilbert Burnet, *History of My Own Time,* vol I pp. 263–4.
3. Hutton, pp. 203–4.
4. J. S. Clark, ed, *Life of James II* (1816), vol 1 pp. 307–8; NA: SP 9444; SP 31/3/108, ff. 1–148; SP 31/3/109, f. 12.
5. Richard Ollard, *Man of War: The Life of Sir Robert Holmes,* 85–131.
6. Paul Seaward, 'The House of Commons Committee of Trade and the Origins of the Third Anglo-Dutch War' in *Historical Journal*, vol 30, 1987, pp. 437–52.
7. National Archives: N.A. 31/3/114, f. 126.
8. Hutton, pp. 218–20.
9. R. Ollard, *Pepys: A Biography*, pp. 160–6.
10. P. G. Rogers, *The Dutch in the Medway* (1970) p. 55.
11. Rogers, p. 87.
12. Hutton, pp. 242–4, 248–9.
13. C.H. Hartmann, *La Belle Stuart*, pp. 124–8.
14. Hutton, pp. 250–3.
15. Keith Feiling, *British Foreign Policy*, pp. 371–2; Thomas Peregrine Courtenay, *Memoirs of Sir William Temple* (1836) vol I p. 133–40.
16. Courtenay, pp. 192–7; Feiling, pp. 262–4 and app. vii; Bryant, *Letters of Charles II*, pp. 215–16.
17. NA: SP 29/243/11; BL: Egerton Mss. 2539, f. 195; Additional Mss. 36916, f. 103; Additional Mss. 28093, ff. 168–77; Bryant, pp. 357–80.
18. Rowen, *De Witt*, pp. 715–16; Feiling, pp. 267–9; C. H. Hartmann, *Cliffor of the Cabal* (1937), p. 137; Calendar of State Papers Venetian 1669–70, p. 60; NA: SP 31/3/121, ff. 247–9.
19. B.L. Egerton Mss. 2543, f. 129; BL Additional Mss. 28078, f. 14; NA: SP 29/243/102; Hutton, pp. 263–4.
20. Feiling, pp. 277–9; CSPV 1669–70, pp. 37, 62–3; Bebington, *Arlington's Letters,* pp. 391–402.
21. Rowen, *De Witt*, pp. 725–30.
22. Ugbrooke Park: STD Papers, 'Minette' to Charles II, 23 September 1669.
23. Ibid, 'The Project'; Hutton, *Charles II*, p. 266.
24. NA: SP 29/284/22.
25. C. H. Hartmann, *The King, My Brother*, p. 39; HMC Report: Bath Papers, p. 144.
26. Jenny Uglow, *A Gambling Man: Charles II and the Restoration*, p. 512.
27. NA: SP 31/3/ 125, ff. 225–316; Sir John Dalrymple, *Memoirs of Great Britain and Ireland* 1790) vol I pp. 115–19; BL Additional Mss. 28040, f.5.

Chapter 4. Did Charles II Marry Twice – and Was the Duke of Monmouth his Rightful Heir?

1. Ronald Hutton, *Charles II*, pp. 74–5.
2. Maurice Ashley, *JamesII*, pp. 91–2.
3. Gilbert Burnet, *History of My Own Time (*1835 edition) vol ii p. 317.
4. Ashley, p. 92.
5. Hutton, pp. 186–7.
6. C. H. Hartman, *The King, My Brother* (1954) p. 44; Hartmann, *Charles II and Madame* (1934) p. 47; Antonia Fraser, *Charles II*, pp. 210–12.
7. Ashley, pp. 97–8.
8. Burnet, vol 2, pp. 15–16.
9. Historical Manuscripts Commission: Ormonde Papers, vol iv, pp. 557–8.
10. See J.G. Muddiman, *The Mystery of Edmund Godfrey* (London 1924), the first book to blame Pembroke for the murder, and Alan Marshall, *The Strange Death of Edmund Godfrey* (History Press 1999).
11. J.N.P. Watson, *Captain General and Rebel Chief: The Life of James, Duke of Monmouth* (Allen and Unwin 1979) p. 5.
12. BL Additional Mss. 28094, f. 71.
13. Watson, p. 4.
14. Watson, p. 5.

15. Ibid.
16. Ibid, p. 4, quoting from Clarendon State Papers, Bodleian Library, Oxford.
17. Watson, p. 276.
18. BL Additional Mss. 32095, ff. 198 and 200.
19. Historical Manuscripts Commisison: Finch Papers vol 2, pp. 76–7.
20. Calendar of State Papers Domestic 1680: 26 June 1680.
21. Somers Tracts vol 8, pp. 197–210.
22. John Carswell, *The Porcupine: The Life of Sir Algernon Sydney* (John Murray 1989) pp. 41–2.
23. Watson, p. 4.
24. Ibid, p. 6, quoting Thurloe State Papers (7 vols, London 1742).
25. Ibid.
26. *Mercurius Politicus* newsletter, 16–17 July 1656.
27. Watson, p.7.
28. BL Additional Mss. 28094.
29. *Pepys Diary*, October 1662.
30. BL Lansdowne Mss. 1236, f. 128.
31. *Pepys Diary*: 20 April 1663.
32. *Pepys Diary*: 29 December 1662.
33. Watson, pp. 275–6.
34. Ibid, p. 276.
35. John Lingard, *History of England* (1849) vol 12, p. 241.
36. BL Additional Mss. 32095, ff. 198, 200.
37. Watson, p. 127.
38. Ibid, pp. 146–9.
39. Ibid, p. 215.
40. Burnet, vol 2 pp. 39304; John Oldmixon, *History of England during Reigns of the House of Stuart* (1740) vol 1 p. 690.
41. Watson, pp. 276–7.
42. Ibid, p. 277.
43. See Frederick Holmes, *The Sickly Stuarts: The Medical Downfall of a Dynasty* (Sutton 2003) for the theory that Charles II was killed by mercury poisoning from his laboratory experiments.

Chapter 5: James II – Progressive Promoter of Religious Toleration or Determined to Turn Britain Catholic?

1. BL Additional Mss. 46961, ff. 216–17. J. Whiting, *Persecution Exposed (*London, 1791 edition) p. 267; Thoresby, Diary, vol I p. 180; Rutt, ed, *Life of Edmund Calamy* vol I p. 117; *The Autobiography of William Stout of* Lancaster 1665–1752, ed. J. D. Marshall (Chetham Society 1967) p. 82.
2. Evelyn, *Diary*, ed De Beer, vol iv p. 419.
3. NA: London Gazette, 19 March, 26 March, and 6 April 1685.
4. John Whiting: *Persecution Exposed*, 2nd edition (James Philips, London 1791) p. 267; Ralph Thoresby, *Diary*, vol 1 p. 180 (February 1685); *The Life of Sir Edmund Calmy*, ed. Rutt, vol 1 p. 117.
5. Sir John Lowther, *Memorials of the Reign of James II* (H.C. Bohn, London 1857) p. 450.
6. P. Braybrooke, ed, *The Autography of Sir John Bramston* (Camden Society, 1845). p. 166; Pincus. P. 97.
7. Ailesbury, *Memoirs,* vol I p. 100; BL Additional Mss. 71691 f. 57v; Buckinghamshire Record Office: Verney Mss., 16 March 1685; Pincus, 1688, pp. 100–01.
8. J.R. Jones, *The Revolution of 1688 in England*, pp. 189, 197–8.
9. Commons Journal vol ix p. 756; BL Additional Mss. 34508, f. 89; Leopold von Ranke, *History of England,* 6 vols, `875, vol iv pp. 276–9.
10. H. Horwitz, *Revolution Politics,* 1968, pp. 39–41.
11. Pincus, p. 172.
12. Ibid, p. 181.
13. Ibid, p. 182.
14. Gilbert Burnet, *A Collection of Papers Relating to the Present Juncture of Affairs in England (1688/9*, pp. 26–7; Evelyn, *Diary*, entries for 4 December 1688, 9 January 1686, 12 June

1687, 24 August 1688; Charles Jackson, ed, *The Diary of Abraham de la Pryme*, Surtees Society, vol 54, 1869–70, p. 1686; NA: SP 31/3/166, f. 361; 31/3/170, f. 13; SP 31/3/172, f. 155.

15. Von Ranke, vol iv pp. 219–20, 282.
16. NA: SP 31/3/ 166.
17. Pincus, p. 188.
18. Adrian Tinniswood, *His Invention So Fertile: A Life of Sir Christopher Wren* p. 281.
19. Pincus, pp. 132–3.
20. *The History of Father La Chaise* (London 1693), p. 342; Ailesbury, Memors, vol I p. 152.
21. Pincus, pp. 125–6.
22. NA: SCA: B 1 1/105/8; Gilbert Burnet, *A Collection of Eighteen Papers Relating to Affairs of Church and State during the Reign of James II* (London 1689); Burnet, *A History of His Own Time,* 1706 edition, vol ii pp. 595, 700.
23. Pincus, pp. 132–3.
24. NA: SP 31/3/160, f. 701; 31/3/164, f. 36; 31/3/160, ff. 39–40; 31/3/167, ff. 11v, 40v, 47–8; 31/3/168, ff. 11, 1 31/3/171, f. 671; Hales, *Treatise on Government* (1692), in *Old Brotherhood Papers*, Book 3/ 258.
25. Pincus, pp. 143–56.
26. Ibid, pp. 372–3.
27. Ibid, pp. 372–3, 378–81.
28. NA: SP 31/3/168; Dr Williams' Library Mss. 31 Q, f. 210; BL Additional Mss. 34512, f. 78.
29. Ailesbury, *Memoirs* vol I p. 99.
30. Pincus, p. 155.
31. NA: SP 31/3/161, f. 66v. N A 31/3/162, f. 66v; 31/3/162, ff. 3, 42r; Privy Council Registers (PC) 2/71, f. 77v'; BL Additional Mss. 28569, f. 56r; BL Additional Mss. 70013, f. 280r; 31/3/163, ff. 1, 2; 31/3/166, f. 29v; 31/3/167, ff. 14v, 29v.
32. NA: SP 31/3/ 160, f. 70r.
33. NA: SP 31/3/ 169, f. 66r; N A 31/3/160, f. 70r; 31/3/164, f. 36; 31/3/160, ff.39–40; 31/3/167, ff. 404, 47–8, 50–1, 58v; 31/3/171, f. 67r; 31/3/174, ff.41–2.
33. N. A. 31/3/167, ff 50–1; 31/3/164, f. 361; 31/3/166, f. 22r; Pincus p. 204; Jones, p. 81.
34. Pincus p.204.
35. James to Dartmouth, 8 May and 25 July 1679, quoted Pincus p. 125; also Pincus p. 205; N A/3/ 169, f. 66r and 31/3/ 163, ff. 120–1.
36. Defoe, *Letter from a Dissenter* (The Hague 1688), pp. 1–3; Maximilian Novak, *Daniel Defoe: Master of Fictions* (Oxford UP 2003) pp. 89–90.
37. Pincus, p. 207–8; BL Additional Mss. 34515, ff. 47–8; NA: SP 30/ 53/8, f. 117.
38. Pincus, p. 204.
39. BL Additional Mss. 34512, ff. 82–3; Additional Mss. 34515, f. 65; NA: SP 8/1/ Part 2, ff. 203–4.
40. A. T. Hart, *Life and Times of John Sharp* (1949) pp. 92–3; Jones, *The Revolution of 1688 in England*, pp. 70–1.
41. Barillon, French ambassador in England, to Louis XIV, 5 March 1687 (NS) and 24 April, 12 June and 9 October 1687.
42. Jones, *Revolution of 1688 in England*, p. 85.
43. Ibid, p. 99.
44. NA: SP 31/3/ 172, f. 151; 31/3/174, f. 11; Burnet, *History of My Own Time,* 1724 edition, p. 701.
45. Longleat House; Thynne Mss. 15, f. 190; J. R. Bloxam, ed, *Magdalen College and King James II* (Clarendon Press 1886) pp. 222–3.
46. D. Lemmings, *Gentlemen and Barristers: The Inns of Court and the English Bar, 1680–1730* (Clarendon Press 1990) p. 65; D. Goldie, 'James II and the Dissenters' Revenge', p. 61; BL Additional Mss. 4194,f. 126v; BL Additional Mss. 28876, f. 23.
47. Jones, pp. 177–8.
48. Ibid, pp. 51–3.
49. NA: SP 8/1/ Part 2, ff. 198, 203
50. NA: SP 31/3/ 175, ff. 56, 171; 31/3/ 177, f. 16.

51. Ailesbury, Memoirs, p. 170; Bodleian Library: Tanner Mss. 39/28, f. 38v; NA: SP 31/3/ 177, f. 42.
52. Pincus, pp. 193–6.
53. Jones, *The Revolution in England.*
54. Ibid, pp. 150–62.
55. NA: SP 31/3/ 173, ff. 191–4A; 31/3/174, ff. 116–17; 31/3/175, ff. 17, 56.
56. NA: SP 31/3/177, f. 42; Longleat House: Thynne Mss. 15, f. 235; Bodleian Library: Tanner Mss. 39/28, f. 38v.
57. Pincus, pp. 194–7.
58. J. P. Kenyon, 'The Earl of Sunderland and the Revolution of 1688' in *Cambridge Historical Journal*, vol xi, pp. 272–96.
59. Pincus, pp. 202–3.
60. Jones, pp. 85–6. Maurice Ashley, *James II*, pp. 220–1.
62. Jones, pp. 214, 216, 218–21.
63. Burnet vol 3, pp. 173–5; Jones, p. 217–19.
64. S. Baxter, *Wiliam III* (1966).
65. Ashley, pp. 238–9.
66. N A: SP 8/1/ Part 2, ff. 224–5.
67. Beatrice Curtis Brown, *Letters of Queen Anne* (London 1935) p. 37.
68. Edward Gregg, *Queen Anne,* pp. 54–6.
69. Brown, *Letters and Diplomatic Instructions*, pp 57–63.
70. Ashley, p. 231.
71. BL Additional Mss. 41816, ff. 205, 209.
72. Jones, pp. 258–60.
73. Jones, p. 259; Pincus p. 228.
74. Pincus, p. 228.
75. BL Additional Mss. 41816, f. 160; Additional Mss. 41827, f. 90; NA: SP 31/4, f. 841. Defoe, *Memoirs and Public Transactions,* pp. 18–19; Ailesbury, *Memoirs,* vol I pp. 129–30; Sir John Reresby, *Memoirs,* pp. 520–1; BL Additional Mss. 34517, f. 91. Jones, p. 258.
76. Jones, pp. 260–1.
77. S. W. Singer, *The Correspondence of Henry Hyde, Earl of Clarendon* (1828), vol ii, p. 176
78. Jones pp. 294–5; CSP Domestic 1687–9, p. 360.
79. HMC Dartmouth Mss (11th Report), appendix, part 5, p. 220.

Chapter 6: Early Hanoverian Royal Murders and Bastards

1. Ragnhild Hatton, *George I: Elector and King* (Thames and Hudson 1978) pp. 20–2.
2. Ibid, pp. 23–4.
3. Ibid, pp. 31–2.
4. Mathilde Knoop, *Die Kurfurstin Sophie von Hannover* (Hildesheim 1964) pp. 102–3; P. L. Muller, *Wihelm III van Oranien und Georg Friedrich von Valden* (The Hague 1873), vil p pp. 109ff.
5. Edward Gregg, 'Was Queen Anne a Jacobite?' in *History*, vol vii, October 1972, p. 367; E Gregg, *Queen Anne* pp. 23–4; Hatton, pp. 39–40.
6. Knoop, Sophie, p. 103; David Chandler, *Marlborough as Military Commander* (1973) pp. 125–6.
7. BL Additional Mss. 38091, f. 242; BL Additional Mss. 37984, Skelton to Blathwayt 16 January 1683.
8. Hatton, pp. 40–1.
9. Ibid, p. 49.
10. Ibid, pp. 23–4.
11. Sophia of Hanover, *Letters to the Raugravines*, ed E Bodemann (Hanover/ Leipzig 1888), 15/25 July 1694.
12. G. Schnath, 'Eleanore von dem Knesebeck, die Gefangene von Scharzfels' in *Nedersachisches Jahrbuch fur LandLandesgeschichte*, 1955, pp. 13–6.
13. G. Schnath, 'Der Fall Konigsmarck' in Ausgewahlte Beitrage zur landesgeschichte (Hildesheim 1968) pp. 68–89; Horace Walpole, *Reminiscences written in 1788 for the Amusement* of *Miss Mary and Miss Agnes Berry* (Oxford 1924) p. 22.

14. Hatton, pp. 60–3.
15. John van der Kiste, *George II and Queen Caroline* (Sutton, 1997) p. 7; And Mis rew Thompson, *George II: King and Elector* (Yale UP 2012) p. 18.
16. William Coxe, *Memoirs of the Life and Administration of Sir Walpole* (4 vols, 1816), vol 3 pp. 261–2; John, Lord Hervey, *Some Materials Towards the Memoirs of the Reign of George II* (ed Romney Sedgewick, 2 vols, 1931) vol 1 p. 353.
17. Hatton, p. 60–2.
18. Hatton, pp. 129–31.
19. Thompson, George II, pp. 159, 162, 169–76.
20. Van der Kiste, p. 12.
21. Ibid, pp. 119–20.
22. Ibid, pp. 161–4.
23. Ibid, pp. 38–9.
24. Ibid, pp. 86, 107, 118n, 128–30.
25. John, Lord Hervey, *Memoirs* ed Sedgewick, p. 275; W. H. Wilkins, *Caroline the Illustrious, Queen Consort of George II and sometimes Queen Regent (*2 vols, Longmans Green 1904) vol 2 p. 94.
26. See article by Sarah Burton, 'Birds in a Gilded Cage' in *The Spectator*, 5 June 2011.
27. Christopher Hibbert, *Gerorge IV* (Penguin 1976) pp. 184–91, 194–5, 197–200.
28. Hibbert, pp. 271–86; also Eric Christopher, *'Adoption, Narrative and Nation 1800–1850: The Case of William Austin*', pp. 960–91.
29. Brougham Mss. 10, 268.
30. Hibbert, pp. 344–5.
31. Roger Fulford, *Royal Dukes* (Penguin, 2000 edition) pp. 231–3; A Purdue article on 'The Daughters of George III' in *New Dictionary of National Biography, (*OUP 2001); Sarah Burton, 'Birds in a Gilded Cage' in *The Spectator*, 5 June 2000; Anthony Camp, Royal *Mistresses and Royal Bastards*: *Fact and Fiction 1714–1836* (A Camp Publications, 2007). For Princess Amelia and her affair, see: William Childe-Pemberton, *The Romance of Princess Amelia* (New York, 1911) especially pp. 61–2, 66–7, 73 124–5, 136–8, 146–9, 174–5, 200.
32. Fulford, pp. 210–13; also 'charlespearce.org/pub/unsolved-murder-mysteries/chapter-2'.

Chapter 7: George III and his 'Marriage' to Hannah Lightfoot. The Fair Quaker and Royal Bigamy?

1. John Brooke, *King Geroge III* (Constable 1972) pp. 94–5.
2. Ibid, p. 56–7.
3. Ibid, p. 96.
4. Peter Douglas Brown, *William Pitt Earl of Chatham, The Great Commoner* (Allen and Unwin 1978) pp. 145–55.
5. Stella Tillyard, *A Royal Affair: George III and His Troublesome Siblings* (Vintage 2007) pp. 150–1, 180–1.
6. Tillyard, pp. 181–2.
7. Ibid, pp. 71–3.
8. Royal Archives, RA GEO/ 15942: George III to Duke of Gloucster, 19 November 1771.
9. Tillyard, pp. 186–9.
10. Stella Tillyard, Aristrocrat (Vintage 1995) p.123.
11. *The Letters of George III to Lord Bute, 1756–66*, ed. Romney Sedgewick (London 1939) p. 35.
12. Ibid, pp. 35–9.
13. Bute's reply to George III, late 1760: Ibid.
14. Ibid.
15. Tillyard, *Aristoctats* pp. 128–9.
16. Ibid, p. 129, quoting letter by Susan Fox-Strangeways (Holland House Papers).
17. Ibid, pp. 130–1.
18. Brooke, pp. 143–7.
19. Romney Sedgewick article in *History Today*, June 1960.
20. See online article at 'journals.sas.ac.uk/ths/article/viewFile/3453/3404', citing a privately printed account of the Kew incidents by a descendant of the 1766 robbery organiser, 'A

Taylor', in 1973. Also article by Martin Ball on 'The Mystery of Hannah Lightfoot and Isaac Axford' in *Notes andQueries*, vol 57 no. 3 (2010).

21. Stella Tillyard, *Arisocrats* p. 112.
22. See Mary Lucy Penderel, *The Fair Quaker: Hannah Lightfoot and her relations with George III* (D Appleton and co, New York 1911, repr 2013). Also British Library: Egerton Manuscripts no. 1719, f. 81.
23. *The Citizen* (newspaper), 26 February 1776. The political orientation of the paper, i.e., 'radical' Whig and opposed to the government and by extension George III, is not usually considered but may be significant, in using the story to attack the King.
24. Nathaniel Wraxall, *Historical Memories of My Own Time* (1836 edition)
25. As n. 20.
26. Jan Bondeson, *The Great Pretenders: The True Stories Behind Famous Historical Mysteries,* (W W Norton and Co, New York 2004) p. 175.
27. Olive Serres, *An Historical Fragment Relative to Her Late Majesty Queen Caroline* (London 1824).
28. Olivia Ryves legal case submission of 1866, as quoted in Storran book, below.
29. Mary Lucy Penderel, op. cit.
30. Charles Bradlaugh, *The Impeachment of the House of Brunswick* (1872); also on the Hannah Lightfoot 'marriage certificate' claims, see online copies of the *Northern Whig* newspaper (England) for 2 April 1839, of the *Kilkenny Chronicle* (Ireland) for 6 and 13 June 1866, and of the *Limerick Chronicle* (Ireland) for 9 and 16 June 1866. Also see modern review in a *Sunday Express* article on Hannah Lightfoot, 18 June 1995.
31. Patricia Storran, *Geotge Rex: Death of a Legend* (Cape Town, 1974).
32. Ibid; and see 'www.the heritageportal.co.uk' article of 29 September 2017.

Bibliography

Chapters 1 & 2

Andrew Amos, *The Great Oyer of Poisoning* (1846).

Robert Ashton, ed, *James I by His Contempories* (Hutchinson, London 1969).

Bryan Bevan, *King James I and VI of Scotland and England (*1996).

Caroline Bingham, *James VI*: The *Making of a King* (Weidenfeld and Nicolson, London 1968).

——, *James I of England (*Weidenfeld and Nicolson, London 1981).

Thomas Birch, *The Court and Times of James I* (London 1848).

Catherine Bowen, *The Lion and the Throne : The Life and Times of Sir Edward Coke* (1957).

John Bruce, ed, *Correspondence f King James VI of Scotland with Sir Robert Cecil and Others in England* (Camden Society, London 1856).

Gilbert Burnet, *History of My Own Times,* ed. Osmund Airy (London, 1897).

David Calderwood, *History of the Kirk of Scotland,* ed. Thomas Thomson, (8 vols, Edinburgh: Woodrow Society, 1841–9).

Calendar of State Papers Domestic: Elizabeth I, 1581–90, ed Mary Everett Green (Longmans, London 1865).

CSP Domestic: James I, 1603–10, 1611–18, 1619–23, ed Allen Crosby (Longmans, London, 1871–4).

CSP Relating to Scotland and Mary Queen of Scots: 1547–1603 (13 vols, ed Joseph Bain; William Boyd; W Boyd and Henry Meikle; Annie Cameron; HM General Register House, Edinburgh 1898–1969).

Ethel Carlton Williams, A*nne of Demark* (1970).

Algernon Cecil, *A Life of Sir Robert Cecil, Earl of Salisbury* (1915).

The Letters of John Chamberlain, ed. Norman McClure (*American Philosophical Society,* Philadelphia 1939).

The *Secret Correspondence of Sir Robert Cecil with James VI of Scotland,* ed. David Dalrymple (A Millar, Edinburgh 1766).

Samuel Cowan, *The Gowrie Conspiracy and its Official Narrative* (1902).

Neil Cuddy, 'The Revival of the Entourage: The Bedchamber of James I, 1603–1625' in David Starkey, ed, *The English Court: From the Wars of the Roses to the Civil Wars* (Longmans, London 1987, pp. 173–225).

John D. Davies, *Blood of Kings: The Stuarts, the Ruthvens and the Gowrie Conspiracy* (Ian Allen and Co, Edinburgh 2010).

Miriam Allen Deford, *The Overbury Affair* (Philadelphia 1960).

Sir Simonds D'Ewes, *The Diary of Sir Simonds D'Ewes, !622–1624,* ed Elizabeth Bourcier (Didier, Paris 1974).

Gordon Donaldson, *The Scottish* Reformation, London 1960.

——, *Scotland: James V to James VII* (Oliver and Boyd, Edinburgh 1965).

——, *All the Queen's Men: Power and Politics in Mary Stuart's Scotland,* London 1983.

Antonia Fraser, *Mary Queen of Scots* (Weidenfeld and Nicolson, London 1969).

Samuel R. Gardiner, *History of England* 1603–4 (10 vols, London 1883–4).

Julian Goodare and Michael Lynch, *The Reign of James VI* (East Linton 2000).

Geoffrey Goodman, *The Court of King James I* (ed. J. S. Brewer, London 1839).

Charles Gough, *Life and Character of Sir Thomas Overbury* (Norwich 1909).

James Halliwell, ed, *The Secret History of the Reign of King James I* (London 1845).

John Harington, *Letters and Epigrams of Sir John Harrington together with The Prayse of Private Life*, ed Norman McClure (University of Pennsylvania Press, Philadelphia 1930).

T. F. Henderson, *Mary Queen of Scots,* 2 vols, 1905.

Lord Herries, *Historical Memories of the Reign of Mary Queen of Scots and a Portion of the Reign of King James the Sixth,* ed. Robert Pitcairn (Edinburgh, 1836).

Historical Manuscripts Commission (HMC): Report on the Manuscripts of the Earls of Mar and Kellie preserved at Alloa House (HMSO, London 1904).
HMC: Report on the Manuscripts of Lord De l'Isle and Dudley Preserved at Penshurst Place (6 vols, HMSO, London 1925–66).
Letters of John Holles, ed. P. R. Seddon (Thoroton Society Record Series, Nottingham *1Letters of 975*–86).
Proceedings in Parliament 1614: House of Commons, ed Maija Jansson (American Philosophical Society, Philadelphia 1986).
G. P. R. Jones, *An Investigation of the Circumstances Surrounding the Murder of John Earl of Gowrie* (1849).
Robert Keith, ed, *History of the Affairs of Church and State in Scotland from the Beginning of the Reformation to the Year of* 1568 (3 vols, Spottiswoode Society, Edinburgh 1850).
John Knox, *History of the Reformation in Scotland*, ed. W. Croft Dickinson, Edinburgh 1949.
Andrew Lang, *James VI and the Gowrie Mystery,* London 1902.
Thomas Law, 'The Spanish Blanks and the Catholic Earls, 1592–1594' in *Scottish Review* vol 2 (1893) pp. 1–32.
Edward Le Comte, *The Notorious Lady Essex* (1970).
Maurice Lee, *James Stuart, Earl of Moray*, Columbia University, US, 1953.
——, *Government by Pen: Scotland Under James VI and* I and I (University of Illinois Press, Urbana, Illinois 1980.
——, *Great Britain's Solomon: James VI and I and His Three Kingdoms* (University of Illinois Press, Urbana 1990).
Roger Lockyer, *Buckingham* (Longmans, Harlow 1981).
——, *James VI and I* (Longmans, Harlow 1998).
Wiliam McElwee, *The Murder of Sir Thomas Overbury* (1952).
James Melville, *Autobiography and Diary,* ed Robert Pitcarin (2 vols, Woodrow Society, Edinburgh 1842).
Sir James Melville of Halshall, *Memoirs of His Own Life* ed T. Thomson (Bannatyne Club, Edinburgh 1827).
David Moysie, *Memoirs of the Affairs of Scotland !577–1603* (Edinburgh 1830).
Linda Levy Peck, *Northampton: Patronage and Policy at the Court of James I* (Allen and Unwin, London 1982).
——, *Court Patronage and Corruption in Early Stuart England* (Unwin Hyman, Boston 1990).
E. Peyton, *The Divine Catastrophe of the Kingly House of Stuart* (1652).
Robert Pitcairn, *Criminal Trials in Scotland* (2 vols, Edinburgh 1833).
Walter Scott, ed, *The Secret History of the Court of James the First* (2 vols, Bannatyne and Co, Edinburgh 1811).
P. R. Seddon, 'Robert Carr, Earl of Somerset' in *Renaissance and Modern Studies*, vol 14 (1970).
Kevin Sharpe, ed, *Faction in Parliament* (1985).
Alan G. R. Smith, ed, *The Reign of James VI ad I,* New York 1973.
Anne Somerset, *Unnatural Murder at the Court of James I* (Weidenfeld and Nicolson, 2017 edition).
Vernon Snow, *Essex the Rebel: A Life of Robert Devereux, Third Earl of Essex* (Lincoln, Nebraska 1970).
Alan Stewart, *The Cradle King: A Life of James VI and I* (London 2003).
Paul Welsby, *George Abbot, the Unwanted Archbishop* (1962).
Arthur Wilson, *The History of Great Britain, being the Life and Reign of King James I* (1653).
Ralph Winwood, *Memorials of Affairs of State in the Reigns of Queen Elizabeth and King James I* (1725).
Jenny Wormauld, 'James VI and I: Two Kings or One?' in *History*, vol lxviii, 1983.
——, *Mary Queen of Scots: A Study in Failure* (London 1988).

Chapters 3 & 4

George Abernathy jr, 'Clarendon and the Declaration of Indulgence' in *Journal of Ecclesiastical History,* vol 11 (1962) pp. 64–72.
Osmund Airy, ed, *The Lauderdale Papers* (Camden Society, 1885), vol 1
Maurice Ashley, *General Monck* (1977).
John Beresford, *Sir George Downing: The Godfather of Downing Sreet* (London 1930).

L. F. Brown, 'Religious Factors in the Convention Parliament' in *EHR* vol XXII (1907) pp. 52–5.
Julia Buckroyd, *Church and State in Scotland*, (Edinburgh 1980).
C. Burrage, 'The Fifth Monarchy Insurrections' in *EHR* vol XV (1910) pp. 722–45.
Revd J.S. Clarke, ed, *The Life of James II (From notes left in his own hand)* 2 vols, (1816).
Thomas Crosby, *History of the English Baptists* vol 2 (1736).
G. Davies, 'The General Election of 1660' in *HLQ* vol 15 (1951) pp. 211–35.
C. Edie, 'The Popular Idea of Monarchy on the Eve of the Stuart Restoration' in *Historical and Literary Queries*, vol 39 (1975–6) pp. 344–63.
Sir Keith Feiling, *British Foreign Policy 1660–1672* (Oxford 1930).
Revd. G. Gould, ed, *Documents Related to the Act of Settlement of England by the Act of Uniformity* (1862).
Ford, Lord Grey of Werke, *The Secret History of the Rye House Plot and the Monmouth Rebellion*, 1685 (1754).
Ian Green, *The Restoration of the Church of England 1660–1663* (Oxford 1978).
C. Grose, 'The Dunkirk Money, 1662' in *Journal of Modern History*, vol 5 (1933) pp. 1–18.
Thomas Gumble, *The Life of General Monck* (1671).
Kenneth Haley, *The First Earl of Shaftesbury* (1968).
C. H. Hartmann, *Charles II and Madame* (1934).
——, *Clifford and the Cabal* (1937).
——, *The King my Brother* (1954).
Thomas Howell, *State Trials* (1816).
Ronald Hutton, *Restoration: A Political* and *Religious History of England and Wales*, 1658–1667 (Clarendon Press 1987).
——, *Charles II: King of England, Scotland and Ireland* (Clarendon Press 1989).
J. R. Jones, *Britain and Europe in the Seventeenth Century* (1966).
——, ed, *The Restored Monarchy* (1979).
T. H. Lister, *The Life and Administration of Edward Hyde, First Earl of Clarendon* (1837) vol 3.
Richard Locke, *The Western Rebellion* (1782).
Narcissus Luttrell, *Brief Historical Relation of State Affairs*, vol 1 (Oxford UP, 1852).
Alan Marshall, *The Strange Death of Sir Edmund Godfrey* (History Press, 1999).
J. G. Muddiman. *The Mystery of Sir Edmund Godfrey (*London 1924).
David Ogg, *England in the Reign of Charles II* (1934).
John Oldmixon, *History of England during the Reigns of the House* of *Stuart*, vol 1 (1730).
Richard Ollard, *Man of War: Sir Robert Holmes and the Restoration of the Navy* (Hodder and Stoughton, London 1969).
——, *Pepys: Biogaphy* (Hodder and Stoughton, London 1974).
B. Reay, 'The Authorities and Early Restoration Quakerism' in *Journal of Ecclesiastical Historyy*, vol 34 (1983).
Victor Sutch, *Gilbert Sheldon* (The Hague, 1973).
J. N. P. Watson, *Captain-General and Rebel Chief: The Life of James, Duke of Monmouth*, (Allen and Unwin, London 1979).
E. A. O. Whiteman, 'The Restoration of the Church of England' in *Transactions of the Royal Historical Society*, 5th series, vol 5 (1995) pp. 120–35.
C. Whiting, 'The Great Plot of 1663' in *Durham University Journal*, vol 22 (1920) pp. 155–67.

Chapter 5

Memoirs of Earl Ailesbury, ed. Buckley.
An Answer from the Country to a Late Letter to a Dissenter, (1687). Rev. J D Clarke, The Life of King James II and VII, 2 vols, London 1816.
Stephen Baxter, *William III* (1966).
Robert Beddard, ed, *The Revolutions of 1688*: *The Andrew Browning Lectures*, 1988 (1991).
E. S. de Beer, 'The Marquis of Albeville and His Brothers' in *EHR* vol XLV (1930) pp. 397–408.
J.R. Bloxam, ed. *Magdalen College and James II* (Clarendon Press 1886).
Burnet, op. cit.
A Collection of Papers Relating to the Present Juncture of Affairs in England, (London, 1688/9).

John Childs, *The Army, James II and the Glorious Revolution* (Manchester UP 1980).
Clarke, *Life of James II.*
Evelyn Cruikshanks, ed, *By Force Or By Default? The Revolution of 1688–89* (John Donald, Edinburgh 1989).
Daniel Defoe, *Memoirs of Publick Transactions in the Life and Ministry of His Grace the Duke of Shrewsbury* (London 1718).
Patrick Dillon, *The Last Revolution: 1688 and the Creation of the Modern World,* (Pimlico 2007).
Charles Dodd, *The Church History of England*, 3 vols (Brussels 1742).
E. Doebner, ed, *Memoirs of Queen Mary of England 1688–1693.*
Sir George Duckett, ed, *The Penal Laws and Test Act* (London 1883).
John Evelyn, *Diary*, ed de Beer.
K. Feiling, op cit.
Mark Goldie, 'Locke's Circle and James II' in *Historical Journal*, vol 35 (1992).
Edward Gregg, *Queen Anne* (Routledge and Kegan Paul 1980).
Ford, Lord Grey, *Secret History of the Rye House Plot and the Duke of Monmouth's Rebellion*, London 1754.
Tim Harris, *Politics under the Late Stuarts: Party Conflict in a Divided Society 1660–1715* (1993).
Basil Henning, ed, *The House of Commons,1660–1690*, 3 vols (Secker and Warburg 1983).
His Majesty's Gracious Declaration to All His Loving Subjects for Liberty of Conscience (London 1687).
The History of Father La Chaise (London 1693).
Dale Hoak and Mordechai Feingold, eds, *The World of William and Mary* (Stanford UP, California 1996).
H. Horvitz, *Revolution Politics* (1968).
Hutton, *Charles II.*
Jonathan Israel, ed, *The Anglo-Dutch Moment: Essays on the Glorius Revolution and its World Impact* (Cambridge UP 1991).
J. R Jones, *The Revoluton of 1688 in England* (Weidenfeld and Nicolson, 1988 edition).
J. P. Kenyon, 'The Earl of Sunderland and the Revolution of 1688' in *Cambridge Historical Journal* 11, no.3 (1955).
——, 'The Commission for Ecclesiastical Causes, 1686–1688' in *Historical Journal*, no 3 (1991) pp. 727–36.
Sir John Lowther, *Memoirs of the Reign of James II* (London 1857).
Narcissus Luttrell, *A Brief History of State Affairs,* 6 vols (1857).
Thomas Babington Macaulay, *The History of England from the Accession of James II*, 5 vols (New York, 1849–61).
John Miller, *Popery and Politics in England, 1660–1688* (Cambridge UP 1973).
Maximilian Nowak, *Daniel Defoe: Master of Fiction* (Cambridge UP 2003).
Steven Pincus, 1688, The First Modern Revolution, Yale UP 2009.
Memoirs of Sir John Reresby, ed. Andrew Browning (Royal Historical Society edition, London 1991).
George Savile, Marquis of Halifax, *A Letter to a Dissenter* (G.H., London, 1687).
Lois Schwoerer, 'Propaganda in the Revolution of 1688' in *American Historical Review*, vol 82 (1977), pp. 843–74.
W. A. Speck, *Reluctant Revolutionaries: Englishmen and the Revolution of 1688* (Oxford UP 1988).
Adrian Tinniswood, *His Invention So Fertile: A Life of Sir Christopher Wren* (Pimlico 2002).
John Towill Rutt, ed, *A Historical Account of My Own Life by Edmund Calamy* 1671–1731, 2 vols (London 1829).
Melinda Zook, *Radical Whigs and Conspiratorial Politics in Late Stuart England* (University of Pennsylvania Press 1999).

Original Sources

Bodleian Library Oxford: Don. C.38–39: Fleming newsletters.
Eng. Hist. c201: Sir Richard Temple papers
Rawlinson MSS: A266 (Sunderland Letters)
Tanner Mss. 39/28.

British Library: Althorp Mss. 75, 366.
Additional Mss: 2906 (Trade papers), 4162, (Newsletters),
4236 (Tillotson Papers),
4292 (Birch collection),
9735 (Blathwayt papers),
17677 (Netherlands paper)
21483 (Letters to James II)
28079 (Godolphin-Osborne papers)
28087 (Edward Osborne papers)
28875–28876 (Ellis papers)
29594 (Hatton/Nottingham correspondence)
31141 (Strafford correspondence)
32681 (Henry Sidney correspondence)
34508 (Dutch political correspondence)
34519 (Shrewsbury correspondence)
41816, 41827 (MP – letters from foreign envoys),
56245 (Blathwayt correspondence)
Egerton Mss: 1717 (Bentinck papers)
3335–3336 (Danby correspondence)
National Archives: SP 31/3/ 143, 160, 161, 164, 167, 168, 172, 175, 177.
Dr. Williams' Library, London: DW L Q: Roger Morice's Entering Book.
Longleat House Mss.: Portland Papers vol 2.

Chapter 6

BL Additional Mss. 38091; BL Additional Mss. 37984
Brougham Mss. 10, 268.
Sarah Burton, 'Birds in a Gilded Cage' in *The Spectator*, 5 June 2000.
Anthony Camp, *Royal Mistresses and Bastards: Fact and Fiction 1714–1936 (*Camp Publications, 2007).
David Chandler, *Marlborough as Military Commander* (1973)
William Childe-Pemberton, *The Romance of Princess Amelia* (New York, 1911)
Eric Christopher, *Adoption, Narrative and Nation 1800–1850: The Case of William Austin.*
William Coxe, *Memoirs of the Life and Administration of Sir Robert Walpole* (4 vols, 1816).
Roger Fulford, *Royal Dukes* (Penguin, 2000 edition).
Edward Gregg, 'Was Queen Anne a Jacobite?' in *History*, vol vii, October 1972
E. Gregg, *Queen Anne* (Routledge 1980).
Ragnhild Hatton, *George 1: Elector and King* (Thames and Hudson 1978).
John, Lord Hervey, *Some Materials Towards Memoirs of the Reign of George II* (ed. Romney Sedgewick, 2 vols, 1931)
Christopher Hibbert, *George IV* (Penguin 1976)
Mathilde Knoop, *Die Kurfurstin Sophie von Hannover* (Hildesheim 1964)
P. L. Muller, *Wilhelm III van Oranien und Georg Friedrich von Valdek (*The Hague 1873)
A. Purdue article on 'The Daughters of George III' in *New Dictionary of National Biography* (OUP 2001).
G. Schnath, 'Eleanore von dem Knesebck, die Gefangene von Scharzfels' in Nedersachisches Jahrbuch fur Landesgeshcichte, 1955.
G. Schnath, 'Der Fall Konigsmarck' in Ausgewahlte Beitrage zur landesgeschichte (Hildesheim 1968).
Sophia of Hanover, *Letters to the Raugravines*, ed E Bodemann (Hanover/ Leipzig 1888)
Andrew Thompson, *Geoge II: King and Elector* (Yale UP 2012).
John van der Kiste, *George II and Queen Caroline* (Sutton, 1997).
Horace Walpole, *Reminiscences written in 1788 for the amusement of Miss Mary and Miss Agnes Berry* (Oxford 1924)
W. H. Wilkins, *Caroline the Illustrious, Queen Consort of George II and sometime sometime Queen-Regent* (2 vols, Longmans Green 1904).
'charlespearce.org/pub/unsolved-murder-mysteries/chapter-2'.

Chapter 7

Martin Ball, 'The Mystery of Hannah Lightfoot and Isaac Axford' in *Notes and Queries*, vol 57, no. 3 (2010).

Jan Bonderson, *The Great Pretenders: The True Stories Behind Famous Historical Mysteries* (W W Norton and Co, New York, 2004).

Charles Bradlaugh, *The Impeachment of the House of Brunswick* (1872).

John Brooks, *King George III* (Constable, 1972).

Peter Douglas Brown, *William Pitt, Earl of Chatham: The Great Commoner* (Allen and Unwin 1978).

The Citizen, edition of Saturday 24 February 1776.

Holland House Papers.

The Kilkenny Moderator, editions of 6 and 13June 1866.

The Limerick Chronicle, editions of 9 and 16 June 1866.

The Morning Post, edition of 3 June 1806.

Mary Lucy Penderel, *The Fair Quaker: Hannah Lightfoot and her relations with George III* (D Appleton and Co, New York, 1911).

Royal Archives, Windsor: R A / GEO/ 15942 (November 1771).

Olive Serres, *A Historical Fragment Relative to her Late Majesty Queen Caroline* (London, 1824).

Margaret Shepherd, *Princess Olive* (privately printed, Shipston-on-Stour, 1984).

Patricia Storran, *George Rex: Death of a Legend* (Cape Town, 1974).

The Sunday Express, article on Hannah Lightfoot, 18 June 1995.

William Thomas, *Hannah Lightfoot* (London 1867).

Stella Tillyard, *A Royal Affair: George III and His Troublesome Siblings* (Vintage, 2007).

Nathaniel Wraxall, *Memoirs of My Own Time* (1836).

www.theheritage portal.com: 29 September 2017.

Index